THE URBANA FREE LIBRARY

W9-BBQ-310

Portsmouth
Boulogne
Agincourt
Crècy
Arras
Cambray
Guise
Somme
Luxembourg
Harfleur
Honfleur
Rouen
Rheims
Metz
Seine
ÎLE-DE-
Senlis
Marne
DUCHY OF BAR
NORMANDY
Meaux
Châlons
Nancy
PARIS
Vincennes
Marcoussis
Melun
Vaucouleurs
FRANCE
Domremy
Chartres
Montereau
Troyes
Seine
LORRAINE
MAINE
Sarthe
Patay
Orléans
Gien
Auxerre
Cravant
ANJOU
Baugé
Blois
Angers
Tours
Loire
Dijon
Dôle
Amboise
Loire
Saumur
Azay-le-Rideau
Mehun-sur-Yèvre
Chinon
TOURAINE
Loches
Bourges
Nevers
BURGUNDY
Saône
Poitiers
BERRY
Chalon
POITOU
Cher
Bourbon
Rochelle
Charente
Rhone
SAVO
Angoulême
Limoges
Clermont
Lyons
Périgeux
Dordogne
AUVERGNE
DAUPHINÉ
GUYENNE
Cahors
Garonne
ARMANAC
ASCONY
Toulouse
Montpellier
Arles
Aix
PROVENCE
Pau
Marseilles
Toulon
BEARN
Carcassonne
Narbonne
Perpignan
GOLFE DU LION
ARAGON

About the Author

For more than twenty-five years, **Her Royal Highness Princess Michael of Kent** has pursued a successful career lecturing on historical topics. She lives with her husband, Prince Michael of Kent, in Kensington Palace in London.

The Queen of Four Kingdoms

An Historical Novel

HRH Princess Michael of Kent

BEAUFORT
BOOKS

Beaufort Books

Library of Congress Cataloging-in-Publication Data is on file.

For inquiries about volume orders, please contact:
Beaufort Books
27 West 20th Street, Suite 1102
New York, NY 10011
sales@beaufortbooks.com

Published in the United States by Beaufort Books
www.beaufortbooks.com

Distributed by Midpoint Trade Books
www.midpointtrade.com

Printed in the United States of America

Interior design by TK
Cover Design by TK

For my mother, Marianne Szápáry, who had the courage and intelligence of her ancestor, Yolande d'Aragon.

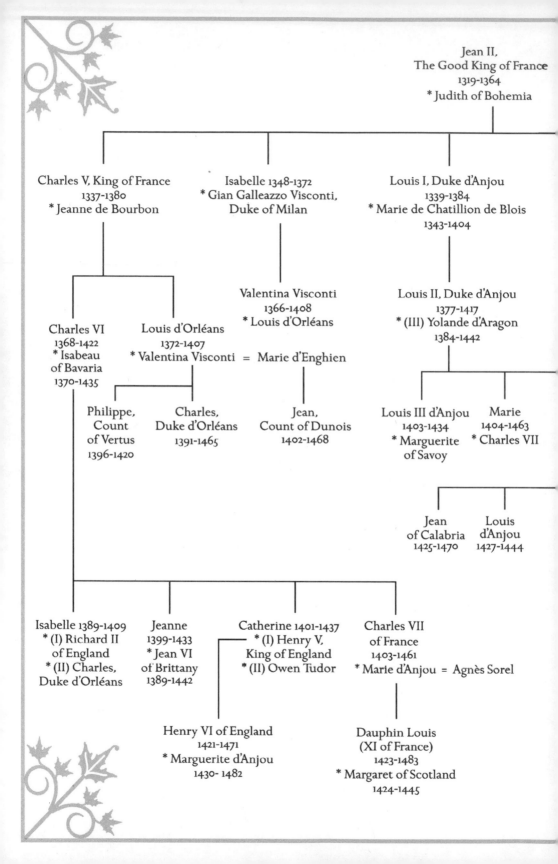

Jean II,
The Good King of France
1319-1364
* Judith of Bohemia

Charles V, King of France
1337-1380
* Jeanne de Bourbon

Isabelle 1348-1372
* Gian Galleazzo Visconti,
Duke of Milan

Louis I, Duke d'Anjou
1339-1384
* Marie de Chatillion de Blois
1343-1404

Valentina Visconti
1366-1408
* Louis d'Orléans

Louis II, Duke d'Anjou
1377-1417
* (III) Yolande d'Aragon
1384-1442

Charles VI
1368-1422
* Isabeau
of Bavaria
1370-1435

Louis d'Orléans
1372-1407
* Valentina Visconti = Marie d'Enghien

Philippe,
Count
of Vertus
1396-1420

Charles,
Duke d'Orléans
1391-1465

Jean,
Count of Dunois
1402-1468

Louis III d'Anjou
1403-1434
* Marguerite
of Savoy

Marie
1404-1463
* Charles VII

Jean
of Calabria
1425-1470

Louis
d'Anjou
1427-1444

Isabelle 1389-1409
* (I) Richard II
of England
* (II) Charles,
Duke d'Orléans

Jeanne
1399-1433
* Jean VI
of Brittany
1389-1442

Catherine 1401-1437
* (I) Henry V,
King of England
* (II) Owen Tudor

Charles VII
of France
1403-1461
* Marie d'Anjou = Agnès Sorel

Henry VI of England
1421-1471
* Marguerite d'Anjou
1430- 1482

Dauphin Louis
(XI of France)
1423-1483
* Margaret of Scotland
1424-1445

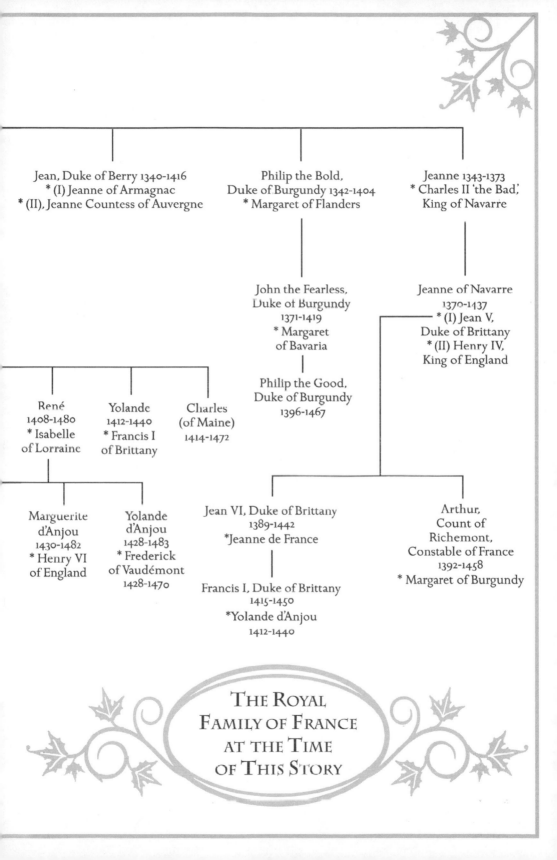

Jean, Duke of Berry 1340-1416
* (I) Jeanne of Armagnac
* (II), Jeanne Countess of Auvergne

Philip the Bold,
Duke of Burgundy 1342-1404
* Margaret of Flanders

Jeanne 1343-1373
* Charles II 'the Bad',
King of Navarre

John the Fearless,
Duke of Burgundy
1371-1419
* Margaret
of Bavaria

Jeanne of Navarre
1370-1437
* (I) Jean V,
Duke of Brittany
* (II) Henry IV,
King of England

Philip the Good,
Duke of Burgundy
1396-1467

René
1408-1480
* Isabelle
of Lorraine

Yolande
1412-1440
* Francis I
of Brittany

Charles
(of Maine)
1414-1472

Marguerite
d'Anjou
1430-1482
* Henry VI
of England

Yolande
d'Anjou
1428-1483
* Frederick
of Vaudémont
1428-1470

Jean VI, Duke of Brittany
1389-1442
*Jeanne de France

Arthur,
Count of
Richemont,
Constable of France
1392-1458
* Margaret of Burgundy

Francis I, Duke of Brittany
1415-1450
*Yolande d'Anjou
1412-1440

THE ROYAL
FAMILY OF FRANCE
AT THE TIME
OF THIS STORY

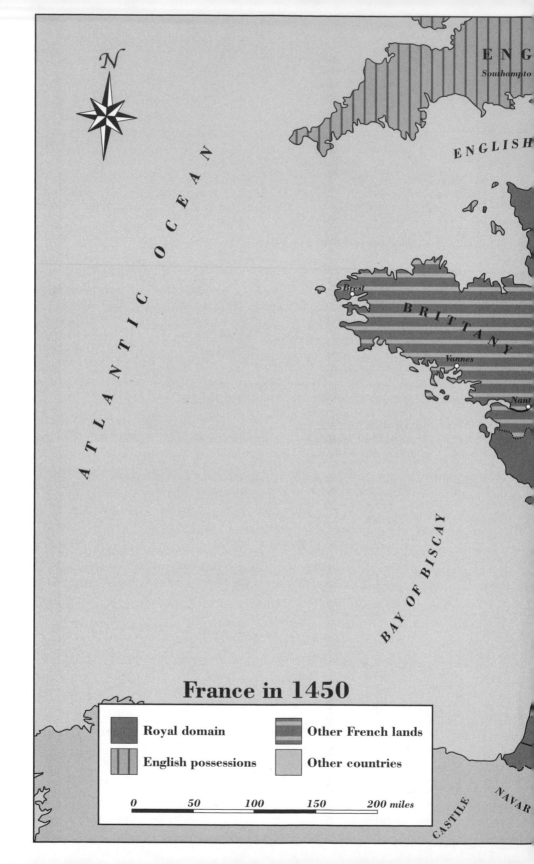

France in 1450

Royal domain

English possessions

Other French lands

Other countries

0   50   100   150   200 miles

Author's Note

This book began with my wish to tell the true story of Agnès Sorel, a girl born in fifteenth-century France. She became the mistress of Charles VII, the king crowned with the help of Joan of Arc, and came to my attention as the mother of Charlotte de France, legitimised and beloved half-sister of the next king, Louis XI.

In my last book, *The Serpent and the Moon*, Charlotte de France appears briefly as the wife of Diane de Poitiers' father-in-law, Jacques de Brézé. When he caught his wife *in flagrante* with his Master of the Horse, he ran the couple through with his sword "at least one hundred times," it was said at his trial. Contemporary chroniclers wrote that Charlotte was as beautiful as her mother Agnès Sorel, a name that meant nothing to me at the time but, intrigued, I began searching for her story. It was during this process that I discovered the remarkable Yolande, "The Queen of Four Kingdoms," and the subject of this book.

My manuscript, decreed too long, became two books—the first dedicated to Yolande's story, the second to that of her pupil, Agnès. Both stories included frequent appearances of a remarkable man whom Yolande had met on her first visit to Bourges in central France. Jacques Coeur was a young merchant of the town; curious, intelligent, enterprising, charming. She marked him well and found in him a reliable friend and then a most essential asset—to herself, her family and especially to her son-in-law, Charles VII. Through his genius and business entrepreneurship, Jacques Coeur became the richest man in France—a dangerous position in an absolute monarchy and one that had dramatic consequences! The twists and turns of his story involve most of the characters in the first two volumes. The wars with England continue as well as the contradictions of treachery/loyalty; cruelty/kindness. His story is too long and intense to be excluded from either the first or second volumes. On the advice of fellow writers, I decided to make him the subject of the third volume.

It was only in the last three years that I learned—through a pathology analysis by a well-known medical expert—that a principal character in my story was found to have died full of poison, and felt the need for some historical improvisation. Difficult to solve a crime some 550 years later! Nor would I claim to have done so, but there are a number of possible clues and much circumstantial evidence that point to a potential villain, at least in the eyes of an unimpeachable character. If the reader agrees with him, then we have found the murderer, but I am afraid the story only ends within the last pages of the third book!

Prologue

As the early-morning sun reaches the tops of the towers of Saragossa, the time has come for Yolande, only surviving child of the King of Aragon, to leave her home, and her country, to marry the French king's cousin, Louis II, Duke of Anjou. By this union, it is hoped her people and his will cease fighting over the Kingdom of Naples and Sicily, which both Aragon and Anjou claim as their inheritance. She is nineteen years old and beautiful, they say—but flattery is commonplace in her world and she pays it no mind.

"Juana, dear one, help me dress carefully," she asks her companion—once her nursemaid, then her governess, now her closest confidante. "I want everyone here to remember me as I look today. Who knows if I will ever return?"

Juana fiddles nervously with the ties on Yolande's bodice. Perhaps she, too, doubts that her mistress will return.

"I thank the Lord that you are coming with me to Provence, dear Juana. I will need your dear familiar face in my new life."

"You should thank your mother. It is she who is insisting I go with you." Her tone is not exactly joyful.

"I wonder what it will be like, our new home."

Juana knows that Yolande is musing to herself, since she has no more idea than her mistress of what awaits; she also knows that her charge is more curious about her betrothed than about the lands of which he is the ruler.

"You must be excited, my treasure," she murmurs

comfortingly as she starts to braid the girl's long blonde hair. "After all, you have been waiting for this moment for nine years."

It is true; it has been a very long engagement. Yolande sighs and tries to hide her anxiety.

"Yes, and he may well look like a frog; portraits can be misleading... Perhaps he has even been disfigured in some way, fighting for so long in Naples for his crown."

"Then our spies would have told us. Stop fretting. Think only of the advantages you will bring to Aragon by this marriage."

Yolande smiles and thinks: *Juana always talks like this—as if she were a great old sage when she is only ten years older than me.*

Juana's capable hands do their work and calm Yolande a little. But still... half of her is excited by the journey, while the other half shrinks from it. How can she be a good, dutiful wife to a man whose subjects have been fighting her countrymen for years? She takes comfort in the sight of her wolfhounds, Ajax and Hector, stretched out by the fire. They will come to France with her. Never leaving her side, they answer only to her call.

"Do you think they may still be permitted to sleep by my bed as they have always done?" she asks.

"I hope so." Juana smiles. "That will depend on your husband, won't it?"

Juana stands on a stool to help the princess into a white linen chemise, her riding habit of brown serge, a white shirt with frills showing at her neck, and a dashing broad-brimmed hat the colour of sand, pinned up on one side, trailing a red ostrich feather. She might not listen to flatterers, but since early childhood Yolande has been conscious of her appearance—and rather vain.

She turns around to gaze at her room, the cradle of her life until this day—the comfortable furnishings, the bright reds and blues of the large Agra carpet, the table where she sat daily at her lessons, the high bed with its red velvet curtains and huge pillows, the view from the tall windows across the plains towards the distant hills. As yet, the sun touches only their peaks. She takes one last look at her room, whispers, "Good-bye, sweet childhood," and blows a little kiss as she opens the door, Ajax and Hector at her heels.

Downstairs, her mother is waiting with the ambassadors from Anjou who will accompany her on the journey. Juana senses the girl's reluctance and takes her arm. Although Yolande is normally afraid of nothing, she is glad of the familiar touch.

As Yolande d'Aragon descends into the Great Hall of the castle, she can smell the heady scent of amber on burning logs, and sees her mother beckoning her into her private chamber. The Queen of Aragon is as tall as her daughter and worn thin from anxiety, having ruled Aragon alone for the past six years, ever since her much older and dearly loved husband died here in her arms. The queen still retains her proud features: the intelligent eyes, fine nose and sharp jaw line; she is a mature forty, well past her childbearing years, and never had any intention of remarrying.

"My darling child, come sit with me for our last moment alone together before we greet the ambassadors and your escort." With a sweet smile that belies her firm grasp, she takes her daughter by the hand. Yolande is the only one left of her three daughters, and it is hard to see her go.

"I have dreaded this moment—and yet I rejoice in it too," she confesses. "I came here to Aragon from the royal house of France to marry your father, and now you are to be married back into France, to the king's cousin." And she sighs as if she is thinking of her homeland. She has not set foot there since her wedding.

Yolande remains silent, looking into her mother's eyes as if to read her mind.

"I know you are aware of this, my darling, but as your mother, it is my duty to say it again, for the last time. Never forget the purpose of this union—to bring an end to fifteen years of fighting between Aragon and Anjou."

Darling Maman, thinks Yolande, *trying to keep me a little longer by telling me what I have heard over and over since my betrothal so long ago*—and she smiles despite feeling her tears gathering. Her mother continues.

"As you know, I have corresponded with your bridegroom's mother for nine years now. I feel I know her—and her son—through her letters, and because of this, I have no anxiety about your future family." Suddenly she clasps Yolande tightly. "But do not forget your home and all whom you love here, and fill your life with that dedication and spirit I have tried to instil in you."

Yolande is torn between sadness and excitement, and she finds that she cannot say anything. Her mouth is dry and she presses her lips tightly together to stop herself from crying out. Her mother kisses her, then holds her away from her and gives her a long, searching look. They both know it is their last private moment. Then they leave the room and go out to face their futures—her mother's here, alone, and Yolande's in a foreign country.

Tall, blonde, and confident in her beauty, the Princess of Aragon takes a deep breath, fixes her smile and greets the fine dignitaries from Anjou one by one; bowing slightly to each as she meets their eyes, trying to read them, her hand and voice steady until she reaches the end of the line. There stands her remarkable mother, head held high. They have said their good-byes a dozen times this morning, but now, in full view of the court and the ambassadors, they embrace again, tears running down their cheeks, and her mother says proudly for all to hear:

"It pains me to see you leave, child of my heart, but never forget, you are part Valois through my family, which makes you half French already. To marry into the royal house of France is your destiny, just as it was mine to leave France and become Queen of Aragon. Remain true to your heritage; fulfil your father's dream of reconciliation between our two lands. May he rest in peace, knowing that through your marriage, the endless, fruitless wars between Aragon and Anjou will be over.

"Beloved daughter, go on your way with my blessing. Write often and put your staunch and joyful heart into all you do. I know you will not disappoint the memory of your father who loved you dearly; or me; or Aragon."

And Yolande curtseys to her slowly, her head lowered, whispering words of commitment and love.

The royal escort is impressively large and would normally fill her with curiosity and delight, but today her heart is aching. Ajax and Hector bark loudly as if they too are bidding their home farewell, running in circles around her horse with excitement.

She turns back time and time again, until she can no longer see those familiar towers of Saragossa.

Part One

Chapter One

During the days of the slow journey towards her wedding in Provence, riding over fields and through forests, along streams and across rivers, meeting other travellers on the road, Yolande finds it hard to hold back the flood of childhood memories. In particular, she remembers the long-ago events that, years later, would set her on this journey.

She can still hear her mother's voice calling from the parapet of their great fortress of Montjuic at Barcelona: "Yolande! Yolande!" and again, "Yolande! Child, where are you? The ambassadors from Anjou are here!"

Even at the tender age of seven, Yolande considered herself an adult, and knew that she had to behave as a young lady to make her parents proud of her. Tall for her age, she stood one step beneath where they sat on their thrones. The first ambassador addressed them with a low bow.

"Your Majesties! We know you are aware of our mission, and we thank you for the welcome you have extended to our suite."

Nods and smiles were exchanged.

"We have travelled some hundred and twenty leagues from distant Anjou in western France on behalf of our widowed duchess, the Lady Marie de Blois. Our mission, and we believe yours, sire, is to bring to an end the long conflict between Aragon and Anjou over the kingdom of Naples and Sicily."

More nodding, and serious faces.

"Our duchess sees the betrothal of her only son, our new

Duke Louis II, to your daughter, the Princess Yolande, as a means of achieving peace and securing thereby our joint interests."

Then they were all smiling as Yolande's mother stroked her long blonde curls, kissed her forehead and asked Juana to lead the princess off to bed. Everyone seemed happy with the outcome of the ambassadors' visit.

In fact, Louis II d'Anjou was not the only candidate for Yolande's hand in marriage. Her breeding and her substantial dowry made her a desirable match, as did her beauty, which the trouvères and poets had lauded since her childhood.

It was on her fifteenth birthday that two ambassadors from Richard II of England came to Aragon to press their king's suit on Yolande. She was naturally delighted with this illustrious proposition, but when the King of France heard of it, he was not pleased at all. His choice of consort for the English king was his own six-year-old daughter, Isabelle. Since the English were always interested in forging a closer union with France to increase their holdings there, they readily accepted Charles VI's offer and forgot about the princess of Aragon.

A year later, when Yolande was sixteen, the sudden death of Aragon's king out hunting changed everything. Her beloved father, who had made her youth such a pleasure, was no more, and his younger brother, her uncle Martin, inherited the throne of Aragon. After her father's death, the subject of the Angevin embassy came up again in conversation at court.

"Darling child, come, sit by me," her mother had invited, patting the cushion next to her while stroking her small grey *levrette*, Mignon, curled up on her other side. And she had told to her again about what Yolande already knew through and through—how her marriage must be a part of the matrimonial game of chess played by the royal houses of Europe—arranging unions between their children to the mutual gain of their territories. That although these could be increased through conquest, it was better to win them peacefully, through alliances sealed by the dowry and the connections of a princess. These were the real bargaining tools of power. And despite her beauty and character, for all that she was the daughter of the king, in this game Yolande was a pawn. These things she had known from her infancy.

"Dearest child," her mother had said again, and Yolande knew that whenever Maman began a conversation like that, the explanation would take time and not please her. "You are the only one left of our three girls and were always the most spirited. Have you not heard it said time and again that Aragon is the first power in the Mediterranean?"

Hesitantly, Yolande had nodded.

"Our other kingdom of Naples and Sicily has been beyond our control for too long because of Anjou—whose sovereign dukes have continually challenged our right to rule there. Your union with their young Duke Louis would solve this problem to the benefit of both our houses." And there she had paused, sensing that the girl had heard enough for the time being.

Stroking her hair, she told her soothingly, "My darling, I know how happy you are at our court, but if and when you leave, you might find an even greater paradise than the one you have here. And if not, you have enough experience to create one for yourself."

As she rides alongside Juana, Yolande smiles a little sadly at the memory. There is no one else in her entourage she wishes to talk to as much as Juana, and she chooses to pass these golden autumn days in her familiar company.

Many years ago, Juana's father died while trying to save the horses when a fire broke out at the stables in Saragossa. In her distress, her mother took her own life, and their child was brought into the castle household. Intelligent and honest, it was not long before Juana made herself useful. When the king married, Juana was appointed to attend his bride, and following Yolande's birth, her good sense and ability put her in charge of the nursery, which would soon house three little girls. They all adored her and she was totally devoted to them and to their parents. With the king and queen often occupied with affairs of state, it was Juana who cared for the children when they were ill, Juana in whom they confided their secrets and who was always their ally, even in their mischief-making—provided it did not go too far.

When first one, and then the second of Yolande's younger sisters came down with smallpox, it was Juana who nursed them night and day, ignoring the danger to herself. When they died, her grief was heartbreaking. She had refused to allow Yolande to stay in the same house, which probably saved her life, and thereafter she devoted herself to Yolande's daily care. It is no wonder that the princess has always trusted her more than anyone else. Juana is the only person to whom she feels able to voice her deepest concerns.

Now, as the two of them travel further and further from home, Juana's Catalan way of speaking is soothing, and her chatter fills the hours as their procession winds its way through deep forests with occasional rays of sunlight breaking through the trees. Only when they come to open ground do they spur their horses to a canter or gallop. How Yolande loves to race the spirited grey Andalusians she is bringing with her to France. People gape at the sight of the proud, arched carriage of their heads, their thick manes flying in their riders' faces, their long, full tails streaming behind. The princess and Juana are accustomed to long journeys on horseback, opting to ride rather than use litters or carriages when travelling.

No matter how tightly Yolande ties on her hat, it will slip back around her neck when she breaks into a fast canter or gallop. The exhilarating feeling of the wind in her loosened hair helps her close her ears to Juana's admonitions, her calls to tie her hat and think of her complexion. As she spurs on her horse, the girl cannot help wondering whether she will ever be able to ride with such abandon again.

Early each morning when the mist slowly lifts and the sun breaks through, Yolande can hear the birds calling and listens to the snorting and shaking of the horses being prepared for another pleasant day's ride. Around midday they find a shady place to sit and refresh themselves with water mixed with a little wine and bread with cold meat. She stays with Juana, a little apart from the others, blankets on the grass and cushions against a tree for comfort. She loves looking up at the red, yellow and gold of the leaves mingled with the dark evergreens overhead—it is her favourite time of year. The air has a special scent, a mix of pine and the fresh smell of leaf decay.

Their route is well planned and not too tiring. Every evening they halt at sunset, spending the night at a welcoming castle or manor. Sometimes, after washing and changing their clothes, the Princess of Aragon will appear before the local people; at other places they just eat and sleep. A number of their hosts have arranged for singers to entertain them while they dine, everyone acknowledging Yolande as the grand lady she is, and as the queen she will become on her marriage.

What will it be like, this new kingdom of hers? And the household she will join? Yolande knows that her mother considers Marie de Blois, her future mother-in-law, to be a lady like herself, shrewd, yet caring for her country and her children. Her husband died long ago, fighting on the Italian peninsula, leaving her all those great lonely castles, huge estates to administer—so much responsibility on her shoulders to preserve the inheritance of her two young sons. And as if that was not hard enough, a cousin of her husband's—Charles de Duras—actively encouraged the great cities of Provence to turn against the Anjous, their acknowledged rulers.

Yolande has heard Marie de Blois left Anjou and rode to Avignon to consult with Pope Clement VII. It was a courageous act, and it succeeded—the Pope confirmed the sovereign rights of Yolande's betrothed, Louis II d'Anjou, to Provence, Naples and Sicily. Next, and without hesitation, Marie de Blois pawned her jewels and her silver, and with the proceeds she raised a substantial army. When she realized it would still not be strong enough for a definitive victory against Charles de Duras, she used her head. Famous for her charm, she travelled throughout Provence with Louis, wooing the towns, ensuring their loyalty to her son. And where charm failed, she used her money. A good lesson: charm first, and if that fails, bribe!

As for her husband-to-be—Yolande's thoughts are both full of him, and shy away from him: he is too large a presence in her mind.

One evening after supper, Yolande and Juana sit before the fire in their cosy rooms at the old stone inn where they are spending the night. Juana knits. She sees Yolande draw a piece of paper from her bag, something she always carries: it is the draft of the first letter she ever wrote to Louis, with Juana's help. With a gentle little nudge of her foot to make Juana look up, Yolande begins to read:

> My lord, my dearly betrothed husband-to-be, my lady mother has told me of your difficulties in your land of Provence and of the efforts your good mother has made on your behalf to regain your inheritance. What a splendid and inspiring lady she must be and how I look forward to knowing her—as I do you, my lord. Please write and tell me of your struggles in the south of France, a place I know little about. If you will allow, I would like to write to you of my life here in Aragon so that you may know something about me, but mine is as nothing in comparison with the excitement and dangers of your life. Your devoted bride-to-be, Yolande d'Aragon.

Juana chuckles—she chuckles often. "Well, that first letter did not inspire a reply for some time, did it?"

She is right. It was not until Christmas that his answer came.

> My dearest Yolande—may I call you so?

In view of the distance that separates us, and will continue to do so for some time, let us know one another through our letters.

I am pleased to be able to give you good news. The people of Provence have sworn loyalty to me and accepted me as their sovereign. No, do not think me a hero or a conqueror.

This past autumn, I made my official entry into Aix, the capital of Provence, and now I am recognized throughout the country as the people's rightful sovereign. So, my dear future wife, this too will be your territory to reign over with me.

Now my indefatigable and brave mother has turned her attention to my other certified inheritance, Naples and Sicily. Will my struggles never cease so that I may come home and marry you?

Reading Louis' letter, Yolande too wondered how long it would take for him to marry her. And what was he like? She was bursting to know. Her mother, who had eyes and ears everywhere, had managed to make some significant discoveries, and reported her findings:

"Louis, at thirteen, is already a young man: tall, strong, confident, his ambitious mind firmly fixed on his objective. He has learnt from his mother's skill and tenacity in reclaiming part of his father's inheritance; he has watched her use charm and diplomacy to regain the loyalty of Provence. Now, with a large navy recruited from his faithful sovereign state, he has set sail for Naples." But until Louis could reconquer the rest of his legitimate inheritance, their marriage would have to wait.

During the years that followed, her mother spoke often of Louis as she shared Marie de Blois' correspondence with her. Yet Yolande longed for more details. How did he manage, this lad with fire in his veins and a will of iron? Who advised him in Naples? Who were his companions? After years spent in and around that large territory—most of the lower half of the Italian peninsula—surely there must be much to tell her? How did the people look? Dress? Eat? What flowers grew? What birds flew in the sky? Did they have songbirds? Good horses? Music?

Troubadours or their like? Was the famous Bay of Naples as beautiful as the poets claimed? The mighty volcano, Vesuvius, was it erupting? Would Louis come for her? Or was she to be sent for? Would they marry in Naples? She bombarded him with letters full of questions, but none came back from Louis, only from his mother to hers.

Then one day, about three years after her father's death, she heard her mother calling her name in a way that she felt was important.

"A package has arrived for you from Naples!"

At last! Anxiously, she tore it open. A letter, a long letter, from Louis:

"My dearest future wife," it began. "Finally, after nine years of constant skirmishes and intermittent fighting, my enemy here, a cousin of mine called Ladislaus de Durazzo, as the Italians call the Duras family, the senior branch of the Anjous, has defeated my forces in a definitive battle." She sat stunned. "I am coming home, there is no more I can do here for the time being. We shall marry at last and I will show you my other beautiful territories of Anjou, Guyenne, Maine and Provence—you will especially love Provence. Wait for me." And he signed himself: "Your Louis."

She had smiled bravely at her mother and said in a small voice, "How wonderful—I shall be married at last."

But Juana knew her heart—and she could not hide some of her disappointment from her faithful governess. Her knight in shining armour had failed to bring her a kingdom, one that she had taken very much for granted. Aragon's right to Naples and Sicily was in her blood, just as much as Louis d'Anjou's rights to that kingdom were in his blood. Complicated as it seemed when she was betrothed, she had long ago learned to understand the situation between Aragon and Anjou. The last queen of Sicily, Giovanna II, a frightful harridan, had named an Aragon cousin as her heir, but disinherited him in favour of another cousin, Louis D'Anjou, before dying herself. Yolande even knew the story that it was the disinherited Ladislaus

Duras, or Durazzo, who was said to have smothered Queen Giovanna between two feather mattresses, so that there would be no mark on her body. He then claimed the throne of Sicily, but died, and Louis I inherited the kingdom. It was indeed a most complicated story and the conflict continued between the Durazzo heir and her Louis' father until he mysteriously died in that faraway kingdom. As soon as he was able, her Louis II went back to Naples and spent the next nine years following his betrothal, fighting to hold onto what he considered was his. And now, after all those years, he was on his way back and she was to appear pleased to marry the loser of her adolescent dreams? Neither the warm looks from her mother nor the excitement of the wedding preparations could lift her mood. Not even her little girl-dwarf Pepita—no matter how much she tried to make Yolande smile as she rubbed her back and shoulders, brushed her long hair into a plait that reached down to the back of her knees or wound it around her head to make a crown—could stop her thinking hard about her destiny.

Yolande had followed every move of the two protagonists through Louis' mother's letters for the past nine years, and she had never doubted his ultimate success. He sounded so positive, so strong in his character and beliefs, so sure of his right to this kingdom, that she had convinced herself he would win. She had often imagined herself there with him in Naples, secure in their position as king and queen. During his time on the Italian peninsula he had won a number of battles, and then, like a thunderclap, had come the final, unexpected defeat. Was it over, or was his return home no more than a respite? Was their planned marriage merely a means of acquiring reinforcements—through her substantial dowry—for yet another attempt at regaining his Italian kingdom?

She realized that she did not know this man at all. Was he still the bold, fearless, young god she had believed in for so long? Or was he a loser, someone she could not admire?

Chapter Two

The leaves are still golden and falling gently as they reach Perpignan, Yolande's last stop on home soil. To her surprise, she is not nervous now; instead she feels a strange and agreeable expectation—or is it just the beauty of the season and the light wind making her favourite mare skittish?

Yolande has heard so much about Aragon's city of Perpignan as a centre of excellent craftsmanship, and of its complicated history as it passed continually between Aragon and France, that she gazes fascinated about her and almost forgets why she has come. But as the Princess of Aragon enters France, she is fast reminded by the appearance of her bridegroom's younger brother, Charles d'Anjou, Prince of Tarente, who has come to be her escort across Languedoc. He arrives with a large suite of elegant courtiers on fine horses—horses always catch her eye—and the French courtiers follow his lead in paying her their respects.

"Greetings, fine princess, my soon-to-be sister-in-law," he begins with an impish smile and a low sweep of his multi-plumed hat as he bends over the neck of his magnificent steed. He rights himself with a jolly laugh. When he bows almost lower to Juana with a more mischievous grin, Yolande is delightfully surprised and barely stifles a laugh. Juana catches her eye and gives Yolande her most knowing look—if her bridegroom is as handsome and has half the merry wit of his brother, she will be fortunate indeed. Charles is a lively companion and chats away without stopping while riding beside her. He is about her age and she cannot help but be entertained.

"What a fancy little dancing mare you have, my Princess Yolande—may I try her?"

"Certainly not," she replies firmly. "I am sure you would gallop away with her and I would be left with that great warhorse you are riding!"

He laughs, and whacks her mare so hard on the rump with his whip that she leaps and charges off, with him keeping up alongside, still laughing—to the astonishment of Yolande's suite, unaccustomed to seeing their princess treated in such a fashion.

"Ha!" he shouts as they gallop. "You think this mount of mine is not up to yours? Just watch me beat you to that great oak in the distance!" And to Yolande's profound displeasure, he does indeed arrive first. "Never judge by appearances," he chortles, pulling up. "This charger of mine may be built to carry armour, but also to let me escape when I need!"

The way he glances at her from under his long dark lashes is most disconcerting for Yolande, his smile always hovering, a tease of some sort in his eyes. Juana can see that her charge is somewhat taken with this young French prince, until her stern look brings the girl back to her senses.

They are heading towards Arles, the old capital of Provence, where the wedding ceremony will take place. Yolande has heard much about this city, which was important in Roman times and is still full of their ruins.

"Tell me about Arles," she asks Charles, and he does, with such enthusiasm that she makes a mental note to visit all the Roman sites here—the amphitheatre, the circus and the great triumphal arch. "Perhaps your brother will bring me back here some day—there is so much more for me to see."

Her progress has slowed as the crowds grow thicker. Everywhere she stops, Yolande is hailed as a queen—she rather enjoys that, waving graciously and acknowledging the greetings, while her equerries toss coins to the children lining their route.

Her mother has made a huge effort with her trousseau. Yolande's bright-coloured skirts almost touch the ground, and she wears a matching hat with a large brim trimmed with coloured ostrich feathers, pinned on with a sparkling jewel. This Spanish princess, an expert horsewoman, has brought a number of horses with her of pure Arabian blood, as well as the larger Andalusians with their strong, thick necks, flaring nostrils, long manes and tails. All are somewhat friskier than the ambling mares most ladies ride, and naturally she is aware of the admiring looks that greet her, especially from Charles d'Anjou.

"Ah-ha, my beautiful soon-to-be-queenly-sister, I see you intend to sweep our streets with your skirts before deigning to set your pretty foot down on foreign soil," he jokes as he rides up alongside on one of his great chargers, which is snorting and blowing and even nipping the neck of her mare.

"Are all you French lords as forward and flirtatious as your horses!" she protests, in mock horror.

"My lady, I am but your humble servant, on my knees forever before you. My back is yours to step onto mount your own fiery steed whenever you require," he answers with sham modesty.

I must not forget my place, she repeats to herself over and over as they ride.

Their huge cavalcade stops at a large inn, and, together with the nobles of both countries, Yolande changes into a more ceremonial costume; their mounts are equally finely adorned. After all, she is a princess of Aragon, about to marry a royal French duke and receive the title Queen of Sicily. The Pope himself crowned her Louis in Avignon and no lost battle will remove that honour from him.

To Juana's distinct disapproval, Charles d'Anjou is already a great favourite with the young ladies of the Aragonese suite, and they chatter and giggle in his presence as if going to a carnival. Yolande tries to remain serene and play her gracious part, but her future brother-in-law's joking with her ladies until they almost cry with laughter makes it difficult.

"Why, whose is that gorgeous hat?" she hears him call as he snatches one from a *demoiselle* and puts it on his own head. "My, don't I look as elegant as any one of you?" and he hides half his face behind a stolen fan, to muffled shrieks.

Yolande's escort of several young ladies-in-waiting, her *demoiselles*, fuss about her as she dresses. She likes her outfits to be made from the most beautiful imported brocades and silk velvets in a multitude of colours, but she insists on simple styles. And so there is little for her ladies to do—no ribbons to tie or flowers to attach, which would keep them busy pinning or stitching. The bodices of her dresses are laced taut to show off her tiny waist—the more so with her shoulders padded wide and the sleeves fitting tight. Her necklines are high and edged in a white frill, and her hats have feathers floating down her back, dyed in colours to tone. Yolande believes in first impressions, and if her clothes are kept to a sharp silhouette all in one suitable, flattering colour, and worn with a good jewel and hat, she considers the impact greater than a display of ribbons and frills.

Once outside, she can hear shouts of "Brava!" from the crowds, and others calling out "Look at her hat!" and they throw flowers in her path as she bows to left and right.

As they near their destination, Yolande's swollen cavalcade stops at a small château prepared for her arrival. Shown to her suite, which she barely notices in her nervousness at the prospect of this first meeting with her future husband, she calls to Juana:

"Dearest, help me choose what to wear, please."

After a number of false starts, they choose a dress of butter-yellow taffeta with two darker shades of yellow for her petticoats. Her fitted waistcoat is of pale mustard velvet with yellow taffeta sleeves, puffed at the shoulder and then tight from just above the elbow. Yolande is attaching a jabot of white lace at her neck when Juana approaches with the jewel case. "Wear the ruby," she urges. The Queen of Aragon has given her daughter some lovely jewels, and Juana pins the ruby brooch onto the jabot at the front. A large-brimmed white felt hat trimmed with long white ostrich feathers completes her outfit. Her blonde hair is twisted simply into a thick coil at the nape of her neck.

As she leaves the château to mount her horse, Charles d'Anjou rides up to greet her—and for once, his appreciation almost silences him.

"Madame, my princess-sister," he says softly, "you are truly beautiful. I rejoice for my brother and for all France." He removes his hat and bows low on his horse. For once, no joke, no jolly banter—just a quiet smile and a look of reverence in his eyes.

As they approach Arles, the crowds lining their route grow denser.

"Listen to them!" shouts Charles over the noise, and Yolande can hear loud compliments about her, and about the ladies and gentlemen of her suite as well. She rides near the head of the procession, with four splendid knights in parade armour preceding her, as well as two buglers. They are there to announce her arrival, and to warn other travellers or farmers with livestock to clear the road. Her suite does not ride quietly; there is much raucous repartee from all sides and she can sense everyone's excitement growing with her own.

She notices some of her equerries tossing coins to the peasants who hail her, and she returns their salutations with a bright smile. As they come closer to Arles, more mounted Angevin noblemen join their procession, each with a bow of greeting to Yolande, their hats sweeping low, before they fall in behind. How elegant they are in their multicoloured parade outfits, and handsome; she can feel the expectations of her ladies. The crowds lining the road have grown yet thicker, and she can clearly hear their shouts of "Godspeed" and "welcome," and blessings on her marriage. "May this union of Aragon and Anjou bring peace, prosperity and many children," she hears repeated from all sides.

Finally, on 1 December 1400, in weak sunshine but under a clear blue sky, the Princess Yolande of Aragon rides into Arles to meet her bridegroom for the first time, his brother Charles by her side. *If he is as welcoming as the crowds, I shall be fortunate indeed*, enters her mind, with a prayer. What a reception they give her—flowers everywhere, and at this time of year too; people are pressing forward so thickly her mare can hardly walk, but aware of her dancing agitation, they do move back a little.

Then, there he stands—her bridegroom. Any resistance she might still have felt towards this marriage disappears the moment she sees him. Louis d'Anjou is more handsome, more gallant than any young man she has ever imagined, with a penetrating gaze from honest blue eyes and a cheerful, friendly smile. She feels her heart beat so fast it may well jump out of her tight bodice. As she brings her mare up to him, he descends the three steps on which he stands, slips her reins through his left arm, and, with both hands firmly on her waist, gently lifts her down from her horse to overwhelming cheers. As he lowers her, their eyes meet, and at that moment, she knows she can love—*will* love—this man as her husband, completely, for all her life.

"May I greet my beautiful bride," he says with a smile and a low bow after he sets her down.

She drops a deep curtsey, eyes lowered demurely, but when she looks up, she cannot help laughing with delight. "It is a joy indeed to meet my bridegroom," she replies, "especially after such a long journey and"—much softer—"after such a long engagement!"

"You must be tired, my dear," he answers with a smile that reaches his eyes. "Come, meet my mother, and then rest," he says as he steers her firmly by the elbow.

The soft grey eyes of Marie de Blois embrace Yolande as

warmly as do her arms. "Welcome, dearest daughter, welcome to Provence and your new family," and Yolande knows at once that they will be friends.

Louis and Yolande see little of one another on that first evening, as she is presented to the great and the good of his provinces. Occasionally they catch one another's eye across a sea of faces, and she can feel herself blushing in confusion and pleasure.

The next day, 2 December 1400, will be engraved forever on her heart. She is to ride "amazon"—side-saddle—to the church on a large, slow white horse, not her fiery little Arabian. Her mother decided that she should wear a long dress of white silk overlaid with a web of fine silver lace; on her head a high tortoiseshell comb also draped in silver lace, worn in the custom of her country. Following Spanish tradition, as a maiden, under the lace her hair will hang loose over her shoulders to well below her waist. Her only jewellery is a beautiful row of pearls left to her by her father, and matching drop earrings. In front of her horse and behind it walk four elegant stewards dressed in vertical red and yellow stripes, the livery of the House of Aragon. Each holds a gold-painted wooden pole supporting one of the four corners of a cloth-of-gold awning held high over the bride's head. Above her she can see her royal arms and those of her bridegroom embroidered at its centre. In this way the Princess Yolande d'Aragon makes her solemn official entry into Arles, ancient city of the Romans and capital of Louis d'Anjou's sovereign territory of Provence.

Soon the bride forgets her nerves as she gazes with fascination at a large Roman arena and then a theatre. As the cavalcade winds slowly through the narrow streets of ancient sand-coloured stone buildings, she cannot stop marvelling at her surroundings. Despite the lateness of the season, every window and balcony is garlanded, and the streets are completely covered with a blanket of flower petals and local herbs. The delicious scent of rosemary and lavender rises up from under the horses' feet, and the loud cheering of the crowds hailing Yolande as their queen quite overwhelms her. Suddenly the procession turns into a wide cobbled street leading to the ancient church of Saint-Trophime, built three centuries ago in the Roman style, with additions to the cloister of tall pointed arches in the new Frankish manner. Yolande has never seen anything like it.

As she nears the steps of the church, she becomes aware of figures standing waiting to receive her outside the intricately carved stone archway of the entrance. Seeing her bridegroom in all his finery, she catches her breath. How handsome he is, so tall and fair, the sun shining on his silver jacket and hose, a large emerald pinning a white ostrich plume to his hat, another emerald gleaming at his throat. His eyes hold hers and his smile has her trembling until she bites her lip to remain composed. As he lifts her down from her warhorse, she closes her eyes and prays silently not to faint. Somehow she walks the few steps to greet Marie de Blois with a deep court curtsey.

"Welcome to our family," says the duchess softly as she raises Yolande, kissing her cheeks. Those kind grey eyes smiling into Yolande's manifest past suffering but also inner strength. Sensing Yolande's nerves, Marie takes the girl's hand and places it on her firm arm as they enter the cathedral, the bride's knees threatening to buckle under her.

As she passes from the sunlight into the darker interior, Yolande is dazzled by the kaleidoscope of colour and glitter from the church ornaments, the glowing tapestries, the clergy's vestments, the elaborately dressed people all staring at her; and by the overwhelming scent of flowers mixed with incense. She remains standing at the door, as Duchess Marie precedes her on the arm of the bridegroom—the bride is to follow alone once they have reached their places by the altar. A brilliant salvo of silver trumpets announces her entry. With a quick glance around at Juana behind her, Yolande is grateful to see her governess's look of encouragement. Clutching her mother's small ivory-covered prayer book in one hand, a pearl rosary in the other,

her hands joined in front, Yolande d'Aragon starts down the aisle towards the altar, her long train of silver gossamer lace held by her six *demoiselles*, each dressed in the palest lilac. She hears the appreciative murmuring from the packed church and is comforted to know that Charles d'Anjou is walking behind her should she need support. But Yolande has regained her composure now and holds her head high, bowing slowly to right and left, her tall headdress with its covering of fine silver lace adding to her slender, almost ethereal presence.

Surrounded by the nobility of Provence and Anjou, and many of her kinsmen come from Aragon, the Princess Yolande, daughter of the late King of Aragon, is wed with considerable pomp and formality to the son of Duke Louis I d'Anjou, younger brother of the late king, Charles V of France. She hears little of the sermon and moves as instructed, while floating in some kind of trance. The rousing singing of the "Te Deum" brings her back to herself, along with the echoing clarion call of the many silver trumpets. As Louis and his bride leave the church arm in arm, all the great bells of Arles begin tolling, a noise to wake the very dead. Conscious she is trembling, she steals a look at him, while flower petals rain softly down upon their heads from windows and balconies, along with happy salutations. It is good to feel the reassuring right hand of her husband stretching to cover hers on his left arm.

Now, as the wife of the head of the House of Anjou, Yolande is proclaimed the Queen of Four Kingdoms—Naples, Sicily, Cyprus and Jerusalem. Cyprus was conquered by her father, and Louis' father bought the honorary title "King of Jerusalem" from the granddaughter of one of its last kings. Even Hungary was claimed by Queen Giovanna II, once conquered by her father, and her brother crowned then as King Ladislaus before he died. Too many kingdoms—and none of them to hold—for the present.

But all that is as nothing compared with the excitement of being the wife of this dazzling young man. *Dear God*, prays Yolande, *may I prove worthy of him.*

The banquet, speeches and toasts are finally over and they are brought to a suite in the royal palace. Alone with her husband in this large room, her nerves return. What should she say to him? No matter how strong her feelings, how can she start to know this dazzling husband of hers?

It is Louis who breaks the silence, holding her by her shoulders at arm's length and saying, "My dearest lady, my own wife, I have a confession to make to you."

For an instant she imagines that her bubble of joy might burst with some fearful revelation, and she forces herself to remain calm as he continues.

"It is true I had heard of your beauty, but princes are often lured into marriages of opportunity this way. I had to be sure. Now I must admit to you that I rode ahead of the rest of my party to await your arrival in Arles." Yolande's mouth falls open in surprise, but she smiles a little as she reads the look in his eyes. "I mingled with the crowd, listening to their comments about you and your entourage. Every voice lauded your beauty; the people were in a state of wonder and awe— and as your cavalcade approached I watched you laughing happily as you encouraged your spirited mare to prance for the crowd. Even before I saw your face emerging from the shadow of the buildings, I noticed your horse—what a mettlesome little Arabian—and how you controlled her with such ease and confidence. I thought to myself, "If she can handle that horse, she can handle anything." And then suddenly you were bathed in sunlight, a golden vision, skirts fluttering at every pirouette your horse made. And then I saw the beauty of your eyes..."

She holds her breath.

"At that moment I bent one knee to the ground and crossed myself, thanking the Lord—and the wisdom of my mother—for having sent me this paragon; then I slipped away to await your official arrival. Will you forgive me?" he asks anxiously.

With tender kisses she closes his questioning blue eyes. This man, she knows now, will fill her heart with love every day, whether they are together or apart. As he carries her to their marriage bed, she swears inwardly he will be the only man she will ever love.

To judge from his ardour, he does not seem disappointed in her either. "My darling wife, you and I will share such pleasures every night of our lives," he tells her with a gentle kiss in the morning—and she believes him.

It does not take her long to gauge his character. She judges him to be generous of spirit and human kindness; gentle yet strong; ambitious; most learned and sound in his judgements. And she too blesses his mother, and hers, for their wisdom in arranging their union; more, she trembles just at the thought of him touching her again.

He loves her, of that she is sure even after their first night together, but she discovers as the days and weeks go by that there are areas of himself he guards fiercely and will not share even with her—his real thoughts on what happened in Naples, his ambitions for the future. She knows his temper is strong and that she would be wise not to cross it. In these early, heady days of love, such realizations do not worry her. She knows herself too, knows that she will find ways to unravel his inner labyrinth and discover what she needs to prove a useful partner and collaborator. She will always be obedient to him, but naivety has never been part of her character.

After several days of ceremonies and celebrations, the bridal couple leave Arles and make their leisurely way by boat to Tarascon, where Louis has almost completed constructing what will be his principal seat in Provence. Situated in a valley, right on the bank of the River Rhône, this high, sheer fortress of white stone is being built on the site of a number of castles erected, destroyed and rebuilt again since Roman times. A few years ago Louis razed the last old fortress and sent workmen to begin building his new *château fort*. Tarascon lies south of Avignon and north of Arles, in a strategic position on a bend of the Rhône that allows a perfect view of the countryside in every direction.

The river is the border of their sovereign territory of Provence, with France on the opposite bank.

Yolande loves this new château at first sight. Its great ramparts and crenellated towers, the whole seeming to grow sharply out of the rocks at its base. Narrow steps lead down to a landing area for small boats, and Louis takes her out on the river. The Rhône is not wide there; they could cross easily to France on the other side should they wish.

Despite the château's austere stone exterior, her clever mother-in-law, Marie de Blois, has arranged the interior to be as dedicated to comfort and elegant living as it is said she has done in her other legendary castles of the House of Anjou. The ceilings are wooden, sometimes decorated with fanciful animals cut out of lead and stuck onto the beams; there is a chimney piece with a lit fire in each room; trellised windows allow abundant light and give views onto the Rhône. How Yolande would love her mother to see this, her first home—but in her absence, she knows that Marie de Blois will teach her how to run and manage such a large establishment.

After their arrival, they are partaking of refreshments in the Great Hall when the duchess takes Yolande by the arm and leads her gently to stand by the chimney piece. Stretching her hands towards the fire, she addresses her with the sweetest of smiles.

"Dearest child, since you are the wife of my son, you are also my child, if you will allow me this privilege?" Yolande senses that her mother-in-law is about to say something that means much to her. "By your marriage you are now the Duchess d'Anjou, Guyenne and Maine, and Sovereign Countess of Provence, but hereafter you will always be referred to as the Queen of Sicily, the highest of all your many titles—and I shall be known as the Queen Dowager." With that, to Yolande's astonishment, the old lady bows gracefully to her before leaving the room.

Chapter Three

Louis and Yolande are in Tarascon with Marie de Blois and Charles d'Anjou, sitting around a glowing fire after dinner one evening.

"My darling," says Louis, "I have decided that when we travel north on our way to Anjou, we will stop in Paris for a few days and call on the king."

Yolande's reaction is a mixture of surprise, delight and apprehension, but she says nothing. Strange rumours had already reached her in distant Aragon about the state of mind of the French king, and some anxiety mingled with her fascination. She hugs her knees with her back against a deep cushion, eager to learn more. But what she hears—as Louis, Charles and his mother take turns to tell the story—is not quite what she expected.

She knows that the King of France is Louis' first cousin, Charles VI, a famously handsome, blonde charmer, whose reign began with such promise that even in Aragon they heard his praises sung. He was only eleven years old when he was crowned in 1380. Everyone was delighted when at the age of sixteen he married the beautiful Princess Isabeau of Bavaria, who adored him. When he came of age, three years later, he decided to dismiss his royal uncles, who had ruled during his minority, and instead appointed sound advisers from the bourgeoisie to help him reign. They were known as "The Marmosets"—wise, decent men who continued the policies of

Charles V, his father, who was justly called *Le-Bon*.

Louis' father, the eldest of the king's uncles, left for Naples and tragically died there. The old king's other two brothers, the uncles both of the king and of Louis himself, were the Dukes of Burgundy and Berry. They, as well as his uncle by marriage, the Duke of Bourbon, King of Navarre were occupied with their own sovereign duchies. It was the king's brother, the Duke Louis d'Orléans, who remained always by his side, loyally supportive, his companion and closest friend.

No one was in any doubt that this was a truly promising beginning, and indeed, for the first four years of his reign, Charles gave the impression that he would become an excellent ruler. Since the personality and the character of a monarch dictates the quality of his government, the French felt blessed by God in the personality and wisdom of the young King Charles VI. But as he reached the age of twenty-four, things started to change. The king began to lapse into regular bouts of insanity. Two incidents seemed to have prompted these; one of them was referred to afterwards at the French court as the "Ball of the Burning Men."

In order to entertain their sovereign, his close courtiers were constantly trying to amuse him, and so they arranged a costume ball at the château of Vincennes, an event that created great excitement. Several courtiers, including the king, decided to disguise themselves as "wild men" who lived in the forests. At least ten of them entered the ballroom chained together, wearing costumes made of cloth soaked in a resinous wax on which was stuck a covering of frazzled hemp to make them look hirsute. They were a great success, instantly surrounded by revellers trying to guess their identities.

Louis d'Orléans, the king's brother, arrived late and had not seen the strange group enter the ballroom. Taking hold of a flaming torch from one of the servants, he moved towards the bizarre cluster of chained men. Somehow, by accident, the torch came too close to one of the "wild men," whose highly flammable costume immediately caught fire. Since the men were chained together, the fire spread instantly to the others, as did the panic in the room.

Even in the retelling, far away in this comfortable castle, the horror of that moment seems alive in the room. Yolande's hand is over her mouth. Marie de Blois has tears in her eyes, and Louis looks distraught. His voice is low as he finishes the story.

"Our aunt, the Duchess of Berry, threw her heavy train over one burning man to smother the flames. Mercifully it was the king, her husband's nephew, whom she had rescued. Another flaming wild man jumped into a tub of washing-up water and saved himself. Other courtiers tried to put out the flames with their bare hands and were badly injured. Four of the wild men, all friends of the king and the court, were burnt to death in front of everyone at the ball. The king was distraught and took to his room alone for some time."

There is a pause as Louis throws another log on the fire, and then the three take up the second tale, describing how not long afterwards, while the king was out hunting with the court, a hirsute peasant, a real wild man, ran out from the undergrowth and grabbed the reins of his horse, causing it to rear. He would not let go, gabbling hysterically about a plot to kill the king. Charles's companions, mistaking the deranged man for an assassin, drew their swords and killed him. "But he was only trying to warn me," exclaimed a confused Charles, visibly shaken. For several days afterwards he locked himself away in his room again.

Following these two incidents, the king would descend regularly into bouts of deep depression. These developed into sporadic outbursts of insanity, which increased in frequency and intensity thereafter.

Sensing Louis' anguish at telling her these things, Yolande moves next to him and makes him drink the warm wine a servant has left by the fire. It is as though a view distantly glimpsed has suddenly come into focus. Some of the story is not new to her—at her parents' court in Saragossa they had heard of the French king's condition, his sudden terrible rages when he lost all control, even killing some of his servants in unprovoked, frenzied attacks—but she had never known what to believe. Her parents had already received the ambassadors from Anjou proposing her marriage to their young duke, and the King and Queen of Aragon became concerned when they heard that the cousin of their daughter's betrothed had turned into a madman. They did not tell her any of this at the time, but as she grew older, she could hardly fail to hear the rumours, and she began to wonder. Did Louis have the same mental illness in his blood? Would he become like his cousin and try to cut off her head as the French king had done to one of his courtiers?

Despite Louis' distress, Yolande is relieved to know the full story. Warmed by the wine, she leads her troubled husband to their room and holds him close in her arms as he weeps. Instinctively she knows that he worries for the sanity of their children yet unborn.

When Louis himself exposed these revelations about his king and cousin, she understood he wanted her to know the worst possible scenario that could result from their union. Through this uncomfortable disclosure made by such a proud man, Yolande knows that she has come another step closer to understanding the man with whom she has so easily fallen in love.

After two weeks in Provence, Louis has seen to his various duties in the region and, together with their enormous suite, they leave Tarascon for Paris. Their journey by river is made in flat-bottomed boats with sails that catch the wind from above the river banks, which in some places are impressively high. Ingeniously, their masts can be lowered flat to the deck to allow them to pass under bridges. Yolande is fascinated. They row north on the Rhône to Lyon, changing to boats waiting on the Saône to take them to Châlon. From there they transfer to horses and carriages to reach Paris. It is a long and complicated journey, but as everything around her is new, Yolande finds it thrilling.

"Where possible we always travel by river," Louis tells her. "The roads are often impassable during the cold season."

"And Charles has told me about the brigands," she says, with a little too much excitement. He laughs at her as he indicates the number of soldiers they have travelling alongside them.

It is December, midwinter here in the north, and Yolande can feel the growing chill as they head away from the warmth of the south. In the boats are soft fur rugs and small brass braziers filled with hot coals. The ladies slide under their fur covers and push heated bedpans down towards their feet. Yolande is as excited as a child; wearing fur mittens and a hood, she can enjoy every moment on the river, the banks lined with trees, their branches often sweeping down into the water.

Their entourage is large, but she and Louis manage to be alone quite often. They picnic on the banks of rivers and spend their nights in comfortable quarters, ignoring everyone else, selfishly absorbed in one another. Louis tells her about the members of his family she will meet, the king and queen especially, so that she is prepared.

After three weeks of travelling, by river and then by road, finally they reach Paris. Their reception is noisy—soldiers stamping to attention, and many barking dogs leaping on their master with joy. Louis' magnificent manor house on the banks of the Seine is almost a small town in itself, with a great inner courtyard, separate houses within, and stabling for many horses. The staff, beautifully trained by Louis' mother, stand in a long line, each greeting their new mistress with a bow or curtsey.

With warm smiles, they make Yolande comfortable in her spacious quarters, the windows overlooking the river as well as the courtyard. Her suite is beautiful. Primrose silk hangs from the posts at the four corners of her bed, forming a ceiling over it, and there is a bedspread of ermine, with white fox furs draped on large cushions and laid on the floor by the fire on top of the exotic oriental rugs. Painted clay figures and bowls and silver candelabra decorate the surfaces, and the gold dressing table is set with a standing gilded lookingglass. With a small intake of breath, Yolande sees her own initials entwined with those of her husband on the backs of all the brushes and engraved on the vermeil lids of the crystal jars. The care and loving thoughtfulness shown by Marie de Blois must be unique, she thinks to herself, recognizing that there is so much she can learn from this extraordinary lady. Little sachets of lavender lie in each clothes chest, and the wardrobes are lined in sandalwood to keep away moths. The smell is delicious and brings back recent memories of her days and nights with Louis in Provence.

The royal newlyweds are constantly invited and feted. Yolande barely has time to take in the sights of this great city as she passes her days and evenings smiling, bowing, allowing her hand to be kissed again and again—some of the peasants even kiss her feet. She tries hard to pay attention to the people she meets during these early days of her marriage, all the while attempting to read their minds, their hearts, and gauge their loyalty to her husband, as well as to their king.

She is happy, swept up in Louis and his love. She finds she has almost forgotten Aragon, and at times even her dearest mother grows faint in her mind, filling her with guilt. Sometimes it seems that only the sight of Juana and her wolfhounds remind her that she had a life before the day she married.

*

As the day of her presentation at court looms, Yolande pleads with Louis to be excused so that their formal life does not yet need to begin. "Let us continue in private a while longer," she begs him. Then she recognizes his expression and reassures him quickly: "No, my love, I am not nervous or afraid in any way. I just do not want this time alone with you to end too soon."

But she knows it must end, and Louis wants his bride to meet the king and queen, as well as other members of his family and a number of the important courtiers, before they leave for his duchy of Anjou.

They arrive at the Louvre in great style, surrounded by Louis' liveried attendants. The building is enormous, and severe. "My darling, I had no idea this palace would be so impressive," says Yolande, marvelling at the finely cut honey-coloured stone, the main facade facing the river and the great courtyard within where their carriages draw up among many others. Their attendants all hold flaming torches; horses agitate, more guests arrive. "Will the king be normal?" she asks nervously.

Louis laughs. "We shall see!"

Yolande has chosen to wear a dress of green velvet, and as she enters, she removes her matching cloak lined in dark sable. As Louis' new duchess, she wants to make a good impression. She prays that her dress, train and headdress are appropriate, and that she will do her husband justice before the critical eyes of the court. How could they be otherwise? She is a *foreign* princess, after all.

They are shown into the glittering Great Hall, her discerning eye lighting on the huge, exquisite tapestries lining the high walls before Louis leads her to the throne. Her court obeisance is low and slow, as she was taught at home in Aragon, and only on rising does she look. She sees a pair of smiling blue eyes, very much like Louis', a charming face and a hand beckoning her forward. Louis whispers: "Go up and sit by him on the stool," and she obeys.

Charles VI is still a very handsome man, only nine years older than her husband, but he has a certain vacant expression that makes her unsure of his awareness. This is dispelled at once when he addresses her loudly enough for the nearby courtiers to hear.

"Ah! My dear new cousin Yolande! Welcome to Paris! How was your journey from distant Aragon to Provence? And another long journey to come to visit us at our court in Paris, for which I am grateful." He smiles endearingly, looking so like Louis. "I hear you speak perfect French, due to your Valois mother. What a pleasure," he says, as he takes her hand and lightly kisses it. Then, more softly, just for her ears: "I hope you will visit us often."

He examines her with a cool, appraising gaze.

"Hmm, I am beginning to think you are someone with whom I can talk freely, someone I can even trust." He says this so quietly that Yolande is not sure whether Louis can hear him.

"Sire," she replies just as softly and sincerely, looking into his eyes, "with pleasure."

At that, he removes a ring from his smallest finger, a gold ring with a fine, smooth sapphire engraved with his crest, and slips it onto her slim index finger. "This ring is my gift to you, my beautiful new cousin. It will remind you of our first meeting and can always gain you access to me should you need it." Again he smiles into her eyes. "Now you may greet Isabeau."

She bows low again and turns to his queen, Isabeau of Bavaria, who is sitting on a throne a little distance apart from her husband. Seeing her, Yolande is taken aback somewhat, although she gives no sign. In Aragon she was told that the queen was beautiful, but if that was so, only a hint of beauty now remains. After giving birth to ten children, Isabeau has lost her figure and is swathed in copious finely woven silks to hide her shape, so that she resembles a pyramid of multicoloured spun sugar. On her head she wears several ropes of pearls entwined within her hair, and her ears are weighed down by a pair of large rubies. When she looks at Yolande's slim waist, there is regret in her eyes, but also a certain sympathy, as if she recognizes no malice in Yolande, a foreign king's daughter like herself, newly arrived in a potentially hostile environment.

"Yes," she says graciously, echoing her husband, "come

and visit us, beautiful Yolande. You will always be welcome wherever we hold our court." And she beckons Yolande to approach and kiss her.

Louis has exchanged friendly words with the king; now he too kisses the queen's hand and cheek, and they withdraw from the dais. He takes Yolande to one side. "Now you must meet the king's brother, Louis d'Orléans, the greatest charmer in France."

He is right. Apart from her Louis, the king's brother is the handsomest man in the room—no, in France; certainly the second-handsomest man she has ever seen.

"Where has my cousin been hiding you, ravishing new member of our family?" he says. "Yolande—a name to roll on one's tongue with delight," and he laughs merrily. "Come, meet my Valentina—we have both heard of you and want to be satisfied that your charms have not been exaggerated!"

With that, Louis d'Orléans steers Yolande by her elbow towards a dark-haired Italian beauty as tall as she is, with a disarming smile and flashing eyes. "Welcome to Paris, and France, and this court, our new cousin Yolande. May you find peace outside it—for there is certainly none within!" she says with a laugh, but Yolande detects a trace of sadness. "Now that we are family, I hope you will visit me and meet my children—and have some of your own soon as well! In your Louis you have won the best of this family, for only he has no interest in acquiring more power here—it is the curse of this court." To Yolande's surprise she says this quite openly.

"Pay her no mind, beautiful cousin. My darling wife is from Milan, where they thrive on intrigues!" interjects Louis d'Orléans, caressing his wife's cheek fondly with the back of a finger. "Now, there is one more cousin for you to meet, at least so you know whom to avoid," says her husband quite frankly. "I am amazed he has shown his ugly face here, but I can see he is already making his way towards you. Be warned—despite appearances, he is not a giant toad, but our cousin, Duke Jean of Burgundy."

Standing before her is quite the ugliest man she has seen in company—gross, pockmarked, with small eyes, a mean expression, and large, wet, protruding lips; his unsightliness the more marked standing between the two beautiful Louis—and all three of them first cousins. Jean-sans-Peur, John-the-Fearless, as he is known, bows over Yolande's hand, which he wets with his kiss, and she instinctively recoils.

Thankfully her husband is at her elbow and steadies her, saying graciously, "Cousin Jean, I am pleased to present to you my wife Yolande. I trust you will pass our good wishes to your dear father." And with that he smiles warmly and bows, as he turns easily on his heel towards a fine-looking older man. "Ah, my dear uncle of Bourbon! Meet Yolande, my bride from Aragon. My dear, this is the king's and my uncle, Louis of Bourbon, husband of our aunt Jeanne. I know you will be friends."

There is something about the older man's face that appeals to her instantly, an apparent goodness and calm. They greet one another warmly, and then Louis whispers in her ear:

"My darling, I have saved the best until last. Now you will meet my favourite uncle, Duke Jean of Berry, my father's younger brother and the most cultured of the whole family. There he is by the window—let us move towards him and then your ordeal will be over."

"Louis, my dearest nephew," says the older man as they embrace warmly. "And this must be your bride from Aragon about whose beauty the whole room is talking." He bows to her with such a sweet expression—how could anyone not like him instantly? "My dear Yolande, I do hope you will visit me at Bourges. It is a most agreeable city, the capital of my land of Berry. Do you enjoy books? I have a library that will delight you. Won't you please come?"

"I shall, dear new uncle, I shall come to Bourges with great pleasure if you promise to show me your famous Book of Hours

I have heard so much about?"

"Ah, you know of my *Très Riches Heures*! So its fame has reached Aragon?" he asks with evident pleasure. "It will be my delight to show it to you, my dear." And with an all-embracing smile he is swallowed up into the crowd as Louis takes her elbow again and steers her determinedly to a door, and they slip away.

For this evening's event, her introduction to the court of France, Yolande took considerable trouble with her appearance, choosing a dress of green silk velvet, the colour of the emerald necklace and earrings Louis gave her as a wedding gift, but he made no comment before they arrived at court—just when she needed a word to give her confidence! Only now does he say:

"You looked so breathtakingly beautiful when you entered the Great Hall that the room fell silent. Did you notice, my darling? I was very proud." He squeezes her arm. "The king and queen clearly liked you. Show me the ring Charles gave you? Yes, it *is* fine. It will indeed give you access to him should you ever have need. Believe me, this is not a gesture I have seen him make before. I was pleased to see that even our Queen Isabeau, the Whale, took to you. But I am glad that is over. You have met my family, the good with the bad. Now we can move on with our own lives away from the court."

To her surprise, he doesn't ask for her opinions about his family. She will wait.

Her first visit to the court of France is behind her. But she knows that wherever she is, that strange court, with its intrigues and pall of suspicion, its atmosphere soured by the fear of royal madness, will lie forever at the heart of her marriage. For Louis is sworn by blood, birth and fealty to uphold his king, and this duty is something he cannot stress enough to Yolande.

"My beautiful, beloved, intelligent wife: never forget that our most important duty in our lives is not to each other, nor to our children should the good Lord grant us them, but to our sovereign king, who has been placed on earth by God to rule us, and we to obey."

He is adamant about this and speaks totally sincerely when emphasising their duty to their sovereign. Yolande, only half-French and educated in Aragon, a wife and soon, she hopes, a mother too, learns to follow him in his obedience to the crown of France and promises, on his insistence, to place this loyalty even before him and her future children.

"My lord and husband, this is a big step for me to take, especially on foreign soil, but if it is your will, I promise to make your values and loyalties my own as much as Aragon's were." And he holds her, because he understands.

Chapter Four

They leave Paris in clear, crisp weather with glorious blue skies, heading south-west on horseback. Theirs is an impressive caravan, and it takes them a week to reach Orléans. Louis delights in showing Yolande this great city, second only to Paris in wealth and importance. They visit the vast Frankish cathedral, a magnificent building with tall towers and slender pointed arches.

His duty done as her guide, their short visit over, he says: "Come, my darling, our boats are waiting and I long to show you my home and now yours." With that happy thought, they embark on Louis' comfortable boat and travel downstream on the Loire. Her husband points out landmarks, fortresses, defensive towers, and tells her the names of the villages they pass, to greetings from all sides. Yolande sees only smiling faces; the people look well fed and content, going about their business tidily dressed and not in the usual rags of the peasantry in Aragon.

They disembark at Les Ponts-de-Cé, not far from Angers, where Louis' people meet them and take them to a large wooden inn by the river, smoke billowing from its two chimneys. In warm rooms they change out of their travelling clothes into formal attire, to make their official entry into Louis' capital.

Seeing how excited and happy his wife is to be arriving at her new home at last, Louis explains: "A page will carry my ducal crown on a cushion while I will leave my head bare so the people can see me." He is dressed in a beautiful suit of burgundy velvet with collar and cuffs of sable fur against the cold, a shining brooch of many colours at his throat—"A gift to my grandfather Charles Vfrom an Ottoman sultan," he tells her proudly. To complement him—and she marks his approving look—Yolande wears a burgundy velvet tight-fitting short jacket, with a sable collar and cuffs like his, and a long skirt of burgundy velvet to hang down the side of her horse, also hemmed all around with sable. To keep her head warm, yet more sable turned like a crown around a burgundy velvet cap. On the side of it she pins a large golden topaz surrounded with diamonds, which gleams in the brown fur. Their horses are caparisoned in quilted ornamental ceremonial cloths almost to the ground, bearing the red and yellow colours of Anjou. Husband and wife smile approvingly at one another—he to reassure her, she full of admiration.

For the short distance, they are preceded by a company of dashing Angevin knights riding four abreast, fully armed and carrying pennants. Soon they see people lining the road, the crowds becoming thicker as they near the city. They hear the high-pitched blast of silver trumpets—a fanfare of welcome—as they walk their horses slowly through a sea of smiling, waving, cheering citizens. Throughout the ceremonial entry, Louis and Yolande often glance at one another and smile. They do not need words at moments like this—they already know one another's hearts and minds. Many emotions fill her breast: delight at the people's warm reaction to her; excitement about the challenges ahead, the new life unfolding.

After Louis has presented to her a long line of servants with a word about each, he leads her, followed by Ajax and Hector, around the great castle of Angers. Only now does she begin to appreciate the might of the House of Anjou. Angers is a massive, powerful fortress, almost a city in itself, rising majestically from huge rocks at the edge of the River Maine. Looking down, she can see a substantial parade area within its walls and many buildings. Not a talkative man by nature, Louis points out the seventeen enormous pepperpot towers high above them: "A castle strong and large enough to house an army, my darling," he tells her proudly. Never before has she seen anything to match its dramatic alternating horizontal stripes of what she later learns is black schist and white tuffeau stone—and the sheer scale of it overwhelms her.

"Angers," explains Louis, squeezing her hand reassuringly, "is the most important fortress in all France." And Yolande can do nothing but nod in wide-eyed wonder.

In contrast to its severe military exterior, once again, the luxurious and surprisingly comfortable interior—with the exception of the immense stone Great Hall—is due to the taste and elegance of her mother-in-law.

To Yolande's relief, Marie de Blois herself arrives at Angers not long afterwards, to teach her daughter-in-law how to become the absolute mistress of her great house.

"Yolande, my dear, come, I will have you meet the people who run Angers in my absence. I hope they will serve you as well as they have served me," she says with her sweet smile as she presents the staff. "This is Vincenzo, my major-domo, who has been here since he was seven years old. He learnt everything from his father, who had the post before him." A tall man of about thirty years bows low before her and meets her eyes with his own honest pair. *Yes, I will keep Vincenzo. His clear intelligence will prove most useful.*

"And this is Carlo, whose father and grandfather were both factors at Angers. They are a most experienced and loyal family." Carlo is another whose face Yolande likes instantly; she judges him to be intelligent and willing to serve her as his new mistress here. Another clever face. Yes, she is pleased with these two on sight.

An idea is taking shape in her mind. Among her mother's household, she remembered three servants who were more than that. With time and quiet observation, she came to know their extra duties. They would travel with her parents wherever they went, and sometimes one of them would be "lent" by her mother to another important household for a period of time—to help train a new wife's staff, or to fill in for an absent servant. With her sharp eyes and ears, Yolande soon understood that these three were also working in a different capacity. Yes, her gentle mother had them *spying* for her! One day, not long before she left Saragossa for her marriage, she asked her mother if this was true.

"Dearest child, come and sit here with me quietly, because your question is a serious one and it concerns something I have wanted to talk to you about for some time.

"You may be surprised that your mother, whom you look on as some kind of saint—yes, I know you think me without fault—could do such a thing as plant a spy in another household—even that of a friend." She looked at Yolande, her head tipped slightly to one side. "Now listen to me, and listen well. Life can be dangerous for anyone, whatever their station. But for a *ruler*, knowledge is the key to survival. He who knows wins!—never forget that. For this reason I have trained three loyal members of my staff to watch, to listen—and to report to me. I never even shared this with your father when he lived, although he had such people of his own. Find similar trustworthy individuals among your servants and you will be in a better position not only to survive, but to win!" With that she smiled and left Yolande digesting the importance of her words. She made herself a promise then that she too would find trustworthy people to work for her. And, after all, she had brought Juana with her, whose eyes and ears had been well trained by her mother.

Marie de Blois leads Yolande to the kitchens, where about thirty staff rush about preparing food. She sees several carcasses rotating over hot coals—sheep and lambs as well as fowl. There is a delicious smell of baking, and someone passes them with a barrow of apples from a larder.

"The kitchens can feed an army, though luckily that does not happen too often," smiles Marie de Blois. "But we do entertain constantly when in residence and there are never fewer than fifty sitting down to dinner. This is Giacomo, my head chef and overseer of the kitchens. He came as a boy to learn from his father, and now his son works in the pantry just as he did." Yolande faces a round, beaming, red-faced man of about thirty-five, who snaps his fingers. Immediately a dish is brought with something freshly baked.

"My lady, please do me the honour of tasting this small delicacy," he says, in an accent she can hardly understand.

"Delicious! What is in the filling?"

"Ah, Madame"—he seems to burst with happiness at her approval—"it is the liver of one of our special home-bred white geese. We force them to drink strong wine, and then the dogs chase them to make them run and the alcohol enters their bloodstream—especially the liver—before they meet their end." He draws a line with his finger across his throat with a toothless grin. "That and the almonds I grate finely into the mix!" he adds proudly.

"Poor goose. But perhaps it is better to die drunk than sober?" Yolande asks Louis when they meet again, and he falls about laughing.

"But we always give our fowl a good drink before a jolly chase, and then, chop! Just like I am going to do to you now..." and he chases her around their bedroom with a small glass of something that, when he catches her, she finds is delicious and made from plums.

"Is this what you give your geese?" she asks, amazed, already feeling the effects of the strong spirit.

"Yes, it is made by our local monks. Do you like it? They make wonderful spirits from the fruits I send to Anjou from our orchards in Provence."

Louis d'Anjou is known as a most hospitable duke and the château of Angers is constantly full of guests, as Yolande learns from her excellent major-domo Vincenzo, whom she watches carefully. *Yes, I think he might just make a useful informer within my household—like my mother's in Saragossa...* Once their guests have retired after dinner and entertainments, she and Louis sit alone in the cosy sitting room between their bedrooms, comparing notes about the guests with just the dogs for company. This is their time, when they learn about one another, their cultures and childhoods.

"You know," she tells Louis, "my father so loved music at his court, he would send his agents to entice the best musicians and poets from the courts of Europe to come to Aragon. What music we had, and how we would dance!" And she shows him how they would twirl in their particular Spanish way, stamping her feet, clicking her fingers and moving her skirts to one side like a toreador baiting a bull.

Louis is entranced. "Darling, do that again! Will you teach me?"

She laughs. "No, that is how the ladies dance; for the men it's like this"—and she makes herself very straight and stamps her feet, which frightens the dogs and makes Louis roll on the bed holding his sides.

"My mother knew of your French troubadours from Champagne, Picardy and Artois, and begged Papa to send for them as well. They taught us to play their instruments—I could play for you if you asked me very nicely?" Only when he begs her does Yolande agree to play the guitar—which she does rather well. Sometimes when she sings, Hector and Ajax accompany her as she taught them, by howling, their long noses in the air, and the three of them make a terrible noise until she and Louis fall off their cushions, laughing like children.

"Imagine, my mother sent our Catalan musicians to Flanders and even here to France to learn new songs, and they would return with their own special blend of exquisite sounds. As children we were allowed to join in and sing with them."

"And I can see how well your musicians taught your dogs to make their own special blend of exquisite sounds!" says Louis, highly amused.

At other times he sits spellbound as Yolande tells him about Barcelona's fame as one of the most cultivated royal courts of Europe. "My mother used to tell us of her upbringing at the fabled court of Burgundy, and how it influenced our own at Saragossa. Can we visit your uncle Philippe in Burgundy one day?"

Louis nods. "We will, I hope. However important our court at Anjou is, I know it is not as full of culture as my uncles' courts at Berry and Burgundy. My father was always much more interested in his distant kingdom of Naples and Sicily, but his younger brothers filled their courts with the greatest treasures they could find, and live with a sophistication unequalled in Christendom."

It is during one of their fireside evenings together that Yolande gathers the courage to ask Louis the question she has been pondering ever since receiving his letter telling her he was coming home from Naples to marry her. She has often wondered whether he would have come if he had not lost his precious kingdom. Or would she have sat spinning and embroidering for years before he sent for her? What if his answer is not to her liking? She has tried so often, but finally she feels the moment is right to ask.

"Tell me my darling..." she begins with trepidation, then hesitates.

"What is it?" Louis fondles her hair.

"Well, I have often wondered... I have wondered about your hopes of returning... with me... to rule one day in Naples." There. She has said it.

Silence.

Louis looks serious and throws another log on the fire. He does not reply at once. It is as if he has to work out the answer himself first, although he must have thought about it often. She bites her lip as he gets up and walks to the window, pours a tumbler of wine, returns slowly and sits.

"Oh, my darling wife..." He pauses and looks at his wine, and then his words come in a rush. "If only I could show you

Naples: the great harbour that can hold hundreds of ships, and high above, the mighty volcano Vesuvius belching smoke." He looks up as if he can see it. "The vegetation in every direction, so green and lush; the pretty houses clustered up the mountain's slope and around the harbour, painted in different pastel shades, each with its own portico growing grapes; the streets filled with laden donkeys; the animation of the locals, singing and talking loudly while they work—and most of all, the genuine welcome of the townspeople as they row out to greet me in countless small craft when my galleon appears, flying my flag as their king." He hardly draws breath. "Such voluble, kind, expressive people, full of laughter and gaiety, very different from the French of the north or our subjects in Provence. I have enormous respect for them, and love, yes, love. Of course I want to return with you one day." He stops, astonished at his own outburst, and taking her hand, he presses her palm to his lips.

Yolande listens wide-eyed as this man she has come to adore talks about Naples as if he has lost a woman he loves passionately—to another. And he wants her back! She feels icy fingers touch her heart. *Can I not make him happy here in his own land, where he has so much?* she thinks. *This must be my goal. To make Louis forget Naples unless he can have her back without cost or pain—and with me by his side!*

"Naples is not just a port city, you know—it is a large kingdom with landholdings stretching down to the heel of the Italian peninsula, all the way into Calabria and beyond into Sicily. You cannot imagine the glorious weather, the flowers, the animals." He sighs. "How I love it there." As he talks on, describing Roman ruins, caves along the shore with water clearer than glass, sunrises and sunsets seen from different sides of the bay, fish, orchards, vineyards, fields and forests—and more—Yolande realizes how much *that* is his true realm and the place where he has left his soul. Only now has she grasped the strength of Naples. His love of the kingdom will not fade easily.

Chapter Five

𝕬s Yolande follows her husband about his duties in his domains—meeting his representatives, joining the ladies of every town and village they visit, observing their children in the care of the clergy, surveying their livestock, their crops, orchards, vineyards, fisheries—she continues to absorb the complexities of his life. But it is the discreet presence of her mother-in-law, Marie de Blois, that makes her task of learning to manage such an enormous responsibility very much easier. All her life Yolande has lived in large castles, but until her marriage, she has never been involved in their administration. Each morning the two Duchesses of Anjou draw up lists of what needs to be done or learnt that week, whether domestic tasks or the demands of the countryside: harvests; fairs; roads to be repaired; villages to visit; parishes to attend; widows and abandoned children to be housed; rivers to be cleared of fallen trees; the breeding of horses, sheep and cattle; even of hounds for the hunt.

Yolande has come to love Angers, that colossal fortress with its large reception rooms, the glorious series of tapestries of the Apocalypse commissioned by her father-in-law, their toiles painted by a master from Bruges. When she first commented on their beauty, Louis told her with pride, "Do you know, my darling, it took the best weavers in Paris five years to complete them. I do believe they are among the finest tapestries in France." She is intrigued by the intricacies of their design and workmanship, never tiring of walking along slowly beside them, tracing their story with one finger as she passes.

Despite the château's remarkable treasures—and there are many to appreciate and admire—her greatest delight lies elsewhere.

"Louis, come, see this," she called to him in excitement on her first day. Louis came to stand by her side on the castle's arched balcony, gazing down onto the lazy Loire snaking past the city's feet. "Look! Look! From here I can see *three rivers* joining! Surely this is an astonishing sight!" she exclaimed, wide-eyed.

"Yes, my darling, they are the Maine, the Mayenne and the Loire," he told her, smiling at her pleasure.

Of course he has known this view for years, but she can sit for hours, fascinated, watching the river traffic coming from all directions, learning to recognize the different types of crafts and their origins, even sometimes correctly guessing their cargo. The rivers bring not only produce to Angers; they also bring an endless stream of visitors and merchants, with wondrous goods acquired from all over the country, from the Mediterranean and even beyond.

Soon Angers' new duchess comes to understand that within this mighty city-château lies the source of the House of Anjou's great pride. Only at Angers can she—or anyone—fully appreciate the tremendous power of this family. She has long heard of the "douceur Angevine," spoken of softly and with wonder; now she understands what it means. Despite its granite-hard majesty, Angers manages somehow to incorporate in its surrounding countryside a unique tenderness, if countryside can be so described. Living here, Yolande believes it can.

Each Sunday they walk with their retinue to the cathedral of Saint-Maurice, an awe-inspiring mix of low, round Roman arches and of the modern style of soaring pointed arches, sweeping heavenward and tempting her eyes to stray from her Book of Hours. One Sunday evening after dinner, as they discuss the magnificence of the cathedral, they arrive at a simultaneous inspiration.

"Why don't we commission a fine chapel," announces Louis, "to be built in the cathedral in our joint name? We shall have the arms of Sicily, Jerusalem, Aragon and Anjou carved in its vaulted archways. In it, we can house Angers' greatest relic, a small piece of the True Cross brought here by Saint King Louis IX himself." And they embrace in their delight at this shared concept.

When Yolande tells Juana, her deeply religious companion is greatly impressed. "Oh! Madame! You do realize that once built, your chapel will be designated a *sainte-chapelle*, since it will enshrine a relic of Christ's Passion?" Yolande is delighted and runs to tell Louis.

Within the enormous château, Yolande and Louis' two establishments run separately; hers includes quite a number of ladies and "women of the household." In addition, she has a dozen young *demoiselles*, maids of honour from the noblest families in the duchy, in attendance on her. Not only is she obliged to keep these girls, but it is her role to dress them as well. The choice of fabrics allocated to her staff gives an exact indication of their status within her entourage. *How could she have managed this without the guiding hand of Louis' mother?* she thinks.

"Your own ladies, dear Yolande, should wear silks and velvets from Italy or Paris, whereas the rest of the household wear simpler cloth in strict accordance with their positions," Marie de Blois instructs her.

At this time, the fashion in society is for bright colours—scarlet; pinks in tones shading from the most luminous skin colour to fierce flamingo; purples—royal or mourning; deep blue or navy; several shades of gold; and strong greens of emerald or peridot. Wherever she sees ladies gathered at receptions in the neighbouring château, Yolande is thrilled to see the company weaving a colour palette of rainbow brightness. She sends at once for fabrics from Paris—and a seamstress—so that she and her ladies can be fitted out appropriately at home.

Even outside Paris, ladies are fashion-conscious, and they have quite different rules and customs to those of Aragon. In France, ladies who frequent the court wear heart-shaped hollow bonnets, or *bourrelets*, covered in delicate gold gauze and often studded with pearls or precious stones, their hair mostly tucked away inside. Some of Duchess Marie's younger ladies wear the fashionable *henin*—a tall, pointed cone, with a slight veil floating from its tip. This diaphanous veiling trails over brows and down backs, or it might be drawn modestly across a face. Hair is also tucked out of sight inside the *henin*, except for a little showing at the brow. Elegant as they are, these headdresses make entering rooms very difficult. Louis and Yolande catch one another's eye and watch with barely suppressed glee as ladies wearing the *henin* become acrobats, twisting their heads down and sideways to get through some of the low doorways.

The early spring arrives, and with it news of a forthcoming visit from the king's delightful brother, Louis d'Orléans and his wife Valentina. Yolande and her mother-in-law fill the state rooms with flowers—whole branches of blossom trees in places—and the royal suite is prepared for their first illustrious guests. Musicians, jesters, and a splendid *trouvère* famous for his poems and songs of love have been engaged. They will have dinners and dances and ride out into the countryside. Louis tells her that his cousin and wife enjoy the chase as much as they do, especially with falcons.

Most of all, Yolande wants to get to know Valentina and make of her a friend with whom she can exchange confidences. From the moment they met at court in Paris, she felt they might share a strong bond.

"Welcome, dear cousins, welcome," calls Louis as they arrive—both on horseback, although two carriages follow with their luggage. To Yolande's surprise, they travel with very few attendants, all mounted, and just a dozen soldiers. And their own three wolfhounds.

"My dear Valentina, you have no ladies in attendance?" she asks in surprise—no grand lady from Aragon would travel so lightly.

"Yes, of course I do," she laughs. "See the two young gentlemen riding astride on that pair of greys? They are really ladies who can dress my hair as well as my clothes—and my horses! I hate to be fussed over and my clothes are always as simple as possible. Is that not also your custom?" she says with a smile.

Yes, she knows me already, thinks Yolande. *We will be friends.* Valentina's riding habit is superbly cut, and Yolande tells her so.

"Ah, thank you, my dear. I brought my tailor with me from Milan and will lend him to you willingly. Now, show me our rooms and then take me around your kingdom of Angers!" And they both laugh with the complicity of their new-found alliance.

The two cousins Louis—who both reply when addressed by either wife, since none but their family is so familiar—plainly enjoy one another's company. Their talk is largely of the political and economic situation in the country—"man talk," as Valentina puts it—while their two ladies relish finding out one another's tastes in literature, art, music, gardens, cuisine and animals. Valentina joins Yolande in the kitchens and they discuss menus at length with Carlo and Vincenzo, the under-chefs hovering. Some culinary triumphs emerge from these sessions—and a few disasters as well, to their shared mirth.

On a brilliant spring day they ride out together on the chase. It is not too warm, with enough scent for the deerhounds, and the hunt ends at sunset with two stags at bay killed by their huntsmen. On the second day they ride out with a falcon each on their left arm to bring down game birds. They start early, their horses fresh and frisky, and it gives Yolande great pleasure to see how well Valentina rides.

"I like your mounts, dear cousin," Valentina calls. "The

Andalusian bay gelding was superb, and now this clever little Arabian stallion."

"I could see how well you rode and so I dared to put you on him. He is called Ismail and comes from the Barbary Coast. He is the king's wedding gift to me and I have never allowed anyone else to ride him," Yolande says with pride, before they take off after the huntsmen, who have sighted their prey.

The two Louis are competitive and never stop their games, whether on horseback or in front of the fire: silly guessing games, or chess, or cards, or mimes to entertain their ladies when they are alone after dinner and the guests and musicians have left.

It is a shared sadness when Louis and Valentina leave, as they must, but with firm friendships formed between them.

To their delight, Louis' uncle, Jean of Berry, also comes to stay and accompanies Yolande when she follows her husband going about his official duties within Anjou. She walks some paces behind Louis as she should, and notes his people's devotion to him. "Our good and generous duke," she hears from all sides with genuine appreciation. Louis is not an actor like other lords she has observed; he is sincere, and the people can see it in his eyes. Yolande finds herself admiring him more each day.

"Uncle Jean, it makes me so proud to watch Louis in action as Anjou's ruling duke. Since he was just a boy when his father died, was it you who taught him?"

"Dear child—forgive me, you look very young to my old eyes—Louis' mother, our dear Marie de Blois, was astonishing in the way she coped with both her sons, but yes, I did come to Angers and often went around his estates with him, giving him my advice on how to judge and choose people to work for him. I think I opened his eyes a little, although he quickly found his own style of governing."

"I have noticed how cleverly he deals with his subjects," she ventures, hoping to hear more.

"The thing about my nephew that I have always admired," says Uncle Jean, "is his common touch. He knows how to speak to every level of person and make each one feel comfortable, whether the simplest peasant or the grandest duke," and he points to himself and laughs. "You see, my dear, he has always been curious. His mother taught him that. A curious child will learn, and he had a lot to learn and quickly, particularly to avoid knaves taking advantage. His father, my older brother, was shrewd, but too kind for his own good. I am sure that is why he lost the throne of Naples—and his life," he adds with sadness.

Yolande sees his eyes welling with tears. "I can see you loved your brother very much," she says softly.

"Oh yes, I worshipped him. He was the eldest of the brothers after the king, and such a heroic figure, very like your Louis— tall and blonde. And kind, very kind to me, the youngest of his siblings. The rest you know—his elder son, your Louis, set out to conquer that mirage of a kingdom when still very young. Dear Marie will surely have told you the story?"

"Yes, indeed she has," answers Yolande, but her thoughts stray once again to that faraway kingdom. *What a challenge I shall face to win my husband away from this powerful intoxication called Naples,* she thinks to herself.

Ambassadors are frequent visitors, and Louis shows his exquisite manners by descending from his tall chair on a dais to make their obeisance unnecessary. He is well briefed by his staff to remember details about each person's life, but he makes it appear so natural, as if he himself remembers. His visitors melt under the effect of his attentiveness. He has notes made during and after each meeting that are carefully kept to brief him for the next visit, and he makes it seem as if concern for his visitor is all he has on his mind.

But he can also be firm. If an ambassador or important visitor takes liberties in conversation with him, most especially if they hint at or speak disparagingly of the king's mental illness, his eyes flash and the visitor quickly feels the razor slice of his tongue. "Good sir, I believe you are mistaken," he says softly but with acid, and the offender is quietly, discreetly removed from his presence.

Yolande notices that Louis does not shy away from his power; on the contrary, he enjoys it to the fullest and shares his good fortune liberally. At council meetings, which Yolande is permitted to attend, she is repeatedly surprised by his magnanimous gestures, granting privileges and favours to supplicants. Marie de Blois, her guide in all things to do with the court and its inhabitants, further surprises her.

"My dear, do not imagine that all our French dukes behave like Louis d'Anjou! I regret to tell you that a great many of our feudal lords hug their power and wealth to themselves—almost furtively."

Louis' estates and great houses are countless, and one by one he takes her to visit them all. There is much for her to learn. But sometimes at breakfast he will announce: "Enough of work, wife of my heart—today we play!" Then horses are brought and they ride out together in the countryside, taking wild gallops over fields and into forests, at times with hawks on their arms; or they join a hunt with neighbours, their hounds following. Often they will ride out alone with only their dogs, their grooms following at a discreet distance. They picnic under trees by a stream, and she sings romantic songs taught to her by troubadours in Aragon, or tries to accompany him on her Spanish guitar as he serenades her with the old love ballads of Anjou.

As part of her marriage portion, Yolande has been given the beautiful château of Saumur in the Loire district of Anjou, and there they are as much at home as in Angers. With its roofless towers, crenellations and bold panache, the château sits high, dominating the town. Although strongly fortified, it does not intimidate—at least not Yolande. Since it is hers to do with as she chooses, she makes a number of changes to the structure both inside and out, adding a tall tower with a pointed roof at each of the four corners. "They look almost like the *henins* worn by my ladies, but without the veils!" she tells Louis. For entertaining in the summer months and to allow in more light, she creates several courtyards and edges them with orange trees in square tubs. How delicious is the scent of the blossoms trapped within the four walls as it wafts up to the open windows. For comfort in the colder months, chimney pieces are installed in every room and blazing fires burn day and night. Fur pelts of all kinds lie in profusion on the rugs covering the stone floors; and on the beds are soft coverlets of marten, mink, or otter. Many candles stand in clusters on every surface to throw light on the glorious tapestries hanging on the walls—not only for their beauty, but to cover the cold stone. Saumur, the most striking of their castles, is the home of Yolande's youthful marriage into which she tries to incorporate the elegance of her native Aragon. Her mother has sent her a number of tapestries, carpets and clothes chests from Saragossa, and she houses them easily at Saumur.

Throughout the summer months they move between Angers and Saumur, remaining in each place for some weeks, making their way overland to the nearby Loire, then sailing when they can, or else being rowed in barges, theirs in front and the household following. They take everything with them they need—bed linen, tablecloths, plates, silver, chests full of clothes and hangings, tapestries and carpets, as well as some of the servants. Yolande takes Carlo and Vincenzo from Angers to test if they will become her eyes and ears among the staff and their guests.

Come the autumn, they make a longer journey—to Tarascon, their capital in the south. The voyage is only feasible for most of the way by water. With a few stops it can take up to seven or eight weeks, their barges or galleys resounding to the songs of the sailors as they row in rhythm, the lyrics often so bawdy Yolande blushes. The long river journey south from Anjou is such a happy time for them all—the promise of an adventure as they leave the growing chill of the north and follow the sun to the warmth of their land of Provence.

They plan to arrive at the end of the hot local summer, at the time of the lavender harvest. From the boat Yolande can see row upon row of the thick mauve bushes and watches the women cut and tie bunches, tossing them into the baskets on their backs to be dried at home. How delicious is the scent of lavender as their boats pass by, all their goods infused with the aroma. They will spend the winter and spring at their château in the south, at Tarascon, Arles or Aix, and there is always a visit to the port of Marseilles for business. These are magical times, and cherished. Then, when the blossom appears in the orchards, and the lambs, foals and calves arrive, they know it is time to move north again.

One lovely afternoon, Marie de Blois and Yolande are sitting in the recently completed walled garden at Tarascon, admiring the sunlight filtering through the trees. Chilled glasses of elderflower juice mixed with water refresh them, and they both work slowly on their embroidery as Marie talks about Louis' nature—punctual, exact, almost military—which is often at odds with the more relaxed Mediterranean ways of Provence.

"Believe me, my dear, I made every effort to have him absorb the Latin ways. But as you may have already noticed, he is a precise man; his life is dominated by control and order, with everything and everyone in their place."

"You are right, dear Maman; it's true, he is punctual and consistently keeps to his word, and I have observed how reasonably he deals with his tenants and listens to argument."

"Have you noticed that when someone has a convincing point of view that he finds valid, he will change his original opinion and agree with them?"

"Yes, it is one of the traits I admire the most—his humility when he realizes he is mistaken, or another has a better idea."

"Ah, my dear, this flexibility is not the custom of the south, and as a result, he has had some difficulty in coming to terms with the more rigidly feudal existence within Provence. You will see soon enough that it will be your role to smooth his path in dealing with some of his more intractable subjects."

It does not take Yolande much time to appreciate that the massive commercial power of the Anjou family originates from the south, for here they have access to the sea with their great port of Marseilles; they have ships; they can trade the produce from the rich soil of Anjou as well as from Provence, and import goods from all over the Mediterranean to sell throughout France. Provence is the heartbeat of this family she has married into—the principal source of their great wealth; of men for their armies; of ships for trading, or to carry their soldiers to Naples to fight for their distant kingdom. This sovereign territory produces twice the income of Maine and Anjou. Trade and taxation, and the salt mines—a valuable export—as well as the efficient government handed down from Louis' father all contribute. To maintain order in his southern territories and to impose his will, it is important for Louis to show himself regularly in Provence, especially since the people here have not long been governed by the House of Anjou.

Chapter Six

It is while they are in Provence, about three years after their marriage, during the autumn of 1403, enjoying the weather, picking wild flowers amid the scent of lavender and the delicious aroma of the ripe harvest in the fields, that Yolande tells her husband she is expecting their first child. Louis surprises her with his enthusiasm. "Oh my darling wife—this is the best possible news! Of course the baby will be a boy, I know it! And he must be named Louis, yes, Louis III. My darling, clever, beautiful wife!" And on and on he goes, describing his plans for his son's first ten years.

Yolande never expected her husband to be such a keen father-to-be, and they delight in her pregnancy. Perhaps they both thought she would conceive sooner, but God chooses his time and she considers herself fortunate—she is strong and healthy, and she feels no sickness. Much as she would love her mother to be with her and share the excitement of the baby's birth, Aragon's queen is nursing a badly broken leg and unable to travel. Her letters full of maternal advice fill Yolande with expectation, and Juana is with her, which comforts them both.

It is during her pregnancy in Provence that they hear Queen Isabeau has given birth to her eleventh child, a son. Since his brother's madness began, Louis d'Orléans' unstinting support of the queen has been remarked upon, somewhat insidiously, by some courtiers. Inevitably, malicious tongues wag about the paternity of this new royal birth, but since the boy is the queen's third surviving son, he is too distant from the throne for the gossip to be of importance. Both Carlo and Vincenzo have been fully trained by Yolande to listen to the staff of the many visitors to Anjou and Provence. From them Yolande has heard all the gossip of the royal court, possibly more even than Louis, since he is more interested in the government.

During the past two years, Yolande's friend Valentina d'Orléans has visited her twice in Anjou, and now she is coming to Provence with two of her little ones to escape the cold of the north. Yolande rejoices in her friendship—they have no secrets, no qualms about exchanging any apprehensions— and Valentina's servants have become good friends of her own house staff, especially Juana and Valentina's principal maid, Eduarda. Much useful information has been absorbed by Carlo and Vincenzo from the others.

After they are settled, and she and her hostess have sat down to refreshments, Valentina says: "No doubt the gossip from the king's court has reached you? No, please don't disappoint me by looking so bland. You must have heard about Isabeau's new son?"

"Oh yes, that—but I paid it no mind. With a wife like you, no man could look at our sadly obese queen, certainly not your dashing Louis! And I expect him, in his kindness, to console her—as much as he decently can in her tragic situation. I really admire Isabeau for continuing to give Charles children, especially since she never knows when a new fit will start."

"Yolande, you are so strange sometimes! I know my Louis has a mistress, though it is not the queen. Yes, don't look so surprised! Like the people of Aragon," she smiles at Yolande, "we of Milan also have our agents, and they are quite as good as yours."

"Valentina—listen to me, please. We are friends. You believe that, do you not? Then I can tell you that my people—and yes, I do have two reliable agents at the court—have assured me that your Louis is *not* the father of this latest of the queen's children—or indeed of any of them. He is too loyal a brother, and I know that to be true. In our many conversations together, the thing that has struck me the most is his devotion and sense of honour where the king is concerned. That is why I paid this silly gossip no mind."

"Dearest Yolande. Yes, you are a good friend, but do not count on his sense of honour to me! I know that his mistress—a pretty, decent young lady from what I hear—has recently given birth to a son. My Louis has even given him a title. Don't look so surprised; it is quite the norm for royal princes!" she says with a wry laugh.

Not mine, Yolande thinks to herself. *Not mine.*

With the coming of summer, they have arrived in Anjou, with everyone ready for the birth of her first child. Valentina has told Yolande in great detail how it has been for her and what to expect. Juana has not had a child, so although she knows a lot, she cannot know how it actually feels. Yolande's birthing rooms are made ready, something she enjoys supervising; and Marie de Blois has produced beautiful lace from a huge trunk in the nursery wing for the crib.

When Yolande's labour begins, she cannot help wishing: *If only my mother could be with me!* But the Queen of Aragon has still not recovered from her broken leg and can hardly walk. *I am blessed to have dear Juana; I can hear the birds singing and rejoice in our child's birth, despite the pain.*

The midwife rushes about, and maids carry clean towels and sheets, buckets of warm water, watered elderflower juice for Yolande. Time seems to stand still. And then, at last, the cry of the newborn baby brings smiles of relief to all the anxious faces.

As Louis III d'Anjou greets the world and the midwife holds up the screaming child to be washed and swaddled, Juana whispers, "Thanks be to God the birth was uncomplicated." Louis is admitted, and sinks to his knees beside Yolande's bed.

He kisses her palm, nuzzles her neck and buries his head next to hers on the pillows, wiping tears from their eyes while she sinks back exhausted, happy for Louis, for herself, for the baby, for Anjou!

The new father appears overwhelmed—as if no child has ever been born but his. He kisses Yolande's hand again and again, and strokes the tiny one of his son, sleeping happily after his first feed from the bright-eyed local girl brought in as the baby's wet nurse.

Now that all has gone smoothly, the midwife delights in telling Yolande horror stories of all the stillbirths she has attended, and the wet nurses waiting ready for a newborn that does not live. Juana is busy counting the baby's fingers and toes, and cannot stop smiling at her mistress.

The summer passes sleepily and with the contentment that only a healthy growing baby can bring. When the weather starts to turn chilly, the family begins the long, peaceful journey to Provence with the little boy held snugly in Yolande's arms.

The joy of motherhood—writing letters and playing with the baby—has so totally absorbed Yolande that she has not appreciated what has been happening in the country since their return to Tarascon in the sleepy South. Carlo has remained in Angers this time and Vincenzo has come with her instead, but, involved with the baby, she has not taken the time to question him. She is aware that Louis and Charles confer constantly and quietly with their mother, which does not seem unusual, and it is to be expected that visitors come to see the baby, including a number of Louis' people from Paris, who, she presumes, also have business to conclude. But slowly, Yolande begins to notice Louis' absent looks and preoccupation with something, though when she asks, he brushes her questions aside with kisses for mother or baby. No, something is happening; Yolande has recovered from the birth and her antennae are alert. She knows that couriers arrive frequently, perhaps too frequently, from

Paris, and she is beginning to feel that there may be trouble of some sort brewing.

Finally, she summons her agent to see her privately. "Vincenzo—I have been so blissfully distracted in the nursery I have not called you to ask if you have anything to tell me."

"Madame, Your Grace, I also have not dared to approach you, but there is much movement at the court in Paris of which I think you should be aware, as it will affect my lord."

"Well, I am strong and well now, so do not spare me any details."

He seems reluctant, but realizes her determination. "Madame, it is not my place to do more than to tell you what I have seen. The court is dividing into two distinct parties—that of Duke Philippe of Burgundy, who favours the English established in Normandy, the better to ease his trade with Flanders; and that of the Duke of Orléans, who favours the French interests of the king. This is not a new situation, and wise Duke Philippe has always ensured that the two parties have never come to any form of confrontation, but you may not realize how ill he is, and the condition of the king."

"Duke Philippe is old, that I know, but is he really ill? And the king?"

"Madame, forgive me, the duke is dying, and his heir will not prove as wise, I hear. As for our good king, he has lapsed into the worst of his seizures to date and cannot be controlled. I dare not say more." And he looks at his feet in discomfort.

"Thank you, Vincenzo, this information has been very helpful. Continue with your observations and let me know all you hear." And she dismisses him. There is nothing more she can glean from him, and though a part of her quails at what she has to do, she knows that the only person who can really enlighten her is her husband.

Yolande is sitting embroidering next to her sleeping baby under the shade of a great old oak tree in the garden when Louis joins her. This time, she hopes, he will not brush her anxiety away.

"My darling, I sense something is wrong—I know your look and you are more troubled than I have ever seen before. Please tell me what is worrying you. I want to help, but I cannot unless you tell me the true situation at the court in Paris. I know you trust me, so let me share your burden."

Louis is never willing to discuss his family; it is hard for him, but he forces himself to explain.

"Dearest wife, I have tried to keep the worst from you for some time, especially since you had such a pleasant introduction to the king. It will be hard for you to imagine, but his viciousness, bad language and filthy habits have finally driven away his queen. You look shocked—you did not know what happens when he has a seizure? His cruelty knows no restrictions. He attacks not only with his tongue but with his sword! Isabeau has tried everything and sent for every doctor and soothsayer, and all the charlatans of the world have taken advantage of her. She loved Charles deeply until his madness took a real hold.

"When the king loses his mind, the government is taken over by ministers who are often more interested in their own causes than in those of the country. The steadying Marmosets have been dismissed, and the king's power is divided between two distinct parties—that of our wise and powerful uncle Philippe of Burgundy, and the king's loyal brother, our friend and cousin Louis d'Orléans. The king's remaining uncle, Jean of Berry, as you know, is a dear, mild man and a scholar, who prefers not to interfere in affairs of state and stays mostly in his own territory in central France, studying the arts."

"So what is the problem, if the leaders of both parties are so wise and committed to the good of France?" she asks.

Louis continues gently: "Inevitably the two politically minded dukes, Burgundy and Orléans, have a conflict of interest in forming the government's policies. Because our uncle of Burgundy has substantial business interests in Flanders, he leans favourably towards our traditional enemy, England, whose trade routes match his; whereas our cousin Louis d'Orléans firmly supports the French interests of his brother the king. As yet, discussion between the parties has continued in a rational vein—both are reasonable men, as you rightly say, with the interests of France at heart. But my uncle of Burgundy is old, as you know, and daily I receive disturbing reports that he will not live long. Meanwhile his son Jean, "the Toad," who you met at court, has been stirring up trouble behind his father's back."

"Are you saying that the party around cousin Jean of Burgundy is working against French interests and therefore those of the king?" she asks, aghast, but one look from Louis silences her. Yolande has no leave to criticise members of his family. But this news shocks her. *Such disloyalty among the king's closest family members. I see now why Vincenzo would not go further with his information. I wonder if Valentina would dare let me know by courier what is going on. Louis treats me still as if I am made of fragile glass. But I am made of steel!* Fully recovered from the birth, her mind is as sharp as before.

Another courier arrives when Yolande has retired with her baby. Louis receives his visitors and does not come to bed until she is asleep.

The next morning, he joins her for breakfast with the little one.

"My darling wife, I have grave news," he begins. "A courier last night brought me the report I have been dreading for weeks. Philippe of Burgundy, whose mighty power managed to control the other factions at court, has died. I regret I must leave at once for Paris. Please understand. Charles and my mother will remain with you."

"My darling, you look deeply concerned. Tell me what this really means. Yes, your uncle kept the peace as you say, but what do you expect to happen now? What will you do in Paris that requires you to leave so suddenly? How do you think you can keep the peace—if it needs keeping?" she asks, in some confusion.

"Jean, "the Toad" as you call him, is the new duke. Burgundy is the largest and the richest dukedom in France. He has money and an army. In other words, if he is so minded, this cousin of mine can make a great deal of trouble. To what end, I do not yet know, but I fear him. All will be well I am sure, but the king is having one of his worst seizures and our dear Louis d'Orléans, his staunchest ally, needs my support. As the senior peer of the realm, I must go to Paris to sit at the head of the Council of State and keep the peace within my family."

After hasty arrangements have been made and the journey prepared, he comes to her with a kiss on her forehead and that of the baby.

"God bless you both," he says, and is gone.

Chapter Seven

The situation among the contentious factions at court has not improved by the time Yolande's daughter Marie is born, a year later in Angers. Again she is fortunate: the birth is easy and the baby is an instant delight, not only for herself and Louis, who visits regularly from Paris, but also for his mother, in whose honour she is named. Even Ajax and Hector are gentle with the little ones and show no signs of jealousy. Instead they are fiercely protective and growl at anyone who is not a familiar of the nursery.

Marie de Blois is a grandmother made in heaven, never tiring of playing with the children. Yolande's passion for animals, soon shared by little Marie, inspires her to keep a small menagerie at Angers, with ostriches, Araby goats, curly-haired sheep, rabbits and exotic birds. Louis indulges her whims with stoic patience. She does not want the animals too far away—the children must be able to visit them often—but at the same time they do need sufficient space. She consults with Juana and the farm managers, and despite their dislike of the idea, it is done to her satisfaction. In fact, it is such a success that she decides to construct another menagerie in Tarascon when they are next in Provence. "I shall send instructions ahead and surprise the children. They can choose their animals when we arrive," she tells Juana.

"Goats, sheep and ostriches! We'd prefer to eat them than keep them," she hears one of the workmen mumble, and gives him a fierce look.

"Juana dear, please make sure that everyone understands these animals are for *our* pleasure and not for the pleasure of their table!" And Juana roars her good-natured laugh.

"That I will, Madame, that I will!" With Juana in charge, Yolande is confident that the animals will be well treated during their frequent absences. There is no one in the household who is not a little afraid of Juana, including sometimes even Yolande herself. Childhood discipline is hard to forget.

Knowing her love of dogs, her mother has sent them three of her home-bred *levrette* puppies. Yolande calls them Circe, Castor and Pollux, and they too love the children, not minding their pulled tails or ears. The Queen of Aragon has also sent her daughter a wolfhound bitch, Calypso, to inspire Ajax and Hector to produce some legitimate progeny. Thus far the dogs have populated the area surrounding Angers and Saumur, not to mention Provence, with their cross-breeds!

Yolande recognizes that to have had the benefit of Marie de Blois' guidance and affection in the first four years of her marriage has been a great privilege. No one could have taught her better how to run and manage her husband's many houses; and yet Marie herself had to do it all alone.

Time and again Yolande asks her mother-in-law to tell her the story of her own life, but she always finds a way of changing the subject. Then one day, they are resting by the fire, exhausted after playing with the children, who are sleeping at last. Yolande pours some homemade juice for them both and notices Marie's vacant gaze into the fire as she hands her a goblet. Then the older lady turns to her daughter-in-law and says:

"My dearest, you have often asked me about my past life, and now I feel ready to tell you." They settle themselves comfortably, Yolande sitting up to give her full attention. "My dear daughter, I have lived long and my life has not been as easy as many would imagine, but the most important lesson I have learnt in my many years, and which I want to pass onto you if you will allow, is that of patience."

"Patience?"

"Yes, learn to be patient, since young people are always in a hurry and circumstances can change quickly. Without patience, often the wrong decision is taken and regretted. I have decided to tell you about my life, as there may be something in my experiences that could help you to manage your own," she continues with the sweetest of smiles, nestling herself more comfortably into the deep velvet cushions. "We live in such uncertain times, and our future, particularly now, is unsure. Perhaps my challenges will help you triumph over adversity, should it, God forbid, come your way."

Yolande remains silent for fear of breaking the spell.

"I married at fifteen and immediately, on our wedding day, my husband was called upon to be one of forty noble hostages in exchange for his father, France's King Jean II, and his brother, both captured at the Battle of Poitiers in 1356 by England's Black Prince. 'Six months,' he called out as he left me, his bride, still standing at the altar. I shall be home in six months to take you into my arms.'"

She looks so sad, Yolande wants to take her into her own arms even though it all happened long ago.

"But, my dear, France's treasury was empty; there was no money to pay the hostages' ransom. That was when I learnt patience, the lesson I want to pass onto you. Desperate to see me, six months later my husband escaped and came home as he had promised me at the altar. What a night we had, our first..." A dreamy look comes into her eyes, and Yolande dare not interrupt her—Marie is far away, reliving her memories. After a pause, she continues.

"The second hard lesson I had to learn was that of fortitude. My father-in-law King Jean was deeply shocked to find that his son had returned home unlawfully. He felt dishonoured by such unchivalric behaviour. The only solution he would consider was that both he and my Louis—and we had spent just one night together—must redeem their joint honour by returning together to detention in England." Yolande cannot help her hand slipping up to cover her mouth as she listens. Marie's vacant look and monotone telling making it harder to bear.

"King Jean died in captivity in England and was succeeded by my Louis' older brother, who became King Charles V. As heir to the throne, he had not been permitted to be a hostage, although he did offer himself." She pauses, as if it is hard to go on. "I had to wait ten more years for my husband to come home."

Her sigh is slight but it cuts deep—only one night together, and then ten empty years. *I could not have borne it*, Yolande thinks, and instinctively embraces Marie.

The duchess composes herself and continues:

"At last Louis came home, and we were blessed when our first child, a girl we called Marie, was born less than a year later. Then Louis, your husband, arrived in 1377, and Charles in 1380. When Charles V died that same year, his eldest brother, my husband Louis I d'Anjou, served as regent for his son, our present king, Charles VI, too young at the time for the throne. While my Louis sat at the head of the Council in Paris, I remained in Anjou, and when winter was approaching, I travelled alone with the children to Provence. Two years later, following the death of my husband's cousin, Queen Giovanna of Naples, I was again left behind, this time with the two boys, while my beloved Louis sailed to claim Giovanna's throne—his inheritance—the kingdom of Naples and Sicily.

"Naturally I wanted to go with him," she says ruefully. "My eldest, little Marie, had died, Louis was five, Charles only two, and my husband refused to allow me to travel with him and his army for fear some harm should come to his heirs. He was obsessed with the idea of ruling Naples—the distant kingdom he felt was his by right of birth and inheritance. He knew it would be hazardous to travel by ship with a wife and two small children, and then there was the danger of the inevitable battles on his arrival."

Yolande finds herself imagining sailing with her own two little ones with Louis on his epic journey to claim *his* inheritance, just like his father did. Or being left behind! How well she can understand Marie's pain.

"But my dear husband's optimism was short-lived and he failed to defeat his cousin, Duras—or Durazzo, as the Italians called him—the other claimant to his throne." The duchess sighs. "I never saw Louis again."

Yolande sits, totally overwhelmed by this heart-breaking story. She looks at her face and sees a mask of tragedy, realizing how much Marie had loved her husband. Her heart goes out to her for the misfortune of her life. She remains motionless, waiting to hear more.

"Some months later word came he died suddenly north-east of Naples. I like to think he was coming home," she almost whispers. But Yolande has heard the rumours, and no doubt Marie had as well—that Louis I had been poisoned.

They sit silently for a while, sipping their drinks, Yolande desperate to embrace her mother-in-law, console her, but not sure how. Then, taking a deep breath, Marie de Blois continues with her story.

"There I was in Anjou, a widow, thirty-nine years old, with two young sons and a huge inheritance to manage for the boys until they came of age. Such a challenge taught me survival, and that the most useful attribute—not only to survive, but to succeed—is common sense. I want this to be my legacy to you, my dearest Yolande. You know, I hope, that I have come to admire you and hold you very dear." She looks at Yolande and says with great dignity. "May you never have as much need of common sense as I had."

Yolande embraces her dear, sad mother-in-law and imagines herself repeating her heart-rending life, loving her Louis as Marie loved hers, his father. She must push away to the furthest reaches of her mind the spectre of that kingdom that ensnared him.

As if Marie de Blois shares her foreboding, for she holds Yolande's hand and says: "I sincerely pray that you will be spared a future like my past. May the chimera of Naples never reach out and touch your precious life."

Not long after this conversation, Marie de Blois takes to her bed. Yolande visits her daily but knows that she has no great will to live much longer. Telling her daughter-in-law her life story was important to her; she wanted to advise Yolande how to help her son, *her* Louis, to survive his own destiny, especially if it included Naples.

But it is not Marie who dies; to their shock and anguish, it is her second son, Yolande's enchanting brother-in-law, Charles d'Anjou, who falls prey to a sudden illness. Charles, who met her as she entered France, who lightened her nerves with his charm and wit. Charles, her Louis' greatest supporter, and to Yolande the brother she never had. Charles, who has never been long from her hearth or her side, constantly explaining, reassuring, positive and entertaining, her companion in Angers during Louis' absences. How can he be gone?

For Marie de Blois it is, perhaps, the final blow. She has completed her silent promise to her husband. His heir is married, with an heir of his own. The duchy of Anjou is in good and capable hands. She suffers the death of her second son, grieving silently. There is no more for her to do. She has no particular illness, but is simply worn out by a life of struggle. One evening, some months later, after she has finished her light supper on a tray in her room, which she has not left since the death of Charles, Marie de Blois sends for them.

"My dears, I have called you to say good-bye. To you Louis, my beloved first-born, I go to my Lord above in the same knowledge that I leave you in the loving and capable hands of Yolande, the wife I chose for you."

She takes their right hands in hers and holds them together. "Hold each other close to your hearts, and bind your children together so that they too will support and love one another as you do. You are young and still have not experienced the great trials that will surely come your way. But you can survive anything—the greatest heartbreak and loss—as I have—if you live your lives with care for your own and others, with honesty, loyalty, patience, fortitude and common sense. Do not grieve for me my darlings. I am happy to join my beloved husband at last."

With that she kisses the palms of their right hands and they kneel and kiss hers. Neither Louis nor Yolande are surprised when she dies that night in June 1404, at the age of fifty-nine.

Chapter Eight

*F*ollowing the death of Marie de Blois, Yolande is based at Angers alone with the children. Louis' absence is hard. She no longer has the good and wise counsel of Louis' mother to rely on, nor the strong and reassuring presence of Charles d'Anjou by her side. But she does thank God for Juana's familiar, comforting presence. No longer the young bride, no longer the protected wife, with Louis in Paris at the Royal Council, she has new duties at home now, and must pursue them with vigour. With her husband's consent and encouragement, Yolande must rule both Maine and Anjou, head his council, make decisions on his behalf, and receive regular couriers from him in Paris to advise her how to run his business at home and to keep her aware of events as they develop at court and on the King's Council. Looking in her mirror now, what she sees is no longer a girl whose realm is the hearth and the home, but a woman who must steel herself to be her husband's effective regent, to wield his power justly when he cannot. When Juana helps her dress each morning, she feels she is donning her armour for the day's battle ahead.

Meanwhile, the political strife deepens. Anjou, Berry and Bourbon, all with the best of intentions, have done little to defuse the worsening situation in Paris. The enmity between the two factions, led by the rival cousins and royal dukes—Orléans and Burgundy—is growing daily more tense.

Couriers arrive several times a day from Louis and her informers as well as friends like Valentina, bringing Yolande news of the growing aggression between the Orléanists and Jean-sans-Peur's Burgundians; small skirmishes here and there, inside the walls of Paris and without, until the local people are too afraid to go outside the city's walls to work in the fields or harvest their crops.

As if this constant fracas between princes, lords and their supporters is not sufficiently harmful to the people and the land, nature is punishing them as well. France is experiencing exceptional droughts, which ruin harvests, and livestock is starving. The result is famine, and worse: disease is spreading— cholera, smallpox, diphtheria and the greatest killer of all, the bubonic plague. Whole villages and most of the citizens in some towns are succumbing to it. In less than a hundred years, France has lost half her population.

To Yolande's relief, she receives word that Louis is coming home. She has given his affairs her utmost attention, but she misses him and needs him to guide her. He arrives a day before he is expected and she has not had time to prepare herself or his welcome as she would have wished.

"Welcome home, my lord," she says hurriedly as she runs to greet him, smoothing her skirt and tucking back a loose curl. "We expected you tomorrow."

"And are you sorry I raced to be with you as quickly as I could?" he says with a teasing smile. "My poor horse is lame with the effort and you admonish me?"

"No, no, my darling, you misunderstand! I wanted everything perfect for your arrival," she quickly corrects herself as she embraces him with all her heart.

"And it is," he says in her ear as soon as he can close the door behind him. He holds her tight and breathes her in, sighing deeply into her neck.

He is home; my strong, loving husband is home.

That evening, after they have dined, Yolande can see he wants to talk seriously. And as they talk, she realizes that there has been a change in their relationship. No longer is he shutting the door on important affairs, family affairs, and leaving her on the other side of it. Now, he is actually seeking her counsel. Has she proven herself? Or is it that, without his mother and brother, he has need of a listening ear? It does not matter—it is the opening of a door she is eager to step through.

"The sparring between the two royal factions is growing out of control and I fear for the consequences. You are fully aware of the situation—I have written to you almost daily and you have your own sources I believe." He raises an eyebrow, but Yolande says nothing. "As you know, I have always held back from taking sides in my family and their differences. Now I am being pushed into aligning myself with one side or the other—and there is no contest; my loyalty will always be with the king—but how can we stay out of this rapidly growing feud, or defuse it somehow?"

Now that she has Louis at home, it might help him in making a decision if he learns more about their troubles in the countryside.

"My darling, allow me to tell you what is going on here on your estates. You should know that anxiety for our family in this time of plague has prompted me to send couriers in every direction, but in particular to our several houses in Anjou, Maine and Provence. I am deeply concerned about the fate of our own people, not only our administrators and household staff, but the families of our workers, our loyal Angevin and Provençal peasants with whom we have such good relations."

"Yes, I know, and that is one of the reasons for my return. I must see for myself how things are here, my dearest, though I can tell from my factor's report how well you have coped." And his heartwarming smile of approval fills her with pride.

"I believe I have done, and am doing, all I can. I send medicines and doctors wherever I hear of an outbreak, give advice on hygiene and basic treatment. I join my own staff visiting the villages and bringing them food or medicine where needed. Why, only last week I called on the family of your good foreman at Saumur, and his wife begged me to send yet more help to their town, where there is a serious outbreak of plague. Her children are so small and sweet, I could not bear it if she lost them. Husband dearest—you should know—so many men are affected that harvests are not being brought in even when the crops do grow. I have had several accounts of vessels arriving at Marseilles bringing infection with them—rats are seen running down the ropes attaching ships to the docks..." She would have gone on, but he presses his finger to her lips and hushes her like he would a baby.

After a long pause, she turns to him.

"My love, I agree with you completely—in the midst of so much misery, these personal family quarrels between the princes cannot be allowed to continue."

"Then you will understand why I can only remain fleetingly with you. I could not bear another day without reassuring myself that all was well here and with our children, but tomorrow I must return." And he takes her in his arms before she can utter a word of protest.

In the morning he is gone again, and she wonders if she dreamt their wonderful night of love.

A week later, Louis' courier arrives.

"Madame, I bring good news. Duke Louis has asked me to tell you that he has succeeded in brokering some sort of peace between the Orléans and Burgundian factions—confirmed and sealed with a High Mass in the cathedral of Notre-Dame in Paris!"

Eagerly she reaches for Louis' letter, certain it contains details of the peace within the family. There is much family gossip and information, and then she reads the words that make her blood run cold:

To validate this remarkable peace between our cousins, something we have all wished for, so that together, our armies united, we can face with confidence our enemy approaching our threshold once more. With this unity in mind, I have arranged a marriage between our son, Louis III and Catherine, the second daughter of my cousin Jean of Burgundy, to be concluded in seven years' time. I know you will appreciate the importance of such a strategic union between our two royal houses.

Reading these words, Yolande sinks to her knees, lost in impotent despair. Every part of her recoils from the idea of this alliance. Short as her acquaintance with Jean-sans-Peur has been, she has never forgotten the loathsome atmosphere he exuded. Nor is she unaware of the trouble he has caused at court. To connect their families may be good politics—Louis may be acting in the interests of France as well as of their family—but she shudders at the idea of joining her family with that of this repulsive man. What can she do? Little Louis may be her adorable son, but his fate, his future, belongs to the world of men.

I do not know the little girl and have no reason to dislike a child I have never seen, but to be linked by marriage to that man, her father, repels me. Perhaps she is becoming a little cynical, but she reminds herself that since part of the girl's dowry will be paid in advance, Louis will also have the necessary funds to mount a new expedition to Naples. Her mind is in turmoil. She knows her duty and it is one she dreads—she knows that she must confront her husband about his decision. Recalling the harmony of his last visit, when their minds seemed as one, she could weep. But face it she must.

On Louis' next visit home to Angers from Paris, Yolande steels herself to broach the subject. They are in her favourite corner of her sitting room, dinner was delicious, the mulled wine has relaxed him and they talk of this and that concerning his farms, the workers, their health and, most of all, the children. Since she began managing Louis' estates during his absence in Paris, her confidence has grown immeasurably—she has done well and he is proud of her achievement. Then, when she feels the time is right, gently she taxes him.

"Louis dearest, I wonder, something has crossed my mind," she begins.

"Yes, my clever wife, what is it?"

She looks at her hands, "Could it be that you have it in mind..." and here her nerve almost fails her, though his smile is warm and encouraging, "to use some of Catherine's dowry to mount a new campaign... to regain Naples?"

Instantly, there is a chill in the room. The hard, cold look he gives her makes her hold her tongue and lower her eyes at once. It seems that the door in his heart has opened to her only so far; he will discuss family matters, politics, court intrigues and affairs of state with her, but there is one thing that lies in a secret chamber beyond all this, one thing he will not discuss with anyone. His dream of Naples, it seems, is territory she cannot cross. In the future, she now knows she will have to learn to find a different approach in order to avoid a conflict with her husband. Louis d'Anjou is not a man even she would dare cross again once his mind is fixed on a particular goal.

But although she holds her tongue, inwardly Yolande is unmoved. She remains convinced that the betrothal of their son and heir to a daughter of the loathsome Toad of Burgundy is not right for their family. And for what? For that accursed kingdom of Louis' dreams.

Chapter Nine

The royal court of France is peripatetic; the government is based wherever the king is in residence, and sometimes that is in Paris. At these times, it pleases Louis that Yolande joins him at their town palace, and they also receive the great and the good there. Present on this night are Louis d'Orléans and Valentina, as well as the Dukes of Berry and Bourbon. The queen has arrived; the king is unwell. Yolande finds she is rather intrigued by Isabeau. Since their first meeting, when Yolande arrived in Paris on her marriage journey, Isabeau has become even larger, and Yolande pities her sincerely. What insecurity she must suffer.

"Madame, welcome," she says, and, queen to queen, she merely bows her head, though not disrespectfully. Isabeau embraces her warmly.

"My dear Yolande, it is always a pleasure to see your sincere face—unlike most in my palace," she says more softly.

Then there stands cousin Jean of Burgundy: he has come with his son Philippe, whose appearance is the opposite of his father—quiet, polite and secretive. In the three years since Yolande first met him, Jean-sans-Peur has not improved. If anything, he is even more brutish of face and manner, but with a slyness that hints at a certain kind of intelligence. From the way he looks at her—as if measuring her abilities and strength of character—she can tell he sees her as an obstacle to his plans, and he will surely cause trouble.

"Well met, cousin Yolande," he greets her, and she does not pull her hand away this time. "How are the affairs of Anjou and Provence?" he asks, though, it is clear from his face, without any interest in her reply. He is going through the conventions, nothing more, and does not bother even to mentioned the betrothal of his daughter Catherine to their son, a topic that should please him.

"Well enough," she says. "Much like Burgundy, I imagine— there is always the threat from England in the air," she remarks and watches him carefully; she knows from Louis that Burgundy's interests are nearer those of England than of France.

"Ah, yes, the threat from England—I do not see this as being quite *so* serious as my cousins seem to," he replies nonchalantly with a raised eyebrow. "Why, dear cousin Yolande, do *you* feel threatened by England?" he almost smirks.

"No, I suppose we of Anjou do not as yet," she answers, "but then you have much in common with English interests in Flanders, I understand," and moves away at once as she catches his sharp intake of breath. *Am I accusing him of treason? Not yet...*

When the king is in his right mind, he is a most engaging man. Whenever Yolande attends the court, he seeks her out and places her beside him at meals. What she can see is a lonely man, as those who were close to him, even the queen, are afraid to be near him now in case his madness suddenly descends and he turns violent. Their eyes show their apprehension, which he too must see—and Yolande does her utmost to ensure that hers do not. His own eyes light up whenever he sees her, and he beckons her to go to him. "Welcome, beautiful cousin Yolande! I see you wear my ring. Does it please you?"

"Indeed, sire, it does, as much as the splendid white stallion you sent me as a wedding gift."

"My dear, the horse was indeed a wedding gift; the ring was not. It is your passkey to me and I want you to use it. Now tell me about your children—you have two, do you not? A boy and a girl? We must find marriage partners for them among my own or our cousins' offspring. I have so many children I cannot keep count any more. Dear Isabeau comes from good Bavarian breeding stock!" he says with a laugh, not unkindly.

But Yolande finds a poignancy in his words, for in some of their personal audiences together, Isabeau has brought her memories of her beloved homeland to life. How in the summer months she would wander in the beautiful mountain valleys, the cows munching grass with their great brass bells around their necks tolling gently to tell the herdsmen where they were. The mountain flowers—edelweiss and blue gentians; the food—a simple meal of sausage and dark bread in a mountain hut—and then the walk down at sunset before the nights became cold. It is clear she was very happy as a girl. Isabeau becomes quite animated during these conversations and Yolande catches a glimpse of the pretty girl she must once have been. "I think hills and mountains are my natural element—not a French court," she says bitterly.

They do not, perhaps, quite become friends, but they are friendly. So it is not such a surprise when, on a visit to the court, Isabeau seeks her out by royal messenger. The queen, it soon becomes clear, is troubled, and needs to unburden herself.

"Dearest Yolande, forgive me sending for you like that, but I do need to confide in you. You see, I feel able to trust you because of our similar backgrounds and you are the only one who will understand what I want to say." She stops and looks around furtively, then shifts her great bulk nearer to Yolande on the sofa and takes her slender hand between her own two pudgy ones. "I... it is hard to say... I don't know what to do... but I can no longer be... a *real* wife... to the king. You must have heard how he behaves when his fits are upon him? His dirty habits, his filthy language and swearing and his violence frighten me—everyone else too.

"My priest says that I must continue to lie with my husband if he wants, but I cannot. Believe me, I have tried, I have tried." She is weeping now. "I loved him so much and now he repels me."

Yolande puts her arm around the queen to comfort her, and Isabeau wipes her eyes. "Please, dearest Yolande, give me your support to help me arrange separate quarters in our palaces." She looks lost and desperate and clutches at Yolande's hands. "What is your advice, my dear? How can I go on? I have no one of my station but you to ask something so delicate. I would... I would welcome your thoughts," and Yolande can see the wild desperation in her eyes.

"Madame, my dear Isabeau, I understand. Yes, I do... Allow me a little time to think on this difficulty of yours—which I assure you I will keep between us." The relief in the queen's face is pitiful, and by the time they part, with a smile of gratitude from Isabeau, and warm embraces, Yolande has decided to help her. Nor does it escape her that a grateful Isabeau could be a good ally. The more Louis trusts her with his affairs, the more Yolande is realizing her own ability to manoeuvre. Yes, she must think on this conversation with the queen.

Isabeau's problem has been exercising Yolande for some days while she stays at their manor by the Seine. Louis is at the King's Council when she has an idea. One of her husband's growing concerns has been the way in which the balance at court leans heavily towards the Burgundian faction, with two of the king and queen's children married into that family. For some time Yolande has been thinking how she can attempt to redress this problem and also find a way of calming the king and improving his state of mind.

It is clear that Isabeau can take no more of the king's abuse. And yet the priest is right—the king does need someone to console him, comfort and guide him, in particular when he is sane. He is a young man, after all, and must at times have need of a woman to share his bed as well as his table. He listens to Yolande, but she is not there at all times, and he needs more than she can give him.

During several of her attendances at court, and after some time spent pondering this problem, Yolande has observed the queen's ladies and *demoiselles* carefully. They are all of good family—minor nobility—and most of them are really quite pleasing in appearance. She notices that they are also rather flirtatious with the young courtiers, and rightly surmises that the queen's court is not as amusing as that of Louis d'Orléans or Jean of Burgundy.

The question occupying Yolande is who from the court could or would be a substitute for the queen. Isabeau has no lady-in-waiting of real character or imagination, or of sufficient devotion to try to fulfil the poor king's desires. Without a word to Louis, Yolande decides to take on the task of finding a companion for the king, for the sake of France. Among the queen's *demoiselles* she has been watching a young girl named Odette de Champdivers. She is intelligent, good-looking, gentle, caring, and clearly devoted to her king. Moreover, Yolande has not seen her flirting with the young gentlemen of the court like most of the others—she just seems to get on with whatever is required, in a quiet, gentle way.

Yolande has weighed the options carefully. If she is to fulfil her husband's directions for the future of the monarchy, then there is, she believes, only this solution. Still, it is the first time she will be acting on her own initiative—and without discussing her intentions with Louis first. How could she? As a man he would never see the logic or the necessity—or even the benefit. And yet....

Her mind made up, she sends for the girl to come to her chambers. When she enters, Yolande is pleased to see she is not afraid, but stands confidently by the table where the Duchess d'Anjou is sitting.

"Odette, my dear, sit down," Yolande begins gently. "I have observed your amiable manner with everyone at court, from the highest to the lowest, and this has impressed me." The girl blushes—good: she is modest. "I have been wondering about your aspirations, my dear. What do you hope to achieve here in royal service?" Odette looks confused. Yolande continues, sweetly and full of concern: "Are you, perhaps, hoping to find a husband?"

Odette studies her hands, folded in her lap. Then she looks directly up at her duchess: "Madame, I fear I am not sufficiently well-born, nor do I have a dowry that would attract a member of the court. No, I see my role as making myself as useful as possible and serving the king and queen in any way they require."

Yolande likes her honest answer, and after spending some more time alone with her, she is convinced that her only interest is the genuine well-being of her king and queen. Confident that she has made the right choice, she says, very gently:

"Odette, my dear, do you know how lonely and sad your king is at times? How much he needs a kind word, a kind touch?" Odette nods. "He is not always out of his mind, you know, and when he is sane, he longs for a gentle word from a pretty young lady like yourself." Odette looks slightly confused, and Yolande realizes that she needs to be clearer. "My dear girl, I am asking something of you that is of great importance to the kingdom, as well as to the king. He needs someone like you, someone who really cares for him, to spend time with him—even to the extent of spending the nights as well as the days by his side."

To Yolande's surprise, Odette looks up at her, into her eyes, and with her open, frank face says, "Madame, I have not thought of that. Forgive me; I do not know what to say. I have seen the king when his illness is upon him and he can be... difficult." Yolande can see she is anxious, and with reason. This will need a different approach.

"Odette, listen to me—please. Do you see me as the Mother of Anjou, your home territory—the person who has the well-being of all the people there at heart?"

"Oh yes, Madame, you are almost worshipped in Anjou for your care of the young, the old, the sick—everyone."

"Well then, could you imagine my asking you to do something that was in some way against the well-being of your king or the kingdom?"

"Oh no, Madame."

"Good. What I am asking of you is something that is extremely difficult, I know, but I am asking for the kingdom, to preserve the country that we love. France must have a king who, although he is not always like others, is comforted and content when he *is* like others."

Odette is silent for some minutes. Yolande can tell from her expression that she is weighing her options.

"My dear Odette, I give you my word that if ever there is a problem, you can count on me, your Duchess of Anjou. Send me a messenger at once, and I will have you placed in comfort and safety. Naturally, I shall also be financially responsible for the children should anything happen to the king, or to you." She expects Odette to recoil in shock at the meaning of her words, but she does not. No, she is mulling over in her mind the advantages and disadvantages of Yolande's proposition. *After all, what are her choices? To remain at court and become an old maid, or to help her country and perhaps even have children with the king whom she can bring up herself and be independent.*

"Madame, I understand now what it is you are asking of me. I give you my word: I will not fail you, the king or France. It is true, I have observed the king's sadness and his need of comforting. He is a good man who suffers terribly when his demons descend. I will give him that comfort, by day and even at night should he so wish."

It is settled, and Yolande assures her again that she will be available should she ever need help. Although she is aware that most of Odette's family are in the Burgundian camp, her devotion to her king is solid and she understands what it is she has to do.

With the use of the king's sapphire ring with his crest, it is not difficult to arrange for Odette to be introduced into the private chambers of Charles VI, and it is also the first time that Yolande gains access to them by using the ring. Every door opens, and while Yolande goes to tell the king she has brought a young friend from Anjou to read to him and sing should he require, she leaves Odette waiting for him.

"Sire, her name is Odette, and she awaits your pleasure in your apartment to which I gained access using your ring." The king smiles at Yolande and embraces her—but she is not sure if he has understood.

Not long afterwards, Isabeau lets Yolande know of her relief at Odette's existence and of her gratitude. Whether or not the queen realizes that it is Yolande who procured the girl is not clear. Yolande hears stories of Odette wearing Isabeau's clothes in bed so that the mad king does not notice the difference, but she puts such tales down to the usual slander aimed at a disinterested, authentic spirit such as she has encountered in Odette. She corresponds regularly with her, and promises again that she will arrange a dowry for any child she bears the king. The girl will serve all their purposes: the king's, the queen's, the country's—and Yolande's, by easing her dear husband's concerns.

Have I done wrong in procuring Odette de Champdivers for the king? No, I have no qualms whatsoever about doing what is right for the kingdom of France. Louis has made me understand that that is my role in life, and I intend to fulfil it.

Chapter Ten

ate one night in November 1407, Louis and Yolande are
at their town palace in Paris when they hear a commotion
in the street, the loud slap of shutters flying open nearby and
the alarm being raised. Accompanied by his guards, Louis
races out into the night, while Yolande remains on their first-
floor balcony, leaning out, watching flares being brought
and a confusion of people running to and fro, shouting. She
cannot imagine what is happening and is greatly afraid that
her husband might be rushing into danger.

But when he returns, the news is far worse than either of
them could have imagined. His face white, his mobile features
rigid and shocked, Louis is almost unable to tell her what has
happened. The story comes out in short bursts—how Louis
d'Orléans left the queen's court this evening in good spirits
for the short ride to his own residence. Entering the narrow,
high-walled lane that separates their respective palaces, he
and his small escort were set upon from above by some fifteen
masked men and brutally attacked. When Louis raised his left
hand to shield his face, a savage sword-slash cut it off at the
wrist, before an axe cleaved his skull, spilling his brains onto
the cobbles.

Aghast, Louis and Yolande gaze at each other. There is no
time to absorb this horror. Within minutes, their own house
becomes a maelstrom of noise and movement. There is much
that needs to be done. The Anjous' palace is the nearest to

the murder scene, and Louis sends messengers at once to the Provost of Paris and the other royal dukes—Burgundy, Berry and Bourbon—summoning them to convene at his house at once and plan how to capture the assassins.

The atmosphere is strained as the dukes—though not Burgundy—meet with several of the suite of the murdered Louis. And at the centre of this terrible whirlwind of activity, there is a still, silent, dreadful presence. The body of Louis d'Orléans himself has been brought here. His horribly distorted, bleeding body lies on a table in the hall, covered with a thick velvet curtain. Yolande is in shock. Their beautiful, gallant cousin, he who embodied all the qualities a prince should possess—courage, courtesy, high ideals—lies murdered in their house. She is too angry to cry, too full of rage at the injustice of it all.

And through her shock, and that of all present, a dreadful knowledge is forming. Everyone's finger is silently pointing at the dreaded Jean of Burgundy. Yolande is in no doubt—there is no one else who refused to see Louis d'Orléans for the patriot he was.

In the presence of the dead prince's body, the men confer hurriedly; messengers are being sent in every direction as the Duchess d'Anjou silently offers strong wine to each of the group as if in a daze. She will not break down in front of them. She will keep her sorrow to mourn him in the quiet of her room, alone. Louis d'Orléans, together with her husband, was the best of this family. Poor darling Valentina and her children—and poor France.

With each goblet she fills, a terrible sense of foreboding grows in her—this can only be the beginning of more outrage to follow. By now, no one doubts the guilt of Burgundy's men—a number were recognized despite their hoods while they fled. As she brings another flask of wine to the gathering, Yolande dares to ask: "Have the Provost's men gone to arrest the Duke of Burgundy?"

No one replies. *What ails them?* She asks again:

"Have men been sent to summon the Duke of Burgundy. Who will enquire into the outrage committed by his men?" And again no one speaks; they only shake their heads. She understands. No one dares move against the powerful Jean-sans-Peur!

She walks away from them and retires to her rooms—what else can she do? She is new to this family and they have their own rules. But she knows what she would do were she in their place! Louis thinks her rash, and he may be right, but to stand by and watch such blatant aggression—and now the murder of a loved family member—is beyond her comprehension. *Have they milk instead of fire in their bellies?* She feels her Spanish blood rising, and a part of her curls her lip at their judiciousness, their diplomatic caution. Surely this terrible deed will be reason enough to cancel the betrothal of their heir with Burgundy's daughter. They can never join their blood with his after this horrible murder.

Yolande spends the next day at home while Louis is leading the service for his beloved dead cousin in the absence of the king, who is sick and cannot attend. He returns, ashen-faced with barely controlled rage.

"You will not believe it—all three royal dukes, Berry, Bourbon *and* Burgundy, joined me in the church. We each held one of the four poles supporting the golden awning over the catafalque."

She is stunned. "How is it possible that Burgundy dared to appear? How did you and the others allow it? You all know it was his men who murdered our dear cousin." She stares at him, wide-eyed with disbelief.

"Can you imagine it?" he gasps. "And what is more, that gross Burgundy was the only one of us correctly dressed in the black robes of royal mourning!"

"*Of course*," she almost hisses. "Only *he* would have known they would be needed today!" And she spits out her words with all the venom in her heart.

But there is worse to come. Following the funeral, Louis has invited all the major mourners to come to their palace and, to Yolande's breathless astonishment, Burgundy dares to appear! Anxiously she looks about for Louis among the company, and cannot see him. *How can I receive this monster?* She has no choice but to move towards him as protocol demands.

"Ah, my beautiful cousin Yolande," he says, taking her hand—which she has not offered—and kissing it in a way that draws attention. "What a sad day indeed."

Yolande's face is frozen, lips shut tight, and she scans his face with cold eyes, chafing at the protocols that prevent her from accusing him outright. Not a shadow, not the slightest hint of any emotion—no, he has applied an actor's mask expression of sorrow, the corners of his mouth turned down. She is so shocked at his presence that, despite her training, she is completely lost for words, certainly of welcome, and just stands looking at him.

At that moment, Louis arrives at her side, with him the two other royal dukes, Berry and Bourbon. "My dear, there are guests in the gallery who need you"—a signal that she is to leave. She moves to go willingly, but as she turns, she hears her husband say clearly, and not too quietly:

"Cousin, you have no place here, neither in my house nor in this city. We, the three senior members of the council, order you to leave Paris at once."

All conversation in the room has ceased, the guests facing Burgundy and the other three dukes. Jean's face is a study; a mixture of hatred, anger, disdain—and superiority! He turns on his heel, makes a slight motion with his head to his followers and marches his great bulk out of their home. A trembling Yolande moves quickly to take Louis' arm, praying that this will signal the end of their family's proposed union with that monster!

"That man would like to kill all of us—you, me, Berry and Bourbon. Darling husband, frankly, he terrifies me." Louis is calm as he pats her hand, but Yolande is barely able to contain her anguish before the remaining guests. "How can this shameful murder of a loyal prince of the blood be accepted so readily? Banishing him from Paris is not enough!"

But Louis' lips are tight and he gives a slight shrug as if to say, "That's the way things are."

Burgundy knows that the Duke of Orléans was disliked by the Parisians, and his people set about spreading the word that he has done them a great service in ridding them of the tyrant. It is true they were taxed heavily by the dead duke, and from what Juana tells Yolande she is hearing in the streets, the Parisians are actually celebrating Louis d'Orléans' murder.

The next day, her dear friend Valentina, the newly widowed Duchess d'Orléans, calls on her. Her eyes look haunted, her face drawn and thin. *Where is the flashing-eyed beauty?* Yolande asks herself. The shock of her husband's murder has Valentina shaking as she asks:

"Dearest Yolande—would you be willing to help me?"

"Anything, anything!" Yolande's inner rage on Valentina's behalf—and on their own too—would indeed make her capable of anything at this moment.

"Would you accompany me to call on my brother-in-law the king? I must beg for his support against his cousin of Burgundy to avenge my husband's murder. Would you do that for me?" she asks, as if unsure.

"Of course, it is the very least I can do. And I can guarantee he will see you—I have his ring that allows me to pass anyone at any time to reach him, and you will be by my side. But to gain the king's support we must plan carefully. I have a young friend near him I can count on, and I will first find out when he is well. We must make our entrance at court dressed soberly—in black velvet and pearls, I think." Yolande knows that appearance is all-important—both the king and the queen are easily swayed by the court's reaction to the appearance of petitioners. Valentina will have the sympathy of more than half of them, she is sure, but to move the king to act against a member of his own family will be difficult. His awareness of Burgundy's immense power could discourage him.

When she receives Yolande's message that the time is right for her audience with the king, Valentina d'Orléans returns to the Anjou mansion. Her strong colouring has faded and her flashing eyes look utterly desperate, but Yolande knows she has more fire in her belly than pain at her loss. On her friend's advice, Valentina has brought her young son, the new duke, so like his father—may his youthful blonde beauty sway the king to listen to her plea for vengeance.

There is murmuring as they enter the great audience chamber of the Louvre palace. Yolande, as a queen, walks slightly in front of Valentina. Both are conscious of the stir they are causing and aware of the approval of their audience. They make a striking pair, both tall and slim, Valentina so dark and Yolande very fair. Yolande is beckoned to sit on a stool near the throne, while Valentina stands facing the king, her young son beside her. Despite her courage, and her straight posture, somehow Valentina looks very slight, very alone, lost in all that multitude of faces. But her voice is firm, strong, an appeal not just to the king, but to the whole room:

"Sire, I bring you my son; as you see, he is too young to avenge his father, and so it is to you I come, on bended knees." She drops to the floor on her knees to gasps from the assembled courtiers, not used to such a scene. "My lord sovereign and brother-in-law, I beg you to avenge this shameful murder of my husband, this young boy's father and your beloved brother Louis d'Orléans, your beloved brother who never failed you." And with arms outstretched, she turns to her left and right in an elegant gesture of supplication to the assembled courtiers.

Deeply moved, Yolande watches the king. But she sees, with a falling heart, that he is not really here with them—his mind has wandered, as it so often does. She knows he loved his brother, yet he shows almost no emotion. Has he understood what has happened? Has he forgotten who Valentina is?

"My young son, your nephew," Valentina exclaims, and Yolande can hear the rising desperation in her voice, "deprived of a loving father and guide through this vicious court, this country divided by its factions. I know, as you do, sire, who is responsible for my husband's murder. Avenge it, I beg you!" she cries out, turning to the assembled court again. But all Charles VI does is raise her from her knees and embrace her, a loving gesture, but he utters no word of retribution against his cousin Jean-sans-Peur.

Yolande cannot blame the king. He is not in his right mind again, but to her shame and forcibly suppressed anger, not one of the royal dukes, not even her own husband, says a word or makes a move to support Valentina's plea. *They are afraid,* thinks Yolande, *afraid of their rebellious cousin of Burgundy.* Each of them knows that Jean, if alienated, is quite capable of giving his duchy's mighty support to the English, who they know are waiting for an opportunity to launch another invasion. *How typical of men,* she seethes as she makes her way home, *to choose the lesser of two evils.* Perhaps it is the wiser choice, but it makes her boil with anger.

Later, in her disappointment and anguish for Valentina, Yolande dares to voice her distress to Louis.

"Beloved husband, was not Valentina brave today in front of the king and the court? Do you think Charles understood what has happened, or was he merely trying to console a grieving widow? Why did none of you support her plea for vengeance? Is this only a woman's desire, to avenge her slain husband? Do you not feel that your cousin Jean of Burgundy should be apprehended? Interrogated at least?" she asks apprehensively.

"Madame," he replies—always a bad start—"this affair is the business of *my* family!"

"My lord," she replies, piqued, "am I now no longer of your family? May I not have an opinion when I see wrongdoing among them?"

Louis says nothing, but he gives her one of those chilling looks from his blue eyes turned to ice, and leaves the room. Her heart is beating so fast she has to sit, as she feels the sun of his approval fade from her and the realization dawns that Louis will not take a stand against his vile cousin.

To make matters worse, this murderer, this so-called "fearless" duke, although now banished from Paris, has gathered about him a large number of grandees and supporters and has returned to the capital. He is even planning to make a solemn entry into the city in tremendous style, ostensibly to pay official court to the king.

Yolande is bewildered. Why does not *one* of the royal family try to stop him? A solemn entry is the greatest honour a king can bestow on an important visitor, even if he is a cousin. Charles VI is unwell and must be excused, and it is left to his eleven-year-old dauphin, together with his father's uncles and cousins, her husband among them, formally to receive that odious murderer. Happily Yolande herself is not obliged to attend court to watch this degrading spectacle.

When Louis comes home, he has mellowed enough to tell her, "My dear, it will astonish you even more to hear that Jean was dressed most extravagantly for his entrance at court, and that the Parisians—no doubt urged on and paid by Burgundy's own men—shouted the royal salutation of welcome as he passed: 'Noël! A tyrant has been slain! Welcome the slayer!'"

And yet she still cannot read her husband's intentions. By now she knows better than to react angrily to anything he tells her about his family, but there is something she needs to know. She asks him softly:

"My dearest, word has reached me that the Parisians have been told that Louis d'Orléans was plotting to take the crown from his enfeebled older brother, and that therefore he was guilty of treason! Is there any truth in that at all?"

"No, my clever wife, and your face tells me how the entire

episode troubles you," he says, annoyingly perceptive. "You wonder why I have not done more—no, do not stop me, I can read it in your eyes—to avenge the foul murder of our cousin Louis d'Orléans, whom we loved. But I am looking at the bigger problem facing France. We have it on good authority that the English stand poised to invade us once again. If we princes of the blood unite against the mightiest of us in terms of men and wealth—namely Burgundy—we will have civil war. Not only is that a catastrophe for France, but it opens the door even wider for England to march in again."

Louis is thinking with cool reason; but she is Spanish, hot-blooded and angry, but she knows he is right. The more she hears of Burgundy's manipulations, the more she realizes how his power has grown in direct proportion to the horror of his crime.

While the Royal Council debates their next move, it does not surprise Yolande to hear that Jean-sans-Peur has mobilized his Burgundian army and is heading for Paris. He can only have it in mind to take the king's place at the head of his council, which governs the country.

While Louis and Yolande sit at breakfast in their town palace overlooking the Seine, busy with river traffic, they are joined by Louis' uncles of Berry and Bourbon. There is tension in the air, the sense of a storm coming, so that it hardly comes as a shock when Louis says, in heavy tones: "My dear family, it is time to make an important decision. The royal family must abandon the capital. It is clear that the Parisians prefer to oblige the wishes of Jean of Burgundy rather than those of their monarch. Our only option is to leave—do you agree?" All murmur their assent. "You, my darling wife, will travel with the dauphin and the queen—and try and talk some sense into her. Now that her great protector Louis d'Orléans is no longer there for her, I notice that more and more she looks for a strong replacement and begins to take the side of our cousin of Burgundy, who, she imagines, will protect her. Without cousin Louis to guide and comfort her, she appears totally lost. I fear she will indeed gravitate towards the strongest of us to safeguard her future. If only she could be made to see he will merely use her for his own advancement. Do what you can to persuade her to stay loyal to her husband and his late brother—she has such a high regard for you, my darling wife."

The carriage is too small for Isabeau and Yolande to sit side by side, and she finds it impossible to speak privately, let alone charm or persuade the queen not to turn to Burgundy for support. It looks as if it will be a long, tiresome journey, but fortunately the dauphin is a splendid young man, interested in everything. Yolande can see he is registering the miserable state of the crops in the fields, and the meagre-looking livestock. When they arrive at Tours, the queen, the dauphin and Yolande install themselves with the court in the royal castle. Yolande watches the queen scanning the crowd of servants noticing her relief when she sees Odette de Champdivers among the royal household. Odette's inclusion has been secretly arranged by her patroness for everyone's benefit, but especially the king's. Yolande has never admitted her part in this unusual arrangement to Louis. She does not want to keep secrets from her husband, but there are some things about women that men cannot understand or appreciate. It is better so.

With the king and queen no longer in Paris, they are not obliged to receive the murderous Duke of Burgundy. If they did, it would only serve to give the people of Paris, and the country, the impression that they accept him and condone his shocking crime. Jean-sans-Peur makes another triumphant entry into Paris and will wait there, like a patient predator, for the eventual return of the king and the court.

Chapter Eleven

For the past eight weeks that Yolande has been with the court at Tours, she has been trying to conceal her third pregnancy, which is now in its sixth month. Already three months ago she removed the little bag of feathers that ladies wear under their dresses in front to give them that fashionable rounded look, but now she is beginning to appear larger than when she does wear the bag. She wants to help Louis, but after a month spent at Tours listening to the endless negotiations between the king's staff and the couriers relaying the Duke of Burgundy's terms from Paris, she tells him she needs to return to Angers, to her little ones, to await the birth.

When she leaves Tours in December on the Loire, the weather is still not really cold, and as yet there has not been a frost. The river journey is a pleasant change from the atmosphere of uncertain confusion that she has left behind. She is enveloped in furs and the warmth coming from the braziers inside the barge while the boatmen sing merrily. After two days they leave the Loire and she rides sedately home to Angers.

Her reception is predictably welcoming; despite the cold, the village girls, dressed in their finery, perform a short dance, recite a poem they have written themselves and present their duchess with a small basket of dried flowers and holly. Yolande extends the traditional formal greeting to the dignitaries, and is overjoyed to see her dear Juana there to receive her, her arms open wide to enfold her in a loving embrace. Ajax, Hector, and

Calypso bound up, and she has to be stern so they do not jump on her stomach. Calypso is pregnant as well—perhaps they will give birth at the same time! As she enters the great doors of the castle, she makes her way down the line of servants, the women bobbing, the men bowing, hats in hand. She has a word with each, remembering every name, making a comment here and there, and their faces beam with pleasure at having their duchess home.

It is too cold outside for the children, who are waiting by the fire in the Great Hall. They rush to hug her around the knees, almost knocking her over. "Come, my darlings, come and sit with me in my room and tell me all that has happened since I left."

"Maman, you are so big!" says Louis, eyes wide, and when she tells him there is a baby in her tummy for him and Marie to play with, he jumps up and down and rolls on the fur rug like one of her wolfhounds. Yolande marvels at how her golden-haired children have grown, and at the progress they have made.

The *levrettes* are waiting in her little sitting room next to her bedroom, bottoms wriggling with pleasure and excitement. The room is warm, with a good fire and the delicious smell of roasting chestnuts. Her children fill her with delight and she listens to their stories while Juana prepares her for bed.

"Papa is coming for Christmas with lots of presents," she tells them, "and we shall have games and play-acting and gypsies and..." She pauses. "The rest is secret!" How their eyes light up with anticipation. They are laughing, healthy children, full of mischief and merriment. The journey and the pregnancy have tired her and, although almost dropping with fatigue, how good it is to be home. The terrible events in Paris and Tours seem like a distant nightmare. Back in Anjou with her children and Juana, her own rooms welcoming her, her own household surrounding her, it is almost possible to forget the ever-encroaching fear of the invasion and push it out of her mind. Almost, but not quite.

Louis arrives two weeks later and in time for Christmas, to the children's exuberant joy. The great fortress resounds with the songs of the visiting troubadours, the musicians Louis has commissioned from Paris, the gypsies and actors as well. There are squeals of delight from the children at their presents, their father's mimicry and storytelling, followed by rough-and-tumble games.

On 16 January 1409, under the watchful supervision of Juana, Yolande's second son René is born, mercifully as easily as her first two children. Two weeks later, despite snow so deep that many of their neighbours are unable to attend the baby's christening, they make merry nonetheless. A pale winter sun shines from a cloudless blue sky onto the sparkling snow as they present their new son to the good Angevins from the town and the countryside after the ceremony. Only the baby's nose and eyes can be seen from his cocoon of fur, but the visitors are happy just the same. Hot spiced wine is given to all, children as well, and some of the town's elders and their youngsters have been invited to join them for a celebration in the castle. Louis invents short sketches for the children and Juana make costumes for them to wear as they perform in front of the guests. Louis always takes part himself—he loves to act and the children adore it. His best role is that of a witch, his face blackened by the giggling girls in the kitchen, who also give him a broom to ride, while Yolande's ladies make him a tall black *henin* to wear on his head, the tip bent forward. He even blackens some of his teeth so they look as if they are missing, to more shrieks from the young ones when he bares them. It is a happy welcome for baby René into the family, and the children's merry laughter allows Yolande and Louis to forget for a while the troubles facing France.

But following the happy interlude of René's arrival into the world, reality intrudes. Louis must return to the King's Council. He has been chosen to act as intermediary between the two camps, the Burgundians in Paris and the king's party in Tours, until a compromise is reached. Not long afterwards, word comes from Paris that there will be a "Ceremony of Reconciliation" on 9 March, and Yolande wants to attend to support Louis. Six weeks after René's birth, she sets out to join her husband in Chartres, travelling by road. It is a tiring, slow journey, the horses carrying her litter unable to manage more than a slow walk, but she arrives within two days.

They both know that this ceremony is a farce, but according to the council it is a necessary one. Together in the soaring cathedral of Chartres, with its tall pointed arches resembling praying hands, they witness the sham settlement between the rival royal factions. Burgundy and his followers stand on one side of the aisle, the Orléans supporters on the other. Duke Jean's mediator asks for—and obtains—a pardon of sorts, and by virtue of this travesty the king and his court can return to Paris. The result? The Duke of Burgundy takes over the government. The remaining wise and helpful Marmosets are banished at once, and he appoints himself guardian of the dauphin, a role that belongs by seniority to the old Duke of Berry. And no one murmurs! Yolande dares not vent her feelings to her husband, but to herself she thinks: *We of Aragon would not have been so spineless!*

Chapter Twelve

The murder of their beloved Louis d'Orléans has left not only a political tangle, but a domestic one as well. And here, Yolande realizes, she can be of help. As well as Valentina and their children, he has left behind his illegitimate son, the seven-year-old Count Jean de Dunois. Since fathers "own" their illegitimate children and there are no other men left of the Orléans family who could care for him, Yolande has been in contact with his mother, a most pleasant lady, and offered to take her son into her keeping so that he may be brought up according to his position, something his mother could never do. Yolande understands it would be too painful for Valentina to take the child to bring up with her own, and since the boy is the son of their dearly loved cousin, she feels it's the least she can do for his memory. With Valentina's consent, it is arranged.

When Jean Dunois arrives at Angers, the children are visiting neighbours and Yolande has him alone for half a day. As she waits for him, she surprises herself by feeling nervous—how will she react to this young boy, the son of someone she held so dear? What memories will he stir in her, and can she put Valentina's hurt out of her mind enough to love him as her own? But his entrance disarms her completely. Although he is the king's nephew, he greets her on one knee as would the son of one of her employees, or a village lad. She raises him, and with her hands on both his shoulders, she looks him in the eye and says:

"Welcome, young cousin Jean, and you are most welcome indeed. There is no need ever again to be on one knee to me or my husband—you are the king's nephew and we recognize you as such. Also, we loved your father, and you are made in his image," she says with a smile, and embraces him.

"Madame, I thank you for those generous words," he says in a very grown way for such a young lad. She takes to him at once; likes his frank look and honest eyes.

"I am sure you have begun to ride to hounds? Well, tomorrow, if it does not snow, that is what we shall do. In the stables you will surely find a pony to your liking, and my eldest, Louis, who is almost your height, will help you. None of the children will go far, but it's such fun to be at the meet. Tell me, how is your mother? I had the pleasure of meeting with her in Paris to ask if you would like to join my young family here."

"Madame, again I thank you. She is well and most grateful for your kindness. She has asked me to give you this letter."

Yolande takes it to read later in her room. "Now young Jean, although you will be treated as one of ours, never forget your dear mother who loves you and will miss you. It would make me happy to know that you remain in close contact with her, and should you want to meet, that can also be easily arranged. Our wonderful Juana has prepared your room and a supper is waiting. You cannot have eaten all day."

He nods, bows to her with his father's natural elegance, then walks backwards three steps and turns towards Juana. Yolande casts an appreciative look after him. Yes, he is very much like his father, and she can detect a great strength in him too—his mother has brought him up beautifully, from what she has seen so far.

Later, she watches her own son greet Jean. "Well met, good cousin," he says as he puts his own arm around Jean's shoulders. "What fun it is to have you to play with and chase and be chased by. I can see you are stronger than me or my sister—are you much older? Do you have your own pony? No?

I have several and you may choose which you like the best. Did Maman tell you we are going on the chase tomorrow? You will love that here. This is my little brother, René, too small to be fun yet, and this is my sister, Marie, who is five and definitely fun to be with! Oh, I *am* pleased that you have come to stay with us!"

This is quite a long speech and it comes bubbling out naturally from six-year-old Louis. Yolande is touched and proud that he is so pleased to have a cousin, and one to play with him as an equal. Jean's eyes shine and she can see that the boys will become fast friends.

Juana comes to claim the children, and they follow her upstairs to the nursery, the new nursemaid, Tiphane, carrying baby René. Tiphane is a good strong country girl, fresh-faced, rosy-cheeked and smiling—typical of the local lasses. Juana assures her mistress that she is almost as tough as "we of Aragon!" This she will wait to see! Juana has become quite stout since coming to Anjou, and Yolande has had to let her ride one of her very strong Andalusians, sitting on its back in a wicker basket facing sideways. She complains of aching bones in the winter, but her room is warm and she sits with Yolande often in hers. Yolande has offered to send her home to her mother the queen, but Juana simply won't leave her or the children and says she has no family left in Aragon. Wherever Yolande is, that is her home. She still sees well and reads, although she does have fewer teeth.

Unlike many mothers of her station, Yolande spends a lot of time with her children—talking, joking, playing games— and in the following days and weeks she notices that Jean Dunois' personality and physique are stronger than any of her children's, but also that he never abuses that privilege. He follows when he could easily lead: on horseback—already at seven he rides well; at games—she can see he actually tries not to win too often, instead helping Marie and often Louis as well, but not so that anyone would notice. And if there is a job to be done, he is the first to quietly offer to do it. Somehow, instinctively, he knows his place, and defers to the others, as would a guest. It does not take them long to love this boy, who shows enormous talent and goodness even at his very young age.

However much Yolande loves to spend time with the children, she accepts that her duties must also take her elsewhere. Louis has done her the honour of appointing her his regent in Anjou while he remains with the court. And so she sets about her tasks—repairing roofs in the city, building where necessary, not least a substantial bridge over the Loire, the first to allow traffic between Nantes and Saumur. The Loire can be a raging river especially in springtime, and often bursts its banks. There are few crossing places for this reason, and the need for a strong stone bridge to gain access to the other side is essential.

From Provence come shipments of seeds for crops, and Yolande puts more and more virgin land under the plough. The country needs food and children, and she encourages her villagers to sow and to breed. As mistress of all she surveys, she enjoys the work of improving their land, of helping the people become productive and healthy, but all the while she knows that the more confidence Louis places in her judgement to govern his French holdings, the keener he becomes to reconquer his kingdom of Naples and Sicily and she hears from her agents that his plans are gathering apace. It mystifies her how he finds the time during his work on the King's Council even to imagine conducting a campaign in Italy.

Despite all the distractions of her work as regent of Anjou and undertaking preparations for the defence of their territories against the inevitable English invasion, Yolande still struggles with the moral dilemma of the betrothal of their eldest son and heir to the daughter of Jean of Burgundy. It is with considerable unease that she steels herself once more to confront her husband when he joins her at Angers. She begins subtly, softly, a plea in her voice:

"Dearest husband, may I unburden myself to you about a matter that troubles me?" And of course his dear face melts from whatever was absorbing him, and he takes her hand and sits her down next to him.

"What is it, my darling?" he asks gently.

Yolande well knows how angry he can become when she interferes in family business, and that is exactly what she is about to do. Rather nervously, she proceeds.

"As you know, my beloved, all your desires are also mine, whatever you command I am ready to obey, and I do this with all my heart and energy." Still she hesitates.

"Yes?" he says sweetly, kissing her palm.

"Beloved, I do not sleep well when you are not by my side, but also, during your absence at court..."

"Yes?" he prompts.

"I have been searching my heart and mind to find a way to accept..." Immediately she senses him stirring, and hears his intake of breath, "the betrothal of our son Louis." There—it is said—and she looks down at once, afraid to meet his eyes.

Louis' hand tightens on hers, then lets it fall. "And why is that?" he asks, in a different tone of voice and with an expression of almost feigned surprise.

Her focus is again on her hands in her lap, like a child in the nursery. She looks up. "Dearest, be not angry with me for discussing what I am aware is truly your business, but as you well know..." She pauses, then finally blurts it out: "Since none of your family is in any doubt that the shocking murder of Louis d'Orléans, the cousin we all loved and the king's staunchest supporter, was orchestrated by Jean of Burgundy." She can hardly believe she has managed to say as much, and almost pants for lack of breath.

There is a moment of silence.

"And?" he says, with an edge that could cut glass. "We have spoken of this before."

"Well..." Again she wavers. "I am of the opinion that... it

would not be correct to have our eldest son and heir... align our house with that of your cousin's murderer." With that she sets her jaw and looks him direct in the eyes.

Louis' face is dark with suppressed anger.

"Madame"—and she trembles; he rarely addresses her formally—"do you imagine that I am prepared to cause even greater strife within my family by publicly humiliating my powerful cousin of Burgundy in this way? By cancelling this official betrothal? An agreement made between our two royal houses?"

She quakes and bites her lip, but takes courage from somewhere and dares to continue. "But surely," she stutters, "the... the shame of joining our family to that of a murderer is greater than that of cancelling even a royal betrothal?" She says this as firmly as she can, while shaking inwardly. She knows her husband's temper well.

She catches a look in Louis' eyes she has not seen before, as if he is far away with his thoughts. Then he faces her squarely and says crisply, barely controlling his anger:

"No, my dear, I cannot agree to this, although I do understand your misgivings. As Duke of Anjou, I simply cannot afford to alienate the Duke of Burgundy." And with that he walks away from her. Yolande feels crushed and humiliated, shut out from his mind—and his heart.

The next day Louis leaves Angers for Paris as planned, but she is bid only a formal farewell, and in public—no private good-byes for her at all.

The result of their altercation is that her husband sends a courier to Angers from Paris with a letter:

"My dear wife and most effective regent! I hear daily from various sources how well you manage my estates and I am thankful for it, particularly as I am in the process of preparing to mount a second expedition in order to reclaim my kingdom of Naples and Sicily. I know you will wish me luck when the time comes."

How can he be so sure? Yolande is thoroughly dismayed. She has always known in her heart that he will try again—why does it affect her so much now? And a little voice inside says: *because you love the man you married with all your heart, and fear for him fighting far from home.*

The expedition to Naples is to be a large undertaking and will require a substantial fortune to finance it. As she suspected, this money is to come from the dowry of Catherine of Burgundy, second daughter of Jean-sans-Peur, now officially betrothed to their eldest son and heir, Louis III d'Anjou.

Despite her pride, Yolande strongly feels the need to confide in someone. It is at times like this that she is aware of the solitude of her position. But, as always, there is her dear, trustworthy Juana, who she finds tidying the nursery while the children play outside. Juana's dark hair, which she wears in the same bun at the nape of her neck, is now streaked with grey, her cheeks are rounder, but as rosy and shiny as ever, and her brown eyes are still full of expression. Yolande throws herself on little Marie's bed, hugging a pillow to her chest to stop herself from shaking with silent sobs.

"Juana, Juana, what kind of a man have I married?" she cries in dismay. "Has he no moral compass within to guide him against taking this murderer's money for his own selfish ends?"

Juana puts her arms around Yolande's shoulders as she weeps out her frustration and sadness on the older woman's ample chest.

"Do not cry, my little one." She still, somehow, thinks of Yolande as a little girl, despite all they have been through together. "Have you not realized yet, after so many years of marriage, what it is that drives your beloved husband?" She takes Yolande's face in her hands and wipes her tears. "His one real goal is, and has always been, his Italian kingdom. Surely you have understood that by now? This dream realm of Naples, which killed his father, draws him relentlessly. It is like the sirens in the ancient myths I told you about when you were young. Yes, he loves you, and the children, and his home, and his country. But his kingdom of Sicily and Naples has a greater hold on his mind and heart than all the rest put together. Once you accept that, you will be able to manage your life and your heart's desires."

And Yolande's sobs shake her body as the truth of Juana's words, of her own inadequacy and of his betrayal, fills her being.

Reluctantly she accepts Louis' decision. What choice does she have? To herself she admits her deep disillusion that this man who until now could do no wrong in her eyes is still prepared to go ahead with what she considers the dishonourable betrothal of his son and heir. It presents her with a whole new aspect of her marriage with which she must come to terms. *Do I love him less for what I regard as a moral lapse? No, I could never love him less than unconditionally. But am I disappointed? Yes, yes I am.*

Chapter Thirteen

On 12 March 1410, Louis d'Anjou, Yolande and their three children, Louis, Marie and fourteen-month-old René, as well as Jean Dunois, journey up the Loire to Gien, a château belonging to Louis's dear old uncle, Jean of Berry. They are there to collect the seven-year-old Catherine of Burgundy, taking her into their family and their care.

She is a splendid sight, a tiny figure in a cloak made of cloth of gold, edged with ermine. With both hands she carries her marriage crown studded with precious stones as she walks gingerly towards them. Her trousseau contains many elegant clothes, jewels, dinner services of gold and silver, tapestries, furniture, horses, birds in cages, dogs and much else.

Yolande detects a slight tremble of the little girl's bottom lip as she curtseys and gives her hand, surely terrified as her new guardian towers over her. And despite her misgivings, despite the child's parentage, despite the hurt she bears in her heart, Yolande finds herself bending down and saying, with genuine warmth: "Welcome, my child." She embraces the small frame, feeling the girl shaking inside. Stroking her hair, Yolande tells her with sincere feeling: "You will be very happy with us, my dear, because we will love you as one of us, which you will be when you marry Louis. Here he is." The two children kiss stiffly on the cheek. "And this is Marie"—who hugs her—"and my baby René." They turn to look at the sleeping baby. "And this is our cousin and yours, Jean Dunois"—who gives her an impish smile that she finally returns.

Yolande can see that the child has relaxed a little, and ventures: "Catherine my darling, we have a surprise waiting for you." The little girl's eyes begin to shine. "A pony—and some baby rabbits!" And Marie adds at once: "You can choose which one will be yours and only you will feed him—would you like that?" Yolande wants to hug her daughter for this sweet gesture. Catherine nods and her little face transforms at last. She is a pretty child, very small for her age, but Yolande can see already that she will grow into a beauty. The betrothal is still a bitter pill, but Catherine herself? Yolande and the children have taken her sweetness to their hearts.

Louis has decided that Yolande will return to Angers tomorrow with her suite, the children and her new charge. He too will leave tomorrow and take part of Catherine's dowry south to Marseilles to assemble his army and sail for Naples. Without any idea how long he will be gone and what kind of dangers he will face, Yolande has forced herself to accept his departure. He is a man who makes his own decisions and does not always discuss his plans with her. She knows her role: take care of his children, rule his territory, and wait. *Patience and fortitude said Marie de Blois. Well, I have need of them now.*

Tonight, as every night, he comes to her room. Gien is a pleasant enough château, warm and well appointed and full of exquisite *objets d'art* chosen by Uncle Jean with his renowned taste. Her room has a large chimney piece and the fire will last all night. It is not home, but it is near enough, and it is kind of Louis' uncle to have accommodated them so well in his absence. The bed is large and the mattress is comfortable.

"Why so anxious, my love?" says Louis as he takes her in his arms, brushing her hair from her face.

"Why not?" she replies softly. "I have believed since we met that I am your only lover; the one who rules your heart... as you have told me so often."

He tries to kiss away her words and whispers tenderly, "And

so you are my darling, my dearest wife," but she breaks free.

"No, sire," she says firmly, and he looks up, astonished at her tone. "For you have a mistress, and you are running from me to her." Louis looks at her in astonishment. "Yes," she says, low and hard, "it is true... Her name is... Naples." And with that she turns her head away and cannot help her tears.

Louis knows of her fears, just as she knows of his ambition. But they also both know that neither of them can change. This night he holds her fiercely and makes love to her like a man possessed. And so he is with her, but also with that kingdom she regards as her most dangerous rival.

Yet his parting from her the following day is as tender as she knows his heart to be. He takes her in his arms in front of the children and says:

"Light of my life, you know of my ambition to rule again my kingdom in Naples and to have you there beside me. I go not only for myself, but for you and the children and for the future of our house. Be content, my dearest wife, on my behalf. Know that I am following my destiny as my father would have wished. I leave in your hands and your care all that I have, the most precious being you and the children. Keep all safe for me and await with joy my return, successful in my quest. I will write regularly—and all of you write to me!" And he makes a cross on her forehead and on those of each of the children with his thumb.

Yolande bites her lip, which makes him smile—a quick stroke of her cheek with the back of his forefinger—and then he is in his boat and gone to meet his destiny. She waits for a backward glance, but there is none. He is already lost in his own world.

Back home in Angers, Yolande hears that when they collected Catherine at Gien, they just missed the arrival of her husband's family. Was this by accident or design? She thinks hard but cannot be certain. Later that same day, she learns that Charles, the new young Duke d'Orléans, and his brother, sons of the slain Louis and her dearest friend Valentina, were the principal guests at Gien. They were accompanied by their supporters, among them some of the most powerful nobles in France. All were guests of the king's senior uncle, Jean of Berry, their dear friend, who came with the party.

Why was my husband Louis not invited to join them, his closest family? she wonders. It certainly seems strange.

All too soon Yolande discovers the purpose of that meeting at the château of Gien. It was a war party—a gathering of the highest in the land. Their purpose: to seek revenge for the assassination of Louis d'Orléans. Their plan: to find a means of eliminating his murderer, Jean of Burgundy. Since the Count d'Armagnac was the senior military figure among the group, the former Orléanists will henceforth be led by him and known as the Armagnacs. At first Yolande asks herself why her husband was not approached to join the family cabal. Then she realizes that Louis' uncle Jean, among others there at Gien, knows of his burning ambition to reconquer Naples—and his need of Catherine's money to make that possible. She surmises that, loving him as she knows they do, they were unwilling to present him with such a difficult choice.

Despite his family's generous consideration, Yolande knows that Louis would have had no difficulty in making his choice. *Nothing* would have been allowed to stand in the way of his determination to conquer and rule again in Naples—more than determination, she knows now; it is an obsession.

Chapter Fourteen

ll Yolande can do is wait, resigned and anxious, for news of his progress. True to his promise, Louis sends her regular packets full of descriptions of difficulties, of battles on the Italian mainland—some large but none definitive. The seasons come and go: spring and summer in Anjou, autumn and winter in Provence, always accompanied by the growing children lightening the heavy burden of worry and empty nights. Catherine has become an integral part of their lives, her sweet nature winning love on all sides. She worships young Louis, refers to him as "my future husband" with giggles, and follows Marie like her shadow. The children are a blessed distraction from the packets from Italy, which she receives with anxious foreboding, always containing descriptions of more small victories, and small defeats.

A year has passed and Louis' army and navy have swollen to such a size that this enormous force needs more money than even Catherine of Burgundy's dowry allows. Like her mother-in-law, Marie de Blois, before her, Yolande offers her jewels as an added guarantee. At least she has the comfort of Louis' choice of second-in-command—Tanneguy du Chastel, a tough Breton captain who acted as his bodyguard in Naples during the years Louis spent there before their marriage. An Angevin, he returned with Louis, and, once they were back in Anjou, he came whenever he was summoned. Tall, strong as an oak, a chest like a barrel and a thick red beard, even his gruff voice is enough to frighten strangers. Tanneguy is well known as a wrestler among Louis' bodyguards and heavy bets were often placed on him to win—which, invariably, he did. When asked by Louis to accompany him on his visits throughout his territories, he always called at whichever of their castles they inhabited, and despite his rough appearance he learned courtly manners, always greeting her respectfully but amiably. There was something about him that she instinctively liked—from the first day she noticed him in Louis' bodyguard as they left Arles for Tarascon, she felt she could rely on him and trust him. Tanneguy's reputation among their soldiers is stalwart, and it comforts her to know that he has not left her husband's side since embarking with him from Marseilles. Also, having been with Louis to Naples before, he knows what to expect.

Is she anxious about the outcome of this expedition on which so much depends? Yes, oh yes! She lives in fear and dread that her beloved husband might be captured, injured, or worse, killed. But what can she do? This is the path he has chosen and it is her role to support him with all her ability. And with her prayers! How she prays each day for his success and safe return. But even if he does succeed, surely he will *not* return; he will stay and rule, and what then? Will she be obliged to remain in France as his regent instead of sharing his throne in Naples? Yolande does not much care for either outcome, but she prays most fervently for his safety.

As the autumn turns chill in Anjou, and she prepares to leave for Provence with the children on their annual migration south, she finds herself faced with an inheritance problem of her own.

On the death of her childless uncle Martin, King of Aragon, as the next in line in accordance to her father's will, Yolande proposes that her eldest son Louis be accepted as his heir in her place. Her son's rival for the throne is Ferdinand of Castile, the thirteen-year-old son of an Aragon cousin. Despite his youth, he is already a successful cavalry officer, who has fought against the Moors. Louis is only eight, and the council of Aragon, faced with a lengthy regency in the case of her son, decide to give the throne to Ferdinand. Yolande feels cheated. As her father's ablest, eldest and then only living child, she had always hoped that she would rule in Aragon one day, and if not her, then her son. For the second time she has been deprived of what she considers her rightful inheritance, but there is nothing she can do.

The weeks and months stretch over a year and it seems that the time passes both slowly and quickly—slowly because she longs for Louis' return; quickly because she is constantly occupied, divided always between administering his estates and ensuring that the brood in her nursery, oldest to youngest, are being brought up as he would wish.

There are daily lessons for the older ones in the schoolroom. Louis and Yolande insist that they receive religious instruction from their dear house priest, Father Jean-Charles, that they hear Mass with them every Sunday and read the family's Book of Hours (rather more than they care to). Louis and Marie are pious, but René is only interested in the music in church. Jean Dunois is cautiously religious—to please them, Yolande thinks—and little Catherine of Burgundy just follows Marie everywhere in silent adoration.

René loves the songs and lyrics sung by the minstrels who come to their court, and Yolande explains to the children how their inspiration comes from the troubadours, with their romantic tales of chivalry and of rescuing beautiful maidens from dragons. All the children love history, and that is usually the subject of their bedtime story. Marie is very attentive at her schoolwork, and so is Louis, but their cousin Jean Dunois is easily the cleverest of them all. How René hero-worships him! Catherine is adorable, never utters an unkind word and is the first to hug and give sympathy to the wounded, learning from Tiphane how to wash cuts and tie bandages. She is loved by them all and Yolande can see that she and Louis are already great friends and accomplices in some things, especially when he teaches her the finer points of schooling her beautiful ponies. To Yolande, she is as a second daughter, bringing her little bunches of flowers after a walk, painting pictures for her and doing everything she can think of to give pleasure. She has brought an extra ray of sunshine into their lives, and Yolande trusts that she can feel how much they all love her.

The spring of 1411 is late, but Yolande has received wonderful news that fills her with joy. Victory at last! Louis has defeated his cousin Ladislaus Durazzo in a definitive battle outside Naples and reconquered his kingdom! Oh, how she rejoices for him! She has trembled at the arrival of every courier, and agonized through Louis' letters full of descriptions of battles on the mainland peninsula and endless negotiations. Now, this news of a definitive victory has made the endless anxiety worthwhile.

The children celebrate at home in Anjou, making costumes and restaging the final battle after dinner tonight, and Yolande has given all the staff a free day to toast their master, once again the ruler of Naples! All his dreams and the years of hope and prayer have come to fruition! Thanks be to God.

Weeks pass in the euphoria of achievement; then another letter arrives. It is not possible! Their celebration was premature. Louis' victory was far from definitive, since Durazzo managed to retreat into the walled city of Naples and, by prolonging the campaign, has succeeded in bleeding Louis' coffers dry. By August, Louis writes that he can no longer afford to support his huge army. Even though Yolande has promised her jewels as a guarantee, with frustration and great sadness he has been obliged to abandon his reconquered territories and sail for home. How she cries for her poor dear husband. So many hopes dashed again. The children have never before seen her weep and are tender in their concern, especially little René, who throws his short, fat arms around her legs and buries his curly red head in her lap. Drying her eyes, Yolande tries to explain things to them.

"My darlings, I am not in pain or crying for myself. My tears are for your beloved father and his vanished dreams." But she is talking more to herself, as she can see they do not understand. How can they?

She determines to travel to Provence and meet Louis when he arrives in Marseilles—to console his wounded pride in her arms. They will all travel south together, and Tiphane can stay with the children at Tarascon until she and Louis come back there. Seeing her blonde hero return defeated will be hard, and she will need Juana's quiet strength to help her.

They meet on the pier at Marseilles. As Louis steps off the boat, she runs to embrace him. They need no words. Their tearful eyes say it all. With a lump in her throat, she notices how much this expedition has aged her handsome warrior, but says nothing. To have him near is all she wants.

"How beautiful you look, my dearest," he says in greeting, and that brings her more tears since she is sure she does not.

"You must be tired, beloved," she replies. "Stay and rest awhile with me here in Marseilles."

They make for their large turreted palace in the port, magnificent with its towers of sandstone glowing in the sunset. She bathes him herself in her copper tub lined with a linen sheet, and pours oil of lavender into the water—the scent of their beloved Provence, to remind him of home. She watches as he closes his eyes and breathes in the aroma deeply. May it bring him happy memories, she prays silently. She does all she can to soothe him with her words, and tenderly massages the oil into his neck and shoulders. As the sea air is cool this night, they sit on cushions by the fire and drink the warm broth that Juana brings in to them. When she sees his eyes begin to close, Yolande leads him to the bed, where she holds him all night long. He sleeps without once moving.

In the morning, she finds him awake and refreshed beside

her, looking at her in a way she knows so well.

"Come home to Tarascon, my love," she whispers, her finger tracing new scars on his chest and arms. "Tell me everything so that we can plot and plan, and take comfort in our good health and renew our energy to fight again. At least I am to be paid a considerable sum in token compensation for the loss of my father's throne, and that may help your attempt to secure yours in Naples for our son." A year earlier she would never have believed she could utter such words! Naples! That curse on the family of Anjou and on her marriage! But Louis' tired, aged face makes her suffer for his loss, and instinctively her heart goes out to him.

Tarascon, she knows, cannot be a refuge for him to recover from his campaigning for long. She is conscious of the gravity of the situation at the council in Paris and wrote him nothing of the troubles the country was facing. He had battles enough of his own to fight in Naples. Why burden him with those at home. Although he is still banished from the capital, Burgundy has used his popularity with the Parisians—and, no doubt, some hefty bribes—to sway them to his will from his camp outside the city. As a result, the people have refused to allow entry to the king's supporters—the combined armies of Berry and Orléans—as well as Armagnac and his terrifying troops from Gascony. She watches as his eyes stray somewhere far away—perhaps to Paris—or even Naples.

"I am afraid there is more, and it is worse," sighs Yolande. "Jean-sans-Peur has gathered a loyalist army from his own region of Burgundy and advanced with them towards Paris. By some miracle, a clash between the two factions has been avoided, but for how long?" Louis' lined face distorts in anguish, and then turns red with anger.

"How can they all be so utterly stupid!" he exclaims, jumping up. "Surely the nobles realize the futility of these petty squabbles for supremacy at court. Fighting a civil war between their own territories, French against French, can only benefit our enemy the English!" He is shouting now, and she tries to calm him by massaging his shoulders as he slumps down in his chair.

"Where is my wise uncle of Berry? What has got into the head of Armagnac? Is Bourbon blind?" and with those words, he jumps up again and strides down the Great Hall and back, heels and spurs scraping and clinking as he stamps his fury into the stone.

"Yes, I see," he starts again, more slowly. "They are trying to protect the king in Paris, trying to keep Burgundy away from him and the queen. But this is sheer madness; even in Naples I heard that the English are planning a new campaign. What defence measures have been taken to protect the north if the armies of the royal dukes are gathered around Paris?"

Yolande takes a deep breath: "I am afraid the situation is even more serious, my love," she replies sadly. "*Both* factions have been trying to enlist the support of the English, sending them couriers—with incentives. Your agents and my own have confirmed it to me," she almost whispers.

Silence. Then:

"I have no choice," he says decisively. "I must leave for Paris and see what I can do to drive some sense into my family."

Yolande has feared this response, but she insists that Louis remain with them for a week to rest—he still looks less than his usual self and she thinks it will cheer him to enjoy the children a little. More than that, though, she cannot do. Once again it seems she is destined to be without her beloved husband by her side.

Chapter Fifteen

Louis has been gone some weeks, and his frequent letters have not enlightened Yolande more than to confirm the preparations being made by the English to launch a new offensive across the Channel. On Louis' instructions, she has remained in Provence with her family; safer in the south, at least for the time being. Who knows what this new offensive may mean?

Today, to her delighted surprise, Louis has arrived at Tarascon and promises to remain with them for some months! The children rush about, overexcited and out of control—and she can see how pleased Louis is with his little ones. When he returned from Marseilles he had hardly time to kiss them before leaving for Paris.

It is Juana who comes to tell her how the master is impressed by what she has done in his absence. How he marvelled at all the improvements, and especially at the account books.

"Madame," she bursts out, "he is overwhelmed by how well you have administered his estates and has nothing but praise for you."

Yolande is quietly delighted, but waits to hear it from him. That night, in his arms, he tells her, and shows her, himself.

The next day, he praises Yolande in front of the assembled household staff.

"As you all know, my wife, the Queen of Sicily, has been acting as my lieutenant general in my absence. No doubt you also know what I did not until my return, and that is how brilliantly and efficiently she has succeeded. I must tell you that I am very proud of what has been achieved on my behalf by all of you, my competent administrators, and by your workforces."

Yolande never expected public praise! Louis' surprised delight is infectious, and the children hug her and everyone is kissing everyone else, and tears of joy well up again, even in Tiphane's tough young face!

What happiness it is to have him back amongst them. When he set sail for Naples, René was just a year old. Now he is a boisterous three. Marie is seven. Louis is nine and Jean Dunois a year older. Although much smaller than the elder boys, Catherine is a year older than Louis, her betrothed. The nursery is a lively place where Yolande has made sure that the children are unaware of the conflict within the two branches of their family. Even the older ones were told only that their father was away fighting somewhere; they know from children's tales that that is what knights are supposed to do: fight in battles and tournaments. They race their ponies, play ball, and hide-and-seek—with prizes that Tiphane and Juana somehow produce for them all. Or they steal into the kitchen and raid the freshly baked biscuits they smell from afar, a furious cook chasing after them. How the rest of them laugh!

Louis has ordered a tree house built, and then a walkway to the next tree and another house in that too. Yolande trembles that the younger ones will fall, but Louis just laughs and says, "It's good for them, toughens them up." He says the same when they fall off their ponies or hurt themselves in their mock battles and tourneys—which sometimes turn earnest, especially with their neighbourhood companions. In the evenings, the children perform plays Yolande makes up for them during the day, and Tiphane, Juana and the maids make costumes for them from old clothes. The plays often have a princess who needs to be rescued, a bad knight with followers and a good knight— in white—with fewer followers, but who has to win. Yolande insists that good always wins over evil.

After dinner in the evenings, the children sit with their father by the fire and he recounts the details of his battles around Naples and on the peninsula, which thrill them. He spares no details—the horrible food (to encourage them to eat whatever is put before them), the dirt, the wounds, the lack of sleep, the discomfort—and he recalls great acts of courage and unselfishness by knights and soldiers alike, and some amazing rescues and happy endings.

How Louis loves to describe the city of Naples and its surroundings; the volcano Vesuvius and what happens when it erupts, fire bursting from its centre, red-hot boulders flying out into the sky, and thick lava, like glowing golden-fired tomato sauce, sliding down the mountain, covering everything in its path. They sit open-mouthed, and all swear they will climb Vesuvius one day.

"On the docks, brought on ships from Arabia, I have seen camels with one hump and with two, looking like this," and he draws them for the rapt children—"and giraffes with extraordinary long necks, and a tame lion," he tells his enthralled audience, his eyes rolling, and he draws those animals for them too.

Sometimes Louis shows the children his suits of armour, his lances, his swords, his shields and the armour for his horses. Their faces glow at the telling, and Yolande can see they think their father the most thrilling man alive.

Chapter Sixteen

After years of hearing their threats, the time has come when the English really are on the march. Louis must leave the relaxed, easy life of Provence, heading north again to prepare to defend his duchy of Anjou. He leaves Yolande expecting a child she is sure was conceived in Marseilles out of sympathy for their shared loss—his of Naples and hers of Aragon.

Louis knows the time has come to make a momentous decision, one he has always sworn he would never make. It is finally clear to him that as a family they cannot stand aside another day and watch their evil, bullying cousin of Burgundy incite insurrection against the king, and in his own capital of Paris. The Dukes of Anjou, Berry, and Bourbon band together, and with force of arms take over the main strategic posts in the city and quell the rebellion, forcing the Duke of Burgundy to flee to Flanders.

That the English dare to threaten Anjou, Louis' own province, is for him the final indignity. Without hesitation, he informs Yolande that he will come to the aid of his lawful king—thereby joining forces with the Armagnacs.

Having gathered his Angevin army, when Louis arrives in Bourges, he writes to Yolande:

My dearest, imagine what I discovered as I entered my uncle's capital. The dauphin, a bright lad if ever I saw one, has instigated a peace process, which is being negotiated as I write!

Yolande replies:

Did you not receive my letter about the birth of our daughter on 12
June? What a sweet bundle of joy she is! And once again, such an
easy birth. The children are as excited as if they have another litter
of puppies—and they have had plenty of those. Marie has taken the
baby over and become her nurse, telling both Tiphane and Juana
confidently what to do. Didn't she learn it all with baby René? And
little Catherine is her nursery assistant.

On 15 August, another letter arrives, again without mention
of baby Yolande. When she opens it, she realizes that her letter
to Bourges must have missed him.

My beloved wife, the impossible has happened. I am at Auxerre,
where the Dukes of Berry, Bourbon and Burgundy have come to
celebrate a Day of Reconciliation and Peace with Charles d'Orléans
and his brother.

She cannot tell from his letter if he believes in it or not—or
whether he is afraid his letter might be intercepted. The situation
is too delicate to take any risks. She prays that this High Mass
will have more success than the last.

Since her evenings at Tarascon are mostly spent alone with
her books and her dogs for company, Yolande begins to think
about the future. There is a situation that keeps troubling her,
eating away at her self-assurance. The king's two elder sons
are married to Burgundian princesses. One of his daughters is
married to Burgundy's heir. With Charles VI's heirs entrenched
thoroughly on the side of Burgundy, she knows she must find a
way to even out the balance. If she could arrange for one of her
children to marry a child of the king's, that would help—and
she sets her mind to thinking about this possibility.

Her concern about the validity of the reconciliation is
justified, as Louis' next letter makes clear. Somehow Jean of
Burgundy has managed to keep control of the government *and*

the treasury. Any opponents are swiftly removed and replaced with his own choices.

> There is only one persistent voice of dissent, and that surprises not only my cousin of Burgundy, but everyone. It comes from the seventeen-year-old dauphin, Burgundy's son-in-law, who alone has the courage to oppose him.

When Yolande reads these words—written by her famously brave husband—she smiles. *That boy has valour and will make a great king once his mad father dies!*
A fast courier arrives:

> My darling sweet wife, how could this wonderful news have missed me—another adorable Yolande in our family! I am so very happy to hear of your safe delivery of a healthy child and a second delicious daughter for me to spoil as I do, and will again, her mother. May God bless you both, my darling. Your devoted husband, Louis.

At last he knows. As she sits with her baby on her lap, surrounded by her other children, as well as Jean Dunois and Catherine, Yolande feels blessed indeed. With each new baby in her arms, she tends to forget or ignore the world outside the nursery. But she is brought back to the daily struggle of events in Paris with the next letter from her husband:

> We have victory and it belongs wholly to the dauphin, who has stood calmly at the helm within the capital, while the great armies of his kinsmen have been forced by the Parisians to remain outside. To our relief, finally the capital's citizens, despite their preference for Jean of Burgundy, have opted for peace over conflict. My uncle of Berry and I have been permitted to make our official entry into the capital—not in armour, but wearing the purple robes of celebration. You can imagine how relieved we feel. Now we can plan for the defence of the kingdom, since we hear from many sources that the English are advancing.

Indeed, all France knows that the English, who have considerable forces based in their own territory of Normandy, have begun to plan a move southwards.

Chapter Seventeen

$\mathcal{I}$n January comes more reason to fear the English. This new year of 1413 has seen a vibrant young king mount the throne. He is Henry V, formerly Duke of Lancaster—young, intelligent and, by reputation, confrontational and ruthless. He has failed to extract the concessions he has demanded, and word comes that he has begun preparations to send his main army across the Channel to Normandy and regroup with his troops already there. The situation has developed into a national conflict between two kings—Henry Plantagenet of England and the Valois Charles VI—each of them claiming sovereignty over certain areas of France. When Yolande hears this from Louis in his letters, she trembles, because she knows what it means for their family. For the French to have a chance of defeating the English the royal dukes must be united, and that is impossible if the Anjou family is aligned to Burgundy, England's ally. Louis has finally understood her initial resistance to the betrothal of their eldest son to a daughter of Jean of Burgundy. At last he can see that they cannot continue with the planned marriage. It is what Yolande wanted from the start, but now? What a cost to their family, to Catherine, whom they have all loved for the past four years. She feels her heart tearing in two.

"I love this child," she says to Louis when he returns from the council to tell her of his decision, "and so does our son, and they would be happy." Louis nods, but he can see from the set of her face that what he has decided, tough and unpleasant as it is,

124

must be.

"You do realize, my darling wife, that this is tantamount to a declaration of war between Anjou and Burgundy, two royal first cousins?" And she answers simply, "Yes." There is no other way.

"Louis," she says, taking his hand, "beloved husband, I know you have never wanted to become involved in your family's quarrels, but the time has come, hasn't it, when we must take this tough and shaming decision, no matter what it costs us?" Louis nods forlornly. "We must nullify the formal planned marriage contract between our eldest son and Catherine of Burgundy, mustn't we?" Again he nods.

Yolande knows that Louis loves little Catherine as much as she and the rest of their family do. "What an asset she would have been in her own right—if only she did not bear that accursed name," he says with genuine regret.

She can sense that she must strengthen his resolve. "It has been four years now that she has lived happily among us, but we must do this. I have taken my decision and I know from your face that you have done the same." And they embrace in joint grief for Catherine and for themselves. Yolande says nothing about their altercation when she last broached the subject of their heir's marriage, nor will she, but however much her heart bleeds for Catherine, part of her rejoices that they have taken their stand against Burgundy at last.

First Louis must inform their son. Young Louis understands at once—though he is young, the rumours of war have reached his ears, and he has somehow divined their significance to him. Then Yolande sends her husband to tell Catherine. When she hears, Catherine comes running into Yolande's room.

"Maman!" she cries. "Why? Why are you doing this to me? Have I not been dutiful? What have I done to displease you? I have never been happier than during these years spent with you. I have grown to love you and your family more than my own, and I have tried so hard to have you love me in return. You have often told me how you love me. Was this not true? Did you just say these words with no meaning? Of all the people in the world, I trust you more than anyone. Whatever you say, I know it to be fact. Can you really be telling me now that you do *not* love me and I must go back to Burgundy? Will I no longer marry Louis, whom I love, and be his loyal wife, the way you have taught me to become?" This all comes out in a torrent of words, her despair heart-rending.

Tears pour down Catherine's cheeks as Yolande holds tight her trembling, fragile body, smoothing her brow and kissing her forehead, but she can say nothing, only shake her head in sorrow. Sorrow for Catherine, sorrow for them all in losing her, and for their son to have to part with this delightful girl who would have made him a good wife. Most of all, sorrow for the House of Anjou, for they know that from this time onwards they will be at the mercy of that vengeful and powerful duke, Catherine's father, Jean-sans-Peur of Burgundy.

In August, with heavy hearts, they send the poor girl home— without explanation and with all she brought with her: the huge trousseau, her wedding dress and crown, her many trunks of clothes and possessions. But not her dowry—that has been spent in Naples and they must find a way of replacing it. The insult to Burgundy is enormous, and universally regarded as such. They know Jean-sans-Peur will be mortally offended and they can be certain his retaliation will be brutal, especially since Anjou is situated between Burgundy and Brittany, both allies of England. *He will not stop until he has punished us and our family, of that I am sure*, thinks Yolande.

"We are doing a dreadful, cruel thing to this sweet child, my husband," she tells Louis, "and we will suffer the consequences. But it is what we must do—for the king—despite Burgundy's vengeance." She remembers the early days of her marriage, how her husband taught her that this loyalty must come above all. Well, the day has arrived, but at what a price.

"You were right, my dearest. I should never have made the marriage contract. It will cost us dear," answers Louis quietly as he holds Yolande's shaking, weeping body in his strong arms.

Chapter Eighteen

It is October 1413, and the Queen of Sicily is travelling from Anjou with her four children, including her youngest, baby Yolande, to join her husband in Paris. During the long nights alone in Saumur, a strategic plan has been forming in her mind: to revive the connection between the House of Anjou and the royal House of France. Now she has set out to achieve it at her own instigation. If she fails, she reasons, Louis need never know. If she tells him, he might forbid her initiative.

On the way to Paris, Yolande makes a planned break in her journey at the château of Marcoussis, where Queen Isabeau is in residence. Her son, the Dauphin Louis, is married to Marguerite, eldest daughter of the Duke of Burgundy. The dauphin's younger brother, Jean de Touraine, is married to Burgundy's niece, the daughter of his sister. And Burgundy's heir is married to one of the king's daughters. These three royal marriages make the odds within the younger generation of the royal family firmly stacked on the Burgundian side. In order to regain a little balance, Yolande's proposal is for her daughter Marie to marry the queen's third and youngest son, Charles de Ponthieu, and she believes that the best way to gain Isabeau's consent is to have a conversation with her face to face. Yolande has helped Isabeau in the past when she asked her; she will not have forgotten.

The Queen of France and the Queen of Sicily could not be more dissimilar. Shown into her room, Yolande is surprised to see how much Isabeau has changed since their last meeting. She has become even larger, and now has difficulty moving. She reclines her great bulk on a day bed, sprawled on her back, draped like a statue under construction with a variety of shawls—some of silk, others of the finest wool. Her famously once-lovely features have coarsened further, her rouge is too intense and her hair unkempt, but vanity has not entirely abandoned her. Isabeau wears an impressive treasure trove of jewels on her fingers and wrists and around her neck. How can she eat with so many rings on? Judging from the size of her, Yolande is confident she manages! The Queen of France has the look of a woman lost, her eyes roaming, unsure of herself and of her place—and she is right. How *can* she be sure of anything—or anyone—in this world so alien to her native Bavaria? Particularly now that she is deprived of the three men in whom she placed her trust, and who maintained her: the late Duke of Burgundy, Philippe-le-Hardi; her brother-in-law, the enchanting Louis d'Orléans; and her husband, the insane king she originally adored. Those others she trusted have either been killed or shown themselves to be disloyal. Isabeau is forty-two, and one would never know she had been a great beauty. Yolande, at thirty-three, knows from her own mirror that, happily, this is not so in her case.

As a queen herself, Yolande does not bend her knee but comes forward and embraces Isabeau affectionately.

"My dear, what a pleasure to see you again," she says as she kisses her cheek.

Isabeau smiles warmly—they have always understood each other. They are familiar with one another's stories, there are no secrets between them, and Isabeau sees that Yolande has come with a purpose.

"Dear Yolande, as beautiful as ever, unlike me," she says, but without rancour. "What can I do for you? You surely have something on your mind."

Politics was never Isabeau's natural world, and once the

old Duke of Burgundy was no longer there to guide her, she floundered in the Council of State, unable to make decisions or even to influence others. That she turned for comfort and reassurance to her captivating brother-in-law, Louis d'Orléans, Yolande found completely understandable. *I doubt she has any idea how her friendship with him has shaped the politics of France.*

Yolande's approach is subtle. "Dear cousin, you and I have much in common," she begins. "We may come from different countries but we are both queens, each the daughter of a king, and we have made our homes and borne our children at the court of France. Our roles are the same—to live our lives solely for the benefit of our king and our adopted country. I know that has always been your goal," she lies, "and you know it has always been mine." At this point she pauses to see if Isabeau is listening. Her eyes appear glazed—or is that just the failing light at the end of the day?

"We have each left behind the kingdom of our parents and our childhood, the safety and comfort of our father's hearth and our mother's knee, and become mistress of our own house, mothers of children. And, if you will allow me, we have both tried our best, in the difficult situations in which we have found ourselves, to make peace among our husbands' followers."

At this point, Isabeau shifts her great bulk somewhat uneasily on her bed, but says nothing.

"Our adopted country is on the brink of invasion from across the Channel, and within, the people are tormented by civil war between members of both our husbands' factions." More discomfort from the queen as she reaches for a sweetmeat. "Your two elder sons are married into the family of Jean of Burgundy, cousin to both our husbands. One of your daughters is married to his eldest son. The future generation of this royal family is, for the moment, totally allied to Burgundy."

Before Isabeau can demur, Yolande continues:

"Give me your youngest son, Charles de Ponthieu, and let him be betrothed to my daughter Marie. Let us join once again our two royal houses of Valois and Anjou, and with this union create some measure of balance within our fractious families."

Isabeau sighs as if with relief. Yolande cannot think what she expected her to say, but whatever it was, her request for the queen's youngest son has come almost as a reprieve. How mentally frail she appears—almost as if she does not know who she is, or where. Without the support of her husband or his brother, Yolande believes Isabeau has lost her sense of her own value and power.

Yolande is persuasive; Isabeau is pensive. And then, to Yolande's masked pleasure, Isabeau nods and agrees. "Yes... why not... Valois and Anjou, Anjou and Valois. I agree with your plan, dear Yolande. You were always a sensible young woman. Come, embrace me. It is done."

Yolande sighs inwardly. This decision gives the House of Anjou a real advantage. She has succeeded.

The formal betrothal of their children is to be celebrated in Paris on 18 December. Louis has come to join his wife at Isabeau's château of Marcoussis, and they all travel onto Paris together with their three older children and cousin Jean Dunois. At the gates to the city they are met by Charles VI on horseback, and alongside him, his third son Charles, Count of Ponthieu, Yolande's future son-in-law.

"Well met, dear cousins," says the king in friendly greeting. "I am delighted with this betrothal and have brought you my youngest son to place in your care."

As both of their escorts fall back, Louis returns the king's greeting while Yolande observes her daughter's intended bridegroom, a small, miserable-looking ten-year-old boy, sitting awkwardly on a splendid white pony. She smiles down at him.

"Would you like to come to live with us and our children? I have two your age," she says, pointing to her children riding behind with Jean Dunois, "and more growing."

Instantly his eyes brighten and he replies with a shy smile.

"Madame, yes, yes please." Yolande doubts that Charles, as the youngest of his siblings, has enjoyed any games with other children. From this day he will be in her care and under her protection. *"Je le garde, moi,"* she announces, and will repeat it to anyone who may doubt that it is her vow. *I will keep him safe.*

*

The queen has graciously invited Yolande and her eight-year-old daughter Marie to stay with her in Paris for the celebrations. She cannot help but despair for Isabeau as she studies her across the table—gross, her face an expression of self-disgust as she shovels food into her mouth, some of it falling onto her clothes. No pride or interest even in the betrothal proceedings earlier, with their beautiful music and poetry read by the court *trouvères*. She attempts to be hospitable and welcoming, but Yolande is so conscious of her apathy it saddens her. The king is unwell again, and they are seated alone at the top table with young Marie and her new betrothed—who exchange not one word in their shyness. Yolande has no difficulty in talking to Isabeau and draws her out on her childhood and her own betrothal—all happy memories that bring her back to life a little.

The following evening, Yolande returns to their mansion on the Seine, leaving Marie and her betrothed together at Marcoussis with Isabeau, while the other children leave for Angers with Juana.

"Well, my dear wife," murmurs Louis in her ear when they are in bed, "you have always been beautiful, and I know from experience that you have been a clever administrator of my estates, but now I can appreciate your true genius. You have achieved something I would not have imagined possible, not in this climate of suspicion and intrigue. Although Burgundy has married two princely heirs to the throne of France into his family, there is one he has missed. This last one belongs to Anjou!"

Yolande smiles with pleasure at his praise. Especially, she has to admit, as their clever, wise-for-her-age daughter Marie is really rather plain—and that is putting it kindly. But her intelligence and her bright expression compensate for her long, narrow face, pointed chin and rather small eyes. Marie has other virtues, and Yolande hopes they will become useful to young Charles de Ponthieu.

Chapter Nineteen

To take possession of the prince as her daughter's betrothed is normal procedure—his older brother Jean of Touraine lives with his future parents-in-law. In February, with the queen's permission, Yolande returns to Anjou with Marie and the young Prince Charles. Meanwhile, her husband has decided to remain in Paris to help prepare for the ever-advancing English.

Their return to Angers with the young prince is a pleasure. Yolande, together with Marie and Charles, descends from the carriage and hugs the others, whom she had sent ahead with Juana. The children are lined up in their best clothes and have clearly been schooled by Tiphane as to how to make their new arrival feel welcome. Jean Dunois shakes Charles's hand and gives him a friendly pat on the back. Otherwise, Yolande can see that this exercise is not an immediate success. Since Charles is shy and prone to standing on one leg looking awkward, Yolande takes him firmly by the hand to show him his new quarters, followed by Tiphane fussing over him—to the clear annoyance of René. He pays more attention to Charles's white pony tied to the back of their carriage than to the prince, a fact not lost on his mother. *I must speak to him.*

That night, Yolande kneels down in front of the little altar in her bedroom and makes a solemn vow to Our Lady that she will take good care of this new son of hers. In effect, she has adopted the shy young prince as her own, and no Duke of Burgundy, regardless how strong or ambitious, will be able to take him from them. *Je le garde, moi,* she says to herself, and she knows it must be a vow for life. This will not be another Catherine; it would break her heart. Having taken him in, she will guard him for ever, as a son, as a son-in-law, as a prince of France.

From the moment Yolande took the unfortunate royal prince into her care, she was determined to right the wrongs of his wretched childhood. Unlike her own boys, he is rather stunted, with short, very thin legs. His inclination is to look at people sideways, and she cannot call him an attractive or even an appealing boy. It was the way he smiled at her when she first spoke to him, sitting disconsolately on his white pony, that endeared him to her, and somehow she understood from that first moment that she would spend her life doing her utmost to help him.

The prince's childhood has been miserable, punctuated by the terrible scenes he has witnessed during his father's insane rages. He knows about the violent murder of his uncle Louis d'Orléans—servants never spare children bloodthirsty details— and he has seen his mother's distress. Worst of all, he may even have heard the whispers that he was born illegitimate, something Yolande, for one, has never believed. Her agents within the king's household have assured her of that fact.

Young Louis and Charles, his future brother-in-law, are of an age, and together with Marie and their cousin Jean Dunois they make a cheerful foursome. Jean is particularly kind to the young royal prince, putting him at ease, and she sees him scold René, albeit gently, for misunderstanding this shy, thin, unloved lad. Yolande overhears him telling her son:

"You know, my young friend, I have noticed that faces can be deceiving. Sometimes the nicest-looking people turn out to be the least so. Give him a chance. He has had a miserable enough childhood. It's our role to make him enjoy himself, and you will see, you may change your first opinion."

Inwardly she thanks Jean Dunois, and loves him even more. So much wisdom in one so young, also damaged from birth, though less than their royal charge.

It will take time for René to change his mind about Charles de Ponthieu, though he hides his feelings well. Several times Yolande has to remind him that Charles has never known what it is to have loving parents like his own. A few days later, she hears that René has taken Charles to the stables to show him Calypso's new litter, and she begins to feel better about them bonding. When René asks her that evening at bedtime if they can give Charles one of the puppies, she hugs him and agrees.

To observe the shy, thin lad grow daily more confident and comfortable in his surroundings seems to please everyone. But it saddens Yolande to see her darling Marie becoming no prettier, and she fears it is true when Juana says—not unkindly—that she resembles a ferret. Marie, however, is discreet, intelligent and kind, and she and Charles have become instant friends—at first through their love of dogs, and especially the puppies. Yolande realizes that Charles will never be as robust as Louis, Jean or even young René, and she focuses on encouraging his mind with excellent tutors. He is a good pupil who enjoys history and literature, and some Latin. She sees to it that he learns a clear, legible hand—and most of all, a decisive signature.

Unlike most parents of their class, and particularly at the royal court, Yolande spends time with her children each day. She knows everything about their lives—and she cares. A caring parent is something Charles has never encountered before. As his mother's eleventh child, Yolande doubts that Isabeau ever addressed a word to him in his early years, let alone showed him any affection. Surrounded by Yolande's free and easy brood, their friends, and their pets—especially the dogs, which she has never succeeded in banning from the nursery—Charles de Ponthieu blossoms, and gives every impression of enjoying his new life. It is easy to understand why this neglected prince openly adores and trusts Yolande and her family. She gives him love and attention, and realizes that he is quite overwhelmed by the mere thought that anyone could care for him at all.

The fact that the young prince is flourishing under Yolande's care and vigilant tuition gives her great satisfaction. He has become more confident, more self-assured—and has begun to call her *ma bonne mère*, "my good mother." She treats him as her son, and, as with her own children, she has authority over him, guides him, teaches him to trust her and her judgement. She gives him all the attention she can to help him curb his natural weaknesses—which are many and very apparent to her. For her daughter to be happy—but more importantly, perhaps, for him to be of use to his family and his country—there is a great deal of work to be done with this oversensitive, easily impressionable, essentially weak-charactered young prince.

Charles de Ponthieu is my raw material. I am the sculptor, he is my clay. I pray I have enough skill and tenacity to shape him into something of value, someone of value, and against all the odds.

This is a happy time for Yolande as she watches her family take shape again after the trauma of losing Catherine. But sad news reminds her that it is not only domestic happiness that matters. Valentina Visconti has died. She was her dearest and only friend at the court of France, and they remained close even when Yolande was far away in Provence, exchanging regular letters and visits. Her death leaves Yolande without a close confidante of her standing, and she mourns the loss of her wonderful caustic Italian wit and her unique way of observing the world. Valentina never recovered from the murder of her husband, Louis d'Orléans, which did not surprise Yolande— she had loved him deeply.

Her elder son Charles, now Duke d'Orléans, has written to tell her that his mother died in her sleep with no pain. Among other details he mentions that Queen Isabeau has taken on his mother's excellent lady's maid, Eduarda. This interests Yolande since she has observed Eduarda carefully on several visits to Angers. Eduarda's replies to the questions she asked her reassured her sufficiently for the maid to benefit from her generous payments, and now they continue to correspond, since Eduarda is willing to inform the Queen of Sicily of all that might be of interest. She is quite an accomplished spy, and Yolande is pleased to have her join her service, albeit unofficially.

Chapter Twenty

By the spring of 1414, Louis d'Anjou believes he has done all he can to prepare the King's Council to counter the inevitable invasion. All the royal dukes have made their plans and organized their followers and personal armies, and the country is on full alert. To Yolande's relief, Louis sends word that he is returning to Angers. The danger from England is growing, and having done what he can for Paris, he must now prepare Anjou and his other territories. Despite the English threat being the reason for Louis' return, Yolande rejoices in having him with them. It is some compensation for the fear the approaching confrontation brings.

Back in the rhythm of their family life, her beloved husband takes her in his arms at night, and after making love, they watch the moon's reflection on the river below.

"You do realize, my darling wife," he says with mock seriousness, "that a child made on such a night would be born... a water sprite." He laughs, and becomes an ogre, who chases her about their bedroom. What the servants must think of her squeals, she knows not—nor cares!

Since childhood, and one without brothers, Yolande has recognized that she has something akin to a man's character and likes to make her own decisions; after all, her father brought her up to believe that one day she might have to take on a man's responsibilities in Aragon. But with Louis, she becomes all woman.

Their convivial family summer in Anjou passes all too soon. September is over and the first signs of autumn appear; the chill nip in the late-afternoon air signals that the time has come to move their household south again on their little fleet of barges.

They break their journey in early October, stopping at their château of Montils-les-Tours for the birth of Yolande's fifth child. He is born without any complications, a healthy, fat little boy whom they name Charles, with his royal namesake standing as one of his godparents. The children are delighted to be somewhere new; there are plenty of neighbours with lots of young to distract them, as well as the many dogs and ponies travelling with them. They explore a different countryside, making new friends among the locals. Charles de Ponthieu is a happy, boisterous part of their young group, and it is clear to them that their royal charge has changed beyond recognition.

Christmas is a joyful time for them all, especially with a new baby, and by the end of January 1415, Yolande feels ready to continue their journey south to Provence with their growing family.

The spring passes quickly, and in July they are brought unsettling news. Finally, the endlessly threatened invasion is under way. King Henry V of England is said to be on the point of crossing the Channel with a considerable army to add to his forces already based in Normandy. The English offensive has brought their peaceful family summer to a premature end. Louis d'Anjou is one of the first to answer his king's summons to go to him and prepare to repel the invasion.

The scions of France's great families have been waiting for this day and are eager to confront the new invader from England, but Yolande cannot deny she is afraid—afraid for her husband, their country, and their future. Women see war as a time of waiting—waiting to hear which of their men have perished, been injured, captured, or, thanks be to God, survived. But survival is not enough—there is loss of pride and possessions to fear as well. If a ransom is demanded for the return of a captured loved one, in many cases financial ruin is the result. Although she has always supported all her husband's military endeavours—what else can she do?

It seems to Yolande that England and France have always been at war or planning it. This time the King of England is coming with eight thousand men, their horses, their cannon and all their supplies. Henry V has never made a secret of his intention to reclaim what he considers to be his; he has called himself "King of France and England" since his coronation, and refers to Charles VI as "our dear cousin of France"—no title. Moreover, he demands the right to the hand in marriage of the king's daughter Catherine, with Aquitaine as her dowry.

While ambassadors have gone back and forth between France and England since Henry V's coronation, seeking a peaceful solution, England's new king has been quietly constructing his navy. Meanwhile, every man and boy in the land has spent his free time practising archery with the longbow. This the French have learnt from their spies.

In Angers they are kept informed of King Henry's steady advance, but Yolande has received little news from Louis, who is with Charles VI. Finally, a letter reaches her in Anjou telling her that Louis is seriously ill. What is wrong with him? Why does no one tell her? Is it the plague? She sends couriers to him and to his adjutants. Tanneguy du Chastel is with him; perhaps he can give her details. She is deeply worried, not least because she cannot leave the children and go to him. All she can do is pray and keep the couriers busy with her frantic letters. *What is this illness of his?*

Encouraging news comes from the front. It seems the French garrison of Harfleur is resisting despite all forecasts; and one in four of the English soldiers has succumbed to dysentery, reducing the enemy's numbers to the French advantage. But Harfleur desperately needs reinforcements, and despite the city's pleas for help, Charles VI vacillates. Yolande writes to her young agent, Odette de Champdivers, who she knows is with the king, to find out about his mental state. "Not good," she replies. "He does not yet seem to be aware of the danger." Yolande passes this onto Louis.

As for France's own warring dukes, Burgundy, the strongest, has not appeared with his troops. Brittany cannot decide what to do, but at least he has sent his able brother, Arthur of Richemont, to serve the king; and young Charles d'Orléans, Valentina's son and the king's nephew, like Louis d'Anjou, has obeyed the call to arms.

Inevitably, on 22 September Harfleur falls and is occupied by the English, while their king heads for Calais, his port of provisions from England. Yolande is grateful to be kept informed of the invasion by her numerous agents, the most reliable being Tanneguy du Chastel, but she also depends on Carlo, who has accompanied Louis to take care of his personal needs. According to a message she receives from Carlo, it appears that Louis is suffering from what seems to be acute dysentery.

Apart from this worry, it is with considerable relief that Yolande hears from her various sources that the royal dukes have put aside their own quarrels and combined in the great plan for a decisive battle to rid France of the English once and for all. For some reason she is convinced that with victory within the grasp of the French, Louis will soon recover. The Duke of Burgundy's two brothers, the Counts of Brabant and Nevers, have joined the king's forces, although it is said the king has forbidden the field to Burgundy himself. Even the Duke of Brittany has arrived with five thousand men to fight with the royal army at Rouen. Since neither Charles VI nor his dauphin can risk being captured, the French army is led by the Constable of France, Jean d'Albret, head of the armed forces. From every direction, the French are uniting with the king's army for the crucial battle to come. There is a new decisiveness in the air; every missive Yolande receives is full of positive news and encouragement, and Louis' letters to her are constantly more heartening. Her husband has always been a man of action, a man of strong physique, whom she has never known to be ill, and therefore she has total faith in his recovery.

As for Henry V, what does she know of him? Only what her own agents have told her—that he is a fine-looking young man, tall, well built, intelligent and hungry for success. His father usurped the throne of England, and Henry needs to confirm—if only to himself—that he is a conqueror and worthy of the crown. She has heard tell that, as a teenager some twelve years earlier, he proved himself an admirable soldier at the Battle of Shrewsbury, and that he has not stopped fighting since, even quelling the rebellious Welsh. He also succeeded in crushing an attempt by another claimant to his throne. When last at court, Yolande was shown a drawing of the English king and had to admit he looks quite a man—he has the face of a conqueror and, she hears, the spirit of one as well. It seems he possesses a natural gift of leadership and that his men will follow him anywhere—to hell and back, should he ask. This will be a dangerous foe, but the constable is able and each of their dukes has such numbers under their banners, brimming with confidence, that Yolande is persuaded to believe in an imminent mighty French victory.

For the past two years as King of England, Henry V has let it be known that France will be the scene of his greatest victories. Yolande has always sensed that he is the most dangerous enemy they will encounter, the one they must defeat, and resolutely, for in his hunger for glory he will fight to the death to regain what he is convinced is England's right—the throne of France.

Chapter Twenty-one

Many mothers, friends of theirs, have written to Yolande to tell how their sons—scions of France's great families—have begged to be in the front ranks, craving battle honours in what will be France's historic victory over this plaguing enemy, continually snapping at their heels like an aggressive little dog. "Our army is jubilant," writes her agent Carlo. "The soldiers are confident of a great victory, with odds on our side of more than five to one!" She hears how the young gallants are parading in their finery, their armour more suitable for tournaments than war. This battle's honours are considered a foregone conclusion; can they not afford a little glamour in the ranks? God willing, their hopes will be fulfilled, but so much confidence among the men gives her a sense of foreboding. She pushes it away until a message from her fast courier relays to her that the English army has found a place to cross the river Somme and is marching north in continual torrential rain to meet reinforcements from the coast.

On 24 October, Yolande receives news from Valentina's former manservant Mario, who is with her son, Charles d'Orléans. He reports that the English troops, exhausted at the end of another day's trudging through heavy mud, have found themselves on a rise near the semi-ruined château of Agincourt, and have gratefully bivouacked there.

All through the next day and a half Yolande waits impatiently for news of a glorious victory. None arrives, even though she knows Louis has posted several of their stewards within and on the edges of the army to report both to him and to her on the battle's progress. She plays with the children, visits the dairy, and cuts flowers. Suddenly a courier gallops into the courtyard and almost collapses off his horse, holding out a package to her steward. Yolande snatches it from him, her fingers fumbling with the string, and sits down to savour the details of victory. Her eyes scan quickly down the salutations and preambles, until she reads:

"After a week spent marching in mud and rain, heads down, following in the footsteps of the man in front, trudging up a miserable incline to arrive on top of a hill with a ruined castle, the English army finally found a place to rest. With the dawn, to their dismay, they saw below them in the valley, blocking their route, our huge French army stirring, their armour glistening in the early light."

Did fear grip the English? she wonders. What a shock it must have been to awake and find themselves facing an unavoidable confrontation with a huge army of aggressive men—fit, rested and ready to fight for their homeland.

She seizes another agent's account in the package and skips to the next part:

"In the tradition of chivalric warfare, our cavalry, led by our senior knights, multicoloured plumes on helmets waving in the gentle wind, ducal banners fluttering, gathered in their ranks in full armour, waiting for the signal to charge, while sitting on their heavy warhorses. These, too, felt the excitement, and, despite their size and the weight of their own armour and that of the fully armoured riders, pranced skittishly in the early-morning chill. As the mist lifted, our troops could see the English archers massed in tight formation on the rise by the ruin of Agincourt, and how scant their numbers looked to our serried ranks."

She can feel the tension. The English archers are famous, but surely they are too few for their number to have a significant effect?

"Our leaders knew the enemy had almost no cavalry, and only their archers were left in any number. Confidence swelled in our warriors' breasts, and then came one trumpet call after another to attack and charge up the slope towards the hated English! There was some confusion, as it was the royal dukes' trumpeters who blew 'Charge,' whereas the constable's trumpeter did not. Only he seemed to consider what the heavy rain of the past week would have done to the ground.

"The large, cultivated rising plain between our troops and the enemy, despite the covering of grass, had softened beneath to the consistency of butter. Our heavy horses, carrying knights in full armour, soon felt the strain and became mired in the ground, their hooves turning the grass into plough, unable to charge up the hill towards the enemy. Seeing disaster unfolding before him, the Constable, Jean d'Albret, official commander of all the French forces, tried to recall the dukes' cavalries, but was unable to countermand the orders of their royal leaders, eager for battle."

Her hands begin to tremble as she continues to read, a dreadful foreboding growing inside her. Where was her husband during the battle? Is he recovered? Did he take part after all? She has heard nothing from the king's camp, and the courier she sent there has not returned.

There is another account in the package—it is from Hubert, her faithful Carlo's brother, who somehow managed with great courage to slip behind the English lines. She skips through what she already knows, and then reads:

"When the English King Henry saw the sinking spirits of his soldiers at the sight of the massed French army, he made a rousing speech, urging them to fight for him and their country on that St. Crispin's Day. With his rhetoric, their dashing young king managed to put courage back into the hearts of his soldiers, wasted with dysentery."

Yolande trembles. *I knew that ambitious young usurper king was dangerous. Why were our men so confident?* Palms sweating, she reads on:

"The English longbowmen, famous for their ability to fire up to ten arrows a minute, began to target our riders and horses. So accurate were they in their marksmanship, their arrows pierced visors and passed through the softer parts of our knights' armour. They even pinned riders to their saddles through their thighs. These longbowmen are an elite force, the best chosen from every village in their country, where their training begins from the age of seven. Their arrows are well crafted from oak and ash, their sharp metal heads cast with side barbs, making them impossible to pull out."

Yolande can feel herself beginning to panic, her stomach churning, but she must continue:

"Our horses, weighed down with their own armour and that of our knights, struggled, plunged and stuck in the heavy going. Some of our knights dismounted, only to flail about in the mud, a foot deep, unable to make headway in any direction."

Her breath is coming in a mixture of gasps and sobs. She pictures the flower of the French nobility, many of them relations and friends, riding out in front of their troops, certain of taking part in a glorious victory and carrying back its spoils. She feels desperate—but she cannot stop herself reading.

"When our knights fell from or with their horses, their vision hampered by their visors, the mud impeded their movement. Seeing this, the English soldiers took off their shoes and ran down the slope, slipping nimbly in and out of the deep mire in bare feet, their tunics marked for recognition with a large red cross of St. George front and back. Wielding daggers and short swords, they stabbed our helpless knights up and under the plates of armour covering their hearts. Those that the daggers missed were dispatched by the ferocious English pike men."

Yolande sits as if turned to stone, tears pouring down her cheeks, her stomach in knots, unaware of anyone or anything around her, seeing in her mind's eye the carnage at Agincourt.

"Where is my Louis?" she hears herself cry. "Where are you, my love?" She realizes she is shouting and feels the strong arm of Juana around her shoulders, pulling her up from where she has dropped to the ground and taking her indoors.

"My dearest Madame, what can be the matter? Let me help you. Why, of course, you must have had a shock; come, rest on me, I will carry you if I must. Come, come, to your room and your bed, we will bring the papers..." but Juana does not understand what has happened.

"The era of the glorious knight is over," Yolande keeps repeating. "Chivalry is dead. Where is Louis? *Where is my Louis?*"—and all the while Juana is making soothing noises and leading her to her room. She undresses her, lays her on her bed, covering her and brushing her hair.

"Tell me, dearest lady, what has caused this upset?" she says softly.

"Juana... Juana... the battle... it has been a slaughter... and we have lost!" Yolande cries. And: *I do not know where Louis is*, she repeats over and over to herself, until the draught Juana gives her sends her into a deep sleep.

When Yolande wakes, she insists on hearing more. Juana must bring all the papers to her. When she has read and absorbed them, the truth overwhelms her in all its brutal reality.

A young equerry of Louis', Pierre de Brézé, who was sent by him to observe the battle, has written to her:

"Madame, I was instructed by Duke Louis to watch the battle from the edge of the field at Agincourt and report to him. I have done so, and now he has asked me to relay to you all the details, although it pains me to do so. King Henry V, fighting in the midst of his troops, saw that he had more prisoners than he could afford soldiers to guard them. To avoid the French escaping and re-arming, he issued the chilling order: 'no prisoners.' And none was left alive."

She chokes as she reads on:

"The two brothers of the Duke of Burgundy; Madame, your close relations the Duke of Bar and his brother; the Duke of Brabant; the Duke d'Alençon; the Count of Nevers; even the constable, Jean d'Albret—all are dead, along with so many others of your friends and relatives. Five thousand eight hundred French have been buried in mass graves; those waiting in the reserves and away from the action were captured at the end of the battle and have been taken for ransom. Among the captured, a prince of the blood, our king's nephew and yours, the young Duke Charles d'Orléans. He was in the forefront of the attack and was found in his heavy armour, stuck in the mud, pinned down by the bodies that had fallen on top of him. Fifteen hundred prisoners from the rearguard are being transferred to English jails.

"Madame, I can imagine what a shock this information must be to you, but I have my instructions. The horror of this battle is unbelievable, not only the numbers slain, but the shame to France's honour and the price there will be to pay. My lord, your husband Duke Louis was too unwell to sit his horse and is safe with the king in Rouen."

Tiphane comes into her room to relieve Juana, and Yolande finds herself crying helplessly in her generous embrace. She can hardly take it in. War has always been dangerous, but honour and chivalry have been natural considerations for both victors and losers. With this battle at Agincourt, it seems that they have been swept aside for ever. The shorter firing power of the French crossbows was no match for the English arrows fired from their longbows. The enemy's boast before the battle that the density of their many arrows would blot out the sun and turn the bright day into night were easily dismissed by the French. Heavily armed horses and men became useless against nimble bare-footed soldiers in the thick, deep mud, stabbing with their short swords into the hearts of the scions of France's great houses. So much has changed... The honour has fallen out of the world as it was known before this terrible battle.

And Louis, my darling love? A courier comes at last with his letter. She thanks God he is alive. He writes how he remained in Rouen with the king, the dauphin and dear, ailing Jean of Berry, all waiting for news of a triumphant victory. "The couriers who raced to us were almost incoherent with their reports of the terrible defeat and the massive slaughter." His letter detailing all this horror is so blotched with his own tears that much of it had to be rewritten. Carlo is with him and adds that, numb with the shock of the disastrous outcome, her husband has embarked on the Seine for Paris, accompanying the defeated king and the stunned dauphin. "To make it more tragic, Charles, our king, for once is sane and understands perfectly what has happened. All we can do is sail for Paris to seek the advice of the elders in *parlement*."

Chapter Twenty-two

As Yolande reads the lists of the friends and relations who have fallen, her first reaction is relief that Louis at least is safe. Then slowly the overwhelming horror of the implication of this English victory begins to sink in. England has *won* France. This was the decisive battle. What will be the price? Apart from the nobles, who else from among their own people, from their households, staff, and workers on their estates, is among the dead? Who has been taken prisoner?

Yolande has never known such a feeling of dread—as if she has been struck a mighty blow to her stomach and cannot breathe. Somehow she composes herself and calls for her son Louis, for Marie, for Prince Charles and Jean Dunois, to tell them all she knows. The young prince weeps with them at the fate of many of their relatives, friends, and countrymen, and at the spectre of the future. None of them will ever forget this day. The country is ruined, their cousins are killed or taken prisoner, and Henry V of England is the conqueror of France.

And my poor dear Louis. Yolande feels his overwhelming distress through his carefully worded letter and she bleeds for him. What is this illness that debilitates him so? Certainly their defeat will not help him recover. Her anxiety for him mingles with the crushing horror of their defeat. News arrives of many of their workers who have been killed or wounded, as well as a large number of the men of their household staff. René searches for Tiphane everywhere and finds her hiding in the laundry, crying her eyes out. Slowly she gasps out between sobs that her own dear brother has died. It is then that René begins to realize that war is not the glamorous exercise he has imagined from story books. The household continues with the daily routines like puppets, numb in mind and body.

Apart from the children and the servants, Yolande is alone at Angers. All the able-bodied men went to help with the war effort in some way, and most of the women remained at home awaiting their return, to rejoice in their survival, tend to the wounded or bury their dead. But there is no victory to ease the pain of loss; just the thought of the dead and wounded, and their own broken hearts.

None of Yolande's contemporaries is with her to share her grief, and she must be strong in front of the young ones and her household. How she misses her dear friend Valentina at this moment. They could have cried out their grief together and comforted one another. But perhaps it is better she is not there to suffer for her eldest son, Charles d'Orléans. What will happen to him now? To be a prisoner of the English does not bode well.

Although the English losses are few, Henry V's army is too depleted to retain any more garrisons than he has already established within France. He will keep what he can maintain and leave for England—which he does three weeks after the battle. No one has any doubt he will soon return to win further victories and claim more of their country.

The Armagnacs have lost their leaders—Charles d'Orléans is captured, and Alençon is dead. The king's uncle, Jean of Berry, is too old and frail to be of much practical use. The Count d'Armagnac himself did not leave his own territory. He waited, as instructed, with his army at Troyes to cut off the English retreat, but they had no need of escape and he waited in vain. Neither the Duke of Burgundy, the king's greatest soldier but also his most untrustworthy, nor his son Philippe took part in the battle—on the king's orders, it was said, though Yolande hears whispers that the duke and his son withheld their support. True or not, Jean-sans-Peur must feel the loss of his two brothers keenly, and of so many of his men of Burgundy.

1415, the year of France's catastrophic defeat at Agincourt, becomes the year of her greatest shame. Does the Queen of Sicily weep? Yes, and from the depths of her inner being, a shaking to her very core, a silent scream, alone. She steals away from her older children, who are doing the same in their own rooms, comforted at least by their nurses and attendants, who are crying as much as their charges. Everyone has lost someone—there is nobody unaffected. Nor can anyone tell how it will end. When will the English return with reinforcements and repeat their murderous victory all over France? Will Burgundy side with them? They have always leaned towards the English, not least because of their trade with Flanders. But without the support of mighty Burgundy, the French have little hope of repelling their enemies.

If only she could share the pain with her dear Louis, thinks Yolande. When will he come so they can comfort one another? They exchange daily messages by courier, but none mentions his return or his well-being; only more tragic news. The waiting is so hard—trying to keep a brave face for everyone around her, riding into the villages to console the bereaved, making false promises that imprisoned husbands and sons will return, just as she prays her Louis will. Yolande and the children spend long hours in her chapel on their knees, and none of them has ever prayed so earnestly.

Chapter Twenty-three

At last there is news. A courier arrives from Louis. He is coming home. The household is alerted and everyone rushes about—Yolande, children, servants. *He is on his way home to Angers. Oh, for the relief of his comforting arms. Dearest Lord,* prays Yolande, *I beg you, bring him back so that I can mend his heart, his body and his soul.*

He arrives, painfully and slowly, as if carrying the weight of his country's losses. He stands with his arms open and Yolande runs to him. As he holds her, she is instantly aware how thin he has become. Where is her towering giant? He seems shrunken in body as well as spirit, his face so aged, and in those eyes that speak volumes, she can see everything she fears most.

After he has embraced the children—almost silently— husband and wife sit by the fire and eat a little, Louis taking only a few mouthfuls of broth. With his face a mask to hide his grief, he gives her more details of the battle and its aftermath—at least eight thousand French killed and fewer than three hundred of the English; of the reaction of the king and the queen and the court; how it seems as if a great black cloud has descended on them, Paris and all the country.

While Yolande is sitting with Louis by the fire, rubbing her poor husband's swollen feet, a royal messenger arrives in great haste. He has ridden in a fast relay from Paris with an urgent missive from the court.

The news is shocking and totally unexpected: the dauphin is dead. Louis and Yolande sit bewildered with disbelief. He has just told her how he left this promising prince in Paris a few days earlier—and in perfect health. The message says the dauphin died of dysentery so violent that poison is suspected. *And to whose benefit?* she asks herself. Why, surely who else but the Duke of Burgundy's! For a number of years the dauphin has bravely, repeatedly and openly opposed his disloyal and traitorous father-in-law. Now he has paid for his defiance in the traditional way.

This news adds to the general misery in the household, not least for Charles, the dauphin's brother. Christmas will bring no joy to the nursery at all.

It crosses Yolande's mind to wonder whether Louis is somehow being poisoned too. She does not dare suggest it to him, but what is his illness, this slow, debilitating daily weakening and wasting of a strong and energetic man? She has the best doctors tending to him and nothing seems to help restore his strength. *Or am I jumping at ghosts and imagining assassins around every corner?* The land is full of disease, the army rife with dysentery; plague follows in the aftermath of battles— the rotting carcasses of animals are often left lying exposed for the crows, even if the dead soldiers are buried, and that is not always done immediately.

*

One would think that Agincourt had been sufficiently terrible to bring an end to the conflict between France's warring factions; but no, both the Burgundians and the Armagnacs have managed to raise another fighting force from the countryside. The avowed intention of each is to rescue the king and his son, the second dauphin, from the "tyranny" of the other side. The two groups have become so inflammatory that legislation pending before Agincourt has now been quickly passed, decreeing that should anyone be heard uttering the words "Armagnac" or

"Burgundian," such a person is to have a hole bored through his tongue with a red-hot poker!

Louis shakes his head as he stretches out on his usual deep bank of cushions by the fire, Hector and Ajax by his side, his hand caressing whichever comes nearest.

"I just don't understand it. At the very time when the focus of both parties should be on preventing the English making further moves into French territory, the squabbling between the dukes' partisans continues, although they never actually come to exchanging blows. What stupidity is this?" he cries. And then answers himself: "Power, my darling, it is all just a power struggle, and as pointless as two fighting dogs snarling and circling one another with no intention of engaging."

And what is Henry V doing while the Armagnacs and the Burgundians exercise in skirmishes of no particular significance? Louis' spies are good, and they know the English king is preparing for a renewed campaign, which they never doubted he would.

By the end of January, after little more than a month at home, Louis cannot stand doing nothing any longer while daily receiving word of the troubles at court. He has decided, despite his illness, to return to Paris to take up his place at the King's Council, where his astuteness is needed. Yolande cannot dissuade him, but nor can she bear for him to travel alone in his fragile condition and in winter. She must go with him and take care of him. She fears that in Louis' present state of health, without her in Paris he will not survive. Yolande both needs and wants to be with him at the seat of power at this important time, not only to support him but because he is a part of history in the making, and she cannot resist observing, even taking part. And yet to leave the children in time of war is an agonizing decision. At least at Angers she knows Louis' trusted people will defend them to the death, and theirs is an almost impregnable stronghold.

Despite her confidence in their Angevins taking excellent care of them, the parting is hard. Yolande waves from the carriage until their little faces, smiling and crying simultaneously, are out of sight. She knows Louis senses her fears, but he says nothing, just holds her hand. He has always been a man of few words, but his eyes speak for him.

Chapter Twenty-four

Strange as it may seem, in the many years of their marriage, Yolande and Louis have never actually lived together for any long period of time. He has either been on the Italian peninsula or with the king, but now, weak and ill as he is, the time has come for Yolande to learn how to do a man's work—his work—and she remains by his side learning from him while he takes up the reins of government in Paris.

For the first time, these two strong personalities are together in the capital without the distraction of a family around them. Is there any friction? Yes, at times; they discuss and disagree on some political issues, but Yolande always bows to his position and experience, even when sure she is in the right. It is the way she has been brought up.

"The council is full of fools," he announces angrily on his return most evenings. "I have always said it and I will say it again. They are donkeys, and just as stubborn and stupid."

He recounts the absurdities of the day's session while she calms him by rubbing his shoulders or massaging his feet by the fire—despite the comfort of their Parisian home, Louis has begun to feel the cold badly.

"My bones ache, dearest, do light a fire," he will beg, and she changes into a light silk shift to survive the heat he needs in the room.

"Tell me about the council; why are they fools?" she asks, trying to quieten his agitation with questions.

"They think the rise of our cousin of Burgundy to run the country is inevitable, perhaps even desirable! Idiots! If he has the run of the council of state, then he will make himself king quick enough. But they just do not see it coming!" he fumes.

One evening, Louis arrives home from his council meeting ashen-faced, and tells her of a Burgundian plot that has been discovered.

"The two of us, together with my uncle Jean of Berry, the excellent provost Tanneguy du Chastel, and possibly even the queen, were to have been abducted and put to death. The details were prized out of the captured perpetrators in the usual gruesome ways." But for her husband's calm courage in the telling, Yolande thinks she might have fainted. "The plot was planned for Easter Sunday, a day when we would have been either leaving for Mass together or returning—and easy prey for our enemies to catch us all together."

Yolande thanks God then, and even more so when they do get to Mass, that they were saved in time and most of the villains caught.

"Despite his frail health and his age, Uncle Jean of Berry has taken command and appointed Armagnac as Constable of France. He is a wise choice, since he has brought with him to Paris his fierce Gascon mercenaries, six thousand of them—a considerable force for imposing peace," says Louis, almost with a chuckle.

As soon as the new Armagnac constable arrives in Paris, he wastes no time in executing the plotters, and imposing stringent security measures on the populace.

Two months later in mid June when Louis returns from his session at the council, husband and wife are beside the fire in their sitting room, sharing the warmth with the dogs, when Louis says sadly:

"I have news that will grieve you, my darling. It has all been too much for our dear uncle Jean of Berry. He died some days ago at home in Bourges, mercifully in his sleep."

Yolande drops her stitching. *Another death.* Uncle Jean is the last of his generation to go, and she loved him dearly.

."This *is* sad news. Such a dear man, and kind. He told me how he looked after you when you were small and fatherless, and gave you advice on how to rule. We shall miss him." She ponders. "I am truly saddened by his loss. He was always so good to us, and wise."

"I am told that in his wisdom, he has designated our Prince Charles as his sole heir," Louis tells her, "and not the dauphin."

"How strange" thinks Yolande, and remembering the insight of this dear man, perhaps he had an idea that Charles might need his fortune in the future.

For Charles, this inheritance will be an incredible bonus at a difficult time. Louis and Yolande have willingly borne the burden of financing him to date, but now the strain on their coffers will be eased, at least for a while. But the Duke of Berry's death leaves another major gap in the ranks of the Armagnacs.

Later the same evening, Louis turns to Yolande:

"I have been thinking—I believe the moment has come to promote our young royal charge into a useful role."

A slight raising of her eyebrows at this, but she continues with her stitching, waiting to hear her husband's plan.

"We know that Charles has observed how his family members have vied for the right to govern when his father could not. He has watched his royal uncles, and realized how a position of power can be exploited in the granting of pensions, promotions, offices, liberties and immunities, not to mention all the tangible gains that can be meted out to favourites, worthy or not.

"Charles is thirteen. We must send for him and Marie—she is his official betrothed and twelve now. They must join us here in Paris and be seen as a unit under the protection of Anjou."

Louis is right. The time has come for Charles to take his place on the Council of State and learn how men govern.

On the night Charles arrives, Louis takes him aside.

"My young prince, since your brother the second dauphin lives with his betrothed and her family outside Paris, I would like you to come with me to the Council of State tomorrow. Just sit by me and listen, and you will learn much." With that, he pats the boy's shoulder and retires.

When they return the following afternoon, they come at once to see Yolande and Marie in the sitting room. As Louis kisses Yolande's forehead, she can see that Charles is bursting to tell her what happened in council.

"Madame, you cannot believe what I heard today!" and he looks at Louis for permission to speak. Louis has reclined next to Yolande with a sigh and is stretching out his hands to the fire as he nods agreement. "The council has it on good authority that my uncle of Burgundy has promised Henry V he will uphold the English king's claim to the throne of France for himself and his heirs! Further, Burgundy is willing to send Henry military aid whenever he requests it! This is treason, *ma bonne mère*!" Charles bursts out with a mixture of shock and excitement. Seeing the surprised faces of his wife and daughter, Louis nods resignedly and says, "Yes, it is true."

"Henry V can count on the allegiance of my cousin of Burgundy—who would profit handsomely," young Charles adds with shame. "Uncle, what can we do?"

Louis looks at the lad and says quietly, "You must come with me to the council every day from now on, and you will hear all their ideas on how to prevent King Henry from joining with our cousin against his fellow Frenchmen. For now, I need rest, so say good night to your *bonne mère* and to me."

Chapter Twenty-five

Each day Louis appears frailer as he leaves the comfort of their house with the young Prince Charles for the council chamber, and each evening Yolande can see how the day's work has weakened her husband. She sits and listens to what has transpired during the day's proceedings, and worries more about Louis' health. To do him credit, their prince is absorbing all the debates and has sensible verdicts on the participants. But as he thrives, her Louis is fading.

When he comes back with his uncle, Charles spends a lot of his time with Marie. She knows her parents want to be alone together, and she keeps herself busy thinking up ways of amusing her betrothed in the evenings.

By the time winter arrives, Yolande can see that Louis' untiring work for the government during the past months in Paris has taken the last of his strength. To her deepening sorrow, and despite all her loving efforts and the many doctors she has called onto help, she can sense the end is near. He wants to return to his beloved Angers, and she knows the children are longing for them to be there for Christmas, but she cannot move him yet. This December is bitterly cold.

Their sons Louis and René have written a long letter—mostly Louis, but they can hear the voice of little René in it too:

Dearest Maman and Papa,
   We are so happy to hear you are coming home. Christmas was

162

not the same without you, as you can imagine, but we have also been having some fun between lessons and games, teasing kitchen maids, and taking pony rides in the snow. Thank you for sending us the entertainers. They were the best we have ever had.

There have been kittens and puppies to play with as well since you left, and we have been watching the head groom break in the young horses. Even little Yolande and baby Charles are beginning to be fun to play with, so we hope you have not been too worried about us.

With Papa home, we will have stories by the fire again, won't we, and please can he act out scenes from court life in Paris? And Charles and Marie will be back and fun will be the order of the cold evenings again by a roaring fire in the Great Hall! We will roast chestnuts and can we be allowed a little mulled wine after supper? Please do hurry home—we miss you both so much.

All our love, your obedient sons, Louis and René.

How they laugh when they read it—and how Yolande cries inside, knowing that nothing is going to be as the children hope for, or describe.

*

January is even colder than December, not a season to travel, but Yolande knows there is not much time left to get her husband home.

When they arrive in Angers, it is too cold for the children and the household to meet them outside. Yolande takes Louis to his bed at once, and after he has rested, she brings in the children, one by one. They each kiss his cheek and his hand, say a few words and leave. Just this has exhausted him. How thin and yellow he looks, and Yolande can see from their expressions how shocked they are at the transformation of their heroic father. This is far from the jolly homecoming they had longed for, and although young, they can sense their father is seriously ill.

Louis' condition is Yolande's total concern. The journey home has weakened him further, and what little strength he has he spends talking quietly to Yolande, propped up in his bed, which has been moved next to the fire in his room. Couriers come constantly, but she hardly pays much mind to the contents of the packages—she is so completely absorbed in the care of her husband and his wishes. They sit night after night talking, recalling happier times, discussing their children; houses; harvests. So many plans made; many, she knows, destined to be unfulfilled.

Yolande does not want to spend a moment away from Louis and a day bed is brought in next to his so that she can be with him almost all the time.

The winter months pass slowly. Only when a courier comes from Louis' young equerry, Pierre de Brézé, whom they left behind in Paris, does Yolande allow an interruption. His orders are to send them anything urgent, and the package is addressed to her. The letter is in codes which she sits to decipher and gasps, clutching at her throat as its contents are revealed. The news is beyond belief.

> Madame, since I am not confident my lord the King of Sicily is well enough to receive my information, I have taken the liberty of writing to you direct. With deep regret, I must inform you of the sudden and unexpected death of the dauphin, Jean. His father-in-law left him in good health a few days ago at his country house, but returned home from Paris to find the dauphin in a desperate state—his tongue and lips hideously swollen, his eyes protruding from his face. When a large boil burst inside his left ear, he died soon afterwards. Poison is suspected. The courier will wait to return with any instructions you have for me.

France's second dauphin, the eighteen-year-old Jean de Touraine, dead? So soon after the first? Not only has Jean of Burgundy now removed the next heir to the throne, his nephew, but his enemy—Yolande's husband, Louis d'Anjou— has the new dauphin in his care. Now only one obstacle, their very own Prince Charles, remains between Jean-sans-Peur and his obsession to rule once the sick king is dead.

She cannot keep this news from Louis, and tells him gently. It may change his instructions for her now that Prince Charles has suddenly become the heir to the throne.

"Go to him, my dearest, he must know his fate." And with that he turns his head into his pillow and weeps.

Somehow, Yolande knows, she must take Charles aside and find the words to tell him as calmly as possible what will become of him now. As she walks down the path towards where she can see the children playing, it feels as if the very stones beneath her feet know what is happening. *Perhaps I am imagining it, but it is almost as if the birds have stopped singing.*

She finds him with the other children preparing to go out. Taking Tiphane aside, she tells her the news and that she is not to tell the children until they are on their way back. Meanwhile she will keep Charles with her, saying she has news for him. When they leave she takes him by the hand and walks with him in the early April sunshine to sit on a bench in the garden. His eyes are apprehensive and questioning as she takes a deep breath.

"My dearest Charles, I believe you are happy with us, are you not?" She smiles warmly to reassure him.

Charles eyes her apprehensively. "Yes, *ma bonne mère*, you know I am. But I see something is troubling you. Have I offended in some way? Not consciously, I promise!"

"No, no, not at all. It is just that I want to be sure you trust me, and know that we all want nothing but the best for you," she continues slowly.

"Yes, dearest *bonne mère*, but what is it you want to tell me?" Now he takes her hand as if to console her—when she should be holding his.

"Charles, dear boy, you have always called me your *bonne mère*, and that is what I have tried to be. I must tell you something difficult, but you will hear it in the sure knowledge that you are among a family that loves you as if you were a true son."

"Yes, yes, I know," and he bites his lip with apprehension.

She can think of no other way to say it:

"Your brother, Jean, is dead. You are now dauphin."

Charles jumps up, his hands covering his mouth as if to stifle a scream. Yolande rises quickly and gathers him to her, holding his shaking body. They remain there for some time, she stroking his hair, while Charles weeps out all the pain he has gathered since his birth, his head pressing on her shoulder.

The children have returned home from their picnic and the older ones are in a solemn mood. Tiphane has told them the news on the way back and they flood their mother with questions: "Will Charles die suddenly as well? Will he have to leave us now that he is dauphin? One day he will become king—is that good or bad?"

She tries to reassure them in any and every way she can. "No, there is no inherited illness as far as anyone knows. Yes, Charles may have to leave us for a while, but he will come back. Yes, he will become king one day, and they must believe that is a good thing, and as his cousins and childhood friends, they must support him always."

As for Charles himself, he has remained in the nursery all day, shut in on himself—and he stays like that despite all the efforts the children make to cheer him.

In the morning, Yolande receives a message that Prince Charles is to go to his mother, Queen Isabeau, at the royal château of Vincennes. She has sent Tiphane to tell him, and he comes to her running, talking terribly fast and incoherently, his face a contorted mixture of disbelief and fear. She calms him and tells him quietly that this is his duty now. "Have I not taught you about always doing your duty?"

"Ma bonne mère, I know you can do anything. Please let me stay." Again and again he begs her.

By now the other children have joined them, all of them beseeching Yolande to arrange for Charles to remain with them. Carefully she gets up, smoothing her skirts and thinking.

"Very well," she says. "I will go and talk to your father."

When she leaves Louis' room, she finds a group of anxious little faces waiting for her. They gather around her as she sits down.

"Your father has said that we must return Charles to his mother." They stare at her, disbelieving. "As dauphin, it is his duty to go, even if we fear for his safety. There is no more I can do. Charles must obey. As his father the king is too ill to attend the Council of State, it is his duty as dauphin to be present," and she sighs, a sigh that comes from deep within her sorrowing heart. She only hopes they were not listening at the door when she said to Louis:

"*He* has killed two dauphins, and now he will surely take the third, whom I promised God to guard well." She does not agree with the decision, but she must go along with it. She will find a way to bring Charles back, she vows silently. She will protect him.

Even if she cannot keep him at home, she can send a little piece of her home with him, to give him the support he will need at court. *And to make our presence felt*, she says silently to herself. And so, with a heavy heart, she leads Marie into her sitting room.

"Darling girl, I need your help. I cannot leave your father and go with Charles, so you must accompany your betrothed, show Queen Isabeau that you are by his side, his future wife and queen. I will make arrangements to bring you both back, I promise, and you will have our excellent Angevins to take care of you both. Will you do this for your father and me—and for Charles, my darling?"

Marie falls into her mother's arms, sobbing. "Poor Charles, poor darling boy. Of course I will go with him, for his sake more than anything. I will be by his side, Maman, fear not," she says bravely.

Before Charles and Marie leave, Yolande summons her daughter to kiss her father and say her good-byes. She falls to her knees by his bed and washes his hand with her tears. Their eyes say it all—their messages of love and encouragement, gratitude from her and then a faint "Good-bye my sweet child—go well" from him in a whisper, as he makes a cross on her forehead with his thumb. All is said in that shared look between a father and his beloved daughter. Yolande then brings him Prince Charles, who kisses Louis' hand in gratitude, which moves his *bonne mère* deeply. Then Charles and Marie leave for Vincennes and the queen—her domain, her centre of power—safe on their journey at least, in the care of Yolande's chosen Angevins.

During the following week, Yolande allows the other children to sit with Louis for not more than ten minutes in the morning and again at night. He holds their hands one by one and smiles weakly. He has changed so much. The strong hero of her marriage and their childhood has shrunk into a little old man, and his famous flashing blue eyes have faded to become watery and pale. His mass of blonde hair is grey, limp and thin. All the children can do is to come in on tiptoe and kiss his hand, which he then lays on their heads with a light caress.

And so they near the end. Louis dictates his last testament to her and she writes it down faithfully, word for word.

To my adopted son, the dauphin Charles of France: know that I have cherished you as if you were my own flesh and blood, as your children will be when you marry your betrothed, our much-loved eldest daughter Marie d'Anjou. Accept that I speak to you as I would a member of my own family when I beg you—yes, beg you—*never to trust the Duke of Burgundy.* As much as I ask this of you, I beg you with the same strength and more, *never to take revenge* on this man who has wilfully done you so much harm. Instead, do all in your power, for the sake of France, for the sake of your family, for my sake and that of your *bonne mère* who loves you, to live in harmony with your uncle of Burgundy. This will cost you dear and aggrieve your justly vengeful heart, but it is the only way forward, the only way for you to regain the kingdom that the folly of others has put in such jeopardy.

She can see that the effort tires him as he struggles for breath, but the urgency in his eyes makes it plain he wants to continue.

To the children of my blood who share my heart and my love, obey always that treasure, that love—namely, your dear mother. I ask you to obey her in all things, for she is wise in more ways than you may ever know, more loyal to her adopted country than many of France's most loyal patriots, and in possession of a greater heart and will to pursue what is right and good. I ask you with my dying breath to honour and obey her, and respect this great lady, until the day of her death and beyond.

Tears roll down Yolande's cheeks, and she tries to stop her hand from trembling as she writes down this, his last and dearest love letter to her. She knows that Louis loved her from the first moment he saw her, but never has she heard him express his feelings with such tender words and with an admiration intended for all posterity through his dying testament. He takes a deep breath to steady his hand to sign the parchment, and the signature is firm and clear. Then there is no more strength left in him and he sinks back into her arms, sleeping softly, a half-smile on his lips, which she gently kisses.

She holds him like this throughout the night, dozing off herself now and then. When she wakes in the morning, he has not moved; nor does he breathe any longer.

Chapter Twenty-six

No matter how she has tried in these last weeks and months to prepare herself, Yolande feels as if a needle has pricked the balloon of her life and, without air, her being has deflated to no more than a shrivelled bag of animal skin. In her mind, it was the shocking news about the dauphin Jean that hastened the death of her beloved Louis. Yolande sent a message of heartfelt condolence to Queen Isabeau, knowing how desperate she must be to lose her second son and in such a short time, but begged to be excused from the funeral in view of Louis' rapid decline. Now she must plan his funeral.

She reads his last testament over and over. It is his final declaration of love. Her husband Louis, Duke d'Anjou, Guyene and Maine, Sovereign Count of Provence, King of Naples, Sicily and Jerusalem, has, with full confidence, entrusted into her sole care: his house; his fourteen-year-old heir; and his other children, his lands, and all he owns. She is to become regent of his many French territories, and is duty bound to attempt to regain his lost kingdom of Naples and Sicily. As if that is not enough, he has made her the sole guardian of the future King of France, to stand against the combined might and enmity of the Duke of Burgundy and the King of England.

Louis II d'Anjou's funeral is conducted at Angers with all the customary formality befitting a royal duke, though with less of his family present due to their preparations for the imminent war. The new young Duke d'Anjou, his eldest son, Louis III, stands tall and proud with his siblings, his cousin Jean Dunois and his mother, the Queen of Sicily, receiving the condolences of visitors and local people following the ceremony. They then watch tearfully and respectfully as Louis II d'Anjou is placed in the family crypt.

With her husband's death, Yolande finds herself a thirty-six-year-old widow with five children, in control of the House of Anjou, not unlike her admirable mother-in-law, Marie de Blois, before her. Also in her care she has the future of the royal House of Valois. Henceforth her role in the history of France will change. They say she still possesses "imperious" beauty. Well, to succeed in the many charges her husband has bequeathed her, she will need it—and all the intelligence she can muster in order to fulfil her heavy destiny.

Part Two

Chapter One

Yolande will grieve for her husband all her life long; now she must follow his instructions for the sake of France. No sooner is her beloved Louis buried than she sets out for Queen Isabeau's court at Vincennes, where Charles has gone on his royal mother's insistence, taking Marie with him.

The Queen of France graciously welcomes the Queen of Sicily and on 13 April 1417, she watches as the fourteen-year-old Prince Charles, third son of King Charles VI of France and Queen Isabeau, is formally installed as dauphin, heir to the throne. With his new title, the traditional territory and income of the Dauphiné is bestowed on him. From his late brother Jean, he receives ownership of the county of Touraine. These properties are added to the duchies of Poitou and Berry he inherited from his great uncle, the Duke of Berry.

Thirteen-year-old Marie, his betrothed, stands with her mother, each wearing, over their court dresses, a cape of red velvet lined with ermine—Yolande's of blue brocade, Marie's in pink silk. The ceremony is conducted with great solemnity in the royal chapel of Vincennes, its choir in full voice and the silver trumpets blaring. According to Yolande's quick exchange with Odette, the king is quite sane and stands to the right of his son, his mother on the left, both wearing their crowns. Each has placed their hand nearest him on their son's shoulder and they solemnly swear to uphold his rights as the sole heir to his father's throne. This is followed by a trumpet salvo and the bells of the Vincennes chapel ring out to cheers from the people gathered outside. Not more than one hundred—and those, the most senior members of the royal court, are gathered inside the chapel.

Following the death of the second dauphin, Odette wrote to the Queen of Sicily that the king had neither been aware of his second son's installation nor his death; indeed, he had forgotten he existed—there were so many children. But she had carefully explained to him that the first dauphin, whom he had known and liked, had tragically died of illness, and now his son Charles was being installed. He seemed content with that although he had no idea which one he was. When she reminded him he was being brought up by the Duchess Yolande d'Anjou and betrothed to her daughter, Odette wrote that "his eyes lit up and he seemed pleased."

In spite of the pomp and ceremony, the atmosphere at Vincennes is not at all to Yolande's liking. There are too many Burgundians at the court, and she cannot help remembering the fate of the two earlier dauphins, Charles's brothers, and the suspicions of poisoning that implicated the Duke of Burgundy. Worried and alone, she asks herself: *What would Louis have done?*

Sadly, the days of relying on her husband's strength and advice have gone forever. Emboldened by her new responsibilities, Yolande reminds herself: *Je le garde, moi. I will keep him safe.* That was the promise she made to God, and by God she will keep it. Immediately following the investiture, despite Isabeau's protests, and trembling slightly, the Queen of Sicily announces to the Queen of France and the court that Marie and the new dauphin will return with her to Angers at once. She gives no one time to protest. A strong guard of her best Angevin soldiers is waiting to escort them, and she and the children ride for Anjou before anyone can stop her.

It is her first bold decision as a widow and regent, and her reward is the touching relief on the faces of the children when they arrive at Angers.

Yolande knows that Charles and Marie will not stay with them for long. Before her husband died, he advised Charles to take up his new life as dauphin by forming his own court at Bourges, capital of his new county of Berry, since this would be the most appropriate base for him. It is a city Louis knows well from visiting his Uncle of Berry there. Charles has decided to follow his advice and establish himself in the beautiful town, strong and prosperous and with citizens known to be loyal to the monarchy. Marie, who loves precious works of art, will be happy among Uncle Jean's treasures, and the army stationed there will protect them. It is a rich area in the centre of France, its people guarded and reticent. With great forests for the pleasure of the hunt, full-flowing clear rivers, clean, healthy fields, plenty of cattle, vines and orchards, the dauphin's new domains are indeed bountiful, and Yolande is happy for him.

The hardest part for her is to let Marie leave home for Bourges. She knows she must—it is her place now to be near Charles, especially when he does not have his *bonne mère* on hand to guide him. Marie has a sensible head on her shoulders and they are firm childhood friends. It is the strengthening of their bond of friendship on which Yolande is counting—and that Charles will listen to her daughter's advice, but of that she is not so sure. Inevitably, his new position has given him a certain inflated opinion of himself and he might not listen to Marie as he would to Yolande. At least Marie can give her mother an accurate account of what is going on at his fledgling court and ask for her help if need be.

As difficult as it is for her to let Marie leave home, it is almost harder to part with Juana, her mainstay since her own childhood and the last link with her former life. But she wants to be sure her beloved daughter has someone near who is capable and honest, someone she can trust and confide in. Yolande is older now and more experienced, and accepts that she will have to rely on herself.

During the past year, Charles has been presiding over councils and meetings of the estates, taking his role very seriously. Nor does this seem to be a passing phase, but one of resolution and purpose. His signature appears on several important edicts of his father's—it is a well-formed, literary, practised hand with beautiful script learnt with the encouragement of his *bonne mère*; the flourish of his signature made with confidence.

And yet, there is still much that disturbs her about her adopted son, little incidents that seem at odds with his newly assumed princely stature. Charles returns often to Angers or Saumur with his entourage, and she watches him closely, noticing his reactions, especially to the inevitable flattery of courtiers hoping for preferment. Mostly he just smiles—and she can tell from his eyes he does not believe a word. Perhaps it is not surprising that he has become somewhat cynical and yet, at the same time, he is a realist. She has often observed him being charming, even alluring, to groups of people, while knowing how he laughs—inwardly—at their pretentions. He has admitted as much to her and to his cousins, telling them quite frankly how he, too, will charm and flatter almost anyone to gain his own ends.

When she scolds him, he laughs good naturedly. *"Bonne mère,* you know that what I am saying is true. Most people only want to profit from me. Very few are like you and your family, and this is how they deserve to be treated." Tothis she says nothing, but she has been concerned for some time by his lack of basic morals. To her dismay, she notices how, with his new status as dauphin, he has become adept at controlling his associates by dispensing favours—his resources are too limited to buy loyalty—and this new trait also dismays her. Granting positions is easy for Charles and costs him nothing, and yet country gentlemen dream of nothing more than a court appointment. It may be just a useful kind of guile, but his little schemes disturb her. What kind of prince and future monarch is he becoming?

When he was very young and first came to live with her at Angers, the child prince would regale the family with stories of his father's court, where he had witnessed his uncles and cousins creating important-sounding positions and granting them often to plainly unsuitable candidates. When he asked one of his uncles why they did this, he was told: "These men can be useful in some way, and once we have achieved our objective, they can always be dismissed or humiliated into submission." He told his audience this with a laugh, and Yolande hoped then that he would never be in a position to do the same. But now he is.

One day at Angers, she heard Charles teasing Jean Dunois.

"Ha ha! My cousin, although you are the son of my royal uncle Louis d'Orléans, you are illegitimate and can therefore never inherit, and without an inheritance you really are no one at all. But if, dear Jean, you do as I command, perhaps one day I will give you a far grander title and great estates! What do you say?"

She will never forget how Jean Dunois smiled in his lovely mysterious way, so like his father, and replied with apparent sincerity:

"My dear princely cousin, how *good* of you to even consider such an elevation for me when, as you rightly say, I am no one after all."

Although Charles maintains his cousin is "no one at all," his military talents have been noted. Now Jean Dunois has been appointed equerry to the dauphin, a position that requires him to travel in Charles's entourage as he moves about the country ensuring that people are loyal to his cause. But he still manages to report back to the Queen of Sicily at regular intervals. On one such visit she can sense from his very bearing that there has been trouble. They climb the great stairs to the first floor and she calls for mulled wine and cake.

"Sit with me, dear young friend, and tell me your news,"

she says.

Jean looks at his hands, and then at her.

"Madame, as you have ordered me to do, I have come to tell you of an incident of which I feel you should be aware, as it may have repercussions for the dauphin."

"Tell me," she sighs, thinking that it really must be serious if he has gone to the trouble of a special visit. But her fears are nothing compared with the story that Jean struggles to find the words to tell her:

"At his invitation, I was with the dauphin's company to second him as his captain of one hundred and fifty soldiers recruited from his territory of Berry. We were making the rounds of the château of the Loire; the dauphin was showing himself and drumming up support for the Armagnacs in the same way as the Duke of Burgundy's men do. We arrived at the small moated château of Azay-le-Rideau, between Tours and Chinon..." He pauses.

"Yes, I know the place well," she says encouragingly.

He takes a deep breath. "The dauphin sent a messenger in the usual way, requesting to enter and dine with the company. This is what he does to win people to his cause, and he has done so successfully with many others in the area. His messenger returned with a reply, which, when he read it, turned him quite pale.

"Madame, I was alongside him, and without a word he passed me the note. In vulgar language it mocked his pretensions to being the lawful dauphin, saying 'God alone knows who your father might be in view of your mother's gross immorality.'"

Yolande stifles a gasp, biting her lip. Jean Dunois looks at his feet, conscious of his own illegitimacy, and says quietly:

"Madame, you can imagine what effect such a message would have on the dauphin."

She pats his hand but says nothing.

"Believe me, I begged him to leave in peace. But his face was red with rage. He ordered me"—he pauses, taking another deep breath—"in front of his men, to storm the château. I had no choice. As his captain, I could not refuse."

Even at his young age, Jean Dunois is already known as a talented strategist and soldier. He would have disagreed with this decision with all his heart. But Yolande knows he had to obey his dauphin.

"Madame, since you know Azay-le-Rideau, you will recall that it was built more for love trysts than for war. The château was poorly defended and never expected an attack. Although our troops were outnumbered, we easily overwhelmed the stronghold." Here he pauses once more, looking at his feet again, his voice faltering.

"In his anger at the insult to his pride and station, the dauphin ordered me, his captain..." he paused, and swallowed, "to hang... and behead each soldier of the garrison... some two hundred men," he almost whispers.

Yolande is speechless. She has to force herself to remember that Charles is fifteen years old, Jean Dunois is sixteen. Both are men. They are no longer the children she was raising—but how could Charles have turned into someone who would give such an unreasonable order? And just when he is attempting to win allies to his cause?

For a moment she can say nothing and then, quietly, taking his hand, "No, Jean, do not think of it again. You obeyed, as you must, your commanding officer. He is not a monster, but there are some things he cannot stand to hear. You can be sure that will be the last garrison that dares call him a bastard." She, too, almost whispers.

When Jean Dunois leaves, she sits thinking about his story. What a troubled character has their future king. Her guiding principles in the children's upbringing were to give them three great gifts: a good education; impeccable manners and self-restraint; and unconditional, unlimited love. The dauphin can be so gracious, a wonderful host, affable, persuasive, and he has a remarkable way of connecting with simple people as well as with the most educated and important. Despite this, she finds herself wondering sometimes what would have become of him if he had not had her restraining hand and advice to guide him. To be the son of a madman could never hold much promise, and a crazy act like this one at Azay-le-Rideau will only frighten people when they hear of it.

It is not long after this that the Queen of Sicily makes her first visit to the court at Bourges. The time has come to see how Charles is transforming his wonderful inheritance. What a strong and splendid city it is, its huge cathedral with its lofty pointed arches dominating the skyline. As she approaches the ducal palace, there is her darling Marie waiting for her. How they embrace and examine each other's faces; and laugh; and embrace again with joy at their reunion. Marie leads her mother by the hand to a superb series of rooms decorated in the exquisite taste of the late Duke Jean. Her salon has walls covered in gilded Cordoba leather—one of the most ravishing decorative skills of Yolande's homeland and she notices it is stamped with the royal arms of Valois. Wisely, Marie has not changed anything: "Maman," she says, "what do I know of decoration? And here I live in one of the most famous of our late uncle's palaces, he who was known for his exquisite taste. But I have laid Papa's bedspread with his arms in the middle of my bed—come look."

Since Charles has his uncle's suite, Marie has that of his late aunt, the clever lady who threw her heavy velvet train over his father when he was on fire during the Ball of the Burning Men.

Marie gives her mother several rooms next to hers. Yolande admires her walls hung with silk taffeta in an enchanting shade of pale celadon green, with rare Chinese porcelain of the same colour in a dark wooden cabinet against the wall. The hangings of her bed and the curtains at the windows are all of the same silk, edged with a delicate silk fringe dyed to match. It is perfect, and when she tells Marie, how she glows with her mother's approval.

It is a joy to catch up with her daughter on all that has

happened since she came to Bourges with Charles, and it pleases Yolande to see her settled here. Marie is accompanied by four *demoiselles* from families known to them in Anjou. Another three are from good local families recommended to Yolande. They will help the Angevin girls find their way around the city, as well as being company for Marie. Heading her daughter's small household is the faithful Juana, who Yolande knows will be in control of everything. Seeing her beloved Juana waiting in the doorway, she embraces her as she would a favoured aunt— just as she did in childhood.

"Juana, tell me quickly, is Marie all right?" she asks her. "Has she found her feet here away from home?"

"Yes, my dearest Madame, she has matured a great deal and has such a wise little head on her shoulders. And she and Charles are close, although I think our dauphin needs a healthy dose of his *bonne mère* around him!" she says with a disapproving look, and Yolande has no doubt she will hear all later.

Marie's tutors have come from Anjou with her, and an excellent painting master of Uncle Jean's will instruct her. The park surrounding the château is large enough to ride in and has direct access to the fields beyond—an ideal situation as Marie loves to ride to hounds. In addition to this, she has her own horses, grooms, falcons and music teacher—altogether everything a young queen could need. Yolande and Juana will see to that. Her mother has brought her two of Ajax and Calypso's wolfhound puppies as well, and she almost squeezes Yolande breathless when she comes in and sees them.

"Maman, you angel, puppies! Oh, the darling things—and they can ride out with me as soon as they grow! No hare will be safe with Ajax's young after them! Oh, I *am* so glad you have come!" And she overwhelms her mother with affection.

Despite her lack of beauty, Marie seems to enchant everyone with her sweet nature and delightful laugh. In fact, despite her delicious sense of humour, she is quite a serious-minded girl at heart, who reads much and loves to learn, but her quirky jokes and japes entertain her audience—as much as her knowledge when conversing with the older members of the court. When she laughs, it is easy to forget that she is not beautiful; emotion shown from the heart does not fade—something Yolande repeated often to her children and also believes.

Marie's life as the dauphin's betrothed is ideal—with her delightful little court, charming *demoiselles* for company, living in the most tasteful, beautiful rooms one could imagine, as well as good teachers and a library such as Yolande would like to have herself at Angers—yes, she must admit, her daughter would appear to be perfectly installed in her own corner of Paradise. From all she hears, Marie is popular with the local nobility as well as the palace staff—both inside and out—whoall seem to adore her. But her mother's instinct tells her something is amiss—what is it that Marie has not told her? Has Charles changed towards her? Now that he is master here, could he have become someone other than the child she brought up to share the values she taught her own children and their cousin Jean Dunois?

It surprises Yolande to find that she is almost apprehensive about seeing Charles in his own court. She has heard so many conflicting stories about him—will he be changed? Will their old ease with each other remain? Her role in Charles's life has always been the same—to be supportive, encouraging, advising, and to use her power, connections and wealth to his advantage while remaining in the shadows, as invisible as possible. Will he remember this; will her influence still hold sway with him? And yet, it is not as simple as that—not black and white—there are more grey areas she will need to observe, and then ascertain how best to use what influence she still has to ensure he is surrounded by courtiers of the right stamp. Often she wishes that he had come to her at a younger age so that he could have avoided his early childhood—and all its attendant horrors—at his parents' court.

The dauphin has arranged a reception for her, and receives her as always with a deep bow in recognition of her status as queen. She notes with pleasure that he looks much more mature and elegant, more confident and assured. And she will find time to carefully probe his mind and discern how *that* has matured.

"Are your rooms to your liking, *ma bonne mère*? Do you have everything you need?" he asks anxiously—it is the first time she has been his guest. She pats his arm in approval and smiles into his eyes—"indeed, my dear Charles, everything is perfect. Now, let me meet your guests."

He leads her around the company, stopping first of all before the Archbishop of Bourges and a group of clergy. It takes her mere seconds to see this is a wise and practical man. The mayor of the city is another who impresses her—and the senior councillors, lawyers and businessmen. She has done her homework and knows Bourges to be a prosperous city due to the excellent administration of the area's substantial natural resources by the late Duke of Berry's appointees. Seeing Charles at home in this company of the great and good, she is content.

Then he presents her to a man in his mid-thirties whose face captures her attention—chiselled but not aristocratic, with a strong jawline and a fine, straight nose. Most people who meet her bow and keep their eyes cast down. His meet hers, but not in an arrogant way—he seems curious yet respectful, as if making a rapid assessment before he bows. His smile shows even teeth, and his manner is straightforward with no attempt to charm— and all the more charming because of it. His name is Jacques Coeur, and he is a successful merchant of the city.

"Madame and Majesty, it is an honour to be presented to you. I have heard much of your wisdom and abilities, most particularly in Provence," he says quietly, and then explains, "I use your port of Marseilles for my ships."

Charles adds, "Madame, this excellent man has been of great help to me during my first year in my new territory. I suggest you mark him well—I have great hopes for our collaboration." And mark him she does. Jacques Coeur has the look of someone who knows much, and from personal experience. She also observes his respect for Charles's position as much as for her own. Yes, he could be most useful to the dauphin.

As she makes her way among the company, her antennae are alerted to others whose faces she can read as the type of self-seeking young men of fortune she has encountered in various courts; invariably attractive, amusing, young men with a wit honed in order to entertain their principal, all the while studying how they can take advantage. She sees several such in the room as Charles presents his guests and asks to meet one after the other, even though she is aware he would prefer to remain with the "great and the good."

Charles is young, and she does not believe he has yet developed that most necessary quality for a successful monarch—the ability to read into hearts and minds. He must learn to judge the true ambitions and motives behind the more experienced and easily corrupt among the courtiers. Inevitably, those who amuse him the most are the worst. She has noticed in particular, among the figures at the court, companions like Pierre de Giac, older but still attractive and with that nonchalant air of a sophisticated man of the world; George de la Trémoille, another adept at subtle flattery, not physically attractive nor domineering, and yet she can see he has a most winning manner despite his brutish looks; Jean de Louvet, another charmer whose eyes betray his deviousness, particularly since he is in the Burgundian camp. When his name was mentioned she heard one or two suck in their breath and wondered... There are others, but these three she fears the most for the greed and cunning she can read in their eyes.

Perhaps more than anyone, the Queen of Sicily knows the value of good advisers and steady, brave and honest souls for the success of an administration. For her to help the dauphin—and who else is there to do it—she will search out several good Angevins; strong and worthy men she knows she can trust and place them close to Charles so that he can learn from their example and, hopefully, grow into a worthy king one day. In the months that follow she ensures that some of the best, including Tanneguy du Chastel, a long-standing loyal companion of her husband's who took care of Charles in Paris; and also Arnaud de Barbazan, known as "le chevalier sans reproche," stay close to the dauphin and guard him as far as they are able—not only from others, but also from himself, if they can.

Chapter Two

To her regret, Yolande cannot remain in Bourges as long as she would like; family duties need her attention at home in Angers. Her eldest son, now Duke Louis III d'Anjou, has begged his mother to be his regent. Underage, he realizes he has so much to learn. She accepts, thanking his dear father in heaven for teaching her how to rule during his absence in Naples. Tiphane has also taken more on her shoulders to help her mistress and is standing by ready to protect her even more than before.

And indeed, these are dangerous times. The English king has taken possession of Rouen, the powerful capital of Normandy, and with his army of ten thousand men systematically proceeds to conquer his way towards Paris. To protect her elder son's duchy of Maine, Yolande requests—and is granted—Charles VI's permission to enter into a separate treaty of non-aggression with the King of England. To start negotiations, Yolande sends him a team of delegates which includes Pierre de Brézé, her late husband's bright young equerry, the only child of a minor Norman noble family. Being neither particularly rich nor from the high nobility, he would appear unremarkable to anyone opposed to her. And it will be a useful way for her to see if he has talent. He is certainly ambitious, and hungry. There is something irresistible about him—he makes Yolande laugh, a guaranteed entry card into her entourage. He is also quite the most handsome young man she has seen—almost too beautiful—with bewitching long-lashed hazel eyes, dark hair, olive skin, a winningsmile with perfect teeth; and he is both tall and well built for someone so young. Despite excellent manners and a certain way with words, he shies away from being noticed or drawing attention to himself, which she finds interesting. He is worth watching, and Yolande will take her time and see how young Pierre de Brézé develops.

After the lengthy negotiations by her team on her behalf, the Queen of Sicily is finally able to sign an official treaty with Henry V, placing her provinces of Anjou and Maine outside any military offensive he might set in motion against France. Her neighbour the Duke of Brittany, on her advice and also with their king's permission, does the same. For the present, Louis' inheritance is safe, and Brittany, an ally of Burgundy's, has come a step nearer to becoming attached to his king.

While Yolande takes charge in Angers, young Louis has installed himself—at least for the time being—in Marseilles, in order to see how his territory of Provence operates. He travels about the countryside, showing himself as the people's new sovereign, and the reports that are sent back about him bode well. He has his father's vocal reticence, but with his handsome face and physique, his natural way with people, and the same honest blue eyes, he inspires trust just as his father did. Marseilles is essential to the income of the Anjou family—as is all Provence, which Louis knows only too well and it is right that he spends time there. But there is foreboding in Yolande's heart at his extended stay, for the longer he is game, the more she fears he will be inspired to launch an offensive against his cousin Alfonso to regain his kingdom of Naples. She is too afraid to even mention Naples, that chimera that began his father's decline into ill health. He never really recovered after his return from losing Naples and she always wondered what was it that drained the strength of such a good, honest man? What inspires such a burning ambition in both the Anjous and the Aragons to possess it? And has Louis caught the fever? In her heart, she suspects he has, and she begins to fear for him.

Charles and Marie depart for Paris so that he can attend the Royal Council in the absence of the sick king. Yolande has arranged for the young pair to stay in her palace by the Seine, in the sure knowledge that they will be safe there. At her insistence, they are accompanied by a strong guard, mostly of experienced Angevins. The queen has written repeatedly to Yolande asking her to return Charles to her at Vincennes. She knows her last remaining son will only obey Yolande, who has steadfastly refused—she has not nurtured this child to risk his being murdered like his brothers on the orders of the Duke of Burgundy. Yolande has no doubt about the authorship of those crimes, but she is equally sure that Queen Isabeau has no idea of the involvement of Jean-sans-Peur in the horrors perpetrated upon her children. With the madness of her husband and the death of the two men on whom she relied, Isabeau must feel she is drowning in a whirlpool of intrigue and betrayal. In the queen's search for a strong family member to protect her as her husband's regent, she clutched at any straw offered. Tragically the one she has grasped belongs to the despicable Duke of Burgundy. And yet Yolande knows that Isabeau would never have trusted him if she believed he had poisoned her children.

The king's seizures are so frequent now that he is rarely seen and remains in the palace of the Louvre with Odette who keeps Yolande well informed. In his absence, Isabeau's position as regent is of strategic importance to the status of the Duke of Burgundy who places himself at her side. It is a contemptible betrayal by Isabeau, not only of her husband but also of the memory of her friend Louis d'Orléans. Still, Yolande does not hate or even despise Isabeau for her treachery in shifting her loyalty to her husband's loathsome cousin. Rather, she pities her and prays their paths will not cross often.

Back in Angers, Yolande hears from Odette that, in one of his rare bouts of sanity, the king has became aware of his queen's alliance with the traitorous Burgundy and has banished them both from Paris. But this decision is to have appalling consequences, for the king, and for Yolande. In retaliation, the Duke of Burgundy's men steal into Paris under cover of darkness. They take control of the city with such speed that the dauphin has to flee the Anjous' palace on the Seine in the dead of night. Fortunately, he has the best of guardians in Tanneguy du Chastel. As the Burgundians enter Paris, Tanneguy brings the dauphin in haste and in the dark to the Bastille, where two Angevins are waiting with horses and clothes. Charles, the boy Yolande has promised to protect and make into a worthy king, is driven from his capital in terror in his nightshirt! Then begins a dreadful massacre of the Armagnacs, while those who are able flee to Bourges to join the dauphin.

There is worse news to come. It is only when she hears that Charles and his escort have arrived safely in Bourges that Yolande receives word Marie is not with them: the Burgundians are holding her daughter captive in Paris.

A shard of ice pierces Yolande's heart. How has this happened? Her daughter confined in Paris, and she herself powerless in Angers. Praying that Marie will not be mistreated, she sends emissaries both official and secret to find out what she can. Fretting for her daughter's safety, she writes a personal letter delivered directly to Queen Isabeau, still in Troyes with the Duke of Burgundy, but this gets no reply. Finally, and to her great relief, she receives a note from Isabeau in her own hand, saying she was on her way to Paris, and giving her word that Marie would be sheltered by her personally and kept safe. Isabeau added, somewhat touchingly, that she still wished for the conclusion of the marriage of her remaining son, Charles, to Yolande's daughter. With her woman's instinct, Yolande knows that Isabeau will keep her word and, with that, her anxiety eased. After all, had she not helped the queen with the king by finding Odette? Altogether, it is the best result she can hope for at this uncertain time.

By 14 July, Queen Isabeau has made her official entry into

Paris in great style, accompanied by the Duke of Burgundy. Jean-sans-Peur is taking no chances and brings with him an army of three thousand five hundred soldiers, for the protection of her incapable royal husband. No one imagines that the queen has had any influence on the duke's decisions. Her presence merely gives the lie that they are made with the regent's blessing and that is sufficient to justify his actions.

Although she holds Yolande's daughter, the queen's repeated requests for Charles to join her in Paris are certainly made on the Duke of Burgundy's instructions. At the Queen of Sicily's insistence, Charles continues to refuse. He must not forget her husband's dying instructions to them both: "Do not trust the Duke of Burgundy"—and neither will. Nor will she forget her own promise to God that she made when she took the young Prince Charles into her family: *Je le garde, moi*. It is a dangerous game she is playing, urging him to disobey the queen, a queen who holds such a precious card as her own daughter. But Yolande is equally sure of two basic facts: that the queen will not harm Marie; and that the dauphin would not survive long if he joined Isabeau at Vincennes. Then all really would be lost. The Duke of Burgundy would arrange for Charles's death just as he did the poisoning of his two older brothers; perhaps also the king's death—and then Jean-sans-Peur would be able to mount the throne. Hard as it is for her, it is wiser to trust Isabeau to protect Marie, and keep her and Charles away from the Duke of Burgundy.

Marie has been held by the Burgundians in Paris for nine months when suddenly, and without warning, she is brought back home to her family at Saumur by the Duke of Brittany, Yolande's fellow negotiator with England. This, he explains, is a sign of the goodwill of Duke Jean-sans-Peur.

"*Goodwill?*" exclaims an incandescent Yolande. "What business did he have keeping her in the first place?" But what a relief for her to wrap her arms around Marie, while happy tears roll down both their cheeks.

"Child, precious daughter, how *are* you? Did they treat you well? Did they harm or threaten you? Were you in any danger?" Her questions come like a fast-flowing river, and Marie laughs.

"Maman, stop! Dearest Maman, I am well and so very happy to be home with you and my brothers and sister and all the people I love. Be calm. I am well."

Yolande notes that Marie has managed to attain more poise, more self-assurance, despite her ordeal, and her expression is as sweet-natured as ever. She has arrived looking healthy, wearing her own smart clothes and riding a fine grey hackney, a gift from the Duke of Burgundy, no less! She has filled out a little, though still slim.

"Maman, I was not ill treated—please take that worried look off your face!" she laughs. "I was kept in my own apartment at our home in Paris. I was free to move about in the gardens; I merely had to agree to remain within our perimeter walls, which was hardly onerous. I had the dogs, my dwarf, my tutors and all our familiar staff. I even received the occasional smuggled letter from Charles." Now *that* interests Yolande since she has not heard a word from him and surmises that he keeps on the move to avoid Burgundy's men, but how good that he keeps in touch with Marie—and encouraging for their future. If they can share complicity now, it bodes well for their married life. *Oh, the joy of having her back and unharmed.* Nothing else seems to matter—she may be a warrior queen on the one hand, but she is also a very fond mother. Her son Louis, she hears, is progressing well in Provence, and the rest of her brood are flourishing here at Saumur. To her relief, her most important treasures, the children, are all safe—all except her adopted son Charles who is still in mortal danger from Jean-sans-Peur and her anxiety for him has not lessened. If only her darling husband was still with them.

Chapter Three

$\mathcal{N}$ow that young Louis has immersed himself in the dream of regaining his distant kingdom, the Queen of Sicily decides to try to find an advantageous bride for her second son, nine-year-old René. His only inheritance is the earldom of Guise, a fine birthright, but stuck in the middle of Burgundian territory. And yet her jolly, red, curly-haired adventurer, this, her most endearing child, though not as academic as Louis or Marie, does have other gifts. His passions have always been music, drawing, history, soldiery—and he has the kindest of hearts. His earldom of Guise is as good as nothing to offer a prospective bride; he has never even been able to go there. What René needs is a substantial heiress, but to attract such a paragon Yolande must find a way of making her younger son more eligible.

Throughout her youth she was close to her maternal uncle, the Cardinal Duke of Bar. A childhood friend and accomplice of her mother, his sister, he was often their guest in Saragossa and Barcelona. A large man, imposing, with a shiny bald head and a deep voice of dark velvet, he would sit Yolande on his knee while he told her stories from the Old Testament so vividly that she begged for more. His visits to their court in Aragon were always a delight. Since Yolande's marriage, they have corresponded regularly, and she knows he prays for her. Having lost his two elder brothers at Agincourt, he has inherited both the title and the province of Bar, but as a man of the Church, he has no children to inherit from him.

As his nearest of kin, Yolande should be his heiress, but it is for René that she wants to negotiate. Friends since early childhood, it is not difficult to approach her uncle by letter and inform him of her willingness to forgo her inheritance of his dukedom in favour of her second son. To her immense relief, he replies that he is open and willing to accept the idea of adopting René as his heir. This pledge of a dukedom is a worthy bequest for a prospective bridegroom. At last René can be considered almost as eligible as his older brother.

Yolande may be a fond mother, but she believes she is not a fool—she knows the character of her children, and René is smarter than he makes himself out to be. He may not have Louis' obvious talents and beauty, let alone his inheritance, but she feels he has the ability to become someone quite extraordinary one day, and she wants to make that possible. The first step, she believes, is a good marriage.

Having settled his inheritance, therefore, she takes the next step towards her goal. It has been known of old that the Dukes of Bar have always longed to unite their territory with the neighbouring duchy of Lorraine. Such is the delicacy of her plan that she makes a special visit to her uncle in person. This is a serious game, and she intends to win!

As they walk arm in arm in his cloister garden, heady with the scent of jasmine, Yolande gently prepares him. "Is it not so, dear uncle, that the Duke of Lorraine has no son?" She pauses, and as if musing, continues: "And am I right in thinking that he has made his beautiful eldest daughter his heir?" she asks.

Nonchalantly he picks some of the small white flowers, places them carefully in her hair and gives her a shrewd look. Guilelessly she continues, sounding light and conversational:

"Would you not agree that a marriage between your heir, my son René, and Isabelle of Lorraine would be most fortuitous in uniting the two duchies at last?"

Her uncle's eyes shine and he smiles slowly and gleefully.

"My dear Yolande, you were always a clever child, and you have grown into a beautiful, clever woman. Yes, yes," he ponders slowly, "it would be an excellent idea." Although her uncle is a heavy man, his eyes are beacons of intelligence and humour. Moreover, his vocation is genuine, not just the usual destination of the third son, and Yolande loves him even more for that.

Encouraged by his enthusiasm, she proposes that, initially, René should go to spend some time with him, become acquainted, and learn about his prospective inheritance of Bar, and her uncle-cardinal agrees with pleasure.

The Queen of Sicily finds René in Bourges with Jean Dunois, both looking for a possible military career in the dauphin's small army. When he hears of his mother's arrival, he comes at once to see her, and she gives him her news.

"Maman, of course I am delighted to be the heir to your uncle's dukedom of Bar, but then I know that no one can resist your charm or your acute reasoning," he says in a most grown-up manner as he embraces her. He pauses for a moment. "As for a marriage with the heiress of Lorraine... we both know that the duke her father is a confirmed follower and childhood friend of the Duke of Burgundy. Do you think he will take kindly to an Anjou, from a family of Armagnac supporters, becoming heir to the neighbouring duchy, let alone marrying his heiress?"

He has a point. The sovereign duchy of Lorraine is known to have been sustaining the English for some time, and to their considerable advantage. Yolande's hope is to untie Lorraine from the web of English alliances and attach this valuable duchy by blood—her blood—to that of Bar, and their united territory to the crown of France.

The question she must now consider is how to persuade the Duke of Lorraine to choose René, a second son from an enemy house, as the ideal husband for his daughter, the heiress to his duchy? France is full of eligible young noblemen far better suited to win the hand of the beautiful Isabelle of Lorraine.

Desperate situations require desperate solutions. There are few secrets in a court, and Yolande managed to place her versatile lady's maid Eduarda—whom she had taken back from Isabeau—into the duke's household. Eduarda informed her mistress that the duchess never appeared other than in her chapel and led a sedentary life quite separate to the lonely duke. The only pleasure he had was in the company of his old friends, and in the visits of his two daughters. "Then he lights up," wrote Eduarda, "at the sight of them and their friends, begging them to remain at his château at Nancy far longer than they intended."

Yolande is not overly proud of what she does to secure the Duke of Lorraine for France, but nor is she ashamed. She decides to find him a suitable lady companion to ease his loneliness, and to persuade him to be loyal to his rightful king—and not to the English. She believes it would probably be best for her choice of helper to come from Anjou. That way she can have more control through her family, and contact sensible people there to find her a suitable young candidate for her purpose. When Yolande returns to Angers, a meeting is arranged with a young woman named Alison du May.

As she enters the room the girl curtseys low, giving Yolande ample opportunity to study her. Alison du May is a natural beauty, and her curtsey is made with a sure and confident movement, as if she has been at court all her life. She raises her head and her green eyes meet Yolande's without fear, almost boldly.

"Alison, do you have any idea why I have sent for you?" Yolande asks.

At this, the girl stammers a little. "Madame, I have none."

"My dear girl, as your Duchess of Anjou, I have madeenquiries to find the perfect young woman to help our country. You would like to do that, wouldn't you?"

"Yes... yes," she replies hesitantly.

"I must therefore ask you: are you a loyal subject of the Duke of Anjou and of your king, Charles VI?" Again the girl curtseys low, and to judge from the clear, open expression of assent she gives, Yolande believes that Alison du May might just be a good choice.

The duchess and Alison meet several more times, both at Angers and Saumur, and through gentle conversation—a question here, an example there of the ways in which France needs her sovereign dukes loyal to their king—it becomes clear that Alison appreciates that France needs Lorraine and Bar on side, and that *she* holds the key to achieving that. The girl certainly understands the perilous situation of the country and, on a personal level, the loneliness of the old duke, and that he needs comforting by day and perhaps by night as well. Is she agreeable to that idea in order to help save France?

"Madame, following our several meetings, I believe I do understand what you are asking of me, and I too have made some enquiries. I hear nothing but good about the duke and feel confident that I can make him happy. If I can succeed in that, then I know I can persuade him to return his loyalty to his king and country."

Alison du May is not only beautiful and bold, she is intelligent; it does not take her long to captivate the Duke of Lorraine—and govern him. Yolande corresponds regularly with her and knows from other informants that Alison does indeed make the elderly duke happy. Should she give him children, Yolande promises her that she will see to it that they are well provided for, but she also makes it clear that she is relying on the girl to see that Lorraine not only returns, but remains with France.

With time, Yolande can see that Alison comes genuinely to care for Charles of Lorraine. Subtly, with her delightful manner, the girl sets about persuading the duke—who adores her— to sign the papers agreeing to the joining of Lorraine and Bar through René's marriage to his heiress. Another triumph for the Queen of Sicily! René becomes Lorraine's joint heir and the future husband of his beautiful daughter, Isabella.

Yolande summons her son from Bourges to Angers and gives him the news as she sits embroidering by the fire in Angers' great hall. To say that René is overwhelmed is an understatement. He sits down beside her, and says nothing for a few moments, as if digesting his unexpected good fortune. Tall and mature, his mother sees a young man before her. Then he stands, paces up and down the room a few times and, turning to her, says:

"I am glad of it, dearest Maman, of course, and very grateful, but..." he hesitates, "it seems as if I am getting my second dukedom more through pillow talk than as my right."

"Really?" is all she says to that, raising her eyebrows but continuing to look at her stitching.

"I would rather have won it on a battlefield," he adds, almost defiantly. How sweet is youth, and she has to smile at his outraged male pride. She stops her stitching and looks at his confused, dear face.

"My beloved son, you are young and eager to win your spurs in battle, but soon you will appreciate that a dukedom is a dukedom however it comes. As for pillow talk, believe me, it can be as effective, and far less costly, than a cannon." She smiles as he bows to her and leaves the room, looking puzzled and lost for an answer.

In time, René will become the ruler of Lorraine, but the immediate importance of the marriage is that it will remove Lorraine from the enemy's camp and shift the duchy's support to that of France's king. Yolande's methods may be unorthodox, but her goals are the goals of France, and her Spanish conscience never troubles her in this regard.

Chapter Four

Since Yolande is unable to be with the dauphin at all times herself, she has placed the best of her Angevin advisers about him to help Charles find his way in the strange and dangerous world that is the court of France. To judge him fairly, it is important for her to see him in action, and she invites him to Anjou to join her at her château at Saumur, where she will hold a formal court during a meeting of the provinces of Poitou. To her delight, he accepts.

Not surprisingly, Charles, the third dauphin of this reign, is barely acknowledged by the people; to please the Duke of Burgundy and further his own claim to the French throne, his mother had hinted that Charles is illegitimate, typical court gossip bandied about by the Burgundians—and everyone knows that his father is rarely sane. Nor has the young man had an opportunity to show what, if anything, he can do for his country. Yolande can sense his frustration at every turn.

This troubled child she took into her family urgently needs recognition to enable him to fulfil his destiny. She knows his faults better than anyone, but she sincerely believes that, given the right handling and guidance, he can become a worthy king. What doubts he must have when his own mother refers to him as the "so-called dauphin!" Nor does he yet understand that she is acting out of fear for her own life and future. Unfortunately, a performance like the one at Azay-le-Rideau shows the depth of his insecurity, and his genuine doubts about his legitimacy eat away at his self-confidence.

Having Charles recognized as the legitimate heir to his father's throne, not just the acknowledged one, has become the Queen of Sicily's obsession. He must learn to believe in himself and in his right to succeed his father. To this end she never fails to find occasions to do him formal, public homage, with her head lowered as she makes him a deep reverence or curtsey.

It is to this end also that she invites him to Saumur to hold a formal court at her château. When news of his visit spreads, many of the Angevins gather at the entrance to the castle to see how this boy they knew has grown into a man, how he has matured, and if he will make a real king. As Charles rides towards the château with his entourage, Yolande decides to meet him outside in full view of the members of her court and the people. She is dressed for the occasion in a deep red velvet gown, cut at the neck to allow her famous rubies to show, a delicate golden shawl around her shoulders, the long velvet train of her court dress stretched out behind her. On her headdress she wears her crown as Queen of Sicily, but when Charles dismounts and walks towards her, she curtseys very low and slowly, forcing him to raise her with outstretched hands. She can hear the faint buzz from the assembled crowd when they see this. If she, in her position and with all her titles, can show the dauphin such reverence, others will take note and comply. His face speaks volumes, and she can see from his expression that he is moved, his eyes filled with love and appreciation for what she is doing.

As they enter the château together, Charles cannot hide his pleasure at being once again at Saumur. Louis is here, visiting from Marseilles, and Marie and René have come to greet him, as well as the little ones, Yolande and the dauphin's godson Charles. And greet him they do, like the old friends they are— with warmth, real affection and trust. Their mother knows she has their support as she concentrates all her energy on ensuring that Charles is accepted as France's true dauphin and future king. This is her duty, and one she performs gladly. It is what her beloved husband would have wished.

June is in full bloom, and Yolande has been granted the audience she requested with the ailing king. Through Odette, she has been kept fully informed about the king's health, and there is no doubt that his mind is deteriorating, his sanity slipping away more often than not. They meet at the dauphin's beautiful château at Mehun-sur-Yèvre, inherited from Jean of Berry. There is an important matter to discuss with the king concerning Charles, and Yolande knows from Odette that her timing is fortuitous regarding his mind. She gathers Marie, René, young Yolande and Charles, and they leave Angers, rowing upstream on the Loire with its enthralling river traffic, to the delight of the children. Downstream from Tours they join the River Cher. The château of Mehun-sur-Yèvre is famous for its soaring towers, and features in the late Duke of Berry's remarkable illuminated manuscript *Les Très Riches Heures*.

They arrive to see the king in a large gathering of courtiers and their ladies.

"Your Majesty, sire," says Yolande softly, as she drops Charles VI a deep curtsey. How he has changed: he is thinner, with less hair, tired eyes and a sallow complexion. The beautiful, dashing young soldier-courtier is completely gone. She notices a flicker of joyful recognition in his eyes when he sees her, and as he kisses her hand he notices she is wearing his sapphire ring and smiles warmly.

"My dear cousin Yolande, it is an unusual pleasure to see someone of whom I am so fond at my court. Welcome!" and he raises and embraces her. "Since you wear my ring, I trust you have come with a request that I will be pleased to grant you?" he whispers in her ear.

Beside him is a young lady she knows well. "Odette, my dear young friend," she says with a genuine smile to her helper. Yolande reaches out her hand and raises Odette from her court reverence. She can see from the king's face that her warm greeting to Odette de Champdivers (to whom the court refers as "the little queen") has pleased him. Children and dogs are led away to explore and Yolande turns to her host with a question in her expression.

The king understands that she wants a private audience and they withdraw from the gathering to an adjacent area, Odette following. Once settled, Yolande says quietly: "Sire, as you know well, I have had your youngest son, Charles, now your dauphin, in my care for some years." From his eyes and the way he nods, she judges him to be quite sane. "It grieves me that the young prince is not kept as fully occupied as his rank entitles him," she continues, observing with relief that he is listening intently. "He has pleased me and my late husband with his dedication to the Church, his studies, and your governance."

The king turns sharply, with interest, and asks, "How does he show his dedication to the Church?" She tells him of Charles's frequent devotions, of his assiduous studies, his time in Anjou and how the people in their territories react to him. She has primed Odette beforehand, and the younger woman confirms everything she says.

"Sire, friend and cousin, I come to ask you to endorse your son Charles as your rightful heir, and create him Lieutenant General of the kingdom." On cue, Odette whispers to the king: "Dearest sire, we have spoken of this before, as I know it is in your heart to give your son these privileges. You will remember our discussions?" The king nods. "And you agreed it would be an excellent procedure?" Again the king nods.

After some ten minutes more, it is concluded. Charles will be confirmed by statute in his new position. By this Act, the queen will be removed as regent, and the dauphin's future appears secure. Yolande sighs inwardly. Another goal achieved.

The king has been most generous to Odette de Champdivers and given her two fine manors and an estate in Poitou. Odette fully understands that his munificence is due to the Queen of Sicily, in return for her service. When they are alone, Yolande takes the opportunity to ask her some things she would not dare commit to a letter. "How mad is the king?" she begins.

"Oh, at times, very! But he always knows me, and although he can be terrible with some, with me he is always kind and gentle."

This comes as a relief to Yolande, since she has heard of his cruelty and brutality to others. Nor does she know why he is always willing to see her—or perhaps he recognizes a kindred spirit who intends him only good.

"Odette, my dear, you know this already but I want to stress it to you again. Should you ever, at any time, feel threatened by the king, you must promise to let me know at once, and I will see you are brought to safety. Now give me your promise?" This Odette does, and curtseys to the ground. As Yolande leaves, she sees that the younger woman has risen, and she catches the reflection of a tear on her cheek.

In spite of the Queen of Sicily's important achievement with the king on behalf of the dauphin, the spectre of Naples has returned to haunt her family. She always knew it would happen—her beloved eldest son Louis is leaving once again for Marseilles, this time to sail to Italy to chase his elusive inheritance. Yolande has feared for so long that her darling eldest son would follow in his father's footsteps; she has been waiting for this day, dreading it, but knows she must be supportive and understanding, although it breaks her heart to see him so. She has always known he will never escape that irresistible, cursed mistress who had his father in her thrall!

As if his ambition was not enough of a burden, she must also be an integral part of his plans. Louis will need his mother to be on hand in Provence to supply his requirements for provisions, men, ships and armaments. For this reason she intends to base herself there for the next four years with the younger children, to manage their considerable landholdings and raise more funds. When Yolande married Louis II d'Anjou, she saw that her role was to support her husband, and now, as she promised him, she must do the same for their eldest son. Yes, she fears for her beloved golden boy, setting out on an unwinnable quest, but she recognizes that look in his eyes, his father's look before he left for the Italian peninsula. Since she cannot oppose his will, she is duty-bound to support it, no matter her own opinion.

Louis has come to bid farewell to all the family currently based at Saumur. Yolande stands back, looking at them—how they have all grown, especially Louis, as tall as her husband and so like him when they met for the first time. Her son is sixteen now and has filled out, is reputed to be a good swordsman and cavalry officer—quite a young gallant. The children run to greet him and pepper him with questions about his quest—they know he will see the mighty volcano Vesuvius and that is their most thrilling topic. Finally, when she has him alone, Yolande looks at him keenly, deep into his blue eyes withher own of a darker, sapphire blue. "Well, my eldest, the first flower of my love for your father, I wish you success, health and happiness. May you fulfil all your ambitions, win and rule your kingdom with kindness and justice—and write to us often. Many ships pass between Marseilles and Naples and we expect to hear everything. You will write, won't you my darling boy?" And at this her voice breaks and they embrace. She cannot help her tears—she has experienced this scene before. All she can do is pray he succeeds in all his ambitions. With her right thumb she traces a cross on his forehead and blesses him.

Chapter Five

After years of feuding, the Duke of Burgundy and the dauphin have at last understood the need to resolve their differences and unite for the sake of France, for without the two factions joining forces, a comprehensive English victory is recognized by every citizen across the country as inevitable.

Both the Burgundians and the Armagnacs are so paranoid with hatred of one another that it seems impossible for them to agree on a meeting place. In league with the English, the Duke of Burgundy controls the north and the east of France; the dauphin holds most of the south—with the exception of Yolande's territory of Guyenne, which is in the hands of the Burgundians. Finally, a meeting place has been chosen, at Montereau in the Île-de-France region of north-central France.

Charles has excellent captains whom Yolande sent him from Anjou, most markedly Tanneguy du Chastel. And there are others who she is sure will prove their worth. Since Yolande is obliged to remain in Provence, she has sent a number of her best agents—young Pierre de Brézé among them—who are not known to one another, to mingle and scout for her. This is something she learnt at home in Aragon—it is wise to keep one's agents unaware of one another, then they can never conspire against their principals. A small precaution, but one she adheres to. They may see each other in her households yet be unaware of their exact role in her employ.

It is a hot afternoon in September and Yolande sits at her writing table in her château of Tarascon in Provence. The books are refusing to balance and are making her head ache, or perhaps that is because thunder is expected. But the thunder that comes is not from the skies. She hears loud shouts, then many voices and feet running down stone passageways. A courier bursts into the room despite the guards trying to hold him back. The poor man is in tears with exhaustion, and she recognizes him as one of Pierre de Brézé's men.

Waving away her guards, she gives him some water, which he gulps. Mud-spattered and hardly able to stand after riding hard, he hands her a note on which Pierre has written:

"Madame, I have no time to write. Trust this man. Please hear him. My written account will follow with the next courier."

What can this mean? She cannot imagine what is to follow, but forces herself to wait until the man can speak. After some minutes, with difficulty, he begins:

"My lord Pierre de Brézé has asked me... Madame, to tell you as follows... that the first meeting between the Duke of Burgundy and the dauphin... aimed at settling their differences... was a failure. The duke let it be known that he would not even bother... to attend the next summit... to discuss a peace treaty... but his decision was reversed by the presence of a lady... named Jeanne de Giac."

Yolande's face does not change, and gives no indication that she knows the woman as the attractive wife of Pierre de Giac, a member of the Duke of Burgundy's entourage she has seen at court. Still breathing heavily, the man continues:

"It seems the duke... was rather taken with the Dame de Giac... who persuaded him to listen to your trusted Angevin envoys Tanneguy du Chastel and Arnaud de Barbazan. This time their meeting with the duke was a success... gifts were exchanged and a peace treaty was drafted."

Yolande's face still has not changed expression, but how is this possible? How could a woman of such little standing have been able to influence the mighty Duke of Burgundy, especially in a matter as critical as the safety of the kingdom?

Slowly the story emerges, the gaspings of the courier clarified by a letter that swiftly follows in Pierre's own hand. And the clearer the picture becomes, the more horrific it seems. The representatives of the two sides had already agreed to meet on neutral ground, namely in the middle of the bridge at Montereau. This was decided despite some misgivings from the Duke of Burgundy, but with the help of the Dame de Giac, he was persuaded. An enclosure was erected on the bridge, and two parties of ten men—unarmed but for their swords—accompanied their principals, the dauphin and the Duke of Burgundy, to witness the signing of the agreement. Polite greetings were exchanged and both parties bowed to one another.

But from this point, things began to go horribly awry. "Suddenly, an argument began between a group of the murdered Duke Louis d'Orléans' followers—including the dauphin—and the Burgundians. This quickly became heated, and a scuffle broke out. Your faithful Angevin, Tanneguy du Chastel, pushed the dauphin out of the enclosure, saving him from harm, before the first blows were struck."

Instinctively, Yolande catches at her throat. "Blows?"

It seems that the Armagnacs felt that only a horror similar to the vicious murder of their leader, Louis d'Orléans, could avenge that crime. And it was the dauphin's guardian knight, Tanneguy du Chastel, who smashed his battle axe onto the Duke of Burgundy's head, spilling his brains on the bridge. Another sliced off the duke's right hand, just as the hand of Louis d'Orléans had been cut off—as if this had become a new ritual of political assassination.

Tears blur Yolande's reading and she wipes them away angrily to read Pierre's final words:

"In their madness, the assassins of both sides claimed that *their* hands had been guided by sorcery and by the invocation of demons. Madame, forgive me—more will follow my further enquiries."

Dear God, she thinks in her despair, how easy it is to allege witchcraft for the inexplicable. She sends the courier out of the room and calls for Tiphane while she sits moaning, rocking to and fro in anguish, both her arms tight across her stomach. Tiphane tries to calm her, pressing a damp cloth to her forehead—she can see that Yolande is in mental agony. What were the Armagnacs thinking of? How can the dauphin ever inspire confidence in anyone after condoning such a senseless and brutal assassination? This is not witchcraft—it is treachery! The two sides will never be able to unite against the English after this.

Couriers arrive one after the other, and the more she reads from the eyewitness accounts coming in from her agents, the more she hears her inner voice: *The dauphin must have known of this, he must have taken part! How could he not have known? Surely these, his most faithful followers, would not have acted without his consent?* She is beginning to realize how deeply Charles must be implicated, and she wants to cry out in her rage and anguish. So many years spent trying to build him up, only for him to destroy everything at Montereau!

And worse, she begins to understand that not only is Charles implicated, but some of the responsibility must rest with her. Several of those involved are her own appointments—the very Angevins she had hoped would keep Charles steady. In her absence, busy with Louis and his needs, these apparently wise counsellors have become bellicose. How quickly attitudes change when she is far away! Among the authors of this catastrophe are old and trusted members of her circle— Tanneguy du Chastel, and the captain Arnaud de Barbazan. How could her carefully chosen advisers, guardians of the dauphin, have been willing parties to this terrible and damaging crime? She sits, feeling her stomach glued to her spine in silent apprehension.

And as for Giac, what kind of man is he to have let his wife persuade the Duke of Burgundy to go against his instincts and come to Montereau? And what is his part in all this? She has heard the most horrific stories about the man: how he killed his pregnant first wife by forcing her to take poison, and then tied her to him while sitting behind him on a horse, riding four leagues at a gallop until she was dead. When her body was found the next day, it had been partly devoured by wolves. He did this to free himself so he could marry Jeanne, a rich widow with whom he was enamoured. They must have become accomplices, he and his new wife, and entered into some kind of agreement with leading Armagnacs to deliver the Duke of Burgundy to them. What were they promised, she wonders, to commit such treachery—and by whom? From her enquiries, it seems there is no crime too low for this Giac nor his wife if it gains them profit. Will she learn more? What is Giac's hold on Charles, because she is sure he has one. According to the letters she receives he has become Charles's favourite and there is nothing he is unwilling to do for him and will grant him any favour within his power.

Her head aches, and the picture she sees and cannot blot out from her mind's eye is of Tanneguy's axe splitting the skull of Jean of Burgundy and spilling his brains all over the bridge at Montereau. And Charles! What did Charles know about this?

Chapter Six

Philippe, the new Duke of Burgundy, is married to one of King Charles VI's daughters; now his father has been killed by the officers of the king's son, his brother-in-law. What is going through his mind? From what little she has observed of him at court, Yolande judges Philippe to be a young man of quiet resolution. He will weigh up carefully his reaction to this situation. And how much rancour does he carry for his sister's rejection by the Anjou family, supporters of the dauphin? When she heard that her darling little Catherine died of smallpox the year following her return to her father, Yolande grieved very much, but at least it could not be said she died of a broken heart.

In his confusion, the dauphin has written an apologetic but utterly thoughtless letter to Philippe. In it he claims that his men acted in response to the old duke's "threatening attitude." He offers Philippe the same proposition he put to his father—to join with him against the English. What madness is this? Is Charles so stunned he has lost all sense of reasoning? Does he imagine for one moment that the new duke will just ignore his father's brutal murder and unite with the dauphin to oppose the English? This is certainly the last thing he will do now. Yolande has always believed she knows and understands Charles, perhaps better than anyone, but this is a Charles she cannot fathom at all.

Instead, the result of the Montereau debacle is predictable. Far from forgiving Charles, Philippe decides to achieve peace by joining the stronger party, England. Meanwhile, the king and *parlement* have decided to punish all involved in Montereau. The decision is not Philippe's, but since the king needs the support of Burgundy, the new duke's desire for retribution will be honoured.

Back at court, Pierre relays all the crucial information to the Queen of Sicily in Provence. The representatives of the two sovereigns, Henry V and Charles VI, are to meet at Troyes, about a day's ride south-east of Paris. In May 1420, the two kings are to sign a definitive treaty in recognition of France's defeat at Agincourt five years earlier. The Treaty of Troyes is formalized but with one small last-minute adjustment—the king's madness has set in again after he heard about the assassination on the bridge, and in light of this, it is his queen, Isabeau, who will sign in his place.

How can such a treaty be anything but a disaster for France? And so it proves.

The terms of the Treaty of Troyes are harsh and unprecedented. The dauphin, Charles, is formally disinherited "on account of his involvement in the murder of the king's cousin, Duke Jean of Burgundy." In his place, Charles VI of France recognizes Henry V of England as his heir.

When Yolande hears this, she cannot believe it. Queen Isabeau has agreed to sign away the crown of France from the last-living of her five sons? It cannot be true!

The king will retain the crown for his lifetime and then it will pass to Henry V. The King of England is to marry the Valois princess Catherine, daughter of Charles VI. Their son, when born, will rule over France and England.

Throughout her married life, the Queen of Sicily has fought against such a catastrophe—to lose France to England. What greater tragedy could befall her adopted country—and her adopted son, France's rightful dauphin!

She must write at once to Charles and try to give him courage. René must go to him; also Pierre de Brézé and Jean de Dunois.

And she is far away, confined to Provence! How her heart aches for them all, and for her dear Louis' France.

Charles, the prince she has raised with such care, is officially disinherited and banished. All his privileges as dauphin are gone as well as his territories of the Dauphiné and Touraine. All that is left to him is his inheritance from his uncle Duke Jean of Berry. *Parlement* has decreed that the plotters of Montereau must be apprehended and punished—but nothing seems to be happening in that regard.

The king's heralds post the treaty and its stipulations in every town square. There is universal disbelief and shaking of heads. The inhabitants of towns and villages all over the country lament one to another, "Did our sons have to die for *this*? Our daughters become widows? Their children grow up without fathers? And we become old without sons to support us?"

The good people of Anjou and Provence look to their duchess for solace. *What can I do to console and help?* she bemoans to herself. There is no one she can confide in; her only comfort is her three great wolfhounds, who never leave her side.

Not until 1 December 1420 does Henry V of England arrive in Paris to make his official entry. He has come in splendour to claim his lawful spoils from the great English victory at Agincourt. Both Pierre de Brézé and René are in the capital, incognito. Pierre with the order to report to Yolande, René to sense the atmosphere and be in a position to inform not only his mother but his future father-in-law of the true feeling of the Parisians. Then he heads for Provence.

A courier arrives at Tarascon announcing that René is one day's ride away. *The dear boy is coming from Paris to comfort me,* thinks Yolande, and she rejoices. Just the sight of him lifts her spirits. As René is rowed across the narrow neck of the River Rhône opposite the château, she runs to meet him at the steps and embraces him with all the longing and frustration of her missing family life.

"How you have grown, darling son, quite a young man!" *How well he looks, and strong.* His hair is still red, but darker, and she detects the beginnings of a beard. "Welcome home to Tarascon—how long has it been?" she sighs, as they climb the steps arm in arm.

"Maman, dearest—no pleasantries. I must unburden myself to you first with what you want to hear from me, an eyewitness. It will be hard for you to believe when I tell you—so be prepared. But first, I must change and wash."

Now settled in her comfortable sitting room, René takes his mother's hand: "Maman—the Parisians actually welcomed the English king, and with great acclaim!" He looks at her for a reaction, but she merely lowers her eyes—how much more sorrow is there? "I know how this will hurt you, but I saw him with my own eyes as he rode into the city, our dear demented king by his side, together with the triumphant Duke Philippe of Burgundy!"

Now she is indeed in shock. *Are there any more tears left in me for poor France? And what of our rightful dauphin? Who will stand for him except me and my family? Who else can I count onto help me reverse this shameful future for our country?*

Despite all the anguish, it is still bliss to have René at home, chattering like a merry brook. He tells her about life in Bar, and complains mournfully that he has not yet met his future wife, Isabelle. She is still, quite properly thinks Yolande, being kept from him until she has reached puberty. But he is full of colourful descriptions of his hunting expeditions, the countryside, the towns and villages, his horses, his archery, the jousting he has been learning. "Maman, do you know that there are mountains to climb and wild goats and chamois to hunt? I saw lynx and eagle owls, and the forests are plentiful with deer and wild boar," he says enthusiastically.

Jean Dunois, the hero of his childhood, who is stationed at Bourges helping the dauphin with his small army there, has visited René several times and joined him in his adventures in Bar. But his life has not just been about the pleasures of the chase. He tells her of the excellent music and laughter of the court, and of how he himself has taken up painting, under the guidance of the court painter, Mr. van Eyck—even showing her some of his work.

"I have to say, I am impressed. You have a real gift and must pursue it. May I have one of these?" she asks. And in a spontaneous gesture so typical of him, he hands her the lot.

"Maman, my dearest mother, take them all. I find it so difficult to think of ways to bring you pleasure and reward for all you do for us children. Do you *really* like them?" he asks eagerly.

She kisses him in thanks and traces a cross with her finger on his forehead as she always did when they were small, a little private blessing.

"And tell me about my Marie—have you been to Bourges?"

"Oh yes, Maman, several times since I last wrote. Marie is desperate and I try to have her visit me at Nancy to cheer her. But she will not leave Bourges or Charles. Do you think their marriage will ever happen now?" It is a silent worry they share.

"Of course it will, darling! It is only a matter of the right time." But she is not so sure either.

Thereafter, at his mother's request, René divides his time between Anjou and Maine, which he rules for his absent brother Louis, and Lorraine under the guardianship of his future father-in-law, Duke Charles. At other times he is in neighbouring Bar with her cardinal-uncle. Both try their best to educate him for his forthcoming role ruling their duchies. Ensconced in the south, Yolande relies a great deal on René, not only to keep her informed—she has others who do that for her as well—but to be the heart of their family in France.

Stranded, as she sometimes feels, in the south, looking out for Louis' interests, Yolande relies on her correspondence with her children to raise her spirits. René's letters have the power to lift her out of the dullest day. Marie also writes often, although her letters are usually asking for advice and never frivolous as René's can be at times. As for her darling eldest, Louis writes as well, mostly about technical things—landholdings and battle formations, equipment needed for damage caused by his troops or his enemy's. He encloses drawings for the two youngest, Yolande and Charles, who send their own drawings back.

Lonely? Yes, sometimes, although she has her ladies if she wants company and of course her beloved dogs, but it is not the same as having her husband and children sharing her life. If only she had Juana with her to share the silent evenings. When overcome by such moods, Yolande forces herself to remember Marie de Blois and all she had to suffer.

One day, when she has spent hours with the harbourmaster in Marseilles and needs a long bath, she returns to their town palace to find an ecstatic letter from René.

"Maman dearest—at last the day has arrived. Isabelle is here! My first sight of my future bride has me, the so-called bold one of our family, shaking all over. She has come home to Nancy at last and I am in love with her at first sight. She is tall, blonde and slender—like you, Maman; she sings like a nightingale and speaks to me so sweetly and cleverly that I am instantly her slave. Thank you, dearest of mothers, for producing for me, a second son with no great talents and no wealth, not one but two dukedoms. As if that was not enough, you have given me the woman of my dreams!"

And Yolande laughs, and her heart is filled with his happiness.

His next letter is so brief and so typical, it delights her.

"Maman dearest, it has not taken me long to realize that Isabelle is much cleverer than me—no bad thing; it will be her duchy after all, so better if she takes the decisions when the time comes. Your loving son, René."

Chapter Seven

𝓕ollowing the Treaty of Troyes, France has been divided into three zones, all governed separately. Normandy in the north is ruled for the English from Rouen, and many of the Normans find the association with England financially beneficial. Normandy's administrators are French as before, but the defence of the territory is overseen by the English army. However, a number of the Norman noblemen have fled the English and joined the dauphin in his zone in central and southern France, along the Loire and the Cher rivers—at Bourges, Melun and Tours. Charles has become known derisively as the King of Bourges, since the capital of his dukedom of Berry is the seat of his administration, such as it is. The area in the middle of France, between the rivers Somme and Loire, is governed from Paris by the Burgundians, together with their allies the English.

Now that Charles has been disinherited by the Treaty of Troyes, he has only his income from his sovereign territory of Berry to finance his small court. Other than that Charles has only the support of his *bonne mère* to provide for him and his needs. Yolande regards this as her duty, and she does it willingly, even at the expense of her own children. She has explained to them that this was their father's instruction to her before his death, and, brought up to be obedient and loyal, they accept her decision without a murmur.

With the English in such a powerful position, the Duke of Lorraine and the Queen of Sicily decide that for their own security and that of their territories, their children Isabelle and René should marry at once. The wedding takes place on 24 October 1420 at Nancy. Isabelle, who is nearly twelve, and René, almost fourteen, are married by his uncle, the Duke of Bar. By this union, the duchies of Bar and Lorraine are now officially joined, creating a considerable barrier for the potential aggression of Philippe of Burgundy and his English allies.

Yolande is heartbroken not to be able to travel to Lorraine in time, nor can Marie leave Bourges, but Yolande advises René to take Isabelle to visit his sister soon after the wedding. As long as the Duke of Lorraine lives, René is not yet obliged to stay put there, and Yolande wants Marie to remain a stabilizing presence for Charles in Bourges.

René understands, and writes to his mother a few days later:

Dearest Maman,

You have asked me for a full description of my wedding, and I will do my best to tell you how lovely my Isabelle looked—and will forever afterwards. Her hair hung loose below her shoulders with a circlet of small diamonds holding a fine golden gossamer veil on her head, a translucent covering that trailed behind her. Her dress was of smooth cream damask with a high, wide neckline, long in the waist before sweeping back with fullness into a train. Around her waist, hanging low in front from her hips, she wore a delicate but wide girdle of gold thread, and I caught the occasional flash of small diamonds. When I saw her enter the church, I had to remember to breathe, because her loveliness stopped my heart from beating.

I do not recall much of the service—I was so overwhelmed that this divine creature, this gentle young lady, was to be my wife that I prayed for—I think—the first time in my life, *really* prayed, and thanked the Lord and you, my dearest mother, for such a great gift.

Before the wedding Yolande wrote to Isabelle's mother, but it was the duke who replied. They both decided that the young couple, who must marry now for the sake of uniting their respective dukedoms, should not share a bed for at least another year, since Isabelle has only just reached puberty.

René comments to his mother when he hears their terms:

"Looking at her on our wedding day, I hope the year will pass quickly."

Throughout the spring and summer of 1421 following the fateful Treaty of Troyes, Charles is active, appearing in full armour at the head of his troops, projecting an image of his position as dauphin despite his being disinherited by the treaty. He is often seen by the common people riding on the road surrounded by an impressive entourage decked out in his livery colours—white, red and blue—as he moves at a fast pace between his towns, drumming up support wherever he can. Flying his banners, with his device of an armoured hand grasping a naked sword and another of St. Michael slaying a serpent, his troops give a convincing impression of legitimate and prestigious authority.

On the instructions of the Queen of Sicily, Jean de Dunois accompanies the dauphin whenever necessary; he is the ideal older childhood friend, a wise head and protector. At her request, Jean goes with Charles on a visit to one of his further cities, La Rochelle, in the north on the coast. Not long afterwards, a courier arrives with an urgent letter for Yolande from young Dunois, full of concern, to say that he is accompanying the dauphin back to Bourges and must come on at once to give her, in person, an account of an event that occurred in La Rochelle.

The sun is shining when Jean Dunois arrives at Tarascon a few days after his message. Yolande is about to suggest they sit outside under one of the great trees in her courtyard when she notices how muddy he is. He must have ridden hard and without much sleep to reach her so quickly. Usually guests stop at a nearby tavern just before reaching the castle to prepare themselves for their arrival. How he has grown, and into such a fine young man, she thinks, as he enters the Great Hall, the scene of so many childhood romps, of visits from troubadours and minstrels that she wants to reminisce with him about—but his face, showing deep anxiety, stops her.

After he bows to her in greeting, she sends him to wash and change while food and drink are sent upstairs so that they can talk in private.

Jean returns, his stained travelling coat removed and his muddy boots and trousers changed; his hair is brushed and his face and hands washed. She thinks to herself how young he looks. "Now I can embrace you," she says, and does, but she feels his unease like a coiled spring.

"Come sit with me," she continues as warmly as she can, to relax him a little, as he enters her favourite room, the little yellow sitting room between her bedroom and what was Louis' on the other side. The *levrettes* lie in heaps all over the crimson velvet cushions and grunt resentfully as they are pushed aside to make room. The sun is streaming in through the window and onto the carpet and fur pelts on the floor, and Yolande's mind slips back to all the mad frolics she has had here with her growing young family.

"Jean dear," she begins, "do forgive me for looking on you as one of my children, although I see before me a tall and mature young man." Still he does not smile, so she knows his news is grave, though eventually he does sit. She tosses some rosemary onto the fire as her people bring in food and drink. He waits until they have left, then, taking a deep breath, he says quickly:

"Madame, dear Madame, I come in haste because I must inform you of something crucial that may have badly affected the dauphin." He has no time for small talk; it must be serious. "A week ago, I travelled to La Rochelle, at your request, to attend Prince Charles. Madame... there was a terrible accident there."

She stops eating her own cake and puts it down on the plate carefully. Something is badly wrong.

"I know you are aware—or I think you know—that ever since his proximity to the horrifying sight of the bloodshed at the massacre of Montereau, the dauphin has had a terror of wooden bridges. Now his experience at La Rochelle has left him badly shaken—and swearing that he will never again appear in a crowded room!"

Yolande moves herself nearer to her young friend on the long, deep cushions, and takes his trembling hand in hers.

"Jean, my dear, tell me calmly exactly what happened," she says, trying to ease his tautly controlled agitation. Again he takes a deep breath, and looking at the floor, he begins:

"The dauphin and I... we arrived with his entourage at La Rochelle... to a splendid reception from the citizens." He is calming down, she notices. "They had turned out in great numbers to cheer and wave, girls tossing flowers before our cavalcade. Madame, you cannot imagine his grateful reaction to the crowds. His face brightened, and he turned to me in surprise, half smiling, with a question in his eyes, as if to say, 'What have I done to deserve this?' With each cheer it seemed as if his confidence grew. I was happy for him—for his welcome and his joy in it.

"His arrival had put him in high spirits, and during dinner he told me with merry expectation how he would dress for the great occasion the next day when La Rochelle's leading citizens would be presented to him in their town hall. He planned to wear a wine-red velvet tunic, with his great gold chain of office hanging on his chest, matching red stockings and shoes. On his head, a black velvet beret—and a brooch of pearls and diamonds to secure a large white plume. He brought this out later to show me, and tried it on my head, and then on his at different angles, laughing all the while. We joked about the feather: whether it would bob down over his nose, or should he turn it away from his face and risk it tickling his ear? Would it be squashed behind him if he leant back on his throne, and so on." More tension now from Jean, as his breathing becomes faster.

"The next morning, we entered the hall, and the dauphin walked slowly and with dignity towards his high chair of office.

This had been placed in the middle, up against the wall at the end of the room. As he took his seat, I bowed and backed away to join his guards under a stone archway on the side, not far from the throne, for a good view.

"From the doorway, I watched as the room filled with more and more local courtiers, all dressed elegantly, obviously in their best, looking solemn and dutiful, almost gaping in admiration at their dauphin, until the large room was packed and no space left at all. I was searching their faces when I became aware of a low groaning noise, as if the very walls were murmuring." He takes another gulp of wine as if his mouth has dried up.

"Other people must have heard it and began to look around, their faces curious, expectant, apprehensive. Very slowly the noise grew until it became a roar, and in an instant the entire floor of the assembly room collapsed under the citizens' weight, and crashed down to the level below!" He stops, lost for breath. Her eyes are wide and she too is lost for breath.

"One of the guards near me rushed towards the dauphin and fell with the company; the other pulled me roughly back under the stone archway as we stared in horror at the scene below— and at the dauphin."

Yolande sits, her mouth open, as if turned to stone.

"Madame, he was still there, sitting in his chair that had been fixed to the wall! Charles was suspended in space, legs dangling, while the whole room full of people had gone—disappeared— in a great crash of masonry, timbers, terrible screams and moans beneath a thick grey cloud of dust. The cries of pain, howling, shouting, the pitiful wailing—and just the dauphin left sitting frozen on his throne attached firmly to the wall. His face was white, eyes wide and blank, mouth tight shut, and his hands clenched on the arms of his chair. I could not take my eyes off him. His features were twisted in terror as he looked down on the broken, tangled bodies below him, many dead and others seriously injured, only partly visible among the broken timber and stone, some screaming, crying or moaning for help—and he unable to move." Jean Dunois quaffs again from the tumbler of wine before him. Now that the story is out, he seems a little more in control.

"Go on, please," she says, as calmly as she can.

"Soldiers came quickly and brought beams to make a bridge to the dauphin, who at first would not let go of the chair. I went to him and, talking softly, gently eased his fingers free. Then, walking backwards on the beams, holding both his hands, I led him to safety. He told me later that he had hardly dared to breathe and almost fainted with fear. Madame, believe me, so did I."

His hands are cold as ice, and she holds them in hers. Dear Jean, as beautiful as his father and as appealing—and now this terrible incident, after she has placed Charles in his care, has shaken him badly, as if he is to blame somehow.

"It is not a sight I will ever forget, nor, I am sure, will the dauphin," he whispers. "Nor will anyone who survived it. There were so many dead, many others terribly wounded. I saw limbs that had been wrenched off, even some heads. I left the dauphin with his escort to rest and went back to the scene to try to help lift some of the debris covering the dead and wounded. The townswomen brought bandages and splints, but many people were crushed, broken beyond hope, and would surely die, their relatives crying out to the Lord to help them. Several priests and nuns moved among the dead and wounded—no one in that room was left unscathed except the dauphin and me and the soldiers waiting outside. Madame, I came as quickly as I could, as I know you would want to hear the news directly from me."

Of course, Jean is right. Charles has such a superstitious nature, and he will imagine some deserved punishment from God, or that evil omens were involved in this terrible accident. She hopes the story of the "Ball of the Burning Men" will not come back to haunt him—another occasion where innocent lives were lost while trying to please the king.

The events at La Rochelle affect the dauphin badly. He is tortured by his inability to help his stricken subjects, all come in good faith to receive him, as he sat, hanging on the wall, frozen with terror, afraid that the great chair to which he clung would come away from its hinges, crashing down with him on top of the others, causing more injury and pain. Only now does the full implication of the Treaty of Troyes overwhelm him. He went to the city with such optimism, and even there, fate seemed to be against him.

Chapter Eight

Lost and alone, Charles retires to Amboise in the Loire valley to spend his time with the distractions of the court, rather than travelling the country to inspire support. But worrying reports reach Yolande about the nature of these distractions as if seeking licentiousness and oblivion in equal measure.

My poor darling Marie, thinks her mother as she hears this. But can it be true? She knows that courts are often a hotbed of rumour, and there are many who wish the dauphin ill. It is therefore time to draw on those people she knows she can trust. With a heavy heart, because she knows how much he will hate the conversation, she approaches Jean Dunois on his next visit.

"Jean, you have been our dear friend since your boyhood. I am now going to ask you something, and on the strength of the love that you know I have always shown you, I insist you tell me the truth." There is a long pause as their eyes lock. "No matter how bad it is, you must tell me what goes on among Charles's inner circle at his court." She sees Jean blush and look uncomfortable, but then he pulls himself together.

"Madame, it is true, you have known me since childhood and you have always treated me with great generosity. I have seen you do the same for the dauphin Charles, and we and your children are all of the same blood. It is for the sake of our family, the royal blood we share, that I will agree to tell you what I know. I do this for the future of our monarchy, the future of France, and out of my loyalty to you, since I know that only you are able to put an end to our dauphin's decline. But I ask you to understand that because of my respect and love for you, it is painful for me—and shameful as well."

Yolande looks at him and notes his expression—ever more like his father, Louis d'Orléans, the same look. It is said that bastards take strongly after their real fathers, and in his case, that is certainly true.

"Don't be ashamed, my dear young friend. You and I both know it is imperative that we help Charles. Tell me what you know, so that I can try to save him from his demons."

"Madame, Charles's principal favourite is a man of low morals named Pierre de Giac."

She nods. "Yes, I have heard of him in connection with Montereau."

"Madame, have you heard anyone speak of the Pages' House? No? It is not far from the royal château of Amboise on the Loire. Giac was the prime mover in setting it up as Charles's Pleasure House and it is the scene of much of the dauphin's recent dissipation. He has had a small road built from the château that winds its way around to this, his pleasure house, his folly. The house itself faces down upon the Loire in a charming situation. Charles likes to retire there in the evenings with his group of intimates, and there they meet with hired boy and girl prostitutes." Jean looks at the floor. "Go on" is all Yolande says, stitching at her embroidery and not meeting his eyes.

"I have once been a guest there, and René has urged mesince to describe it to you, but I could not, until your insistence now. We both agree you should be aware of the full extent of what goes on in the life of our dauphin, since we believe only you have the power to end it. But until now, I lacked the courage." He says with shame. Yolande gets up to fill his glass, giving him time to compose himself.

Jean Dunois looks very uncomfortable, but he hardens his jaw and, taking a deep breath, begins:

"On the night I went there, I had no idea there would be anything other than a dinner and perhaps some musical entertainment. I was brought into a luxuriously decorated salon with about thirty other young people there—mostly my age, some I recognized, including Pierre de Giac—surrounding what I guessed was a narrow table. As I approached to greet the dauphin, he put his arm around my shoulders and said jovially, "Ah! Welcome, my dear cousin Jean, I have a novel entertainment for you." And he led me through the grinning crowd to the table, on which I saw a young girl of about ten or twelve years, lying on her back and smiling happily. Her naked body was thickly covered with sweet creams. At this point, the dauphin gave a signal, at which six of the company, not all male, proceeded with much mirth and ribaldry to eat from her body, using just their tongues as their hands had been tied behind their backs."

Jean seems stuck for words and cannot look at her when she hands him a goblet of water.

"The girl did not complain, but seemed to be enjoying this as well. I heard a number of the guests beginning to place bets as to who would have the final treat.... Madame, I was so repelled that I left without a word to the dauphin. Later I learned that similar events take place there regularly, with variations: two teams with pairs of girls, or boys, on two tables, head to toe, with prizes for the fastest—and the prize is usually one or more of the girls or boys, to be enjoyed in full view of the company..." His voice fades away and his face is red with embarrassment.

"Madame, I apologize for telling you about these events, but they must be stopped, and René insisted you know," he says for the second time. "I believe that such behaviour, which I hear is not uncommon at the dauphin's court, will ruin all we have worked so hard to achieve. Servants talk, and soon this information will reach the ears of the powerful dukes we have succeeded in enrolling into our cause on behalf of the dauphin." Poor Jean, shaking with embarrassment, cannot wait to leave.

It is shocking, but there is no time to be shocked; it is repellent, but there is no time to be repelled. Yolande withdraws into herself with her new-found unwelcome knowledge and deliberates on what to do. Soon her objectives become clear. She must find a way to remove the abysmal influences surrounding the dauphin and encourage the good ones to return and replace the others. Above all, she must as ever find a way to unite the warring dukes. She has never severed her contact with Philippe of Burgundy and arranges several secret meetings with him. As always, he is measured and calm, but implacable. He too has kept dialogue open with Charles but he has maintained the same conditions since the murder of his father: as long as the plotters of Montereau are still at liberty, safe in the dauphin's sovereign territory of Berry, or outside the jurisdiction of parlement in other sovereign duchies, Philippe can never contemplate uniting his forces with the dauphin.

And now the situation has become urgent. Henry V of England is on the doorstep once again, and this time he lets it be known that his intention is a complete conquest of France. His forces are formidable—far more so than ever before. Happily, a good number of the counsellors Yolande has placed around Charles are sound and able. But how can her excellent captains succeed in battle when they see that their dauphin, for whom they risk their lives, is a victim of venal and avaricious courtiers? How can they respect him as their future king when they hear of these orgies in his private apartments? And as long as Charles is surrounded by the intriguers of Montereau, and allows them to remain safe within his sovereign duchy of Berry and behave as they do at his court in Bourges, there is no chance of rapprochement with Philippe of Burgundy—the only hope of freeing France from the English.

Disregarding for a moment her problems with Charles, Yolande must alert her sons to their duty. She sends a courier with some strong words to René to drag him out of his happy reverie of the newlywed:

"My beloved son, Henry V is coming to claim not only the north of France but our entire country, our way of life, our nation. Since you were a small boy you have been practising for this moment, and now you must fight to defend our lands in France. Although you are young, I know your mettle, for it was forged by the love shared between your father and me. Your father was a warrior prince. Now I ask you to be one as well—like your father, and his father before him. Like my father of Aragon, and his father before him. In your veins flows the blood of heroes; the time has come to live up to their heritage, to fight with your king against the invader, the thief of his just throne."

She can read René's mind even from the distance of Provence. *Yes*, he will be thinking, *this is what I have always wanted to do. No longer a wooden sword, now it will be real war!* And Isabelle will support him, of that she is sure. She knows that war is still some kind of gallant medieval tournament to René, despite Agincourt. This is not a game, however; this is dangerous, and on its conclusion rests all their futures. He must understand this... France is in mortal peril.

René's reply has come by return. He must have made the courier wait while he wrote:

Madame, dearest Mother, of course I am ready to do the king's bidding, and yours, though I hate to leave my darling Isabelle. But I will be the warrior prince you want me to be! I will not fail you, nor my father or yours, and theirs before them. I have heard nothing here in distant Lorraine of King Henry's arrival, but I will make for Bourges and join the king's army. I will tell Isabelle at once.

She has to laugh at his next letter, which follows on the heels of the last—how he keeps the couriers busy!

Maman—I asked Isabelle if she would mind if I left her at home and joined Charles and the royal army at Bourges. She would miss me, of that I am sure—we are inseparable. But I planned to tell her that when summoned to halt the advance of the English king, I must go. She saw my face as I approached her:

"What is it?" she asked me. "You look so odd—a mixture of joy and misery with tears in your eyes but with an ecstatic smile." And all I could answer was:

"It's war dearest; King Henry has landed in France. I must go and defend our country." Again she gave me a peculiar look.

"What are you talking about?" she replied—rather crossly I thought.

"When the king summons his vassals, I must go join the army in Bourges," I blurted out. And then I could see her lip trembling as she said:

"But not yet, we're not at war yet, are we?" And I held her, this delightful, funny, slip of a girl who I have come to love so dearly I would die for her. "I don't want you to die for me," she cried—Maman, she can read my thoughts, I have said it so often—"I want you to live and be here with me in my beautiful Lorraine, where we can walk in the forests and climb the mountains and hunt the game and, and..." She dried up, tears rolling down her pretty face, and her shoulders shaking with sobs. It was then that I knew she loved me and I am torn in half—my love and my duty. Duty won—as we both know it would, and I leave tomorrow to join the Angevin army in Bourges. My father-in-law knows I will wear the colours of Anjou proclaiming my allegiance to the king and he understands. He just said: "Well, see you make me a grandfather before you get yourself killed," and embraced me.

Ah! My son—what a delight he is. Dear God, may he be kept safe.

Then, to Yolande's horror, she hears that the Duke of Clarence craves her own lands for himself. Disregarding her treaty with the king, he is leading an army of seven thousand towards Anjou. Far away in Provence as she is, and constrained by her position and sex, she can feel the warrior's blood of her ancestors rising in her at the prospect of an assault on the heart of her husband's lands. All she can do is write to the dauphin beseeching his help while praying for Rene's victory and safe return.

The couriers ride off, and no answer comes from the

dauphin. Her beautiful palace at Tarascon, flooded with the sunshine of the south, begins to feel like a prison. Day after day she waits for news, until finally couriers begin to arrive and she can piece together what has happened. Despite being badly outnumbered, the Angevins did not disappoint, loyally gathering around one of her own senior officers to lead them. Then, just when the battle looked to be turning in favour of the English, reinforcements arrived—sent by the dauphin himself! Not only the Maréchal de La Fayette, but with him a terrifying band of some four thousand Scots soldiers! So Charles *did* receive her urgent messages, and acted. Thank God. The Scots had not long landed at La Rochelle, and were headed by their fearsome leader, Lord Buchan. René was there too, riding proudly with the Angevin army, by then swollen to some six thousand mounted men and foot soldiers.

Battle was joined at Baugé. The English, led by the Duke of Clarence, were slowed down by having to ford a wide, fast river. The French archers began to pick off the English in the water, one by one, giving their soldiers the time to arrange themselves in battle formation. And René, it seems, was in the thick of it, charging with the others, slashing to the left and right, "without," he writes, "any thought in my head, as if my actions were laid down by years of practising for this moment, or by the heroes in my ancestry you told us about as children!"

She is proud to hear how her son has proved himself in battle, as has her Angevin army joined by the dauphin's and the Scots. The French are hailing this victory in the same light as the English conquest at Agincourt, although the numbers were far smaller. Two thousand English killed, including Clarence himself, with far fewer casualties among the French and Scots.

Following this victory the dauphin heads for Chartres with an army of eighteen thousand men, a proud René invited to ride with him in his own party.

Chapter Nine

The news of a son born to Catherine, the dauphin's sister and King Henry V of England's queen, has at last prompted the wedding ceremony between the dauphin and Marie d'Anjou. The Queen of Sicily decides their union should be solemnized at her city of Tours in Anjou on 2 June 1422, and that she will leave Provence to be present at the ceremony. Charles is nineteen, Marie eighteen, and they have been betrothed for the past nine years—the same long engagement Yolande had with Marie's father. But her daughter has known her future husband all this time, while Yolande's Louis was a miraculous surprise. Sadly, that will not be the case for her darling Marie.

In Tours, the Queen of Sicily has prepared as much as she can with her excellent staff from Angers, led by Carlo, Hubert and Vincenzo, who have been working for weeks. When the bridal couple arrive from Bourges some days before most of the guests, it gladdens her heart to see what good friends they are, chatting and joking together. Charles is surrounded by his courtiers, leaving Yolande and Marie time to discuss her trousseau and the wedding dress.

"Maman, of course I want to look elegant, but not *too* elegant—you know it's not my style. Anyway, no woman alive can look as elegant as you!" Marie is sweet, but sadly still no beauty. Yolande concocts a headdress that she think will do more for her face than most, with a high collar of gauze on the neckline to fill her out a little.

The arrival of Isabelle and René delights everyone, especially Yolande. René has been granted leave by Charles himself, and she knows he has done this to please her, for which she is grateful. It is the first time she has met René's Isabelle, and she is instantly impressed, noting her calm as well as her beauty. Her older children are pleased to see the younger two; Yolande is now ten and Charles eight. They were both tiny when they went south to Provence, and the occasion turns into a happy family reunion. Only her shining eldest, Louis, is missing.

A number of the French dukes come to Tours for the ceremony, and many dignitaries arrive from Bourges to support the dauphin. Yolande has even dared to send an invitation to Philippe of Burgundy; although she doubts very much he will come, at least it shows her public desire for reconciliation. There is a large contingent from Anjou and also from Provence: graceful ladies, prancing horses with elegant riders, young girls from the city scattering flower petals and herbs in front of them, the local people leaning out of their windows unfurling coloured ribbons. The gardens along the processional route are bursting with June flowers, and climbing roses cling to every wall.

The wedding day sees the month of June at its best, and the ceremony is as splendid as the Queen of Sicily can devise. Spring flowers decorate the soaring cathedral built in the flamboyantly pointed Frankish style, and the scent of the many lilies and narcissi lining the aisles is heady and delicious. Marie's dress is of silver brocade, her hair caught up in a golden veil brought forward around her face, and she glitters in her mother's jewels. Her daughter will grow to be handsome rather than beautiful, Yolande thinks, but she is intelligent and cultivated, and has marked her little court at Bourges with a distinctive polish.

Charles, too, wears silver brocade, at his throat the great emerald brooch inherited from Jean of Berry. He looks cheerful enough as he enters the cathedral, walking alone and bowing to right and left. Marie waits for him to reach his place near the altar before making her entrance. She is escorted by her *demoiselles*, each a daughter from a great house, delicately pretty in their pastel dresses of lilac, pale blue, and shades of pink. To her mother's pleasure, Marie has placed her enchanting cousin and friend, Veronique de Valois, in the lead as her chief maid of honour.

When bride and groom stand together before the altar, the silver trumpets in the gallery blast their celebratory clarion call. The congregation rises for the entry of the bishop who will conduct the service. Seeing the way Charles and Marie smile at one another gives Yolande hope for this marriage after all, and she knows Marie will do her duty as she has been taught. She keeps reminding herself: *They are friends, it will be a success—* and she prays sincerely for that.

Everyone is in a jubilant mood—this wedding has been so long awaited that it almost comes as a relief. After three days of merrymaking, the bride and groom leave for Bourges with Yolande's blessing on them both, while she returns to Tarascon with Juana and her young ones, who loved every minute.

Chapter Ten

Yolande's agent has arrived at Tarascon, eager to impart his news: "Madame, when King Henry V realized he was dying"—she is aghast: *dying?*—"he made his last wishes clear to the Duke of Bedford: his young son is to succeed to the throne of England and of France on the death of our King Charles VI; his youngest brother, the Duke of Gloucester, is to be the regent in England; and the Duke of Burgundy is to be offered the regency of France!"

Yolande is speechless. Burgundy to be France's regent! *He will find a way to move up the final step to the throne once his cousin the king is dead, of this I am sure.*

Her agent continues: "Should Burgundy decline, Bedford is to continue to be regent until Henry V's heir comes of age."

This sudden change in their fortunes has left her more anxious than ever before. Some weeks later, on 21 October, comes another dramatic surprise: France's own dear, mad king, Charles VI, follows his English nemesis to his maker. He dies in the arms of the beloved mistress Yolande found for him, his last words a whispered "Odette, Odette."

Yolande has not seen Charles VI for some years now and always thinks of him as he was when she met him on her first visit to Paris—her wedding journey—a handsome man and so like her own dearest Louis. Those kind eyes—the colour of the sapphire ring he gave her—smiling into her own, telling her that if she wore it, she would always have access to him if she needed. How glad she is that Odette de Champdivers has been there to comfort him and make his last years easier. And the poor queen, confined to a manor in the English-controlled part of Paris, no longer exercising any influence on court affairs and, by all accounts, lacking all interest. They say she has become so obese she can hardly move her vast bulk from her bed, and keeps her shutters closed with almost no light in her room. And no mirrors. Odette writes that Isabeau has shown no interest in her husband's death.

Both kings dead! If only she had her dear Louis with her to counsel the dauphin, the new King of France—or is he?

The Duke of Burgundy has rejected the English offer to become regent. Of course! He would far rather be king. The Duke of Bedford, as regent of France once again, accompanied his brother's coffin to England for burial in Westminster Abbey. When he heard of the death of Charles VI, he promptly turned back for the funeral of the French king— but more importantly, to claim the throne for his nephew, the baby Henry VI of England.

Already on the road, a fast courier meets Yolande with a letter from Pierre de Brézé in Paris: "Madame, I beseech you, hurry to Bourges." She must join Charles and see that he takes the necessary steps to mount the throne of France. This is the dauphin's moment and it must not be lost.

The Queen of Sicily arrives in Bourges in the golden glow of early autumn. When her party reaches the outskirts of the city, she is instantly aware of an air of expectancy, of bustle, everyone in a hurry, everyone busy; people arriving, tradesmen, carriages, as well as mounted visitors in attire that ranges from the fashionable to the homespun. The streets seem much more crowded than usual and there is a distinct buzz, an effervescence, in the air. But what this effervescence means, good or bad, as yet she cannot tell.

Her first stop is with Marie at the royal palace. She embraces her, then René, who has also hurried to Bourges with Isabelle from Nancy. But they are not there to rejoice—each of them knows what the death of the two kings means for the dauphin. Henry V's death was surely an act of God in their favour—at the least, an act of justice. Their own king's death has Marie, René and Yolande sharing the same thought: a ten-month-old baby king in England cannot inspire the French nation. And France has a twenty-year-old dauphin waiting in the wings, a dauphin who is, by tradition, now the legitimate King of France—at least in the eyes of many.

"Where is Charles?" Yolande asks, but apart from being with his entourage, no one seems to know.

Suddenly, there he stands before them, the new King Charles VII. As he enters, they embrace, and Yolande traces the sign of the cross on his forehead with her right thumb—just as she would to her son—before making him a deep reverence. Charles bursts into tears, then composes himself somewhat and turns to face her.

"*Bonne mère,* does this mean I am now the lawful King of France? Or will the English crown my tiny nephew of England in my place?" His eyes are wide and red; how she feels his anguish. Without hesitating, she makes another slow, deep curtsey, and bows her head before rising to reply:

"Sire, yes, you are now the lawful king. The English will try to crown your nephew, but we shall have the country behind your legitimate claim, I promise." She knows she is promising what she cannot deliver, but she is determined that this prince will come into his rightful inheritance. Then tears appear in his eyes once more, and he weeps: for his father, for himself, his country and his uncertain future.

Yolande sends out several of her trusted Angevins, who have awaited her arrival, to test the mood of the people. Unsurprisingly, the word she receives back from the streets—her intelligence-gatherers are efficient—is that the people of Berry, and certainly of its capital, Bourges, would be far more willing to accept Charles as their king than an English baby prince. Marie, René and Yolande stress this to Charles, to reassure him as much as possible, but his eyes are vacant and hesitant. That wretched Treaty of Troyes hangs over him and drains his confidence still.

Yolande dispatches one of her Angevins to try to find Jacques Coeur—he may know the feeling of the country from his many agents. The messenger returns with a note:

"Madame and Majesty, with sincere apologies, I beg you to understand when I request that you come to my office for a private meeting. It would be better for you and especially for your son-in-law if I am not seen together with your family at this time."

Yolande hurries through the narrow backstreets of Bourges, winding her way between the many delivery carts. She goes on foot and heavily veiled, accompanied by twelve of her best men wearing disguise so as not to draw attention. On arrival at Jacques Coeur's office, they check the interior and see that it is safe—only his four impressive giant Moors stand guard in the corners of the room, their black, muscled arms glistening; shiny, curved scimitars at their waists. She has warned her men not to be afraid, but they seem happier to wait for her outside.

Jacques Coeur receives her with his usual courtesy, hand on heart and a dignified bow.

"Madame, I beseech your forgiveness for this secrecy, but in view of the dauphin's presence in the town, the Duke of Bedford's agents are everywhere and the English are anxious that he will succeed in declaring his right to the throne."

"And what do you think, Jacques, my friend. Should he announce himself as King Charles VII?" she asks earnestly, pushing back her veil. "I see you hesitate; I give you my word, this conversation between us will remain just that. You have agents all over the country—I need to know your instinct when you have so many informants."

"Madame—you know you have my trust and I have yours.

Yes, I think the new king should announce himself as the rightful heir of his father, but it will not be easy to dislodge the English. The Duke of Bedford has been a fair and good regent during the lifetime of both the late kings, French and English, and there is nothing to say he will not continue in the same way. Whereas our new King Charles is still an unknown quantity and some of his actions do not speak well for him, not least his reputation for—excuse me—debauchery."

She knows he is telling her the cold facts; she cannot dispute them. She thanks him as she makes to leave, and he bows. As he straightens, he looks into her eyes and says: "Madame and Majesty, you know you can count on me always to do your bidding. Know too that I will support the new King Charles VII in any way I am able." He bows again and she leaves, confident in the allegiance of this able man.

Weaving around carts and small children, holding her veil close to her face and over her nose, the Queen of Sicily makes her way back to the palace. More of their loyal people are gathered there—Jean Dunois has joined René and Charles, and a number of her Angevins wait in another room, Tanneguy du Chastel and Arnaud de Barbazan among them. Jean Dunois has news from Paris.

"Madame, you will be pleased to hear that very few French accompanied the funeral cortège of the English king to Paris and onto the coast, but huge crowds turned out for our own King Charles VI's funeral journey to Notre-Dame. Vast numbers of people gathered and cried out their desperation that such a good king should leave them! An even larger crowd accompanied the cortège from the service in Notre-Dame onto his royal resting place at Saint-Denis. I estimate the crowd at around eighteen thousand."

This is good news at last—and a surprise that in spite of his illness, the French still loved their once-so-promising king.

Jean Dunois has more to add, though: "At the end of the ceremony in the crypt of Saint-Denis, the heralds announced the new reign of King Henry VI of France and England, shouting with one voice, "Long live the king! Long live the king!" The assembly, who were all hand-picked supporters of the English, shouted: "Noël!" in the traditional salutation, but I could detect little enthusiasm from the crowds in the streets of Paris, and that despite the Duke of Bedford's personal popularity."

And yet Yolande still wonders how many will leave the court at Bourges calculating they can win more favours in the Duke of Bedford's retinue.

In the early afternoon, she walks with a sombre Charles, wearing a coat of royal mourning, into Bourges' soaring cathedral, followed by Marie and René also in black, and then by Isabelle and Jean Dunois, all of them heavily guarded by Angevin soldiers wary of an assassination attempt. The royal family have come to attend a full Requiem Mass for the soul of the late King Charles VI. Yolande wears formal black velvet robes, pearls and her crown as Queen of Sicily, in this way endorsing Charles's claim as the legitimate King of France. The cathedral is ablaze with candles and heady with incense; tall branches of red and gold autumn leaves serve instead of flowers. At the end of the service, and the moving tribute to the late king by the archbishop, Charles leads Yolande and Marie from the cathedral, one on either side of him, as a glorious "Te Deum" is sung by the choir beneath the tall vaulted arches.

For the first time, Yolande can see something of kingship in Charles. How well he carries himself on this momentous day. They halt on the cathedral steps, Marie and her mother standing a little behind Charles and to either side, as he faces a huge crowd. In his fine, strong voice, then and there he declares himself King of France, and here, too, the heralds proclaim with one voice: "Long live the king! Long live the king!" blowing hard on two dozen silver trumpets. They are all deeply moved, although inwardly each of them is unsure whether Charles's monarchy will ever be established, even though it is his birthright.

Charles is gambling on the support at least of the people of his duchy of Berry, and that, to judge from their cheering—myriad hats thrown into the air as he salutes them—he has. But as for the country, he cannot know. The only thing he can claim by right is that in the established custom of France, the dauphin inherits the throne of his father the king. For the English to challenge his claim is to be expected, but Yolande is assured by her agents that a significant part of France recognizes the son of the late Charles VI as his legitimate heir.

Chapter Eleven

*B*ut a fine ceremony is not enough to make a king. Yolande is soon aware and with growing dismay that Charles takes little day-to-day interest in governing the country. The only person she can tackle about this is Marie, who bursts out immediately:

"Maman, he has little confidence that he will ever be king. His only trust," she says with tears threatening to fall, "is in you, as I have no power to sway him one way or the other."

"But at least he confides in you and talks to you, doesn't he? You tell me in your letters how he pours out his frustrations, but am I to understand he does not seek your advice?"

"Maman dearest, you often ask me to have him do this or that—but you must understand, I have *no influence* on him whatsoever, although he never fails in his kindness to me," she says in a tone of real regret, turning away from Yolande's look of concern. "My main function in the life of my husband is that of a pillow to cry on and to conceive his heirs."

And Yolande holds her darling daughter close, willing her strength of spirit into her.

She contemplates her son-in-law, this new King Charles. He is not a warrior prince, never warlike by temperament; no, he has learnt other ways of winning over opponents to his cause. He has a pleasing manner of speech and his deep, resonant voice can be quite captivating. He is a good listener, and when he replies, always politely, with reasoned and logical arguments, they often succeed. He speaks well and with conviction, and uses understated flattery to turn the minds and hearts of men to his own ends.

When in council, and also at court, he has become more ingenuous in his discussions, to the point of deviousness. He never pontificates; he asks advice constantly, but she knows him well enough to be sure he has no intention of following what he is told. Yes, he disappoints her at times, but she knows instinctively that his manoeuvrings are a part of his desperate plan for survival. Although he makes light of his troubles, she is convinced Charles is very aware of the tightrope he walks daily, and of all the forces ranged against him.

After her absence of four years in the south, his *bonne mère* can see the physical change in Charles, and for the better. At twenty, the young king is rather slim, small and dark, like his mother, Queen Isabeau, was said to be in her youth. His upper body has developed to that of a larger man, and he covers his knock knees and spindly legs with unfashionably long tunics, hanging down to mid-calf, although the current style is for short tight jackets over hose. His posture is straight—he holds himself well and proudly, and he definitely has presence. His eyes are not large, but dark and intelligent, his nose long, his mouth sensual. His deep knowledge of the New and Old Testaments and the Acts of the Apostles surprises many. He values solitude and country life, and as well as attending Mass, he says his Hours each day, and confesses his sins regularly. His appetite is small; he eats and drinks very little. He does not like to see too many unfamiliar faces around him and cannot abide strangers. Overall, the impression he gives is of a sensitive, clever, noticeably cautious young man. And, she thinks, with good cause, considering the upheavals of his childhood.

And yet, and yet... knowing his weaknesses, she can see that many of the courtiers do all they can to manipulate Charles for their own advantage. Favourites succeed one another in rapid succession, while he remains blind to their scheming. Since he has little faith in ruling, it saddens Yolande to see him succumb to most of the temptations put before him.

One of these contemptibles is Georges de la Trémoille. Born into a grand aristocratic family, he is cultured and charismatic, connected to all the great families of France and superior to the other favourites who have manipulated Charles to date. Although he was a former ally of the Duke of Burgundy, even then he saw that reconciliation between the late King Charles VI and the Burgundians was the sole means of defeating the English. This has always been Yolande's clear aim as well, but without the assistance of this greedy brute, who has made himself the richest landlord in the country.

The Queen of Sicily discovers that the immediate goal of La Trémoille is to rid the court of one of her protégés, Arthur of Richemont, the excellent younger brother of the Duke of Brittany, who fought with distinction at Agincourt. To her astonishment, she hears from Pierre de Brézé that La Trémoille has publicly raised with the king the subject of her own truce with the King of England and the Duke of Brittany, agreed years ago to protect her territories. This truce was instigated by the Queen of Sicily *to protect her territories* and made with the late king's sanction. It was Yolande who suggested to her neighbour of Brittany that he do the same!

"Madame," Pierre informs her, "La Trémoille referred to it as an act of treachery, and pointed the finger at Arthur of Richemont as the prime mover."

"If this is so, then why has no complaint, or even mention, been made by La Trémoille to Charles VII of my having done the same, and with his father's sanction! It is becoming clear to me that the young king is already under the spell of his new favourite!" No sooner said than she hears to her consternation that Charles has banished the good Richemont from the court.

During her absence over the past four years, these powerful lords, La Trémoille and Richemont, have devastated their province of Poitou with their private war. Since her return,

Yolande has daily become more aware of the number of the king's nobles pursuing their own interests throughout the country, some behaving no better than robber barons: minting false coin, kidnapping heiresses, robbing peasants and raping their wives.

It doesn't take her long to assess the court and its courtiers, and what she sees and hears does not gladden her heart. It is plain that even those men who she put in place to guide and help Charles have been corrupted by power and an easy life. Apart from the despised bully La Trémoille, one of the worst is Jean de Louvet, whose wife is one of Marie's ladies, and whose daughter—known mockingly as "Louvette"—is said to be Charles's mistress. Louvet, she hears, was deeply involved at Montereau, and has become immensely rich—too rich, too soon, for an honest man. Further, it is commonly known that Charles has presented him with a magnificent flat diamond called "Le Miroir" as a gift. The court gossips that this was the price of his daughter's virginity.

Then there is Pierre de Giac, who with his wife was also culpable in the conspiracy at Montereau, arriving there with the Burgundians and lending the duke his wife to reassure him. Giac has become particularly close to Charles and is thought to be the worst influence of all. It is rumoured that he has made a pact with the devil, offering him his right hand in return for a successful career at court. Yolande has met Giac several times; although forty-four years old, he is still attractive and charming. Like many fraudsters, he is entertaining and good company, and has managed to ingratiate himself thoroughly with the king—and, she knows from Pierre de Brézé, it is Giac who is responsible for the infamous *Pages' House* and has the role of Director of Entertainments there.

Nor has Charles grown out of his childhood habit of playing favourites; worse, she realizes that he is making his chosen ones spy on each other. His aim may be to show that no matter what he owes to his friends, he is bound to no man, but the result is a court that fosters suspicion and intrigue. The atmosphere is rife with bad blood—hatred—and in the middle of it all, the king ensures his personal security by surrounding himself with his Scots archers.

Only now does Yolande fully realize how confused Charles has become. Here is a young man who no longer knows whom to believe or even who he is. At times he seems almost to be two different people. When he was young, she never knew him to have a bellicose nature—if anything, the opposite—and yet he has proved his courage in the past by confronting not only his own father and the King of England, but even the terrible Jean-sans-Peur. Despite this, she knows from Marie and René among others that Charles still has moments of great timidity, trusting no one except his *bonne mère* and Marie. Then, when he does take someone into his confidence, he makes the wrong choice. Some decisions he makes too quickly; at other times, he cannot make any decision at all.

Worst of all, it does not take her long to discover that all her hard work to surround Charles with steadying influences would appear to have been in vain, as one by one, the men she chose so carefully have been corrupted by the power they wield. To her shame, she realizes how often she has mistaken the character of those she selected for Charles. *How can I have been so wrong—I who have always believed I can read the most secret desires of men's hearts and minds?* The situation is such that Yolande feels as if her labours of the past five years in Charles's interests have been for nothing.

She visits his chambers to find his staff half asleep, not springing to attention as hers do. She asks for certain documents; they cannot be found. Everyone gives the Queen of Sicily her due, but only just—as if they are not quite sure who she is, and yet they know full well. She asks for his personal administrative staff and they are not in their places despite the lateness of the morning. When Tanneguy du Chastel arrives, she finds herself turning on him in anger. "Tanneguy—where is everyone? It is past ten o'clock in the morning. Why are the secretaries not at their desks? Surely there is a great deal of work to be done, especially in the new circumstances?" To her amazement, even her dear, loyal Tanneguy shrugs his shoulders as if to say, *That is the way things are at this court.* "Well," she exclaims furiously, "it is not good enough—and before I leave again for Provence, I will have to make some changes." With that, she strides angrily out of the new king's chambers.

Soon she must leave again for Marseilles and finish the work there for Louis so he can sail for Naples, but she vows that before she goes she will replace a number of the unsuitable, grasping courtiers—and greedy mistresses—installed at the new king's court. She interviews around six or seven candidates a day for a variety of posts, and by the end of a week she is quite pleased with those she has chosen. Her scouts have done well to select those she screened. By far the more difficult task is to *remove* those courtiers who surround Charles and whom she considers unworthy. Yolande does not make such decisions lightly or based on hearsay or gossip—no, her choices are made from a vast amount of evidence presented to her. But their removal, she knows, will take both tact and patience.

After some months back in Marseilles, by June 1423, everything is ready for Yolande's beloved eldest son, Louis III d'Anjou, recently returned from his base in Calabria. At last he can sail from Marseilles for Naples, fully equipped to meet with his enemy. There is no more she can do. Everything is in place; all the preparations have been completed. After working for him throughout almost five years, mostly in his absence, financing his trips to Calabria and back in preparation for this major expedition, Yolande will be able to return to the court in Bourges and try to solve some of the problems there.

Once again she embraces her eldest son on the docks of Marseilles. "Go well, my son, as your father would have said. Make this expedition to reclaim your kingdom a triumph. Win and rule what is rightfully yours, and then send for me to glory in it!" She tells him this with as much encouragement and conviction as she can muster, despite her sinking heart.

"Beloved Maman, any credit there might be from this campaign will be yours, for I know how you have sustained me these past five years here in the south to the detriment of my siblings, and the king. I thank you with all my heart," he says solemnly, but with a smile from those so-familiar blue eyes. One more embrace—they cannot bear the pain of another— and he is gone, without a backward glance, just like his father when he left her for Naples so long ago. She prays that he will triumph; what else can she do? Her heart is breaking and she fears the worst. If only the heirs of Anjou were not in thrall to that irresistible siren's song of Naples.

Chapter Twelve

Marie is to give birth to her first child. Yolande has been so excited about this event that she has worked harder than ever to complete all her labours in Provence to arrive in time. And she does—on 3 July 1423 she is there to witness her sweet daughter delivered of a healthy boy. He will be christened Louis—what else could they name him but for the father she loved and the uncle who rescued and guided Charles? France has a new dauphin and there is much rejoicing. Isabelle and René arrive to attend the splendid christening in the Great Hall of the palace, conducted by the Archbishop of Bourges. Standing beneath the golden canopy used at Marie and Charles's wedding, with the arms of Anjou joined to the royal fleur-de-lis of France, the congregation is almost overwhelmed by the intoxicating scent of countless lilies, as well as the glow from hundreds of candles illuminating even that large space.

The country rejoices at the news; optimism is in the air, fires are lit and people make merry. How proud Charles is, and elated, to be feted as the father of a new dauphin. It is the first time Yolande has seen him look at Marie with a semblance of love!

Her grandson is as delightful as Marie's brother and namesake was at the same age: gurgling, blue-eyed and healthy. For the first time in as long as she can remember, Yolande sees Marie radiantly happy. This is what she lacked more than anything else—her own child to nurture, especially since her influence on her husband is unlikely to grow, no matter how hard she may try.

And there is no doubt that Charles needs some steadying influence. In spite of the air of rejoicing, Yolande regards the court again with a sinking heart. Though her new appointments are in place, the malleable Charles VII is still surrounded by persuasive courtiers vying with one another to influence him for their own benefit—and to his detriment. She decides to remain for some time in Bourges, officially doting on her first grandson while she tries to solve some of the problems besetting her son-in-law.

One thing Yolande knows for certain: if she is to succeed in winning Burgundy over to the side of the king, she must first find a way of removing Georges de la Trémoille. This venal, sophisticated favourite is totally opposed to reconciliation with the duke, and for this among a number of other reasons he must go. But to rid the court of La Trémoille will be a delicate and complex manoeuvre. He is clever, crafty and devious. After much thought, Yolande decides to use the fast-developing skills of her young equerry, Pierre de Brézé. She takes him aside and they work together on a plan. It takes a little time, but with Yolande's guidance Pierre lays a trap for the favourite, one his venal and greedy nature cannot resist. With clear evidence writ in his own hand, Pierre exposes La Trémoille as a liar and a thief—especially in the way he manoeuvred to have the innocent Arthur of Richemont exiled for treason. Confronted with irrefutable proof, the king banishes La Trémoille and his colleagues from the court.

Following this successful exercise, Yolande judges the time has come to bring Pierre de Brézé to the king's attention. At her request, her youngest son, Charles d'Anjou, now aged twelve and the king's godson, has been appointed to his staff. As a royal prince, he is able to confer a knighthood, and does so on Brézé. Thereafter, Pierre is eligible to attend the Royal Council and be admitted into the king's presence: another able ally to add to his circle at court.

Acting as regent for her eldest son Louis during his absence in Italy, Yolande visits Anjou to help her people organize their defence against the English, who are advancing once again. On 19 August 1423, the Queen of Sicily makes her official entry into Angers, accompanied by René, who hopes to be of some use.

The situation in Anjou is not much better than in Bourges. The Duke of Suffolk's army is almost on the doorstep, and although the Angevins do not have anything like a substantial army with which to confront the English, everyone who is able-bodied has volunteered and rallied around the standard of the Count d'Aumale, Anjou's most capable soldier. René is still too inexperienced to be given a command, but after the inevitable confrontation with the English as they attack Anjou and are driven back, his commanding officer informs the regent that her son played his part and fought with energy and verve defending his homeland. She smiles graciously, but inside how proud she is! Somehow the Angevins have managed to defeat Suffolk's army, but how much longer can their forces succeed against such a powerful enemy? Yolande's revenues, primarily from Provence as well as from Maine and Anjou, have been poured into young Louis' efforts to regain his distant kingdom, and there is simply not enough left for her to hire mercenaries.

The most pressing problem hindering a defeat of the English is still the division between the French dukes. Yolande realizes that the time has come for her to become a true queen: to dazzle, be subtle, beguile and use her intelligence to try to dissolve the coalition of French dukes supporting the enemy.

Her first target is the wavering Duke of Brittany, who has changed sides so often; surely she can persuade him once again. A new obstacle has arisen in that his brother, her acolyte, Arthur of Richemont, has recently married the Duke of Burgundy's sister Marguerite, creating a solid connection with the enemy. Undaunted, Yolande has invited herself to stay with her old accomplice Duke Jean at his capital, Nantes. René will accompany her, and learn from her the art of diplomacy.

Nantes is no more than a full day's ride from Angers towards the coast of Brittany, a huge fortress castle of similar proportions to Angers. Constructed around the same time, it has seven towers protruding from its rough-stone curtain walls. But inside the fearsome defensive perimeter sits an elegant ducal palace built of white tufa stone earlier in the century, striking in its elegance and in complete contrast to the formidable exterior. Duke Jean is a fine-looking man in his fifties, with the weather-beaten face of someone accustomed to outdoor life and the wind from the sea. Elegantly dressed in a pleasing shade of ultramarine blue, he is outside waiting to welcome his guests, and does so warmly.

"Madame, my dear friend, what a pleasure it is to have you and your son come to sojourn with me here in Brittany. You will find the sea air bracing and, I hope, the comfort akin to Angers."

Yolande and her son dismount and he leads them along the serried ranks of his staff, who curtsey or bow. Yolande knows that her riding habit of dark green becomes her, as does her large green hat with its long white ostrich feather. At her throat she wears white lace and a large emerald brooch. Somehow she has managed to persuade René to be a little less flamboyant in his dress than usual, and he wears a flattering shade of cinnamon. She can tell from the murmuring as they pass that mother and son make a pleasing impression.

"Duke Jean—I believe you met René at Angers some years ago; now he is my experienced young chevalier!" And René bows, rather too effusively.

"Ah yes, I remember him as a young lad when I brought your daughter home to you from Paris," says Jean, looking up appraisingly at her young giant. "Welcome, welcome to Brittany—I take it this is your first visit? I pray you will come often hereafter."

Jean of Brittany is a most civilized host and makes his many guests extremely comfortable. After resting, they descend the great staircase to dinner, led down by the duke to the agreeable sounds of an excellent group of musicians. Meals are a delight in Jean's company, with sparkling conversation, music and delicious fare. Having exchanged all the usual pleasantries, Yolande gently broaches a number of current issues with her host.

"You know, my dear Duke Jean, I have noticed in Anjou that the people are not happy at the idea of having foreign rulers. How is it here in Brittany? Is it not the same?" And the good duke, spearing a particularly juicy piece of meat with his knife, agrees that he has become aware of the same sentiments among his people.

She continues very slowly, toying with her goblet. "I would welcome your advice. Correct me, please, if I, as a foreigner born, have misunderstood, but do the French ruling families not have mutual interests, as we do in our Spanish territories of Aragon and Castile?" And when her host once again agrees, she smiles and begins to speak of something else.

She continues in this way throughout her stay, which lasts a month—a few comments about the commonality of the ruling families and their loyalty to France, and then off to something quite unrelated but agreeable. Her way of achieving her ends is always understated, but once they leave Nantes, she is able to confide to René:

"Darling son—thank you for your support while we stayed with that vacillating old duke. I am confident I have sown the seeds of doubt in his mind about his recent re-alliance with England and Burgundy against his own country."

"Maman, are you sure? You never once raised the subject of his alliance with the English!" replies René, confused.

"You will see, my darling. I sow seeds and wait for the harvest. Crops do not grow overnight, you know." And she smiles at him mysteriously.

Sadly for her, René must return to Nancy to help in whatever way he can towards the defence of Lorraine, but she can see she has piqued his curiosity regarding her slow manoeuvring.

Her place now is back in Angers to prepare the defence of Anjou, for the English will surely try to engage them again. They work hard and their efforts are not in vain. One month later, in September, the Angevins win a resounding victory against the English at Gravelle.

But such an excellent outcome is tempered by unexpected and shocking news. Yolande's port city of Marseilles has been invaded by a flotilla of ships from her homeland! This is devastating for her. The flotilla was led by her cousin Alfonso, now reigning as King Alfonso V in Aragon, and in conflict with her son Louis over the kingdom left to the Anjous, Naples and Sicily. In a vicious attack, he has taken revenge on Louis' claim by devastating the great port of her son's sovereign inheritance of Provence. *It is just this kind of situation that my marriage was supposed to have prevented*, thinks Yolande bitterly. Alfonso's sack of Marseilles on his way home from Naples was his act of revenge for the city's support of the Anjous. Three thousand houses were burnt, although he did at least give orders to spare the women and children. After four days of pillage, he sailed his fleet away to Aragon. It is a heavy price for the people of Marseilles to pay for their support of the Angevin cause.

In retaliation, Louis is spurred to go on the offensive on the Italian peninsula. Joined by a large number of his men from Provence, determined on revenge, he conquers several of his enemy's garrisons, even Alfonso's largest fortress in Naples itself. Some retribution at least, and Louis has written to his mother how encouraged he feels.

It seems the city of Marseilles has become a ghost town and the morale of the citizens badly needs uplifting. Yolande knows how much the physical presence of a member of their family would help. Before he left for Naples, Louis appointed her youngest son, fourteen-year-old Charles d'Anjou, as his viceroy in his absence. Together with Pierre de Beauveau, a loyal and experienced Angevin, to support him, she sends young Charles to reassure the good citizens of Marseilles. Since René cannot leave Lorraine and Louis is in Naples, Charles' presence will demonstrate how they, as a family, want to show their concern for the catastrophe, and hopefully give the people of Marseilles a measure of comfort. To her great relief, Yolande hears from Jacques Coeur, who is often in Marseilles, what a help her son's presence has been to the unfortunate citizens. Without their support, Louis cannot hope to regain and hold his kingdom of Naples and Sicily.

Chapter Thirteen

Throughout 1423, Charles VII is defeated in a number of conflicts, the most important being the Battle of Cravant, where, to the sorrow of the French, his formerly victorious Scots troops refused to yield to the superior Burgundian forces, and were cut to pieces. The following year, Charles is saddened by the death of James, Earl of Buchan, another excellent Scottish military leader, who fought so well for him that he had appointed him Constable of France. At this critical time, however, fortune chooses to smile on the French; England's powerful and effective regent, the Duke of Bedford, is obliged to return home to deal with problems of his own, and his absence brings a welcome respite from endless battles.

Fighting keeps soldiers and courtiers occupied, but with Bedford gone and peace restored, Yolande begins to exchange urgent letters with Marie about finding ways for her to occupy Charles in some worthwhile kingly pursuits. Since her daughter is continually pregnant and unable to move with the court, Yolande knows how hard it is for Marie to have much influence on Charles. After the birth of her son, the Dauphin Louis, poor Marie has miscarried four times. It is a great disappointment for her not to fill her nursery with companions for the boy.

Without a war to engage him, and despite the good men his *bonne mère* has placed at his court in Bourges, Charles has once again dissolved into his former state of lethargy and self-indulgence. As she witnesses this change in him, Yolande's worst fear is that he will develop his father's madness.

The following year, Philippe of Burgundy signs a truce of four years with Charles VII. This is not a peace treaty, nor has he withdrawn his demand for the murderers of his father at Montereau to be punished. The truce is there to enable Philippe's forces and the population of the rest of the country, to take advantage of the absence of the English to recover. Without the English or the Burgundians breathing heavily down their necks, surely the French can prosper? Unfortunately, Yolande's son-in-law is still influenced by the Armagnacs at court and therefore avoids a complete reconciliation with Burgundy.

How can Charles rule a kingdom so divided?

After much thought, Yolande conceives a strategy. Her first step is to persuade the Duke of Brittany to break his agreement with England; she has sown the seeds for that during her month long sejour at Nantes with René. But she also knows that the strongest unifying force within the French upper classes is a blood alliance. To further persuade Jean of Brittany to return to supporting his king and country, her plan is to betroth her eldest son and heir Louis to the daughter of this vacillating duke. Such an alliance would benefit both families and also neutralize the danger from Burgundy, at least on one side of Yolande's land of Anjou. Louis and his mother correspond; he recognizes the advantages of this marriage for his Anjou inheritance, and from Naples he agrees. Hopefully Brittany will feel the same.

Yolande's next step is to persuade the king to meet with Brittany's brother, Arthur of Richemont, at Angers the following October. If they could meet on agreeable, neutral ground, conversing in a purely social setting, who knows what might come of it? Richemont was a member of the court prior to his banishment through the machinations of La Trémoille, but he had not been admitted within the king's immediate circle, and they never had occasion or opportunity to converse.

Like his brother, Richemont has served the Anglo-Burgundian cause for some time, and Yolande wonders if she will be able to turn him back to wholly supporting his king. Richemont's title and estates are English; his mother's second husband was King Henry IV of England, making her the stepmother of Henry V! Richemont himself was brought up at the court of Burgundy by his uncle, Duke Philippe-le-Hardi, and he is married to the sister of the Duke of Burgundy. His Burgundian ties are strong, and it will be difficult to extract him from his allegiance. *Difficult, but not impossible,* thinks the Queen of Sicily.

During the battle of Agincourt, Richemont was seriously wounded, his face badly smashed. He was captured, taken to England and imprisoned. There his injuries healed, but he was left horribly disfigured with dreadful scarring in particular to his face. He was allowed to see his mother occasionally, but despite her position, he was held in the Tower of London for five years. In 1420, Henry V gave him permission to serve in the English army on condition that he would return to prison should the king demand it. Putting himself at the head of a troupe of his brother's Bretons, he offered his services to Henry V in France.

With the death of the English king, Richemont considered himself no longer bound by his promise made, after all, personally to Henry V and not to England. However, when he married Philippe of Burgundy's sister, his position was firmly established with the Burgundians. Yes, Arthur of Richemont will be difficult to extract from that allegiance. *But not impossible,* thinks the Queen of Sicily.

She decides to invite Arthur of Richemont with a group of agreeable friends to stay at Angers, and to ask the king to join them as well. If Charles were to get to know Richemont, he would see his qualities and realize how useful he could be. When he was at court during the time of La Trémoille, Yolande heard that Charles would not agree to meet Arthur due to his horror of any physical disfigurement. Therefore banishing him from court for Trémoille's lie was easily done.

When there is important work to be done, or a great challenge to be met in the interests of France, the Queen of Sicily's mind never ceases examining every potential opportunity. The death of the Scottish Earl of Buchan has left vacant the post of Constable of France. As the most prestigious appointment in the land, it gives its holder power and authority second only to that of the monarch. René agrees with his mother that if Arthur of Richemont was appointed constable, it would suit all their purposes. Since the councillors of both the English and the Burgundian parties will only transact business with their peers, and never with a commoner, as an aristocrat Richemont possesses another asset. He would be ideal for the post—were he not firmly entrenched within the Burgundy camp.

"Maman, I agree that his *qualifications* for the post are ideal," says René, come from Nancy to join his mother at court, "since he can influence both his ducal brother of Brittany, and his ducal brother-in-law of Burgundy, but how can we move him to *our cause* with such strong Burgundian links?"

Doesn't René know me yet?

"Have faith," she tells him, with her most mysterious smile, "and remember: if you cannot achieve your ends by force of arms or diplomacy, you must work on the *pride* of men."

Thanks to her vigilant agents, Yolande is aware that Arthur of Richemont's vanity has recently suffered a crushing blow. It seems this French earl, stepson of an English queen, loyally attached to England's ally Burgundy, has been sidelined by the English regent. On his return to Paris, and for no known reason, the Duke of Bedford has recently refused Richemont quite a minor command he requested.

"Pride," she tells René, "is one of the great motivators of men. And Richemont's has been badly bruised by Bedford's petty rejection. The Duke of Brittany's forces are top heavy with capable and experienced captains, therefore he has little chance of a great position in his brother's army. But, with my help and yours—if you will join me at Angers—Richemont could achieve the most prestigious, senior military and court position in France! That would more than make up for his humiliation by Bedford."

An invitation is issued to Arthur of Richemont from the Queen of Sicily to join her guests for a pleasant stay of some days at her château of Angers in Anjou during October.

Since Charles has never refused her anything, he agrees to join them. But before Richemont will enter the lion's den, the capital of the Angevin domains, he demands some serious guarantees. Jean de Dunois and Guillaume d'Albret, the king's two most senior captains, are to become hostages in Richemont's stead, and the king's own surety for Arthur's safety is to place in bond four of his most strategic castles. Memories of Montereau have not faded.

"Come my son; Charles will lodge in the abbey and we will line the way there with obsequious citizens—you must show them how to bow low." And she has to do her best not to laugh as René shows them. "Not so low," she hisses, "or they will fall over..."

"Rest assured, Maman," says René, "while he is waiting with us for the king's arrival at Angers, Richemont *will* be impressed—and I am longing to see Charles's face!"

As he rides up the path, Yolande and René can see Charles's curious look at the rows of bowing Angevins lining the road as he makes his royal entry—and his quizzical look at his *bonne mère* as he rides on up to the castle entrance. Yolande has to bite her lip before she makes her deep reverence and gives him her sweetest smile of welcome.

The next day, when Richemont calls on the king, Yolande and René are present. Charles, carefully schooled by his *bonne mère*, appears both affable and royal. René whispers in his mother's ear:

"Richemont is clearly completely seduced by your beauty and wisdom Maman, and by your imposing surroundings. That he has the king's attention as well must *really* astonish him."

With carefully chosen companions in the delightful surroundings of Yolande's formidable yet comfortable and imposing castle of Angers, a place full of happy and secure childhood memories, Charles is relaxed, and he and Richemont have the time to talk and to get to know one another.

Following two days of agreeable entertainments, dances and feasts, with Arthur of Richmont easily absorbed among the many guests, on the third day finally the moment has come. The king, Yolande and René are alone in a large reception room at Angers when Richemont is summoned to join them. He enters, evidently unaware of what is about to happen. Charles, carefully schooled by his *bonne mère*, appears both affable and royal. Pleasantries are exchanged, and then the king turns slowly, and grandly offers Richemont the constable's sword.

"Sire," he looks suitably surprised, "the honour is immense, and undeserving as I am, I thank you for it." He bows low. "Allow me to consult my brother of Brittany before making such an important decision," and he bows low again.

But Charles, Yolande and René know this is just a ruse—Richemont is overwhelmed by the unexpected appointment—and the unimagined heights he is about to attain. *Of course he will accept.*

To Yolande satisfaction, her plan so far has worked—the king decides to accept the presence of Richemont at court once again and, this time, as Constable of France.

By Yolande establishing Richemont as constable, Charles understands that he must dispense with others. Louvet and his group—in fact all those who were involved in Montereau—must go. But these are powerful Armagnacs, and to make enemies of them would not be wise.

After a long talk, it is decided. Louvet is banished to Provence and given a minor post, but with considerable financial compensation to keep him at peace. He agrees to retire to his château there with his family. In a strange twist, Yolande's beloved adopted son Jean Dunois becomes betrothed to one of Louvet's daughters. It is a bittersweet moment when they wed—she is overjoyed to hear of his happiness, but knows as he does that she cannot attend his nuptials. It is almost a relief when she realizes that he has wed discreetly, in secret, and their bond is so strong that her relationship with him is unchanged. Others of the Montereau plotters are banished to various parts of the country, but with generous financial compensations, thus freeing the king from the negative members in his court without embarrassing them.

Tanneguy du Chastel has shown great loyalty to Charles, and especially to the Anjou family over many years, but Yolande knows that for the treaty with Philippe of Burgundy to be implemented, Tanneguy has to be seen to be punished. He too is banished, but Yolande decides to give him personally a very large compensation for his many years of loyal service to her husband and son, and she also creates him Seneschal of Beaucaire in her own sovereign territory of Provence. In this way they will not lose touch. There is no doubt Tanneguy did wrong, but for many years he was a staunch supporter and protector of her husband, and then of the king as a boy. She cannot abandon him.

Following this smooth change of power at court, henceforth the king wants no one within his kingdom to be in any doubt as to who is in charge. Letters are sent out to the principal cities throughout the land to inform King Charles VII's subjects that those who previously exercised control are no more. "From this time onwards," states the communiqué, "only the king, the Constable of France and the Queen of Sicily are in a position to issue orders." Thereafter Yolande begins to take part in the meetings of the King's Council, the only woman to do so, and her place is next to the king. She always tries to remain in the background, but Charles regularly turns to her for advice. He likes to give her the floor, even if he has already made up his own mind. He is keen to establish his *bonne mère* as someone for the other councillors to reckon with. And they do. A good number come to ask Yolande her opinions privately before and after meetings, and she passes on the king's views as if they are her own. In view of how many of his people constantly manipulate him, she trusts she is helpful to him in this way.

Is Charles at last becoming the man Yolande trained him to be?

Chapter Fourteen

At last, Yolande begins to believe, the stage is set for a united France, a country in a position to defend itself against— more—*rid* itself of the invader. At last, through the exercise of negotiations, machinations, charm, diplomacy and hard work, she has placed Charles in a position where he can bring France together. The Montereau plotters are almost all gone, the Duke of Burgundy is set to be appeased. Unacceptable influences have been pruned out, and he can take up the mantle of kingship as he should. How desperate she feels, then, as, with time passing, she senses the momentum slipping away. Courtiers still come and go—her good appointees forced out by a slicker tongue, a more devious mind—while once again the English advance. For his part, Charles continues to play his favourites off against each other—and Yolande is certain he does this in order to keep them dependent on him. After all, royal patronage lies in his sole gift.

Apart from these damaging games he plays within his court, she can verify that Charles VII shows every resolve to become a responsible monarch. With most of the country's nobility united under his control, the time has come for the king to rid France of the English, without the divisive partisans. But there is still one of the Montereau conspirators at court who was absent when the others were neutralized, and hence forgotten.

Pierre de Giac is the most subtly evil of the whole group who allowed his wife to accompany (and certainly more besides) the late Jean-sans-Peur to Montereau. Not only has he reappeared at court, but he has the king's ear and has been appointed First Chamberlain.

Meanwhile, despite his famous courage and leadership, the Queen of Sicily's protégé, Arthur of Richemont—whose men would follow him to hell and back if asked—has not shown himself to be the greatest military strategist. When he loses a major battle against the English, who far outnumber the French, there is some sympathy. When he loses to the English again but with far greater numbers on the French side, he also loses the king's confidence—almost to the extent that the accusations of treason made against him by the former favourite Georges de La Trémoille carry some weight.

La Trémoille, to whom the king gave another chance with an important embassy to Holland, has also failed miserably. He was captured on the road home by a well-known brigand, and by the time he had paid his own enormous ransom, and managed, with difficulty, to rejoin the court, he found his place usurped by Giac.

Due to the power of his position, Giac has succeeded in surrounding the king with a solid group of his own people, many of whom were in Louvet's circle and were dismissed with him. To Yolande's dismay, these corrupt courtiers are entrenched in the court and have succeeded in keeping Charles isolated from everyone else. The new inner circle has encouraged the king to return to his former habits—orgies with lewd women, drinking and eating until he is sick, and for days on end.

Newly returned to court from Anjou, Yolande listens to these stories from a desperate Marie, who loyally resists going into details, and the Queen of Sicily is forced to instigate her own investigations. The results are shocking and shameful. There is no depravity beyond the imagination of this inner circle of the king's—boys are even brought in to dance naked and entertain those who prefer them to young girls. The same decadent behaviour as recounted to her by Jean Dunois is repeated—and worse.

Marie has invited her mother to a dinner in her apartment at the palace, but Yolande needs to talk to Charles beforehand, since she knows he will not be joining them. She makes her way to his private apartments to the sound of laughter and music. To her surprise, there are no footmen or guards standing at the doorway into his suite. Yolande enters and is about to descend the short staircase from the landing to the reception area below when she stops to see what is happening there.

A group of about ten young people, all with their backs to the entrance and so to her, are performing a slow dance in the centre of the room below her, surrounded by courtiers and some women who do not appear to be ladies, all watching. She recognizes several of the men, and there is Giac, acting as the circus master with a long whip, which he waves at the participants, boys and girls of about twelve or fourteen, completely naked, who are miming lewd sexual acts—no, they are not miming!—and then she hears a strange noise, and two goats are brought in to join the performers, to ribald laughter from the audience! With her hand over her mouth, she turns and flees, still no one aware that she has been standing there.

"Maman," calls Marie when she hears her mother arrive. "What is it? You are white. Are you unwell, dearest Maman? Come, sit here." She takes her mother's hand, which is ice cold, and leads her to a sofa, then calls for a glass of water.

When Yolande's breathing steadies, she says, "Yes, my darling, I am unwell. Bring me more water and let me sit here a little while before I join your guests."

She does not know what to think, or what to do. She can tell no one from her world—but she must certainly change the world of the king!

By the time Marie's other guests have left, Yolande has recovered her composure. She takes Marie by the hand.

"My darling, tell me what is going on here. Come, child, you know you can trust me not to tell anyone, but I must know in order to help you, because I can see you are unhappy."

Slowly, and with difficulty, Marie swallows several times, and then she says:

"Maman, you are right, I am unhappy, deeply unhappy. There are such strange people around Charles, courtiers who I thought had been banished, who whisk him off to places I do not know. Often he does not return for the night, and when he does, he looks awful and dazed somehow—not himself at all, almost as if drugged. They are all back, Maman, all the bad influences from before, and also some dreadful young women."

Yolande can see that Marie is desperate and close to tears, but she waits for her to tell her more.

"Maman dearest, at these times, nothing can stir him to any form of action at all." She cries on her mother's shoulder. "I am powerless—please can you help me? You are the only person he listens to."

This boy I brought up is slipping downhill fast, thinks Yolande helplessly.

"Keep to your apartment, my darling," she counsels. "I have to think through these circumstances with all my intelligence, energy and reason. We will meet in the morning and I will have decided what to do. Count on me, my beloved child." With that she kisses Marie, strokes her hair and hugs her.

In the morning, after a night spent searching her soul, Yolande has decided on what action she will take to rid the court of its evil nucleus. She sends for René, Jean Dunois and Pierre de Brézé—her three young chevaliers—to join her at the palace in Bourges. She wants them all to be in agreement with the plan to bring an end to the corruption dragging their king down into oblivion, and France with him.

"Marie my dear, we have met in your apartments, but now I must ask you to leave us—I do not want you to be a party to my plot." And Marie leaves without a murmur. *How well she knows me*, reflects Yolande. "Never question, never explain" was the motto Yolande lived by when her beloved husband was alive, and Marie does the same while her mother is there to watch out for her interests.

When her daughter has gone, the Queen of Sicily turns to the three young men before her.

"Please listen carefully to what I have to say. I want you to know I have not come to my decision in haste or without a very great deal of thought. You all know that I speak the truth and that my love for the king and this country is my first concern, as I was taught by my late husband. And that is how I brought up my children, and cousin Jean, you too. Pierre, you have been with my family long enough to know that as well. Do you all agree?" Yolande looks into the eyes of each of them, and she sees none of them flinch or avoid her sharp gaze as they all answer "Yes" in a firm voice. They know not to say more— there is no need. The Queen of Sicily has spoken the truth and they have agreed.

"During my four years in Provence, I have been hearing stories from my agents, and sometimes from one or other of you three, of what goes on in private with our king's intimates. The stories have been growing steadily worse and have caused me a great deal of anxiety due to my helplessness at being far away. Since my return, and when I am at the court, the king appears quite normal to me—a little vacant at times, perhaps, but otherwise himself. No sooner am I gone than I hear that he slips, without resistance, under the influence of steadily more depraved characters.

"I have instigated enquiries and have discovered appalling crimes being committed by some of his intimates. Those who were banished are back in favour and active in his corruption.

"I have now, inadvertently, seen with my own eyes what company Charles keeps, and witnessed some of the behaviour of these intimates. For this reason I have brought the three of you here to help me solve this serious problem. No one knows him better than you, nor cares more about his future.

"When it becomes known what is happening at court, I fear that neither Brittany nor Burgundy will stand by the treaty for which we have worked so diligently. Until now, in order to neutralize men opposed to the good of the kingdom, I have resorted to the well-trodden path of offering honours and privileges, and bribery. But slowly—and after much thought and agonizing—I have come to the conclusion that it is time for me to take more drastic action." All three shift uneasily in their seats.

"I have undertaken my own investigations and the story is even more horrific than you have told me or I have witnessed. I know now that all I have heard for so long is not only true, but worse, much worse. There is not just debauchery at court, not just bribery, but our king's own chief minister, Pierre de Giac, and his accomplices from Montereau openly rejoice in crime. Theft from lesser noblemen's houses is common practice, since no complaint ever reaches a judge; the chief minister sees to that. I know of the raping of these lesser noblemen's wives and daughters on a regular basis, and if resisted, not only are their servants killed, but also the daughters and then the wives in front of their husbands. I have here signed statements from at least a dozen witnesses to these foul deeds."

She can see she has shocked her audience. It certainly shocked Yolande when she discovered these terrible deeds, and she has agonized over finding a way to counter them.

"I have never employed violence to dispatch an enemy, but this time there seems no other way. France needs to be saved and so does her king." Yolande has educated all of them, and they know she will not countenance argument or opposition. And they can be sure that whatever she says must be true.

Pierre, René, Jean Dunois and the Queen of Sicily gather a small band of her faithful followers. She decides to include the odious Georges de la Trémoille, too. He is strong, a good soldier and he hates Giac. La Trémoille may think he will be given back his position which Giac usurped, but she will see to it that the king will never reinstate him. And if he is a part of the plot to eliminate Giac, they will all have a hold over him by claiming him to be the instigator and solely responsible—thereby neutralizing a potentially dangerous enemy. She tells them her intention. Giac has the king's ear, and since no judge will act against the king, they all agree that theirs is the only course of action for the sake of the kingdom.

That night, Giac is kidnapped, gagged and tied up wearing just his night shirt. He is put into a cart, to be driven to a town four leagues away. Yolande and her group accompany the cart on horseback. When they arrive, a local judge is presented with the evidence of numerous sworn and witnessed statements. When the judge hears that the executioner is on his way from Bourges, he remains deaf to Giac's bribes. The verdict is foregone. Giac's sentence is death.

No emotion shows on the faces of the Queen of Sicily, René d'Anjou, Jean Dunois or Pierre de Brézé. The evidence speaks for itself. They, the jury, are agreed; the judge has passed the sentence. Their decision is unanimous and made for the sake of France and the king. If any of them doubt the validity of their actions, it does not show. They do not speak, discuss or argue. They are united in their aim—to save the king and France. To do that they need the dukes to be in accord and that is not possible if life at Charles VII's court continues as it has in recent months. Their jaws are set, their eyes impassive, their expressions frozen in the little light glowing from the lanterns they have brought with them. The town is asleep, what words need to be said are whispered. There are no furtive movements as with thieves; quietly, they just get on with their unified plan.

Giac once boasted he had made a pact with the devil—to exchange his right hand for material success. This he achieved. Now the condemned man asks for his right hand to be cut off, which is quickly done by axe. He is then put in a leather sack tied tight at the neck, and thrown into the river. His executioners stand and watch. No one speaks. Once Georges de la Trémoille sees the last of the bubbles, he leaves the others and rides back to Bourges. It seems he arrived at the door of the newly widowed Jeanne de Giac, and he marries her!

The following day, the conspirators ask to see the king and Yolande, with the others, tells him how Giac has been dispatched, and the reasons why. To Yolande's surprise he does not really react at all. Not to the crimes committed by his corrupt courtiers, nor to the death of their leader, his favourite and chief minister. It is as if he half expected—or even hoped—that someone would rid him of a man who exercised such evil power over him.

When told, Marie shows no more emotion than the others. Yolande has educated them all, and they understand. When the law fails to protect the innocent, justice must be done another way.

As for Yolande, her conscience is clear. Her husband taught her that there are times when one must act against the teachings of Church and State. This she believes. She has acted for France and the king—the greater good.

Part Three

Chapter One

By 1428, the English are advancing steadily towards the king's territory of Berry, and Charles VII decides it would be advisable to leave his capital, Bourges. His fortified castles of Loches and Chinon in the Loire district offer more protection. It is a major decision and an enormous undertaking, but he moves his seat of government there with his family and the whole court, including the Queen of Sicily. Chinon can easily accommodate an entire army, and strategically is almost impregnable.

No sooner is the large court settled in its new surroundings than there is worse news. The Duke of Bedford, once again appointed England's regent of France, has succeeded in persuading Parliament to grant him a huge endowment to finance a new army. Its commander is to be none other than the Earl of Salisbury, victor of the battles of Cravant and of Le Mans, capital of Louis d'Anjou's territory of Maine.

To general surprise on both sides of the Channel, the English people prove unwilling to continue to fight in France. French agents inform the court that fewer than five hundred and fifty soldiers have enlisted, and together with two and a half thousand archers, they set sail from Calais. However, combined with the troops already in France, the total strength of the English army is still formidable, and there is always the possibility of their being joined by the Burgundians. Since the Duke of Bedford is said to have designs on Anjou and Maine for himself and he does not want to see these, Yolande's lands, destroyed by an invasion, he has issued orders to attack the mighty city of Orléans instead. With its great stone bridge crossing the river and leading directly onto Bourges, once Orléans is taken, the road to Paris will be open, and Charles VII will be obliged to flee—satisfying for the English, but a terrifying scenario for the citizens and the country.

From Chinon, Yolande writes to René at Nancy:

> You cannot know how baffling it is to see the difference between the seventeen-year-old prince who had the courage to stand up to his father the King of France, the King of England and Duke Jean of Burgundy; and this indecisive, feeble twenty-five-year-old that Charles has become, unable to make any move at all. It is beyond my understanding. As you know, I will never give up—no situation is hopeless, no matter how grave it may seem, and I am resolved to find some solution.

But even René, a born optimist like his formidable mother, is not so sure. He too has good informers, and knows the strength of the enemy.

An English army of three or four thousand is marching towards Orléans—the second-largest, richest, most important and powerful city in France after Paris. The Queen of Sicily watches developments from Chinon with growing anxiety.

By 12 October 1428, the English army has arrived at Orléans and immediately occupies the two flanking fortresses defending the city and the approach to the strategic stone bridge. Aged twenty-five, Jean de Dunois is an experienced captain. He is tall, well built and possesses the famous good looks of his late father, Louis d'Orléans. Jean is known to be immensely brave, honest and most highly regarded by his superiors. As the last of the Orléans family left in France, Jean Dunois decides to enter the blockaded city together with a few hundred men, to help with its defence. Once inside, he sends the Queen of Sicily a message:

Madame, you will be interested to hear of a strange accident that has lifted the spirits of the French within Orléans. While the English commander, the Earl of Salisbury, was inspecting one of the strongholds adjoining the city, a stone bullet fired by one of the defenders hit the corner of the window out of which he was looking, rebounded, and smashed into the earl's head. He died four hours later. The majority of the people are convinced this is a positive sign from God. Forgive me, but I think it was just good fortune for us.

The English command has been taken over by William de la Pole, Earl of Suffolk, but he realizes he cannot surround the city with the resources at his command. Until their reinforcements arrive, the English busy themselves building a dozen watchtowers to control the surrounding area. Our men have found a way through between them, and we are still able to use the river to resupply the city. Once the English reinforcements arrive, however, our situation will become critical and I urge you to use your influence with the king to send an army for the relief of this vitally important city. All thinking Frenchmen know what will happen should Orléans fall.

This letter from Jean moves Yolande more than she would care to admit. This boy, who never gave her a single moment of worry during his childhood with her and her family, is so very dear to her. He has all the qualities of his wonderful father—a man Yolande considered, together with her own Louis, the epitome of what a prince should be. Such memories of his father flood back while she reads his words—how the two Louis would banter together and what fun they had in the early days of her marriage. She recalls the way Valentina told her about Jean's birth to her husband's mistress. Never did it occur to Yolande that she would be the one to bring up this bastard son of the king's brother—and what a rewarding experience it has been. Now he has put himself in such danger with the same courage of his father—and probably just as doomed. With the English reinforcements on their way, Orléans' citizens will surely die of starvation or be slaughtered when the city falls.

The Queen of Sicily spends her time writing hollow, optimistic letters to her children from Chinon, telling them privately of her relief that her own territories of Anjou and Maine were spared by the English and Orléans chosen instead, but for their dear friend Jean Dunois inside the walls. But the truth is, she is desperate about the overall situation.

Other good fighting men known to Yolande and loyal to the king join Dunois in Orléans—the generals La Hire and Chabannes among them—each bringing large numbers of soldiers. This reassures the citizens, but knowing they cannot defeat the English without an army to relieve them, they have sent several reliable messengers to the king, asking—*begging*— for his help, and Yolande endorses their pleas, but to no avail. Charles seems in some sort of trance, almost as if he does not care.

One after another of the king's loyal representatives comes to Chinon, men to whom he has always listened in the past, and whom he trusts—the Bishop of Clermont, the Archbishop of Chartres—but all, to their consternation, find the situation at the court as bewildering as does the Queen of Sicily. Charles appears listless and incapable, unwilling to make any decision at all. Without an army, and with no ability to hire mercenaries, he cannot send help to relieve Orléans. It is as if the king sees ruin as inevitable and is mentally absent, watching the disaster as it unfolds from a distance. Yolande realizes that her momentous decision to have dispatched Giac—thereby freeing Charles from the influence of such evil—has been in vain.

Chapter Two

The punishing siege of Orléans is destroying morale throughout France. This once great city, whose inhabitants are starving and at the mercy of the Burgundians and the English, has become the symbol of the depth of the country's despair. No one, and certainly not the king, has the means to help to save the city.

The mood in the country is desperate. Fear herds people into the churches, but also into the clutches of smooth-talking charlatans who peddle so-called "divine powers" to the gullible masses. Faith in God our Saviour and the saints is strong, but when the French see their beautiful country despoiled and the English relentlessly invading, it is hard for them to believe without some sign from the Lord that he is with them. What relief is there to be found in prayer when villages are being torched by the enemy, and rape, pillage and plunder dominate people's daily lives? "Where is God?" is the cry heard uttered more and more.

The only small relief for Yolande at this time comes from letters she receives from René in Lorraine. When a courier arrives from Nancy, her spirits lift momentarily as she takes the packet to her room alone to enjoy slowly, in secret, like a child with a sweetmeat.

And it is from this source, when all appears lost, that it seems an answer comes.

"Maman, please give me your advice," René writes in 1429. "I have heard from the captain of the border territory between our duchies of Bar and Lorraine about a simple yet impressive girl from Domrémy. For the past three years, no one has paid her much heed, until finally her uncle, exasperated by her constant beseeching, brought her to the attention of her feudal lord, our excellent captain Robert de Baudricourt at Vaucouleurs. The captain has written to us several times saying that this girl is determined to save France and I admit we have ignored her requests to meet us. What can a young girl do to save France? It seems she has convinced many of the local people, and Baudricourt admits that even he has been forced to change his mind once he met her. I know you have often found a use for persuasive young women in the interests of France. What would you like me to do?"

Yolande's advice is simple—René must meet the girl and judge for himself. She trusts him to make the right decision.

At once Baudricourt agrees to bring the girl to Nancy to meet René d'Anjou. After the meeting, René writes to his mother at Chinon.

"I was present with Isabelle and my father-in-law when the girl, Jeanne d'Arc, arrived. She is shy and looks quite ordinary. It is her eyes that held my attention; I could see the strength of her mission in them—and her determination impresses me greatly. She must have heard of my closeness to our young king, and that is surely the reason she asked to meet me. While listening to her, I realized how misguided we had been not to see her when Baudricourt initially contacted me. She told us that she had been at home in Domrémy when the Anglo-Burgundian army invaded and all the inhabitants were forced to flee. It was then, she says, that she first heard her "voices."

"Maman dearest, I feel strongly that she could be of use to you. But not in the same compliant way as other girls you have employed in the country's interests. I am convinced she is a maid and intends to remain one. Her mission is for God alone, but her sincere, almost passionate desire to help France has moved me sufficiently to alert you. She has impressed us all here at our court—and in our desperate situation I believe any help may be welcome. Please advise me what to do."

When the Queen of Sicily receives this letter from René, she writes by return telling him to send Jeanne d'Arc, at her expense, from Nancy to join her at Chinon. It is a long way and through enemy territory, but Yolande must decide for herself if there is any merit in her.

To get the girl to Chinon safely, Yolande instructs René to have her hair cut chin-length like a boy's, dress her in a black jerkin and short black tunic, black leggings and trunk-hose, spurs and a black hat with a black feather. In this way she will pass for a young man, and the numerous cords with which the long boots and trousers are tied to the tunic will offer an added measure of security in the company of soldiers if captured. Jeanne should also wear a sword—God only knows if she can use it—and she should have a sound, strong black horse. As a country girl, Yolande is reliably informed, she can ride. Dressed in her man's clothing and accompanied by just six mounted men-at-arms, all in black and on black horses—she will pass for one of their number and not draw attention. It is forbidden by the Church for a woman to dress as a man, but for Jeanne d'Arc's survival, it is a necessary precaution.

Yolande has made her own enquiries about this extraordinary girl. It seems that Jeanne d'Arc was born on 6 January 1412 in Domrémy in Lorraine, the daughter of a fairly substantial tenant farmer; a sensible, plain-speaking, strong country girl. It would not have been hard for her to recognize the pitiless state of the country, or the indifference of her king to the plight of his people. With soothsayers and fortune-tellers in every village, it is not unusual for a maid to claim she hears voices, as Jeanne does. It was in 1425, when her own town of Domrémy— on the frontier between the France of the Anglo-Burgundians and that of the king—was under attack from the Burgundians, that Jeanne claims she first heard the voices of Saints Michael,

Margaret and Catherine, all urging her to save France.

Yolande is informed when the little band sets out from Nancy by night to ride south-west to her at Chinon. She stays quiet as she waits for Jeanne d'Arc to reach her. Secretly she nurtures a tiny, flickering hope in the person of an unknown girl she has yet to meet. This young girl with her small band of guards must reach Chinon, unscathed, from Lorraine, riding hard through enemy territory, in the dark, for at least ten nights! It is too bizarre an aspiration to share with anyone else at the court.

Chapter Three

When—indeed, if—Jeanne d'Arc arrives at Chinon, Yolande intends to keep her hidden for at least two days in order to interview her thoroughly. Should the girl have convinced the Queen of Sicily by then that she has been sent by God, Yolande will set Jeanne d'Arc an almost impossible task: to lift the siege of Orléans.

And there is no doubt the situation there has reached the point of desperation. Jean Dunois, who is inside the city, sends Yolande a message that the siege is reaching a critical stage. Food can no longer get through their tunnels and fresh water is running out. The older citizens are dying of starvation, the very young also. The extra soldiers who came to help did not bring much food and are depleting the stores. They are counting on help from the outside so that they can fight from the battlements, squeezing the enemy in between. If Orléans falls to the enemy, it will totally demoralize the king and the country, and England will have no further obstacle to prevent their conquest of France—no one is in any doubt about that. The atmosphere at Chinon is leaden, along with everyone's spirits.

After eleven nights' hard riding, Jeanne d'Arc and her party arrive at Chinon. Yolande's own servant immediately takes Jeanne into seclusion, with instructions from the Queen of Sicily that the girl should wash, be given dinner and rest a while.

Two hours later, Jeanne is brought to the queen's quarters through a secret passage, and stands waiting. When Yolande enters, she sees before her a very slim girl, not tall, boyish with her short brown hair—neither plain nor pretty. The queen has come from dinner at court and is still in full regalia, although she has just had time to remove her crown. A tall woman in a dress and train of deep blue velvet, sapphires covering her chest, her long blonde hair in an elaborate plaited chignon entwined with pearls, she must appear quite ethereal to a country girl. She sits and asks Jeanne to do the same, to lessen the difference in their height, but the girl seems neither timid nor nervous of the imposing royal personage before her. She is still wearing her black leather jerkin and hose, although her boots were cleaned before she was brought into the suite. Her face and hands are also clean and she has a fresh country smell about her—like a meadow after rain. Yolande studies her for some moments. Can this simple girl have the spirit to save France?

The large, beautiful room is lit by a fire blazing in a huge stone chimney piece, and candelabra with many branches stand on every surface. The smell of smoke is masked by the frankincense the servants have thrown on the blaze, the lavender on the floor and the cloves stuck into oranges on tables. Everywhere the glow of firelight or candlelight is reflected in silver bowls, drinking vessels and objects, and bright tapestries cover the walls. Jeanne is offered a beaker of mulled wine, which she declines.

Yolande begins gently. "Jeanne, my dear, tell me about yourself," and the girl tells her how she has tried for several years to reach someone who would believe in her mission to save France; how she has asked again and again to meet René, knowing he could influence the king (if only that were true), and finally, how her town of Domrémy was sacked in 1425 with great brutality by the Anglo-Burgundian army.

"Was it not then that you began to hear your voices?" the queen prompts her.

"Madame, yes, it was at that time."

"And what did they tell you, my dear," she asks softly, trying not to show even a hint of scepticism. Certainly Jeanne's fervour is beyond doubt. When she begins talking about her voices, her own takes on a different timbre, and there is great confidence in her when she says: "I must find a way of saving France. That is my mission from God, and He has asked my saints to help me convince the dauphin to let me do it."

"And how do you propose to save France, my dear?" Yolande almost whispers.

"Why, with the help of my saints, Madame." There is no argument.

At another time and in another place, Yolande would have dismissed Jeanne d'Arc as a young madwoman making ridiculous claims. But these are desperate days, and she is experiencing the same growing conviction about Jeanne d'Arc that René wrote he felt when he met her.

*

Unbeknown to the court, the Queen of Sicily spends the next two days and nights with her young guest, never leaving her rooms. They pray together and they eat together, but most of the time they talk. Jeanne tells Yolande about her home life, her family, her belief in God, the Virgin Mary and the saints, but using language so simple, so pure and with a conviction Yolande has never encountered in anyone—that God has given her this mission and it must be done. She tells Yolande of the years she has spent trying to find a way to the dauphin, convinced that if she can speak with him, he will believe her. She says she has a message for him that she will not divulge to Yolande or to anyone else but him.

Finally, and without knowing why, Yolande does believe that Jeanne d'Arc has indeed been sent by God. The strength of her zeal and the utter certainty of her faith, her overwhelming desire to serve God and her country has convinced the Queen of Sicily to let her meet her son-in-law the king. But what can Charles do, even if he does believe in her? No, only the Queen of Sicily has the power to take action. Only she has an army of seasoned soldiers, but at this time they are marching to Marseilles to sail for Naples to fight for Louis. Her son's needs—or her king's?

That is the dilemma she is facing.

She promised her beloved husband on his deathbed that the answer to that question would always be her king—but Charles is so unworthy, and Louis is the best of sons. She cannot break her promise to her dead husband, but nor can she abandon her beloved eldest. Yolande lies awake reasoning with herself for the two nights Jeanne d'Arc is covertly with her in Chinon, unable to resolve her conscience.

On the third morning, the Queen of Sicily has reached her decision. Her army must fight in both wars—the king's and her son's. After they have relieved the siege and brought the king through the enemy lines to Rheims to be crowned, then they can march to Marseilles and sail for Naples; and she prays they will have few casualties.

She summons René, and sends word to her army—which has left Anjou and is well on its way to her port—to turn and march north to Bourges instead of south to Marseilles. Changing the direction of an army is no simple matter—and costly. Once again, Yolande is taking an enormous chance on the king's agreement. It is hard to enthuse him about anything—it seems he sees naught but Armageddon.

When they arrive in Bourges, Yolande will meet her captains—who she knows respect her—explain her plan, and then present Jeanne d'Arc to them. René, Pierre de Brézé and the Maid's carefully chosen guards will surround her and ride with the army further north to Orléans.

"Once you have succeeded in lifting the siege," Yolande tells her—"no, don't be afraid; my seasoned Angevin soldiers will be by your side—then, and this is important, instead of chasing the fleeing English, you must turn the army and ride north-east to Rheims, where your dauphin will be crowned king."

Jeanne looks unsure but willing.

"I will equip you. All you need do is sit calm and tall on your charger wearing the armour I will provide, and proudly holding your banner with the red cross of Lorraine I have prepared for you. My soldiers will do the rest. Your role is to inspire, not to fight." When Yolande sees there is still hesitation in her eyes, she continues more gently.

"Jeanne, Jeanne, place your trust in me. Would your saints, who speak to you, not want to see your dauphin crowned at the cathedral in Rheims? It is the traditional place for our kings. You always refer to him as your dauphin, and so he will remain unless he is anointed with the Holy Oil of our first Christian King Clovis and crowned at Rheims."

Jeanne's eyes have a faraway look and begin to glow. She nods enthusiastically.

"Yes, yes, until he is crowned and anointed," she cries, "he will remain my dauphin."

Gently Yolande adds: "And he will remain so to many of the French. You, and all his faithful followers, must know that if he is anointed with the Holy Oil, and crowned in Rheims cathedral, the people will acclaim him as their rightful king. But before he can be crowned, you must help to inspire my army, raise the siege of Orléans and save those lost souls."

Chapter Four

*C*harles has been alerted; he has been told of Jeanne's extraordinary claim and knows he will shortly meet her.

The Queen of Sicily is well aware of her son-in-law's complex mind; he will not be easy to persuade that a country maiden can be of any use to France, let alone the saviour of Orléans. But if this Maid, with her glowing faith in him and in her voices, can convince Charles of his need of her for success, they might have a chance. Yolande has placed another good voice near the king, that of Pierre de Brézé, who Charles knows is there as her equerry and has her confidence.

True to form, her timid and easily influenced son-in-law looks at the cynical, disbelieving faces of his noble friends when they hear about Jeanne d'Arc, and joins in their laughter. But the Queen of Sicily insists. This meeting will not be straightforward and Yolande is sure his courtiers will somehow connive to trick the innocent girl. It is their idea of a jape, an amusement to distract from dire times.

On the afternoon of the girl's presentation, Pierre de Brézé comes quietly out of the king's audience chamber as the Queen of Sicily prepares Jeanne.

"Madame, it is as we thought: the king has been encouraged by his intimates to play a trick for their amusement. He has stepped down from his throne, switched his hat bearing the gold fleur-de-lis for a blue one from a young courtier, and exchanged his purple velvet cloak with a more modest grey one belonging to a page who now sits on the throne in his place."

Yolande looks at Jeanne—has she listened and understood it? Yes.

The Queen of Sicily slips in through a side door to watch as Jeanne d'Arc enters the Great Hall. When she is announced, the room falls silent, all eyes turning to examine the slight, boyish girl who approaches the throne with the Lord Chamberlain. She is wearing a simple white dress of light wool that reaches the floor, with long sleeves and a high neck—somewhat like a novice nun.

"Greet your king," she is urged by the audience as she is led before the impostor placed on Charles's throne. But Jeanne has understood and ignoring the page on the throne, she allows her gaze to survey the crowd. Slowly, she turns and stops. Calmly she raises her hand and points out Charles, lurking behind a pillar.

"There is my dauphin," she announces, and drops to one knee, head bowed, her clenched right hand on her heart.

Charles is swayed, as Yolande knew he would be, and comes forward. He raises Jeanne by her elbows, takes her hand and dismisses the page in his chair of office with a wave. He sits, still holding her hand. A stool is brought for her; he orders music and indicates to the company to continue talking, so he and Jeanne can speak privately. Yolande can see Jeanne whispering to him; as planned, she is telling him that she knows—*knows*—he is truly the rightful heir to the throne. For Charles, his confidence in himself is all-important. Yolande can see her whispering to him closely—is she, perhaps, telling him this precious secret of hers, the one that she kept even from Yolande? His look is serious and absorbed. Yolande does not know what it is that persuades him to believe in such an unlikely saviour, but believe her he does.

Naturally, not everyone at court is as easily convinced by this country girl's enthusiastic belief in her ability to save France. The

Church is inundated with the claims of fortune-tellers, mystics and visionaries. And there is a well-known prophecy made by a certain Marie of Avignon that a virgin will save France.

The Archbishop of Rheims is particularly sceptical, and demands that Jeanne be examined to prove by her virginity that she is not in league with the devil.

"Only a maiden can hear the voices of saints," he announces to the court.

This task falls to the Queen of Sicily. She can hear titters from the court and insists that a screen is erected around Jeanne; she examines her, and is able to pronounce her a maiden.

"And how do you intend to raise the siege of Orléans?" one of the sly young courtiers calls to her loudly across the room. Yolande sees the king turn to look at Jeanne, the same question in his eyes.

"With my army," Jeanne answers simply. Smirks emanate from the younger courtiers.

"What army is that, my dear?" Charles asks kindly.

"Why, sire, the Angevin army already on their way to meet with me at Bourges. I will ride at their head to Orléans," she replies plainly.

With that there is quiet in the audience chamber, and Yolande notices Charles searching the assembled courtiers for her until their eyes meet. Yes, he understands. She is behind this girl and trusts her enough to lend her an army that should be marching to Marseilles for departure to Naples. He recognizes at once the sacrifice she is making, the risk to Louis her son, and the huge additional expense involved. If she, his *bonne mère*, believes in Jeanne d'Arc enough to lend her army to her when he is aware how much it is needed by her treasured son, then there must be something to this strange girl.

Yolande meets with the king privately at the side of the room.

"Sire, yes, it is true. I have offered to arrange the financing of Jeanne d'Arc's Army, as it should now be called, to move on Orléans and save those ill-fated citizens."

He takes her hand silently and nods. "So be it."

What Yolande does not tell the king is that she must sell her wonderful gold and silver plate to finance her own army to divert from their road to Marseilles to march north to Bourges instead and to fight for the relief of Orléans—for Charles VII and *his* kingdom, and not for her son's kingdom of Naples. And then march on further north to Rheims before returning to Marseilles, if they succeed... so many uncertainties, but that has never diverted her from her chosen path before.

Jeanne is ready to obey the commands of her voices, and the Queen of Sicily prepares her for the task ahead. To help with her daily needs, and especially with her armour, she appoints two pages who come highly recommended. René, now Duke of Bar, and Pierre de Brézé have arrived at Chinon. There is no time to waste; together with the Queen of Sicily and Jeanne d'Arc, accompanied by her pages, they set off with their guards to ride east to Bourges.

They arrive in Charles's capital the following day and meet Yolande's Angevins. These hardened men stand amazed and look with awe at Jeanne d'Arc sitting tall on a great white charger, a vision in white armour holding the huge, swirling white silk banner, boldly marked edge to edge with the red cross of Lorraine—all of which Yolande has provided for her. Good. They need a vision to follow. If even these tough, experienced soldiers stare, how much more will the Maid impress simpler minds?

Isabelle has arrived in Bourges from Lorraine to be with Yolande and Marie during the offensive. This is a comfort she needs, since René, for all his courage and bombast, is very inexperienced in warfare, and had a competent guardian on either side in the two battles in which he took part. Despite the confidence the Queen of Sicily has in her Angevins, raising the siege of Orléans will be far from simple. Yolande has instructed two of her most dependable soldiers to ride on either side of her son as his guardians—something which, naturally, he does not know.

The three ladies, with the little Dauphin Louis clutching his grandmother Yolande's hand beside her, bid Pierre and especially René farewell. None of them can stop their tears.

As Jeanne d'Arc sits on her white charger, ready to ride to Orléans in the front rank of the Angevin army, the Queen of Sicily reaches up to give the girl her hand. They smile at one another without a word, while Yolande looks deep into Jeanne d'Arc's eyes. *Yes, she will do well.*

When the army has left, the three ladies, Yolande, Marie and Isabelle, go at once to the cathedral and spend the best part of the afternoon in silent prayer.

Couriers bring notes daily from René describing how, all along the route, local people come forward, tossing flowers in Jeanne's path, clutching their rosaries and calling out blessings. Word has indeed spread quickly. Already a mystical aura has been attached to Jeanne d'Arc's name and presence, no doubt enhanced by the people's desperation.

In Bourges they wait, the days passing slowly, and then their messenger rides fast through the gates where the three ladies linger for news. The message is brief and to the point. "*Mesdames*, Jeanne d'Arc's Army has arrived outside Orléans. Pray for us."

And so it begins—the battle not only for Orléans, but for France. If they lose this city, then all hope for a French future has gone.

Chapter Five

In Bourges, the citizens, like the Anjou family, wait for news.
The days pass terribly slowly. When they are not in the
cathedral praying, they sit and sew, mostly in silence.

Fifteen long days later, a muddied courier gallops hard into
the city, bringing a large package from René. All three ladies
rush to Marie's quarters. It is Yolande who opens it and reads.

Dearest Maman, darling wife and beloved sister,

With her voices—yours no doubt the loudest—ringing in Jeanne
d'Arc's ears, we arrived outside the stricken city of Orléans. No
matter how many horrors our soldiers have seen—severed limbs
and heads, hideous wounds to men and horses, lakes of blood,
burning houses with people shut inside, all the terrible abuses
of warfare—I could see that these tough, hardened men of ours
became lambs around Jeanne, as if they felt some grace emanating
from her person.

She prayed with us before the first onslaught, and I heard from
some of my fellow Angevins that they really felt the presence of
God in their midst—"How can the army of Jeanne d'Arc fail?" I
heard them say.

The men fought hard, with our heroine sitting proudly on her
great horse on a hill overlooking Orléans, surrounded by her guard
of honour, too far for the musket balls or arrows to reach her, a
beacon of white inspiration, the sun shining on her white armour and
with that huge white silk banner swirling in the breeze—visible to
everyone, Maman, exactly as you planned she should be!

It has taken us nine long days of hard fighting to relieve the city—just in time too, before the citizens began to die of starvation. All the dogs, cats, even the rats are eaten, and I heard later that the fighting men's rations were down to two small spoons of tuna a day.

After the fighting was over, with joy I found our dear Jean Dunois, a skeleton who could barely walk. How I embraced him. While he gnawed at the provisions I brought with me, between mouthfuls he told me about the campaign from within the city, and how the people suffered. He really does look desperately thin, as do all the survivors of Orléans, and many starved to death.

Yolande wipes her eyes and gazes at her family around her, and all sigh with relief. "René is safe, Jean Dunois is safe, Jeanne d'Arc is safe, Pierre de Brézé is safe," the three of them keep repeating like a mantra. "Our Angevins triumphed," says a joyful Marie, again and again.

"Now the army must head for Rheims, then at last Charles can be crowned—there where his ancestors have all been anointed and taken their vows," Yolande says, almost to herself. Neither she nor Isabelle, nor pregnant Marie, can possibly reach Rheims to be present at the coronation. That they accept. Rheims is in enemy territory and the army will have to fight all the way there. It never occurs to them that perhaps the council would much prefer to chase the fleeing English!

It was such a wild, impossible hope that an unknown slip of a girl could inspire an army and now a people. Orléans and its inhabitants are saved! Strangers kiss one another in the street, people form rings and dance around a lone piper; others hang out of windows shouting their joy. Hailed by the city's grateful population as the Maid of Orléans, Jeanne d'Arc is rightly lauded by the troops and the people, and she visibly enjoys that. Why not? After years of indifference and ridicule, she has succeeded in fulfilling her unquenchable mission to help save France. The victor's laurels are rightly hers. At just seventeen years of age,

Jeanne d'Arc has inspired a tired nation and a dispirited king.

After the Angevin army raise the siege, the King's Council could see how the slight figure in white armour bearing her huge banner from the top of her white horse terrorized the enemy, and is all in favour of pursuing the fleeing English, following them north to their Norman stronghold in Rouen. "She is said to be a maid—or is she a phantom?" the enemy asked, "Or someone bewitched?" The council feels, with some justification, that this is the moment to take advantage of the shocked English and follow them north to their stronghold of Rouen in Normandy, and many of their leaders agree. It is only Yolande's insistence to Jeanne d'Arc that *her* army must turn towards Rheims, fighting all the way, in order to crown and anoint the king. With the council preferring to follow the fleeing English, the decision will have to await the king's arrival in Loches.

Two days earlier, Marie and Yolande wave Charles off from Bourges, heading west for Loches to meet there with the victorious Angevin army coming south from Orléans. Yolande made it plain that the king must join them before starting the long, dangerous ride north again for Rheims. As Charles embraced them all before leaving, he knows how sad Yolande, Isabelle and especially his Marie must feel that they cannot go with him, but all three understand and accept that the journey to Rheims will not be safe for them. Sadly, that means no coronation yet for Marie; even if the road was safe, her pregnancy is too advanced to take the risk.

The king invites René, as his closest family member present, to sit within the council at the royal château of Loches, and René sends his mother this extraordinary note:

> Maman, I arrived in Loches today with Charles, and witnessed a most unexpected scene: Jeanne d'Arc burst into his private chamber at the château in floods of tears! She begged him on her knees not to hold any more of these endless councils discussing war and following the English to Rouen. Kissing his feet, she beseeched him to come to Rheims to be consecrated, and receive the crown "of

which you are worthy."

Believe me, her dramatic approach to the king on her knees rather took him aback—as it did the rest of us. Can you imagine: here is this slender, almost fragile-looking girl who has done the impossible, albeit with your brilliant soldiers, in tears, on her knees, kissing the king's feet and beseeching him to accept his crown! Charles was converted. Then and there, he decided that the significance of the consecration and coronation outweighed the need to pursue the fleeing English army. He turned to the assembled courtiers in the room and ordered: "To Rheims!"

From Loches, the king rides with Jeanne d'Arc, followed by René, Jean de Dunois and Pierre de Brézé at the head of the Angevin army, as they make their way through enemy territory northwards towards Rheims, knowing that battles must be fought before they can reach their objective.

On 18 June, they find the English at Patay, not far from Orléans. The enemy prepared for this confrontation in the same way as for other battles, with forward-pointing sharp stakes in the ground in front of their massed ranks to deter the French cavalry and allow their longbowmen to pick the French off as they mill about, unable to advance past the stakes. For once this tactic fails. The English give away their position when they put up a hunting cry for a deer that comes into their view. The mounted Frenchmen are then able to circle from both sides around the sharp stakes and a terrifying battle follows, with no quarter given. The longbowmen, with almost no protective covering, are no match for mounted armoured soldiers in close combat approaching from all sides.

René was in the thick of this battle, and wrote proudly to his mother afterwards:

"Maman, imagine, I had *no time* to be afraid. When Dunois, riding next to me, shouted *'Charge!'* I think my horse obeyed *him* as I was unaware of doing anything, and then I was in the midst of it, and exhilarated in some strange way too—I kept thinking *kill or be killed*. I believe my mind was blank throughout the battle.

"My horse was badly wounded by a lance during the first charge and fell, but I quickly caught another running loose, mounted that and fought on. It seemed so natural. And then it was over, and we had won decisively." Yolande, Marie and Isabelle smile at one another with shared complicity.

But even then the danger is not past. The road to Rheims is long and hard, with skirmishes all along the way, unexpected sallies from the enemy as they ride through the woods, with traps laid along the paths, men in the trees shooting arrows, others behind hides waiting to attack at the narrower passes in the forests. But the glorious victory at Patay spurs them on.

Finally, on 16 July, the army arrives at Rheims, only to find that the citizens have barred the gates and are preparing for a siege. Suddenly the mounted vision of Jeanne d'Arc leaves the front ranks and advances alone, riding beneath and along the city's walls, her great banner billowing gently in the light breeze. Behind her rides her bugler, blowing furiously and drawing every eye to the white apparition, defying the soldiers on the ramparts to shoot at her. They look down and see the now fabled Jeanne d'Arc, a pale knight on a white charger, her banner unfurling behind her, an obvious target disregarding the danger. A great cry goes up. "She's here, the Maid of Orléans is here. Open the gates and God is with us!"

And open the gates they do. Jean Dunois and René enter the empty cobbled streets of the city with the army to see the closed doors and shutters of the houses, a chink open here and there so that curious eyes can stare at the columns as they clatter past, heading for the cathedral.

Chapter Six

Yolande, Isabelle and Marie wait at the gates of Bourges every day now for their couriers. Marie receives short messages from Charles, but never in his own hand. Sometimes there is a little gift—a scarf, a decorated tile. At least he thinks of her.

Then comes the day when a letter arrives from René, and they race back to the palace—it has become a tradition to open it together and for Yolande to read to them:

Maman, dearest wife, and beloved sister,

I trust you have received my other packets and know what has been happening before we reached Rheims. Once we entered the city, I knew we had just twenty-four hours to prepare and carry out the coronation. The Bishop of Rheims was expecting us and the king's chosen set to work.

The Archbishop of Rheims could only take possession of his office on the day before the ceremony, and the whole of last night was spent in feverish preparations. As the king's brother-in-law, together with Jean Dunois as the king's first cousin—and the only male member of the Orléans family left in France—we had the honour of being placed near the front. Although it was only just after eight o'clock in the morning when we formed the procession to ride to the cathedral, it was already becoming hot.

After the silence of our reception from the citizens the day before, I was astounded and relieved to see how their mood had changed overnight. It was as if a dense fog had lifted and the local people had decided in favour of their king. Doors and shutters were flung open and a gentle sprinkling of petals fell from above, or were tossed by people in the thick crowds lining the cobbled road leading to the cathedral.

Children were lifted onto shoulders, men and women wore their Sunday best, not the usual dull robes of workers and housewives. We heard them exclaiming with approval at the elegance of our attire and shouting "*Vive le Roi!*"—their excitement and enthusiasm infecting us and our horses, which jigged and sidestepped, snorting and prancing, well groomed and gleaming in the morning sunshine.

We in the king's suite wore all the finery we could gather—velvet tunics, satin sleeves, large hats with long feathers and whatever jewels we had, to add to the shine of the metal on bridles, the trappings of our steeds, our spurs and swords. What a kaleidoscope of colour, so many of the senior nobles carrying banners with every device imaginable; and the smells, some good—rose, jasmine—others less so—horses and sweat, though the strewing herbs and flower petals crushed under the horses' hooves did help!

I rode close behind the king with Jean Dunois, and we could see him clearly under his golden canopy. The expression on his face when he turned to bow to the crowds was one I have never seen before—a mixture of joy, astonishment, humility and reverence as he acknowledged *his* people to the left and right, waving and bowing graciously. Maman, believe me when I say he was kingly.

On entering the cathedral, coming from the bright sunlight, at first I was blinded, the interior still dark despite the myriad candles lit for the occasion. Slowly my eyes adjusted and I could see the glow of the strong reds, blues and silver threads of the tapestries against the stone walls, hastily hung the night before. I became aware of being overwhelmed—almost faint—by the incense and the press of large numbers of courtiers and nobles eager to watch the proceedings, but when I reached my place of honour there was no crush there. We knew that the royal regalia was in the possession of the English at the abbey of Saint-Denis in Paris. We did not have the sceptre, or even the correct order of service for the ceremony, but to our surprise, the crown was found in the cathedral's treasury! And above all we had the Holy Oil, the most important part of it all, which was still lodged in the basilica of Saint-Remi within our own territory.

The choir stood at the back with the Archbishop of Rheims, the senior peer of France, and the Bishop of Châlons in front of them, magnificent in their embroidered robes, together with several bishops blazing in scarlet. The choir was in fine voice for the rousing "Te Deum," which I really appreciated. The Constable of France held the king's sword throughout the ceremony pointing upwards, the handle nestling in a cushion.

The Holy Oil was brought with great ceremony from the basilica, carried by the *abbé* walking bare-footed between four mounted, fully armed captains, each carrying a pole supporting one corner of the golden canopy held over the *abbé*. In that formation they rode their horses right into the cathedral, clattering up the stone steps and to the choir! Ushers held their bridles while the *abbé* presented the ampoule containing the Holy Oil to the Archbishop of Rheims on a red velvet cushion—which a quick-thinking page had slipped underneath it. I found the sight incredibly impressive.

Following tradition, the archbishop anointed the king with the Holy Oil on his chest and back through slits in his shift, and on his head. It was then that the Duke d'Alençon knighted the king—I had no idea he was not a knight already! Georges de la Trémoille, as Lord Chamberlain, laced the king's shoes adorned with golden fleur-de-lys and then Alençon fitted the golden spurs onto the shoes of our kingly knight.

It was moving to see with what reverence both the newly anointed King Charles VII and Jeanne d'Arc treated the ceremony; tears poured down her face as she watched the anointing. Then the king's more formal robes were put on over the shift. As his closest relative there, I stood just to his right, and behind me, Jean Dunois. We heard the king swear his solemn coronation oath in Latin, "to protect and uphold Justice and the Law." Then to great salvos from the dozen silvertrumpets, the Archbishop of Rheims held the crown of Charlemagne high for all to see, and placed it carefully on Charles' head. He then handed him the makeshift sceptre. At that moment he was truly the king, our king, Jeanne d'Arc's king! The choir burst into another bold and loud "Te Deum" and we all bowed our heads in reverence to our newly crowned monarch. When I looked at Jeanne, I swear she had the face of an angel transported.

I was quite close and able to watch the Maid throughout the ceremony, standing near the king. She stood motionless in her splendid white armour, her banner of Lorraine furled and upright beside her, a celestial expression on her face. She really could have been in heaven. This was the moment she has been living for; this was her goal, the culmination of her dream. Her dauphin was now truly her king.

Since the day she came to see me at Nancy, I have met Jeanne a few times with Charles at court, and the difference between the Maid I saw even then and here is extraordinary. By now she has seen battle at close hand: the horror of it, the cries of the wounded men, the screams of injured horses, and the pools of blood from both in which soldiers often slip. She has seen houses burn, children abandoned and crying by the side of the road, begging and lost. She has seen the faces of the dying, and the hard faces of the victors. Jeanne d'Arc has grown up in that short time, just one year since she left her home town of Domrémy.

Another innovation—and there were many for this hastily improvised ceremony—was the handing over to the king of the keys of the city of Rheims, placed on another cushion, in a token of submission to the newly crowned monarch. Following this gesture, Charles VII stood and knighted over three hundred of his most deserving soldiers.

I was told the ceremony would be much shorter than usual because of its improvisation, and I can only say thank the Lord for that, as it was around nine in the morning when we entered the cathedral, and we did not leave until after two o'clock. I found the music superb, the Rheims cathedral choir of the first order, and they fairly lifted off the vaulted roof with their final rousing "Te Deum", sung as we emerged with the king into the bright sunlight, to be met by a scene of wildly cheering crowds.

There followed the traditional laying of hands on the sick by the king, and I slipped away with Jean Dunois to find something to eat.

How typical of him—food before the holy moment—but Yolande and the others had to smile.

Can this great ceremony really have changed Charles?

Yolande dearly hopes so. But she knows that although Charles is sincerely religious, he is also profoundly cynical. So many opposites are contained in him—capable then helpless, strong yet weak, charming then charmless, cruel then breathtakingly generous and forgiving. No one knows him better than she does, but does she really know him? Even to her, this adopted son and son-in-law is still an enigma.

Once crowned, the king sets out on a triumphal journey. Jeanne d'Arc, who has by now assumed mythical status, rides just behind him as more towns in Burgundian territory capitulate to his army and her presence. During one of the recent battles Jeanne was wounded in the leg by an arrow but refused to leave the field, which enhanced her standing even more in the eyes of the soldiers. As for the king, it seems that the coronation in Rheims has confirmed his spiritual status. *I know I was right to insist on his coronation*, thinks Yolande—nothing else would have given him legitimacy in the eyes of his subjects.

Now that Orléans has been saved and the king has been anointed and crowned, Yolande must make haste to Marseilles with her Angevin army and equip them to sail to Louis who is anxiously awaiting their arrival to re-conquer Naples. As far as she is concerned, Jeanne d'Arc's mission is over. Like the rest of France, she is forever indebted to the Maid of Orléans for achieving the impossible, but now that her task has been accomplished—and, as she herself has admitted, her "voices" are silenced—the time has come for her to live her life peacefully again, among family and friends. She has been offered a great house in Orléans and will have the admiration and gratitude of the country, and the House of Anjou, for life.

Yolande sends for her, but her message is met with a gentle determination to continue in the king's service until France is rid of the English. It is easy for Yolande to appreciate her feelings, but Jeanne is young and does not yet know the disillusionment of defeat—or betrayal. Again the Queen of Sicily begs her to go home, but the Maid of Orléans has made up her mind to remain with her king, to fight on with the soldiers who have flocked to his side. Yet without her voices—and Yolande's—to guide her, or the Angevin soldiers to support her, Jeanne will be rudderless.

They meet in Bourges, where Yolande has come to see the king, and embrace. How much older she looks, thinks Yolande to herself, and tired.

"My dear Jeanne, I admire what you have achieved for your king and country," she begins, and as Jeanne bows low and raises herself, Yolande can see the girl's face visibly shrinking before her in anticipation of the words to come.

"How strange you must think it that I would deny the king my army and send my men to Naples instead of fighting on against the English." Jeanne stares at her shoes. "But I gave my word to my husband, and my son's messages are becoming more and more desperate." Still the girl will not meet Yolande's eyes.

"Winter is fast approaching, and soon there will be no more fighting in France until the spring—now is the right time for you to go home. My dear, your work for your country is done." There is no more reaction from Jeanne d'Arc than from a stone wall. *The girl must listen! She is doomed if she stays—the court is pitiless!*

"We all have our duty to do. Mine is to focus on the quest of my eldest son, and I can no longer afford to lend you my army. Louis is fighting for his throne in Naples and has more need of my resources. My responsibility is clear to me, no matter what the cost."

Jeanne bows again and backs away from her silently. Another bow and she is gone. She has not uttered a word—and there is no softening in her desire to continue fighting with the king. Yolande watches her leave and then, with a sense of foreboding, goes to find Marie.

"Dearest child, now that you are her queen, can you not make Jeanne see sense? You know as well as I do that Charles will not stand by her for long. The courtiers do not want her, nor does the clergy—and sooner or later they will convince Charles to abandon her."

"I know you are right, Maman, and I have already attempted to talk to her." Marie sighs, looking at her hands in a new attitude of helplessness.

Yolande does not give up. "Jeanne should leave on a high note, my darling daughter, not as one rejected by the court. This ragged army Charles has collected on her account will drift away to their homes when the snow comes. Will they return in any number in the spring? I doubt it. I will try once again myself before I leave Bourges," she decides.

She calls on Jeanne the next day. The Maid has been installed in a beautiful suite in the palace at Bourges, quite feminine, with light blue velvet on the walls and curtains edged in a gold fringe. The tall windows look out onto fields and a small lake. Soft furs cover the bed and lie on top of sofas and cushions; paintings of various Valois kings and queens hang on the walls, and there are flowers in vases on many of the surfaces. In these grand surroundings, Jeanne looks more fragile even than on the first day Yolande met her at Chinon.

"My dear girl, listen to me," Yolande tells her firmly. "I must leave again for Provence, as you know. You have completed the task God, your voices and I gave you. Do not be swayed by the hero worship you see around you—it will be short-lived. Do not imagine these victories are yours alone. Others will claim their place in them and resent you yours." The girl's face tells Yolande she is talking to a wall, but she feels she must try to convince her.

"Go home, Jeanne: I ask you in all sincerity, and with a genuine affection and admiration for you. Soon you will find yourself isolated in a hostile environment at court, fuelled by envy of you and your success. The courtiers are jealous that a maid has achieved what they could not; the bishops are envious that you had God on your side when the people say the Church did not—and you do not know your king. This man you have seen crowned and majestic before you can change in an instant into another person altogether. I know because I reared him. Once you are of no further use to him, he will abandon you without a qualm."

Jeanne stands looking stunned. *Can I have frightened her? She who has seen the terrible ravages of battle? Can my words have caused her to look so glazed?* Yolande knows that her speech was cruel, if honest, but she is not even sure that Jeanne has heard her. Is she in some kind of trance?

She gives Jeanne a precious rosary, then embraces her and they leave one another, again without the girl uttering a word. *She must take her own decisions about her future*, thinks Yolande. She herself has her eldest son's life in her hands and has no more time for Jeanne d'Arc's. Fame has come to the girl so easily that she seems to accept her own myth as fact. She will have to learn for herself the hard lessons of the court, the army and the world.

Chapter Seven

As the Queen of Sicily starts on her long journey south towards Provence, she begins to regret her sharp words. Jeanne is only a young country girl—how can she understand the court's ways? Again and again Yolande asks herself why she could not make Jeanne realize how quickly envy of her will turn the king's nobles, bishops and confessors against her. Jeanne d'Arc, a girl from nowhere, without family or fortune, who succeeded where they failed? This girl was her responsibility. She gave her the Angevin army and told her what to do. Throughout her journey south from Bourges to Marseilles, Yolande turns these questions over and over in her mind, and is afraid for her young heroine.

Meanwhile, René is so smitten with the Maid that he has decided to join her army—which consists of a motley collection of volunteers, mostly raw recruits, from all around the country.

During her journey south, Yolande receives her news of the Maid's progress through René's excitable letters. At first, her son is buoyant—military victories at Senlis, the honour for him of captaincy at the siege of Paris. But then the tone changes: "The king has sent me with the Count of Clermont to inform Jeanne that the siege of Paris is being withdrawn, as negotiations for a truce with Duke Philippe of Burgundy are in progress."

If the king has been in discussions about the surrender of Paris, what then was the point of ordering the attack on the city—which anyhow was unsuccessful? Sometimes—most of the time—Charles's wily mind totally confuses Yolande. Did he *want* Jeanne d'Arc to fail so he could remove her and appease the courtiers? Not for the first time, Charles's motives worry his *bonne mère*.

Jeanne d'Arc remains with the king of her own volition during the winter ceasefire, and goes with the royal party to Bourges, where another legend is born through her goodness and generosity to the poor. She will join the king and court for Yuletide, and soon Yolande hears that Charles has ennobled the Maid, her parents and her brother: a small recompense for all that she has done for him. He has also given her a great house, servants and horses, as well as precious materials for her court wardrobe. Jeanne accepts all these marvellous gifts humbly and with deep gratitude, always thanking God for providing her with the strength and ability to help her country. And in every statement she mentions the Queen of Sicily, who made her efforts possible.

Yolande hears from sensible Marie that she has been meeting the Maid in her own quarters in the palace, and that she too has been won over by Jeanne's character, simplicity and modesty. She learns from others that Marie and Jeanne appear inseparable, always deep in conversation, and in the cathedral where they go to pray. She hopes that Jeanne is finding her place at court, and yet she has a sense of foreboding. Charles's entourage is no place for a modest, simple country girl, even one as extraordinary as Jeanne d'Arc.

It is while she is wrestling with her doubts on this score that a letter arrives from Marie, bringing news that temporarily empties her mind of the affairs of state:

> I so wish I had good news for you sometimes, but no. Darling Maman, I know this will be difficult for you, but I must tell you that Juana, that dear, good soul who has been a part of your life

since the very early days, and mine since its beginning, has died, mercifully in her sleep. I could see that the last weeks have tired her, and the winter has been hard this year—so much so that I would not allow her to go out except to church on Sundays, since she insisted. I have ordered a High Mass to be said for her funeral and a beautiful headstone for her grave in the cathedral courtyard. I know how much she meant to you and to us all. Even little Louis is crying for her.

Yolande walks alone in her garden at Tarascon to bring back memories of their adventures together—most of all that journey from Aragon to her wedding in Arles. Losing Juana feels like losing a limb—a hole has opened up inside her. She knows she must be practical and accept that Juana's time had come, and a merciful death without pain is something to be thankful for. But they shared so much of their lives; in fact, she almost cannot recall a time when Juana was not there.

Yolande sits and re-reads Marie's letter, memories flooding back together with her tears. *Dear Juana, how you will be missed*. If only she could have been there to comfort her beloved governess and oldest friend at the end.

When disturbing reports reach Yolande from Bourges concerning Jeanne d'Arc, she realizes at once that her complacent hope of her finding a role at Charles's court was optimistic. She can only blame herself. Yolande knows how easily the Maid's honest and perhaps too forthright manner of speaking could upset certain members of the court; and this, she hears, was happening. It was also inevitable that several influential nobles would be envious of the people's adulation for Jeanne, but also, and worse, it was reported to Yolande that a number of the clergy were overheard speaking against her young heroine to the king. Not that they dare to admit what is really troubling them: namely, that their power over their flock has been diminished by this girl! That she claims to have *a direct line* to God and his saints—who speak to *her*—not to them! As if such a thing was possible? As if the saints would prefer to honour a simple farmer's daughter with their confidence—and not them, God's anointed?

The king's religious adviser, the Archbishop of Rheims, told his congregation during his Sunday sermon that Jeanne has "raised herself up in pride." He claims that she believes she is "closer to God than even the bishops." A sure sign of pride!

Some of the king's military entourage, even those who had seen how much she had inspired the soldiers, have had enough of her "stealing their glory." Did she actually fight as they had? No. She sat on her white horse, in her white armour, holding her white flag, on a hill and out of range of the enemy's arrows. What was so remarkable about that? Why should seasoned warriors have "a girl" commanding them? And they have had enough of her revelling in her fame.

Yolande knows the pulse of the court too well, and for her to hear the waves of discontent lapping against the fragile defences of Jeanne d'Arc's heroic effort makes her fear for her survival. But how can she make the girl listen—and leave before it will become too late?

Chapter Eight

From her stronghold in the south, Yolande ponders these difficulties. But she has no notion of the disaster that has in fact already overtaken the maid. In May, during the course of a relatively small battle, Jeanne d'Arc was captured when a soldier hooked his lance into her glittering tunic of gold wire mesh she wore over her armour. Perhaps it was too vain a commission from her to Jacques Coeur and greatly prized—but so too did others! No doubt the ambitious soldier had no idea of her identity, but when brought before the group's captain, Jean of Luxembourg, he recognised her at once. The soldier could keep the gold mesh tunic—Luxembourg's prize was worth far more! This terrible news has taken three months to reach Yolande, since Jean Dunois' couriers kept missing her. Had she but known of it earlier, had she been able to be at Saumur with the king when he held a court in her château during her absence, she would never have allowed Charles to abandon Jeanne, who has achieved so much for him.

Yolande is in despair, pacing up and down, sending couriers in every direction with an offer to pay the Maid's ransom—whatever it is.

Apart from plunder, the only sure profit to be made in war by either side is through the ransom of important officers. To her horror, Yolande discovers that when Charles refused to ransom Jeanne d'Arc, her captor, Jean of Luxembourg, decided to sell her to the English. It seems her own offer got there too late. The Maid has been taken to Rouen to be examined by the

Inquisition. There could be no worse outcome.

The situation is desperate. Yolande knows that Rouen is far too well defended for the king to try to attack the city, even if he wanted to—and in her heart, she is not sure he does. Rouen is Pierre de Brézé's home city, and Yolande sends him there to find a way of bribing someone to get Jeanne out.

When his courier arrives at Tarascon with his letter, she tears it open.

> Madame—I have failed you. There is not a stone I have left unturned in my attempt to reach Jeanne d'Arc's captors. The English have their prize and they are not going to let her go. She is their way of saving face and they intend to prove her to be a witch—how else could this young girl have succeeded and defeated them? Only with the aid of the devil! Not that anyone I hear in the streets here even believes her to be a girl! She has been placed in a male prison, which is against the law, but they say she broke the law by wearing a man's clothing. "But how else would she be able to keep a semblance of modesty?" I answer. I promise to keep trying, but I do not believe any amount of money can help Jeanne d'Arc now the Inquisition have her in their power.

Marie and Yolande are in constant contact now, couriers hastening backwards and forwards between Bourges and Provence, but slowly Yolande begins to understand that she is too late. Neither her daughter, the Queen of France, nor she, the Queen of Sicily, has the power to save Jeanne d'Arc, despite their frantic efforts. France is exhausted by all the fighting, her son-in-law too indolent; his men want her removed, and his councillors are more interested in their own selfish purposes. The English will not give her up no matter how much Yolande offers, Pierre makes that clear—and he offered a king's ransom. This unknown girl from Lorraine has caused the humiliation of the mighty courtiers and the senior clergy of France. To salvage their own shame, just as the enemy must salvage theirs, they will allow the English to condemn her as a witch.

And even Yolande, despite her desperation at what has happened, is not able to give herself wholeheartedly to the Maid's plight. Once again she is embroiled in problems of her eldest son's making. Louis has been betrothed to the Duke of Brittany's daughter since 1417, under the arrangement Yolande made to secure the duke's loyalty to the king. Shamefully, he has now cancelled the betrothal, believing an alliance with a princess of Savoy to be of greater advantage to his kingdom of Sicily. This will not be easy for Yolande to resolve; and she must make the long journey from Marseilles in the very south all the way to Brittany in the north in order to make peace on Louis' behalf. The French cannot afford to lose the Duke of Brittany to the English side again, and Louis cancelling his betrothal will leave that vacillating old duke open to Burgundian offers.

The journey is long and circuitous, taking over four weeks travelling by road and on water. When finally Yolande arrives in Nantes, she has had quite some time to think of a solution. She can see only one way to ease the embarrassment and avoid a scandal: she will suggest an alternative contract to the duke. She will propose that his heir, an ally the king is anxious to keep on the side of France, should marry her own youngest daughter, her namesake Yolande. After so much time given to the problem, she believes she has reached the best possible conclusion.

Reluctantly, Yolande must admit that these long journeys tire her much more now than in her youth. Nevertheless, the result makes it worth her while. To her considerable relief, following lengthy discussions, the duke agrees for his son to marry Yolande's daughter. Once again she has secured Brittany on the side of France.

But due to her departure on the complicated journey to Nantes, Yolande missed the courier sent to her in Marseilles by Jean Dunois. Weeks pass before she finally receives his letter with the tragic news of Jeanne d'Arc's condemnation. How could the judges come to this conclusion? Why has Charles not intervened? Has he no feeling? Another letter from Marie reaches her at the same time that makes her weep with misery and shame at poor Jeanne's conviction.

Having Brittany allied once again to France cannot begin to compensate the Queen of Sicily for having failed Jeanne d'Arc, and she swears she will carry that guilt to her grave. The English paid handsomely for this astonishing girl, and now they will make *her* pay for their loss of Orléans, by condemning her to death—as a sorceress. How absurd, thinks Yolande—and how typical as well. In their egotism, only devilry could have defeated them. Never a pure maid who inspired soldiers well beyond their capabilities! Yolande would have paid as much and more. *Dear God, why did my offer not reach Jean de Luxembourg in time?* she cries out to the heavens. How could the king listen to his councillors and not to her?

Yolande's enquiries reveal that only two of the Maid's judges were English; the rest were French. To be condemned by her own people, whom she saved—*this* is an even greater crime. By all accounts Jeanne's trial was a farce, with none of the correct procedures followed. She should have had a lawyer. She should have been in a women's gaol, guarded by nuns, and not by soldiers in a prison with men. Her judges claimed she sinned by wearing men's clothing—of course she would do so in a men's prison, to avoid being raped. *May they burn in their own hell!* she curses.

Yolande's heart goes out to Jeanne, alone in her cell in Rouen, and she prevails on Pierre to see that at least she receives some creature comforts—writing materials, food and blankets. She pays well to receive constant news of Jeanne d'Arc's well-being and treatment—what else can she do?—while she continues to search in vain for a way of freeing her.

Many months pass before the regent, the Duke of Bedford, delivers the sentence: Jeanne d'Arc is to be burnt at the stake at

Rouen on 30 May 1431.

Immediately when she hears the news, Yolande sends a messenger to Pierre de Brézé in his home town. "Pierre, use whatever influence you have and spend whatever you need to arrange for Jeanne to be given a strong draught she can take before they collect her from the prison, so that she will feel almost nothing." She knows Pierre does her bidding and that Jeanne receives the medicine—but will she take it? Pierre remains in Rouen on Yolande's instructions in case there is something, anything, that can be done.

Following Jeanne d'Arc's execution, Pierre de Brézé feels duty bound to come to Tarascon and tell Yolande the details himself.

"Pierre—you surprise me! But in view of the news, how glad I am that you have come—I was expecting a letter... but I can see from your distress you want to tell me yourself—am I right? And I know it won't be easy. Come, dear young friend. Sit with me here and I will send for refreshment." Pierre sighs his gratitude and gratefully sits, the weight of injustice and his sense of failure weighing down on his hunched shoulders. It was a long ride from Rouen but at least he stopped this time to freshen himself before calling on his patroness.

"Madame, my gracious Lady," he begins, his voice sad and solemn, "yes, I felt I should tell you all in person." And she takes his hand for a moment to reassure him. "Just as you instructed, I did send Jeanne a draught—made by a very reliable man I know—who assured me that some minutes after drinking it, she could still walk but would feel no pain, nothing. However, to judge from the way she walked—firm, straight, almost determined—from the prison, I doubt she had taken it. As she was being led to the square with the post to which she was to be chained, the local citizens cried out repeatedly that she could not be a girl, that they had been tricked and that the Maid was really a boy. The executioner had his instructions, and lit the pyre. Her hair and her clothes had burnt from her body—also the ropes they had used to tie her to the stake—and there she lay, quite naked." At first there was some jeering. Then—silence—and I was aware of the crowd's surprise as all could see she was indeed a girl.

"Poor Jeanne," Yolande cries, her tears bitter. "How shaming to be so exposed, even in death." Drying her eyes, she continues to listen to Pierre's account:

"Then the executioner piled back the logs and burnt her to ashes, which were gathered and thrown into the Seine. By royal command there were to be no relics left of Jeanne d'Arc, who many believe to be a saint, not a sorceress."

"By royal command," repeated Yolande almost in disbelief. "Was that Charles? Surely not, more likely the Archbishop of Rheims," she says quietly to herself.

"Madame, I will never forget that day—30 May 1431 is forever engraved on my conscience—nor the knowledge that I failed you—and her."

"Pierre—no, don't blame yourself. We are all guilty—all right-minded people who know she was not a witch are guilty. You did all you could. If anyone is to blame, then I am. Knowing the king and the court as I do, I came south for my work and left her to her fate." Pierre adds forlornly: "I am certain she did not take the draught I sent."

"At my request, Jeanne d'Arc came to Chinon aged seventeen, to begin her remarkable odyssey, and rightly, she became the country's heroine, saviour, to some, even a saint. At nineteen, after completing her holy mission to 'save France,' the judges of the Church's Inquisition condemned her as a witch, and sentenced her to burn at the stake," Yolande almost whispers, shaking her head in disbelief.

"Madame—the courtiers just say 'war is pitiless,' often with a shrug; that Jeanne d'Arc had outlived her usefulness. Even if this was true in a military sense, she should never have met such a terrible and undeserved end. Of course, once she had been condemned as a witch by the Elders of the Church, who were the people, or even the king's men, to deny the word of

God's representatives on Earth?"

"No one would dare, my friend," and with that sad verdict, Yolande puts her arm around Pierre's shaking shoulders, as he sobs out his frustration and sense of failure.

Is the King of France guilty of Jeanne d'Arc's death? Not alone, not solely, susceptible as he is to any silver tongue, especially as the verdict came from a jury of clergymen. This is not an excuse, but Yolande offers it as an explanation, even if she feels her own guilt heavily in her heart. The time she spends in her chapel in Tarascon brings her a measure of comfort in prayer. Her adult life has been spent following her beloved husband's wish—to work for the salvation of the king and the kingdom—and she believes sincerely she has done all she could in this regard.

Yolande, the proud Princess of Aragon, the Queen of Four Kingdoms, who has never considered failure, whose self-belief has always been firm, secure, strong, must now face the fact that, despite all her efforts with Charles, they have not been enough. For that she can only blame herself—she shaped him. *He was her clay, and the result is no work of art.*

Part Four

Chapter One

With each birthday, Yolande reflects on the previous year as well as on her life in general; it is something her mother taught her as a child, a habit she cannot break. This year, 1431, she has turned forty-nine, and is, say some, still in possession of her famed "imperious beauty." It does not concern her, but the strength and reach of her power, and that of her family members, most certainly does. Earlier in this tragic year of Jeanne d'Arc's death, her beloved son René, Duke of Bar, also became Duke of Lorraine when Isabelle's father died peacefully in his sleep. With a nursery full of children at Nancy, it seemed to Yolande that their life, at least, was settled. She knew of their plans for improving their united duchies, and looked forward to her next visit to them and their latest child, a little girl they named Marguerite.

Her own darling eldest, Louis, writes regularly with his news from his kingdom—always with sketches and amusing anecdotes—and the inevitable list of requirements for his army to be sent to him from Marseilles. Of her two youngest, Yolande is gentle, pretty and harkens to her, and Charles has become a great favourite of the king's and is enjoying his new elevation and coronation bequest. But she worries about Marie, who has still not filled her nursery with playmates for her little Louis. And there is more.

From her agents she hears that it would seem as if Jeanne d'Arc's remarkable achievements on the king's behalf—and her tragic end—have not swayed him away from his life of pleasure for long. How is it possible that Charles, newly crowned and consecrated, has returned so quickly to his old ways? Following that extraordinary and deeply religious ceremony at Rheims, Yolande thought the king would become responsible at last. Most unruly young people become serious when they acquire great responsibility, after all. Marie is quietly desperate, and tells her mother that following the execution of the Maid, something left the spirit of the king. He recognized a life force in Jeanne d'Arc that seemed to flow into him and helped him really become a king at Rheims. With her death, condemned by the Church and burned at the stake as a sorceress, Charles has lost himself again. Was he wrong to believe in the Maid? Or was he bewitched by her? In his confusion, he puts up no resistance to the bad influences around him.

As soon as Yolande heard of René's elevation as Duke of Lorraine, her first thought was that this territory would henceforth be added to the regions loyal to the king. According to the written and verbal testament of the late duke, René and Isabelle would now become the duchy's joint rulers. But her joy is short-lived.

Isabelle is greatly distressed by her father's death, but instead of being able to mourn him quietly, she finds that their inheritance is not as clear as the old duke planned. Her uncle, Antoine de Vaudémont, her father's nearest relative in the male line, also claims the throne of Lorraine. René is indignant. His father-in-law made his wishes clear for many years, and this was known by all his kin. With his mother's blessing and his wife's agreement, René will fight for Isabelle's rights.

Thus it is that at the same time as she finally hears of the execution at Rouen, Yolande receives more terrible news.

René's scouts had come in early to tell him that Vaudémont was gathering his troops to engage René's army at Bulgnéville, a part of Lorraine he knew well. Since his troops had won their last two engagements, René was not anxious; he had no doubt they would do the same again that day. The two armies met on a large field backed by forest, and their combat could not be described as much more than a skirmish. To René's shame, however, his horse put its foot in a hole and he fell heavily on the hard ground. Before he could get up, awkward in his armour, a knight held a sword at his throat and captured him. At first René did not realize who his captor was, and surrendering his own sword said merrily: "Go ahead and claim a big reward for me, you deserve it." Then, to his misery, he saw that it was Vaudémont himself who had taken him prisoner.

As an ally of the Duke of Burgundy—the one man in France with whom the Anjou family have a personal problem despite their political truce—René knew at once that Vaudémont would hand him over to Philippe. There could be no possible worse scenario for him, just as he was about to accede to Isabelle's birthright. As the prisoner of Duke Philippe, Isabelle will be left alone to be threatened by her cousin Vaudémont, just when she needs René by her side more than ever. And what would be his future in the hands of this ruler of Burgundy?

In all their time spent amiably negotiating together, Yolande and Philippe have been acting on behalf of the kingdom. The question of René's imprisonment, however, is personal. Philippe will use René to settle the old family score—that of the Anjou family returning his sister unwed, to die a year later. This new Duke of Burgundy may be different to his loathsome father, but he will not listen to Yolande in the case of her son. The insult inflicted on the House of Burgundy by that of Anjou still burns deep inside him, and he refuses to release René.

Yolande writes at once to her daughter-in-law. "Isabelle— heed my words and act quickly! You have two tasks. First you must summon the council of Lorraine immediately. Dress in deepest mourning, gather your children about you, convene your army and meet with your vassals in the Great Hall at Nancy. Once they have willingly sworn loyalty to you, set out for Chinon to plead with the king. I shall be there and will prepare him." Charles VII likes Isabelle and Yolande knows he can be swayed by a beautiful lady in distress.

Accompanied by her children, Isabelle arrives at Chinon. Tall and slender in her long court dress and train of black velvet, she looks ethereal and frail. Her golden hair is piled on her head and tied up with pearls. With her two blonde little ones, also in black velvet, clinging to her skirts, she makes a great impression on the king—and on Yolande. How adorable the children are, with their blue eyes gazing wide open at the king, and how tragically beautiful is their mother! Isabelle does not need to act out her pain and agony—it is real, and Charles can feel it. Charles is also particularly fond of René, and aware how his capture must be affecting his *bonne mère*. For once he does not disappoint her. As a result of her discussions with the king, Isabelle achieves a truce with Vaudémont regarding her right to rule Lorraine—but René remains a prisoner of the Duke of Burgundy, which tears at his mother's heart.

It comes as a small relief when René is given permission to write to his family—at least they can exchange their news. When they were very young, Yolande taught her brood a code for secret letter-writing developed by her husband, and René has taught this to Isabelle. They can receive and send information between one another that cannot be read by others. Apart from that small concession, René has very little compensation for the loss of his freedom. For some weeks since his capture he has heard nothing from the duke and has no idea about his eventual ransom. But at least it is some consolation to Yolande and to Isabelle that they hear regularly from him and how he occupies himself. He writes of his imprisonment in as light a vein as he can conjure: how for the first time in his life he has time to ponder; when the duke finally deigns to visit him, how their meetings progress; and how, in spite of his intransigence on the matter of Rene's freedom, their relationship is completely cordial. Philippe has allowed him paints, and he has struck up a friendship with a visiting artist, Jan van Eyck, nephew of

Philippe's court painter. Painting is Rene's new passion—as well as reading and writing in earnest, inspired by the legends and romances of his childhood: the tales of Arthur, the Romance of the Rose, Tristan and Iseult. Yolande knows he makes light of the strictures of his freedom, concealing the disappointment below, but she treasures him the more for that.

Her replies are as cordial and light-hearted as his; how can she make this dearest son of hers feel better but by words of encouragement and assurances that she will continue with her negotiations for his release?

Chapter Two

The court is at Chinon. It is the early spring of 1435, and Yolande is walking dreamily in the garden among the flower beds, admiring the fresh green leaves beginning to appear on the fruit trees, when a messenger brings her a long-awaited packet from Naples. It has finally reached her, having been sent to Tarascon and then to Angers. How she delights in receiving letters with news of Louis' activities, her "golden boy," as she has always thought of him. They are always well written and amusing, and sometimes he encloses pencil sketches of a building or scenery, every little event turned into an adventure for her pleasure— how well he writes—another gift inherited from his father, as well as his looks and goodness of heart.

Yolande is quite alone in this part of the garden, and she settles on a comfortable seat to open the letter. This 4 April is warm, but with a slight fresh breeze, bringing her the scent of early-blooming flowers and bulbs. There is not a cloud to be seen, a gentle sun shining, birds singing, and she sits to open her letter full of anticipated pleasure.

But sorrow, they say, never comes alone. She reads the cold words. Her beloved eldest son, Louis III d'Anjou, died on 12 November 1434. It seems he contracted malaria while campaigning on the Italian peninsula. It has taken more than four months for the news to reach her.

She does not cry out; she just sits very still, hardly breathing, trying to take this in. Her thoughts turn immediately to her beloved husband. *My darling, are you with me in this hour of my grief?* she wants to cry to the heavens. She has seen so little of their firstborn in the past years. Her last contact was over his rejection of the Duke of Brittany's daughter, when she left for Nancy once his army had departed for the Italian peninsula. *We did not even say good-bye!*

She turns her thoughts to the happiness he gave her and Louis with his birth, and as a family during his childhood: a sunny blonde boy, serious, and then bursting with playful mischief. He was a good influence on the sad young Prince Charles, making him laugh, possibly, for the first time in his life. He was a wonderful inspiration to René, and always tender with the girls. He inherited his father's looks and was strikingly similar in other ways too—intelligent, handsome, gentle yet strong, wise yet a warrior prince, cultured and full of courage. Yolande admired him intensely, this firstborn son of hers; he was all a royal duke should be, and yet they grew apart with time and distance, less aware of one another's daily lives. She realizes she never met his wife. How often she has prayed that he would come home with her, but somehow she always knew his fate would be entwined with that fantasy kingdom.

She will mourn him quietly away from the court, and examine her inner heart as to how she might have failed him. She needs to be alone to cry out her anguish. *I do not want to be brave! I want to weep and beat my breast in my pain for the loss of this golden, heroic son!*

She goes to Charles to tell him and to ask to be excused from the court's activities. The words stick in her throat when she finds him. Quietly, she says, "Sire, I have sad news."

He sees from her face that something is tearing her apart and, taking her hand, he leads her away from the others. "What is it, dearest *bonne mère*, tell me. I hate to see you distressed. How can I help?"

"Dear boy, forgive me, but my son and your friend Louis..." and she falters.

He knows at once and holds her, and she feels his body shaking with his own sobbing joining hers. Charles hero-worshipped Louis from the first day they met; she knows that Louis seemed to him a shining example of a princely knight. *Which indeed he was!* He takes her onto the terrace so they can be alone. They sit in the shade, and when they are done crying, they recount their memories to one another and discuss the happy times: the adventures, the tree houses, the pony excursions, the fights with the neighbouring children, and much more. In times of grief, this king she has raised can be so gentle and understanding, quite a different person.

Since Louis and his wife, Margaret of Savoy, had no children, René becomes Duke of Anjou, a territory he has ruled for his brother since Louis left more than ten years ago.

For a week Yolande retires to her suite, and Charles imposes a period of royal mourning on the court for the King of Sicily, his cousin and childhood friend.

Louis dead and René imprisoned indefinitely—how alone Yolande feels, and there is no Juana to comfort her. Somehow her beloved dogs feel her sadness and sit by her all the time, but even they cannot do much to console her.

Chapter Three

Spring becomes summer. Yolande has chosen to distract herself from her grief over Louis by spending time with Isabelle and the children, when she receives news from Calabria. Queen Giovanna II of Naples, the last of her line, had appointed Louis III d'Anjou as her co-regent and heir. Following his death, she named René as his brother's successor shortly before she herself died. With the last of the senior branch of the Anjou family known as Duras, or Durazzo, gone, now the throne has finally passed to the younger branch. It is in his prison tower that René learns he has been bequeathed the kingdoms of Naples, Sicily and Jerusalem—a poisoned chalice as far as Yolande is concerned. How she prays those sirens of Naples will not call again and claim her sweet René one day as well.

And still Philippe of Burgundy refuses to set René free to accept his new responsibilities. The Queen of Sicily sends her representatives to plead with him; she offers to buy her son out of prison, but to no avail. He will not even see them. In reply to her written plea, Duke Philippe dares to remind her that Charles d'Orléans has been held in the Tower of London since Agincourt, a battle that took place some twenty years ago. She trembles at the thought of René sharing his fate. *Oh dear God, why am I so punished?*

The only sliver of light on the horizon is the news that Anjou's allies, the Genoese navy, have defeated and captured Alfonso V of Aragon, the claimant to what is now René's throne of Naples, and the monster who sacked Marseilles. But it gives little enough comfort; when the ambassadors from Naples arrive at the end of that same year, 1434, it is Isabelle, René's wife, whom they crown in his stead. Yolande, now to be known as the Old Queen of Sicily, attends the ceremony at Nancy with her youngest son Charles, Jean Dunois and Pierre de Brézé. Together they write to René with an account of what should have been his coronation. Watching this event of which her son has been deprived, Yolande swears she will never find it in her heart to forgive Philippe of Burgundy.

Yolande notes with pleasure that René was right when he wrote to say Isabelle is not unlike her—that she too has steel in her veins. Isabelle acts at once to grasp this opportunity to regain their Italian kingdoms. Leaving their eldest son, ten-year-old Jean of Calabria, in her stead in Lorraine, she has gathered her other children, her ladies and her entourage, and is on her way west across France to Chinon. There she will ask for the king's blessing—and Yolande's—before heading south to Marseilles to take ship for Naples and claim René's throne.

The newly crowned young Queen of Sicily arrives at Chinon escorted by her brilliant train and her ladies; she intends to set up her court with as much elegance as possible, even if she cannot have her much-loved husband beside her yet. Yolande feels a surge of pride in her daughter-in-law as she studies her court. What style she has, and what courage! Isabelle is her younger self—as tall as Yolande, with her long golden hair entwined high with red ribbons. She wears a long robe of scarlet and gold damask covered with a short, tight crimson velvet jacket. At her neck are the wonderful pearls Yolande gave her. Her blue-eyed gaze is firm and the sweetest of smiles belies the strong set of her jaw. *Yes,* Yolande thinks to herself, *she is very like me.*

The gentlemen accompanying her suite come from Lorraine, Anjou and other French duchies loyal to the king. They are a fine sight—young, elegant and unmistakably intent on adventure. Yolande hopes that among them there are some more serious contenders for administrative posts. René has written that a number of the older and more experienced courtiers will remain in Lorraine to govern on his and Isabelle's behalf and to train their heir. Isabelle's is a young court, but then so are its principals. Her ladies and *demoiselles* are equally stylish and come from all over the country. Yolande can see they have been well trained by their mistress and appear both modest and capable. She has chosen only a small number—the rest must remain behind for the time being, at least until her son can leave for his kingdom. Yolande knows from her correspondence that Isabelle went to considerable trouble to choose for her retinue those *demoiselles* she felt would be the most suitable. One by one, at her request, they are presented to the Old Queen of Sicily, by the new queen. There are ten of them, all fair-haired and on the tall side, with laughing eyes and quick to smile—it is important that their approach to the local people shows this court to be warm and friendly, especially in a new country. None is hesitant, all advance willingly. They are a delightful sight, all dressed in pastel colours, with tight bodices and modest necklines. They wear their hair tied back in the same fashion as their mistress, and each curtseys with grace and a lovely open smile.

"Tell me, my dears," the awe-inspiring Queen Yolande says to the group nonchalantly, "what do you expect to find in Naples?" And she looks at the eldest of them.

"Madame, first and foremost we are all aiming to make the life of our young queen as agreeable as possible, to serve her in every way and befriend the existing household if Queen Isabelle decides they should remain."

Yolande turns to another of the older *demoiselles*. "I understand you have all been taking lessons in Italian since you became aware of the plan to travel to Naples. How are you getting on?" And there is a burst of gentle but merry laughter.

"Oh Madame, we are making some progress, but the gentlemen of the court accompanying us tease us so, it is hard! We all have lessons daily, first five of us followed by the other five, and then our teacher asks us to hold conversations entirely in Italian. It is very amusing, though not for him! He scolds us in Italian—which, I am afraid, is even more amusing! I think we have learnt scolding in Italian best of all since we hear the words so often!" And they all laugh with good humour. *How I wish I could go with them* she thinks—just for a moment. Perhaps when René is freed, we can go together. Happy day dreams for another time...

One of the young ladies adds, "Oh, but Madame, we do take it seriously, I assure you, and by the end of our sea journey we intend to be quite fluent." But their happy light laughter does not entirely convince her.

Among these *demoiselles*, Yolande catches sight of a strikingly beautiful young girl—a quiet, intelligent-looking maid who has kept her place in the background. She turns to the obvious leader among them and whispers to her, "Remind me of the name of the youngest among you?"

"Why, that is Agnès Sorel, and she is indeed our youngest at fourteen years old."

Yolande thanks her and becomes aware that she is not alone in noticing Agnès, as she sees the king's eyes stray in her direction. Agnès keeps her own lowered and fixed to the ground as a maiden should. Charles's interest intrigues his mother-in-law—normally he never takes note of anyone among the very young at court unless they are important.

As she watches him, an idea is slowly forming. Ever since Pierre de Brézé surprised her some time ago by confiding that he thought the reason for the king's debauchery was his search for someone younger but as remarkable as his *bonne mère* to love, she has turned this over and over in her mind. She realizes she has been his image of perfect womanhood since he was ten years old, and yes, strange as it seems, this could indeed be the cause of Charles's dissipation and lassitude. Flatterers he has in abundance, and even some friends. But she would be among the first to hear if he has ever fallen truly in love, that purest of emotions. She has long ago ceased to delude herself that his feelings for Marie will ever extend beyond friendship.

Even for the sake of the kingdom, would it not be a cruel betrayal of her darling daughter if she condoned her son-in-law's relationship with a younger version of herself? And where could she find such a girl and, once found, would she be willing to be trained by Yolande to thwart the deviousness of the king's mind? How to hold him to persuade him to heed her advice? Marie is so sound and could be such an excellent counsellor, but he ignores her advice; her job is to breed children. Since the death of her husband and then her darling son Louis, Yolande has been aware that she herself is perhaps the only truly steadying influence on Charles, the only voice of reason that he still heeds. Aware, too, that since she will not last forever, she has been looking carefully at the young ladies of Marie's entourage, as well as ladies who come to court as guests for one occasion or another. As yet, she has not encountered anyone with whom she believes he could fall in love. Such a young lady must not only be beautiful—he has such an admiration of beauty—she must be intelligent, cultivated, and yet not inspire the kind of envy among the court that caused the downfall of Jeanne d'Arc.

Yolande watches Agnès—there is something about her that reminds her of her younger self—and also of Isabelle—strength of character but not willfulness; there was a dedication in those glorious eyes when she finally lifted them, yes, and a *"goodness,"* but also that spark, the sign of a natural intelligence, the kind that observes and reads the character of others. As the youngest, Agnès Sorel is the last out of the door, and her modesty and demeanour strike Yolande as particularly remarkable for a girl possessing such extraordinary beauty. She must receive compliments daily, but, as yet, they do not appear to have affected her. Again she notices Charles watching the girl, and not in his usual lascivious way. *Yes*, she thinks, *it might just be prudent to have Isabelle inform her regularly about this girl's progress at her court in Naples.*

Chapter Four

The next morning Isabelle comes to Yolande's suite with her enchanting little girl, Yolande's youngest granddaughter Marguerite. It has been agreed between them that the journey to Naples is too dangerous for one so young, and that Yolande is to have care of her in Isabelle's absence. Perhaps when René is released, he can bring Marguerite with him to Naples.

Isabelle is desperately sad to part with her youngest one and Yolande sees tears welling up in her eyes.

"And how old are you now, Marguerite my darling?" she asks.

"Grandmama," answers the child quite seriously, and curtseys, "I am five now, quite old enough for the ship, but Maman says I will be sick and there might be pirates and I am so worried for my brother and sister!"

"Well, in that case would you like to stay with me and help me look after my new puppies? I do need your help, you know. I have heard how gentle and kind you are with the dogs at home in Lorraine. Will you help me with mine, and perhaps I will give you one of your own?"

The little girl's eyes light up. "Yes please, Grandmama," she says, and Yolande sits her on her knee and begins a story while Isabelle blows her a kiss behind her daughter's back and slips out of the room. They have said their good-byes and this is easier for the child. Tiphane will come in a little while and take over from her mistress—"Grandmama" is definitely becoming too old for the nursery.

Later she writes to René in his tower:

> The departure of your darling Isabelle and her dazzling court
> was half happy and half sad, but they left with an air of excited
> expectancy and all intend to succeed until you arrive. My sadness
> was tempered by Isabelle giving me the joy of caring for your little
> Marguerite, and I agree that at five years old she is too young to
> travel to Naples. At least the thought of my puppies and baby
> rabbits has consoled her. Trust me—I will make a splendid young
> lady of your daughter and Tiphane is thrilled to have one of yours,
> her darling, in the nursery. I am totally devoted already! If only she
> and I were permitted to visit you!

It is the merchant of Bourges, Jacques Coeur, who has provided
armed ships for Isabelle's journey, and she will be escorted by
several more of his galleons. In René's last coded instruction
he appointed Isabelle as his regent in Naples. She will be
splendid—but it will not be easy.

The new Queen of Sicily expects her position to be challenged
eventually by Yolande's cousin Alfonso, since none of them
knows how long he will be held by the Genoese—they hope at
least as long as René is held by Philippe of Burgundy. Yolande
admires the extraordinary lengths to which Isabelle has gone
to prepare herself for their inevitable conflict. She has sold her
jewellery, her silver, even her warmer court clothes to raise
money. With her other two children in tow, and her ladies,
courtiers and minstrels to give form to her royal entourage, the
new Queen of Sicily is determined to succeed in Naples and
hold the kingdom for René. Yolande suggested another delicate
touch—Isabelle's minstrels are to double as secretagents. They
will become very useful, and she has seen to their instruction in
the Italian language as well.

Mother and son are equally anxious about his family
undertaking this perilous journey and what they will find
there, but do they have a choice? If Isabelle does not go and

stake their claim, then the efforts—and deaths—of both of the Louis d'Anjous, father and son, will have been in vain. What is more, René wants his kingdom. It is his rightful inheritance, and Yolande will do everything in her power to support him. To him, his mother has always been infallible—if she agrees to help him, and with Isabelle taking the initiative by sailing to Naples and installing their court, he might just have a chance of succeeding where his brother and father failed. Perhaps even Charles might help him? All these thoughts—no, dreams—he passes to Yolande in their code; what else does he have to do in his tower but dream? How Yolande's heart goes out to him—and how can he be so sure of his eventual success in Naples, confined as he is in isolation? To get him out of his prison tower must now become her goal—what happens afterwards is in God's hands.

Six months after Isabelle's departure for Naples, Pierre de Brézé, who has been negotiating with Philippe of Burgundy to free René, comes to Angers to tell her the outcome. She scans his handsome face—he has matured, and looks more dazzling than ever—to see if his news is good or bad. "Madame, after much discussion and many meetings, Duke Philippe has finally agreed to release your son," he tells her with a solemn expression despite his honeyed tones. The relief is so intense she can feel tears approaching. But as he continues, she understands his reticence:

"The duke has made it known that he asks for a great compensation in view of the shame inflicted on his house by yours, my lady. His Highness the Duke will release Duke René immediately for your signed undertaking to give him in return the duchy of Bar, and your granddaughter, the lady Marguerite, for the duke's eldest son."

Having held her breath throughout Pierre's speech, for a moment Yolande looks as if she might faint. After a few seconds, she says quietly, almost as if to herself, "So this is how he intends to equal Anjou's insult for rejecting his sister as the bride of my son! The price of his revenge is to be the hand of my next son's daughter Marguerite, thus forcing a union of our houses after all!"

Pierre looks crestfallen. "That is not all, my dear lady. In addition, the Duke of Burgundy demands the sum of three million gold ducats."

Yolande feels as if her knees are melting as she sinks into a chair. "There is not so much money in all France," she cries out. "Certainly not in my dukedom."

Pierre advances and gently takes her hand. "Madame, my lady, there is still more." Her breathing becomes strangled, her other hand at her throat. "My lord René was so shaken on hearing the duke's terms, he declared boldly—and insisted that I tell you—he would rather die in prison than allow you to accept them." Pierre looks at her. Quickly he hands her a goblet of water and is on his knees by her chair, his face anxious.

No, she does not faint, but it takes her a few moments to absorb René's reply. What is he saying? He would rather remain in Burgundy's prison tower than lose one duchy and bankrupt the other? Rather stay in prison than sail to Naples and take up his throne with his beloved wife and children? The sad empty shell of her begins to swell and fill with pride at the courage of her treasured son. How his father would have admired him for this response.

In her own distress she has forgotten Pierre's feelings, and how he too must be suffering to bring her such unhappy news. "Pierre, dear friend to me and my family—grieve not," she says reassuringly. "You have not failed in the task I gave you. It was an impossible charge, and I was wrong to hope for a successful outcome from such an intractable foe as Philippe of Burgundy. I will find another way—somehow. For the present, we must all recognize the sacrifice my son is making for his family and our lands." She knows there is nothing she can say to cheer Pierre— or herself—but she is grateful to have him near.

Chapter Five

Yolande has spent so much time negotiating with Philippe in René's cause that she is beginning to know this duke's heart. His attitude to the Anjou family has nothing to do with the other matter she has been pursuing for so long, the alliance of the French factions against the enemy. She has a feeling Philippe is slowly beginning to understand the need for a united France—and its advantages. Yolande is not surprised he finds excuses to avoid a meeting with her—he senses he might lose the argument regarding René's release if they come face to face.

To her intense pleasure she is proven right in this side of his character at least—even if it has taken until 1435 for Philippe to be persuaded to withdraw his loyalty from the English and give it back to his rightful king. At last he has agreed to sign a treaty, to signal a peace with Charles VII of France. Although this agreement, the Treaty of Arras, absolves the duke from giving homage to the king, he promises Charles VII his loyalty and will return to Paris to place himself under the king's jurisdiction.

For his part, Charles is willing to humble himself before Philippe for his involvement in the assassination of his father, and he gives his word that he will punish those responsible. Most significantly, the king renounces his leadership of the Armagnacs, and thereby finally puts an end to the existence of the two factions that have divided France and enabled the English to decimate the country. With Burgundy on side, a united France has a distinct numerical advantage over the enemy. Finally united, the time and the opportunity have come for the French to rid themselves of the English yoke.

But despite such success, how can Yolande not grieve? René has sent a letter that wrenches her heart:

> Maman, most stalwart and loving of mothers, I rejoice in my prison tower at the news of the reconciliation of the king with Burgundy, but it has only increased my desperation to be free. The only hope of freedom that the Duke of Burgundy has offered is for me to agree to the marriage of my nine-year-old Yolande with Ferry, the son of my captor Antoine de Vaudémont, who continues to dispute my right to the duchy of Lorraine. If I agree, he will receive a part of our duchy, which he craves as my daughter's dowry. As if this is not sufficiently unreasonable, I am constrained to pledge a huge ransom, hand over my two sons as hostages and send my daughter to her future mother-in-law. Imagine my frustration when I find myself unable to raise the ransom and I am obliged to remain in Burgundy and my prison tower.

Is there despair for a mother deeper than this? His letter tears at her heart and she resolves to find a way to have her son released, no matter the cost.

Despite her fighting words and strong intentions, not until February 1437, some six years since René was captured, is Yolande able to reduce Philippe's demands to the still enormous amount of 400,000 *écus d'or*. She has spent almost two years exchanging correspondence—nothing she could do or write would make Philippe agree to meet with her. Although a fraction of his original demand, the ransom has almost bankrupted Anjou, but René is finally set free. He writes to his mother at once on his departure from Dijon.

> It seems impossible, dearest Maman, that I am out of that wretched tower, and I can imagine how you must have struggled to pay my

ransom. Would you believe it, Duke Philippe saw me off as if I have been an honoured guest. I arrived at Dijon on one of my own horses, but for my departure, a splendid mount was waiting for me, a gift from Duke Philippe, who assured me he meant me personally no ill. As if that helps to assuage my years of frustration! My entourage, who have come from Lorraine to escort me home, tell me how well they have been received and how Duke Philippe has stressed he wants no rancour between us following my incarceration. What does he imagine? That I will *thank* him for his hospitality?

René must ride to Lorraine to embrace his son Jean, who is representing him there, and then try at once to raise some of his ransom. Yolande can imagine him free at last—the feeling of the wind on his face; the sensation of a horse under him again; the sight of the countryside covered in fresh snow in the weak winter sunshine—and the thought fills her with contentment. She knows his next stop after Lorraine will be Anjou, then onto her at Saumur.

After what seems like an age of unbearable waiting, the day has come. René has arrived to meet his mother at Saumur. Their embrace is all-enveloping and she disappears into the folds of his huge robes. He holds her in his bear hug for what feels like forever, and though she can hardly breathe, she would happily suffocate with the bliss of having him free.

"Mother, my dearest Madame, the best and most loyal of mothers..." He goes on and on until only her finger on his lips stops the flow. Both their faces are wet with tears, tears of joy and of the sorrow brought by their separation. Eventually they settle by the fire in the pretty yellow sitting room by her bedroom, René jumping up to look at the view once again, or caress another of the wolfhounds, his wonder at his freedom making it impossible for him to sit still.

When he arrived, Tiphane could not stop crying and hugging him and he hugging her. She was unable to speak and he was choking on his own words, laughing and crying at the same time. Yolande's youngest son Charles, now twenty-one, and grown so tall, has come from Paris to meet his older brother. They embrace in awe at one another and instantly bond, both so alike in many ways.

The most moving reunion is with Marguerite. René stands beaming with delighted surprise at the sight of his lovely eleven-year-old daughter.

"My, how you have grown, and quite the young lady," he says, looking at her and turning her about, then holding up her chin in wonder.

"Enough, enough, Papa dearest," poor Marguerite cries. "I am not a filly! You'll be looking at my teeth next."

"Good idea," he says, and makes to grasp her, and she escapes with a laughing cry.

Yolande tells Tiphane to remain with them, and they all exchange stories and laugh and cry again, and laugh, and embrace. Yolande sighs, recognizing this as one of her happiest moments, just to have him safely by her and to see his beaming, good-natured, dear, dear face. For lack of exercise, René is considerably stouter, but he looks well and assures her she does also. Of course she notices the changes—yes, at twenty-six he is no longer a lad, and stouter, but agreeably so, and his extra girth suits him too. His red hair is as wild and copious as ever and she smiles to see a little paint under his nails.

Once in Angers, René visits every corner of his province, catching up on developments—planting, building, road construction, river dredging; everything that he has missed in the governing and administration of his territory. He visits every town, every village, discusses with every mayor and foreman the progress or lack of it. What else has he had to think about in his tower for the past three years? Yolande joins him, but then the evenings are theirs. There is so much to discuss and plan, not least the future of his youngest child, Marguerite. How he has enjoyed coming to know her during the past week, the light of Yolande's life during his absence. Marguerite has shared the nursery and the strict rule of Tiphane just as her own father did and, Yolande believes, has profited as much. As for Tiphane, to have her darling René's child in her care has been her ultimate happiness.

Chapter Six

The following year, the constable, Arthur of Richemont, recovers Paris and evacuates the English in orderly fashion with all their possessions. Another triumph for Yolande's protégé, although the English still occupy Normandy, much of her Guyenne and part of Maine. Furthermore, she notices that the king has taken up her recommendation of Jacques Coeur, which pleases her, and has made him director of the Paris mint.

Following this success, the king installs Jacques Coeur as his Argentier, his personal treasurer and supplier of luxuries to the court. The Old Queen sees her merchant friend not long afterwards on one of his frequent visits to Marseilles. When her agent informs her he was in the port, she invites him to dine with her at her palace.

"My dear Jacques—how very pleased I am to hear of your new appointment—so well deserved." She thinks he is actually blushing.

"Madame, my Lady Queen, I am all too well aware how such an honour has come my way, and once again, I give you my solemn vow to be in your service always." This he says with such a low bow she almost laughs, but manages to bite her lip before he straightens.

This second appointment Charles has given Jacques Coeur pleases Yolande sufficiently to invite the good merchant to join her and Marie's entourage for the journey from Bourges to Paris to witness the king's entry into his capital.

The official entry into Paris will be a momentous occasion, not only for the French to recover their capital, but for the king personally. Naturally, the Queen of France and the Old Queen of Sicily want to look as majestic as possible and Yolande joins Marie in Bourges to plan their wardrobes together. Jacques Coeur has been prepared and is waiting at the palace in Bourges, laden with wonderful cloth and furs. Marie and Yolande exchange glances of mother and daughter complicity—what fun! Now they can really allow themselves some extravagant fantasy for the great occasion when they, two queens, will be in their places of honour to watch the king's entry into his capital at last.

They drape themselves with silks and satins of every shade, furs around their shoulders, gazzars of the finest spun gold thread, as they swirl about in front of a large looking glass forgetting themselves and poor Jacques completely.

"Mesdames, my two dear queens, I fear it may be cooler in Paris, certainly by mid November," he tries to intervene and make some sense out of their pirouetting, "and there will be much waiting about on your litters before the ceremony. And despite the many candles, the cathedral is just as cold inside as out." With that, they drop the lovely sables and other dark furs as he hands them white minks and ermines, and white fox pelts. "I do hope you agree—I think white is the most appropriate colour for queens," he suggests with a low bow.

As Yolande catches Marie's eye they have to turn their heads away so as not to let him see them smile. "Maman, what do you think of this," as Marie spreads a ravishing blue brocade with ermine, "or this," and a burgundy brocade is wrapped with white fox. They both sigh at one another and gaze with gratitude at Jacques Coeur, who sits in the middle of this delicious chaos with a satisfied smile. His lady queens are having fun. Finally they make their choices from an irresistible array of materials for their formal state gowns and their cloaks. As if this was not enough, Jacques then brings out more exquisite pieces—fans of pheasant feathers to go with Yolande's green and gold brocade, and emeralds for her neck and ears to further enhance her ensemble. "Dear Jacquet"—as they have taken to calling him—"I do have my late husband's emeralds, and should not take yours... but they are so beautiful... perhaps just for the one occasion?"

Yolande cannot recall a happier afternoon shared with her sweet daughter—their lives are so serious, and this is sheer, frivolous, delicious folly. They both know that with such exquisite, luxurious fabrics and furs, they will really appear as the queens they are on that important day, and they are grateful to Jacques Coeur for it.

The great event of the king's entry into Paris takes place on 12 November 1437, some nineteen years since he left the city in such dramatic circumstances and in just his night shirt. At last, Paris is *his* city, the capital of his kingdom.

Stands have been erected all along the official route, the place reserved for the two queens upholstered in pale blue velvet, stitched with gold fleurs-de-lis, with gold fringe on the awning above to shade them from the late autumn sun. They can feel the festive atmosphere welling up from the crowd below, and the joyful mood lifts their spirits. Flower petals are caught and spun by the breeze as people toss them from open windows lining the route. The air is chilly but fresh and the sky blue. Marie and Yolande both wear their fur capes, Jacques Coeur's wise suggestion. Yolande's is white mink and Marie's cape of blue and gold brocade is lined and faced with ermine. She is the Queen of France after all, and her mother feels she should wear the royal fur Jacques Coeur has produced. They have added collars and cuffs of white fox. Marie is wearing the sapphires Louis and Yolande gave her for her wedding and looks very much the queen. On her head she has placed a small crown of diamonds, pearls and sapphires—another treasure from Jacques Coeur's Aladdin's cave, which may have to be returned, her mother warns her, unless they can persuade

Charles—or Jacques Coeur himself. Yolande wears her crown as the Dowager Queen of Sicily.

The parade begins with brightly dressed foot soldiers and fearsome-looking pikemen. Next come the knights, most extravagantly attired, wearing parade armour, with tall ostrich feathers in many colours on their helmets. Some hold banners proclaiming their allegiance to a particular duke; others prefer to wear the current fashion of short, tight jackets and hose, and wide-brimmed hats with feathers, often attached with a glittering brooch. Finally, to loud cheers, the king appears, preceded by flower girls casting lavender and other herbs in the path of his prancing horse. Charles rides a snow-white charger, a stallion he particularly likes, which arches its neck and snorts to the appreciation of the crowds, sidestepping daintily despite its size. Named Abélard after the philosopher, it is caparisoned to the ground in quilted pale blue velvet stitched with golden fleurs-de-lis, and from its gilded leather headband tall white ostrich feathers bob along with its bowed head and prancing steps.

As the crowd roars at the sight of its king, "Maman," whispers Marie with a wicked smile, "does Abélard have an Héloïse?" and Yolande has to suppress a giggle.

"Many, darling, many—he has more children than anyone we know! But none of his wives is called Héloïse!"

Yolande cannot deny swelling with pride to see Charles as their king. He is wearing a full suit of parade armour, decorated with finely inlaid gold scrolling patterns, glistening in the winter sunshine; his head is bare for the people to see him better, and he is escorted by his Scottish archers on foot.

"How tall those archers are in comparison to some of ours," marvels Marie. Behind Charles rides the first esquire of the stable with the king's crowned helm on a cushion, and another mounted steward carries the sword of state.

"Oh, look there." Yolande points at a building opposite as she notices that jesters have climbed up onto a balcony and are somehow juggling balls while standing on the ledge.

Charles knows of their viewing position and makes a point of turning his horse and bowing gracefully to his queen and his *bonne mère*. His trumpeters notice too and give them a royal salvo, and the crowd responds with shouts of *"Vive le roi, vive la reine, vive la reine de Sicile,"* over and over.

After a short gap, next in the parade rides Yolande's fourteen-year-old grandson, the Dauphin Louis, on a fine black gelding, followed at a little distance by other princes and nobles. She can sense Marie's motherly pride as she watches her only son; *how she would have loved to have more, poor darling.*

Then her heart fills with joy as she sees her René appear directly behind the dauphin among the dukes, her younger son Charles by his side. How René enjoys himself, turning to left and right with a huge smile, acknowledging salutations with much doffing of his feathered hat. He is dressed quite outrageously in mustard yellow with green facings and trimmings, with a large emerald holding the ostrich feathers on his hat and another at his neck. Young Charles is far more soberly dressed, but also elegant in burgundy velvet and a matching hat with a long white feather. Marie and Yolande exchange glances and smile tenderly at one another. *But do I imagine a shadow in my daughter's eyes?* wonders Yolande.

Marie's son Louis has always been something of an enigma—almost a split personality. Charming one moment and snarling the next, and for no apparent reason; intelligent, and yet Yolande recalls his tutors telling her he wasted his good brain on the rubbish he learnt from disaffected and conniving companions outside the court. Marie has lost so many children; who can know if she will produce another healthy son, and should this one become the only heir, her mother fears she will have no peace.

With René's help, Pierre de Brézé has recently been appointed Grand Seneschal of Poitou and Anjou. How dashing he looks in his armour and black velvet cloak, a great shining jewel holding it on one shoulder and the gold chain of his new office around his neck. Everyone agrees that Pierre is still the handsomest man in France! Marie sighs in appreciation as he bows with raised eyes and a wave, smiling broadly at them as he passes on his high-stepping black Friesian stallion. How the crowd appreciates both rider and horse! Where did Pierre find such a creature? wonders Yolande, but not for long—it could only have been through that magician Jacques Coeur.

The army marches at the rear of the procession, with a noticeable bounce in their step, and stop when they reach the city gates. Trumpets blow, cheers ring out and the two queens have an excellent view as the mayor presents to King Charles the keys of Paris with great solemnity, followed by more clarion calls of the trumpets.

The traditional blue canopy dotted with golden fleur-de-lis is brought forward, supported at its four corners on gilded poles held by four favoured courtiers, all expertly controlling their horses at the same time. To the slow beat of a large drum, King Charles VII makes his official entry into Paris with deafening salvos and the traditional exclamations from his people of "Noël," "Vive le Roi," and "Montjoie."

Marie and her mother exchange kisses and embrace, tears of joy in their eyes. It gives Yolande deep satisfaction that she has helped to heal the open wound between the Duke of Burgundy and his cousin, her son-in-law the king—as well as the rift between Burgundy and Anjou. She vows that in honour of this day she will retract her earlier pledge of enmity towards Philippe of Burgundy. When he passes them in the procession their eyes meet for a moment as he looks up; and he removes his hat and bows, while Yolande inclines her head. *Oh, when I think of the pain this man has caused me!* But today is a glorious occasion of unity and reconciliation. She squeezes Marie's hand and her returning pressure reassures her mother that she understands. Henceforth, all past grievances will be forgiven and forgotten between the royal houses of Burgundy and Anjou, for the sake of king, country and peace.

All about them they see the people continuing to cheer and celebrate the king's entry into his capital. The knights' horses, sensing the excitement of the crowds, prance and fret, whinny and jingle, their metal shoes stamping on the strewing herbs scattered by young girls who curtsey as the king, the dauphin and his lords pass by along the route to the cathedral.

Having arrived early to watch Charles's entry into the city from their specially built stand, once he and the main courtiers have passed, Marie and Yolande descend and settle together on their own litter.

With the delicious aroma of the fields of Provence wafting up from the lavender being crushed under their horses' hooves, the procession winds its way through the thronged, joyous streets of Paris, past a number of *tableaux vivants* in progress. There is music and the sound of excited, happy citizens all around them. Coloured ribbons unfurl from balconies, banners curl lazily in the breeze, and petals drift down on the parade from the windows above.

When they reach the cathedral, their litter is lowered and they are ushered into their places of honour to await the arrival of the king and the rest of the procession. When all are settled in the nave, a "Te Deum" of thanksgiving rings out with all the verve, pomp and formality that can be imagined: choirs and silver trumpets, glittering vestments, incense and candles flickering so brightly they light even that cavernous dark space. Their places are near the king in the front and they listen as the Archbishop of Paris begins his address. Yolande's mind wanders as she looks around at a sight she feared she might never see, of nobles from both sides coming together to rejoice in their sovereign and give thanks to God. At last, a united France; no more factions, no more internecine war. How both of her Louis would have rejoiced—and are, she is sure, in heaven above. But she is pulled out of her happy reverie by the loud ringing of the cathedral's bells, the signal for all the bells of Paris to begin tolling as they follow the king outside, the choir competing with the clarion of the silver trumpets.

The whole occasion has been a triumph for Paris—for the king, his queen and their family and friends. A memorable, magnificent day!

Chapter Seven

In spring, to his mother's joy, René visits her again at Saumur. Now that he has been with his eldest son Jean in Nancy and sorted out the administration of Lorraine and Bar, he finds he has more time to spend with her and with his youngest daughter, Marguerite. René has so much to tell Yolande about his son's successful work in Lorraine and Bar, and his pride in him gives her great satisfaction. They walk arm in arm in her garden under the blossom trees, chatting about nothing in particular, until he says with forced joviality, "Madame, my dear mother." She always knows when he begins this way that he has difficult news to impart. She cannot deny she has been expecting it, and she does her best to understand, hiding her dread.

"You have no need to speak, my beloved son; I know your plans in my heart. Like all the eldest sons of Anjou, you crave your kingdom of Naples, as much as you want to be with your wife and children."

He turns at once and embraces her, and she can see tears in his eyes, which he wipes away quickly, almost in annoyance with himself. He stutters and swallows hard.

"Dearest and most perceptive of mothers, how well you understand me. I know you can sense my longing—especially for Isabelle, who has done all and more a wife should ever be expected to do. How I have missed her! Each night when I have prayed in my tower, her face has appeared in my mind's eye. As did yours, darling Maman, and those of my other children just as I last saw them. I want to know them too—as I have loved getting to know our youngest, Marguerite, with you here. But the others do not know me, and I do not know my kingdom. Maman, can you understand?" he asks so plaintively, his eyes wide with anxiety at her sorrow over losing him again.

"I know, I know, my darling boy—you have no need to explain. The time has come for you to leave," she manages to say, keeping her voice even. "So go with my blessing, and all I ask is that you come back to me before I die."

They embrace and she can feel the tears on his dear face, and he wipes away hers. Then he turns, and her treasured René, light of her heart, leaves for Marseilles, and onto fulfil his destiny in Naples. *Will I see him again?* She stands outside the entrance to Saumur, unable to move or even to cry out. How like his father and brother—"never turn back or you will not be able to leave" was always in the thoughts of these, her beloved men, as they set out. *Her beloved men, whose lives were taken by their quest for that cursed kingdom.* The desire for this illusion of a kingdom has taken from her both her husband and her eldest son, and now she must fear for her delightful, jovial René.

He has laid claim to his throne of Naples, and Isabelle, crowned by the ambassadors in his stead, has held it for him during the six years he languished in Burgundy's prison. This brave young Queen of Sicily has even defeated their cousin Alfonso when he dared dispute their title. Yolande's only consolation is that René has agreed to leave Marguerite behind with her. As he rightly said, "She has a greater chance in France to make the kind of match she deserves since you have brought her up splendidly, and she would do even a king or an emperor proud." Yolande loves this granddaughter who has much of her father in her character although, happily, she looks more like Isabelle and, she is often told, like Yolande's younger self—although she doubts she was ever as beautiful.

The next she hears of René, he is docking in Naples after a trouble-free journey, reunited with his beloved Isabelle and with his children. "Not a very kingly scene, I grant you," he writes, describing his wife's sparkling eyes and the tears that no one held back, "but even the crowds who came to the port to see their king for the first time were wiping their eyes, and they do not even know me yet—what a credit to my regent."

Letters follow this almost daily, asking her to join them, telling of the wonders Isabelle has carried out, how her little court is a byword for culture, charm and elegance—and in truth, Yolande has heard this from many a traveller friend who has been to Naples. All have told her that the palace is enchanting and the gardens a beautiful haven of peace and tranquillity. And yes, there is a part of her that is aching to join them all there, but she fears that her son Charles, her youngest, still has some maturing to do before she burdens him with the responsibilities of ruling Anjou and Provence. Since she is no longer with the court, it is important that one of the Anjou family is there to remind the king with his presence of her many sacrifices on his behalf.

René's descriptions of his explorations of his kingdom give her hours of happy reading, especially his amazed delight that wherever he goes he is welcomed sincerely and spontaneously. Since he took the trouble to learn the language while in prison, he communicates easily with his subjects from nobility to peasants. There is much to see as the kingdom is large, covering the lower half of the Italian peninsula. He writes with such excitement: "Among the first things I have done is to climb Mount Vesuvius, the crown of my great bay of Naples, and what a view from there. I enclose some sketches to give you an idea. How I would love you to come here and see it all with me. Do come, Maman?" And how tempted she feels.

Joining René in Naples is a daydream she enjoys now and then, especially when he sends her pretty little sketches of Isabelle and the children playing with Vitesse, their pet cheetah, their surroundings, the bay, the palace and the dogs. What a strange and wonderful gift of Jacques Coeur's that was: a tame cheetah which still manages to terrify the servants. Their life sounds completely enchanted, but she knows from her own experience how fleeting Paradise can be, and her cousin Alfonso d'Aragon has the devil in him somewhere. She would like to take Marguerite to Naples so they can both appreciate some of its magic, but with Alfonso making threats again on the Peninsular, they must enjoy the life available to them in Anjou.

When in the throes of great happiness, sadness often walks alongside, as Yolande has always taught her children. In the spring of 1440, her darling namesake daughter dies at the age of twenty-eight of childbed. She is the second of Yolande's grown children to die, and it grieves her mother deeply. She was always a good child, gentle like Marie, and uncomplaining. Yolande tries to console herself with the thought that at least her marriage to the Duke of Brittany's eldest son, a compromise to cover their shame at Louis' cancelled union with his daughter, turned out to be surprisingly successful. But even that cannot make up for the fact that now, suddenly, she is gone, leaving a void in her mother's heart.

Her only consolation is in knowing René has found happiness in Naples. He continues to send her letters brimming with the excitement of the ebullient child he has always remained inside—and has become again—through discovering his playground kingdom. His enthusiastic sketches give his mother an even clearer vision of his surroundings. With Isabelle and the children he rides to the vineyards; watches the harvesting; the festivals; the ships coming into harbour with visitors and traders from all over the Mediterranean, the Levant, Near East or even further. Isabelle's young ladies are elegant and entertaining, know many amusing games and dances, and although she keeps them closely protected, they are a delight at her court as many of their visitors inform the Old Queen on their return from Naples. Most of all, she treasures René's sketches of the children as the only record she has of how they grow and change.

Chapter Eight

Do we become wiser with age? Now that Yolande has reached her fifty-eighth year, she feels she has attained a certain peace in her life, not only from the knowledge that René's estates in France and Lorraine are in good order, but because the life of Charles their king has reached a stage where he can be proud of all he has achieved. At last she has secured reliable people around him; the reconciliation with Burgundy is complete; the English are confined to Normandy. All the bad influences that infiltrated his court she has quietly banished or neutralized, and his advisers are people worthy of her trust— primarily her youngest son Charles, who is cleverer than her adorable René, and on whom René has bestowed his own earldom of Maine. Charles has become a close confidant and key adviser to the king. Pierre de Brézé has also risen to a senior post in the royal circle and government. Most importantly, the king has finally taken his able constable, Arthur of Richemont, into his confidence.

Thanks to these sound men, the country's finances are in order, the military are disciplined and ready, and the king is becoming a *real* king, in the eyes not only of the court, but of all his people. He is more confident, more assured, and Yolande likes to think that by treating him as a king since his father's death, she has helped him to become one. It has come as something of a surprise to many that he has chosen to take up the position at the head of his army himself, another proof of his growing self-confidence.

Yolande has decided that the moment has come for her to leave the court, its peculiarly enigmatic king and its varied troubles, and to spend the rest of her days at her beloved Saumur, in the beauty of the Loire district of Anjou. When she informs the king of her decision, he decides to come to Saumur to spend some time with her there. There is so much neither of them can commit to letters.

"Welcome, sire," she says, as she forces her stiffening knees into a low reverence from which he raises her the moment he can jump down from his horse. She smiles at the Charles she came to know here, the dear Charles, caring and considerate and uncorrupted.

"Welcome home to Saumur," she says, and they embrace.

Once inside, by the warmth of the fire, cups of mulled wine in their hands, he says, *"Bonne mère*, you know how much you have always meant to me. I cherish every memory and often sit and reminisce with Marie about our childhoods spent with you and the others. I feel truly blessed to have had your good counsel for many years and I ask you please, even if you no longer feel able to join my court, to continue writing to me with your thoughts."

"Of course, Charles, dearest son," she replies. "You know I will always look on you as my own."

He tells her of his plans for the standing army he intends to create—just as her husband, his uncle Louis, advised him long ago—and then they speak of him and of her darling lost son, and of René in Naples and so much more. She asks about Marie and his dauphin, and she can see he is troubled on both their accounts—Marie because she cannot seem to bear another healthy child, and Louis because of his strange character. She knows it would be so much better if he had siblings. Being an only child, everyone defers to him, and that has not helped.

It seems Charles has some inkling of this himself. "When I look back on all you have advised me to do in my life, and how often I did not follow your wise direction, I realize how misguided I have been. I have learnt my lesson and will listen and obey better in the future! And I promise, with your permission, I will visit again soon, if you will allow?"

Yolande knows he has only come for one night—and considers it an honour he has come at all, with so many demands on his time. In the morning they bid one another farewell, after many assurances on her part that he is always welcome, just as he has been since childhood. Charles looks at her tenderly, and she knows she has a place in his heart.

Chapter Nine

To Yolande's surprise, she receives emissaries from the new young Holy Roman Emperor, Frederick, indicating an interest in her granddaughter.

"My dear child, what do you think? Shall we receive his ambassadors?" she asks Marguerite.

"Well, Grandmaman, why not?"

"Only because I cannot give them an answer one way or the other—that is for your parents to decide."

"But let us see them anyway. You are always teaching me the importance of curiosity if I want to learn—and I am curious to know what they have to say."

The two of them laugh and decide that yes, they will receive the ambassadors—their visit will allow them some distraction.

"Let's dress up for them," Marguerite says with glee, and Yolande sends a courier to Jacques Coeur with a message to supply her with a suitable wardrobe for Marguerite to meet the emperor's representatives. Jacques does as he is bidden, and more. Yolande can imagine her friend thinking: "If this princess is to become an empress, she must look the part." She has instructed him to spare no expense, and he has certainly taken her at her word!

"Grandmaman, look!" says Marguerite when the trunks of clothes arrive, and they play like children at dressing her up.

When the ambassadors come, Marguerite makes her entrance in the most luxurious gold brocade and white ermine. Yolande can tell from their expressions that her granddaughter has made a great impression: beautiful and intelligent as well as superbly dressed. And she laughs to herself, but her laugh is a poignant one, as she remembers the ambassadors who came to visit her all those years ago, those men who set the course of her life.

"Well, my darling girl, what did you make of them?" Yolande asks her granddaughter after their visit.

"Madame Grandmère, I will do whatever you and my parents say," she replies in her peculiar formal way. "I found them agreeable, and from the pictures they showed me of the young emperor, I was not displeased."

"So if your parents were in favour, you would not disagree?"

"Oh no, I think I should like him, and what fun to become an empress!"

Marguerite has a mind of her own, despite the impeccable manners she has been taught, but it is René and Isabelle who must mke the decision; Yolande cannot do it for them. The ambassadors will have to wait for a reply from Naples. But Yolande also knows in her heart that their arrival signals a change in her own life. If she is to make a good marriage, Marguerite must be exposed to court life; she is reaching the age where her beauty, intelligence and position proclaim her a desirable match. Yolande writes to Isabelle in Naples:

> Darling Isabelle, I believe I have taught your enchanting youngest and most delightful child everything that I know to equip her with the ability to enter a union with any prince or great lord. Now it is your turn to expose her to the court life to which my gentle old age no longer draws me. I think it might be appropriate for her to be at the royal court of France in the care of my darling Marie, who would welcome her, I know. Forgive me, my time there is past. May I have your thoughts on this?

But by the time her letter reaches Isabelle, it is too late. By return, Yolande learns that their situation has changed completely. There is dramatic news from René in Naples:

> Maman, my dearest mother, I am sad to say that the enchantment
> of our court in Naples was too good to last. I have lived in a fool's
> paradise these past three years. Once again our cousin Alfonso
> d'Aragon has intervened to try to establish his right to our throne.
> It seems our quarrel will never end. When he was captured by the
> Genoese navy and handed over to the Duke of Milan, remember
> how we hoped he would remain the mighty duke's prisoner for a
> long time? To my amazement, it seems Alfonso convinced the duke
> it was in Milan's interests that *he* rule in Naples, not me, and he was
> released, while I was held for six years by Burgundy!

The threat is real: René cannot afford to maintain a large army
indefinitely, while Alfonso has the backing of the Holy Roman
Emperor and his unlimited resources. In spite of René's courage
and that of his supporters, it becomes impossible to maintain
his army.

> To put it plainly, I have run out of money to finance my troops.
> Despite every effort and the support of the local people, I am slowly,
> reluctantly, coming to the realization that I cannot win against my
> cousin of Aragon. I will fight to the end with my people, but the
> day has come when I must send Isabelle, the children, her ladies
> and any non-fighting staff home to France for their safety. This
> morning, after I hugged the children and said my good-byes to the
> ladies of the court and all the non-combative staff, Isabelle and I
> embraced and parted resignedly, our hearts broken. We both know,
> without words, that it is over.
>
> Something has been torn from me this day: the dream Isabelle
> and I have shared all our married lives, the dream that kept me
> positive during my imprisonment, the endless letters in laborious
> code stoking the flames of that dream—so much effort from
> so many, most of all, by *you*. Dearest Maman, once they reach
> Marseilles, they will come directly to Saumur. Please receive them
> gently.

This letter from her son has come as an insurmountable blow. She has sent René everything she has—there is simply nothing left with which to raise more money. Nor can she appeal to the king—he is not in a position to help at this time. She writes to Marie, but she knows there is nothing her daughter can do. She asks Pierre de Brézé for his ideas; her son Charles of Maine; and the ever-faithful Jean Dunois. None of them can find a way to help René against an enemy with such unlimited credit.

René's next letter is even more bleak.

> Maman, most understanding of mothers, I have been forced again and again to retreat towards Naples, in the hope that somehow, by a miracle, we can keep the city from Alfonso with the help of the local citizens. Our food and arms are running low, and I fear it is really over.

When she arrives in Saumur, Yolande greets Isabelle with open arms. She has worn a little but still looks splendid. And the children, how they have changed, and know their grandmother not at all. It dismays her to have missed out on their childhoods, but then she had the pleasure of Marguerite, who does not yet know her mother or siblings. As they play with Isabelle's *demoiselles*, Marguerite enjoys getting to know their many dogs, their birds, and Vitesse, their old cheetah, gentler than any of the dogs.

"Dearest daughter, yes it will be hard to lose Marguerite, but of course I understand, and we have much to discuss."They settle down with the excellent tea Jacques Coeur sends to Yolande at Saumur.

"As you know, I have always remained close to your eldest son Jean, whom you left in charge in Lorraine, and I trust that has been a comfort to you. You will see—he has turned into a young prince of whom you can both be proud."

"Maman, it was so wise of you to send him to Marseilles after Alfonso d'Aragon sacked the city. I believe it made a man of him to see such suffering at first hand—he wrote to me at length. I know it really did raise the spirits of the people to have a member of our family there to represent us."

"Dearest daughter, it has been a pleasure keeping a family eye on both Jean and Marguerite, who have grown healthy and strong and I believe will prove a great credit to you both. What sadness that, of your other children, only your son Louis and daughter Yolande have lived beyond childhood. I know from Marie how hard it is to lose children in their early years, and you had lost four already in Lorraine, and then buried another two in Naples." Tears fill Isabelle's eyes—she has such a loving attachment to her family, unlike many of their world.

If only Isabelle's visit could last longer, but after two weeks she must leave for Lorraine to go to her son Jean, who needs her. As they sit by the fire in the evenings, Yolande delights in Isabelle's stories of Naples and can understand how sad she and the others must feel to have left such an enchanted place, especially now, with their worry over René's safety. A great sadness for Yolande is that naturally Isabelle will take Marguerite with her when she goes. But the cogs of Yolande's mind are still turning, and she has an idea.

"My dearest daughter-in-law, I have a favour to ask, though I feel guilty for even broaching the subject."

"Maman, anything, after all you have done for us," she answers.

"To help ease my pain at losing Marguerite, would you leave me one of your young ladies for company?" Yolande can see a question in Isabelle's face when she says: "Of course I have my own ladies, but they are old, and I have so enjoyed having the company of a young, bright companion. I remember a girl I met among your *demoiselles* when you came to Chinon to say good-bye who struck me as gifted and kind. When you have mentioned your young ladies in your letters, you often wrote what a help she has been. Would you allow me to keep Agnès Sorel with me? Perhaps you could spare her and she could comfort me in

Marguerite's absence?"

Isabelle gives her mother-in-law a quizzical look—she knows there are several ladies at Yolande's court there to read to her—and she always wondered at her interest shown in Agnès in her letters. Naturally, she graciously agrees.

As always, there is a plan behind Yolande's innocent requests. She believes Isabelle's *demoiselle* Agnès Sorel has the kind of potential she can shape to become of use to her country. In fact, she has kept this girl in her mind's eye for some time. When Yolande met her at the court in Chinon before Isabelle left for Naples, Agnès was a ravishing fourteen and since then has grown even more beautiful. The young Queen of Sicily will have seen to it that Agnès, like all the young ladies of her court, has remained pure. Most importantly, Yolande has made a point of speaking with her on several occasions since she arrived with the others at Saumur and finds her highly intelligent. At times, she has mentioned her to Isabelle in letters, and now Yolande has had a chance to see for herself how she has developed. Yes, she may indeed be able to use her.

Isabelle, her children—including Marguerite—and the rest of her court are ready to leave for Nancy. Their cavalcade is lining up in the large palace courtyard, the dogs and the cheetah all on long lines. Yolande hugs the children, especially Marguerite, and embraces her daughter-in-law.

"Good-bye, my dearest Isabelle—thank you for allowing me the pleasure of your delightful Marguerite. Now take her home to Nancy with my blessing. She has been the best companion I could wish for, and I think she has turned into quite a remarkable young lady. I shall miss her terribly, but I wish you great joy of her."

They all say their farewells and promise to meet again soon, but somehow Yolande knows she will not see any of them again.

Chapter Ten

The old queen settles down into a quiet routine with her new companion. She cannot hide her delight in this young lady. Agnès has grown into all and more than she had hoped. A little shy, perhaps, but after a few days she relaxes. At the bidding of her mistress, she recounts entertaining anecdotes of life at the court in Naples, while Yolande sits and marvels at her beauty under the pretence of drawing her—a beauty that has refined into alabaster perfection. How she enjoys the girl's tales of the officials Isabelle had to deal with in her first years there without René.

"You know, Madame, often they would arrive unannounced, and my queen and we, her *demoiselles*, would be resting wearing only our shifts, fanning one another in the heat, lounging on the grass under a tree," she tells her, doing her best not to change her position in case she ruins the sketch. "Suddenly there would appear a fully uniformed, heel-clicking officer, totally disarmed by the sight of so many young ladies virtually in undress! A quick military about-turn so his back was to us, and despite our giggles, he would impart his message to the wall. Stuttering, and with several quick low bows to the wall, he would leave in a fast high-stepping march! How we would laugh." There is no guile in her, no coquettishness, and yet she is full of fun.

Her stories entertain Yolande for hours: the formal occasions, full of Spanish protocol from the court of Alfonso, rigorously followed by his people at the court of Naples, who trained the local staff. With time, she tells Yolande, Isabelle managed to make the staff adopt a more informal, relaxed manner.

Listening to Agnès' stories, Yolande fully understands how much Isabelle's elegant, small court loved their stay in Naples—which makes it harder for her to imagine how it will be for René when he returns.

Some months pass before Yolande feels she knows Agnès well enough to broach the subject.

"Do you think King René will find it difficult to adapt back to the life of the court in Lorraine, my dear?" A presumptuous question for her to ask the girl, she knows, but she is genuinely curious about Agnès' reply, which does not come quickly or thoughtlessly.

"Madame, yes, I believe it will break his heart to leave Naples. It is his true vocation to rule there; the people love him and he clearly loves them too. This he showed in so many ways—firstly by speaking the language on his arrival; his kindness from the lowest to the highest; making sure that anything unfair or wrong of which he became aware was resolved. He himself often sat in at the magistrates' courts to listen and make sure that correct judgements were given. He would visit the corn markets; the docks; check the cargoes that arrived to satisfy himself that no one was trading slaves, or that pilgrims were being cheated. Oh, he showed he cared for the people in so many ways, and not just for the nobility." She stops. "Forgive me, Madame, my tongue ran away with me."

"No, my dear girl, I want to know, and to understand if I can, what went wrong, and from what you tell me, it was not the wish of the people of Naples to change their rulers."

"Madame, most certainly not!" Agnès exclaims. "Everyone told us how afraid they were of the return of King Alfonso of Aragon! That is the greatest tragedy of all—the suffering the good people of Naples will endure when our king has to leave."

"And you are sure he will have to leave?" Yolande presses gently, not looking at her, eyes on her sketching.

"Madame, I am no politician, nor captain, but I spoke often with both, and no one was in any doubt that the forces of King Alfonso would overcome ours, since there was no chance of any relief from allies or from the King of France. I think the most difficult thing for King René to come to terms with will not be losing Paradise, but the knowledge of the retribution King Alfonso will impose on the Neapolitans on account of their loyalty to King René in preference to him. As you know, Madame, he has such a kind heart."

And so she does, so she does.

When Queen Yolande receives visitors from other courts, she is attended by Agnès as her sole lady-in-waiting. Once the visitors leave, she often discusses them with her. She allows Agnès to stay during administrative meetings as well as social ones, and afterwards Yolande questions her, noting with pleasure the evidence of her sharp intelligence in her assessments. These she only gives if asked, but it soon becomes evident that she is a fine judge of character, despite a generous and forgiving nature.

From her comments about daily incidents at the court of Naples, Yolande can see she is perceptive, her observations well judged, often wise, and she understands restraint. Without showing too much knowledge—though Yolande suspects she knows a lot more than most people she meets at her court—she can enter into any conversation if asked, and quietly hold her own. When confronted by a stupid French courtier who may have had too much to drink, her tact impresses her mistress.

"Well, my pretty, you must have had a free and easy time with the court in Naples," he says rather loudly. "And what did you think of those local lads? They dive into the sea quite naked, don't they? Ha ha! To catch coins that pretty ladies like you throw from boats, I hear. Isn't that so? And what did you make of them? Were they handsome? Did you young ladies invite them to your beach gatherings in the evenings? I am told that in the heat, elegant people there often stroll along the beaches in the moonlight! Ha ha! And what went on then, my pretty, I would like to know!"

Agnès smiles politely and makes to move away, but he detains her, Yolande watching to see if she needs rescuing.

"Good sir, I fear you may have been misled by mischief-makers, for we at the court had no such experience," she assures him. He continues with his silly talk, but with patience and kindness Agnès disentangles herself without causing offence. "Perhaps, good sir, you should go to Naples yourself, for I can see the subject interests you, as would the great volcano there, spitting boulders and hot lava. Now that really is an exciting and dangerous sight." And with that she distracts the boorish man, whom Yolande's stewards quietly remove.

During Agnès' long stay at Saumur, Yolande makes a point of talking to her on their daily walks so that the girl does not feel the need to meet her eyes all the time. She does not want Agnès to imagine she is planting ideas in her head. She knows that her time at Saumur has a limit and that one day she will be returning to the court in Lorraine. In this context, she keeps stressing the importance of the obligations of a lady attached to the court; varying her words and approaches, she hopes the message will stick firmly in Agnès' mind.

"You know my dear, your duty to your sovereign lord and his family, and loyalty to the crown, should be placed above all else," she says. "The King of France should be the most important person in the life of every one of his subjects. His will should be theirs." And Agnès nods. Yolande tells her about Charles's youth with them, how he grew with her children, how they learned from her their duty to his father, and eventually to him.

It is important for Agnès to understand the procedures at the court of the King of France and the names of the good people Yolande has placed there. "After all," she tells the girl, "once King René returns to France and joins Queen Isabelle in Lorraine or Anjou, there will be many occasions when they will spend time with the royal court, and the more you know of its protocols and the character of its members, the more help you can be to Queen Isabelle and the others of her entourage."

Is Yolande indoctrinating Agnès? Yes, she is, because she understands the necessity of laying sound plans to help the monarchy survive, plans that she may not live to see come to fruition. All she can do is sow the seeds, and trust in her knowledge and understanding of Charles, her young protégé and now her king, that these seeds will flower and bear good fruit.

With each passing week during this peaceful time of her life at Saumur, Yolande grows more convinced that she has made the right choice, that Agnès Sorel is the one most capable of helping Charles when she is gone, of turning him away from the valueless women at his court. He has such an appreciation of beauty; hers may just distract him long enough for him to absorb her wisdom and her inherent goodness, and, she hopes, experience ecstasy at last. Yolande will entrust clever Isabelle with bringing this plan to fruition.

She knows it may seem strange that she is discreetly promoting another woman to influence and guide her own daughter's husband, once he has fallen in love with her. Yes, and Agnès must fall in love with him, because Yolande has realized by now that she is the kind of woman, like her, who would have it no other way. Naturally Yolande knows it will be hard for Marie to witness her husband, her king, in love with someone else, but Marie has been educated by her mother to put the needs of her country before all else, and Yolande is confident that she will understand and play her part. To date, she has given birth to twelve children—and buried eight of them. Only the Dauphin Louis and three girls still live. Since her eighth year, when Charles came into her life as her betrothed, Marie has known she could count on his sincere friendship. She has always been aware of her value to him, his unfailing courtesy to her; and Yolande believes she recognizes his needs, as well as those of her country. She has no doubt that her daughter will put the welfare of the kingdom first—even before her pride, if she must.

When his *bonne mère* is no more, without her guidance Charles will need to harvest all his resources, harvest the good counsel from the advisers Yolande has planted around him. If only she could have had him make use of the natural common sense of her daughter Marie, but she can see his highly developed aesthetic side requires beauty, and more than that, she now understands what he feels he has missed. It was Pierre de Brézé who first alerted her to the fact, and over time she has not seen Charles drawn to anyone at court with the potential to guide him, as well as being someone with whom he can share the magic of love. What he needs is for once in his life to fall in love with all his heart. Yolande knew such a love with her husband Louis, and she knows René has experienced it with Isabelle. How she regrets not having had the same success in mating her darling Marie, but she is sound and sensible enough to be an excellent queen consort and mother, without causing Charles any trouble. In the final analysis, sustaining the kingdom is more important than anything else, and Marie is one of the necessary sacrifices Yolande has had to make to achieve that goal. She believes Marie understands that too.

During the years Isabelle spent in Italy, Yolande often wrote to her at length to explain her hopes for Charles and the kingdom, and she concurs.

For the sake of France Yolande has not hesitated to plant useful spies into the households of those she feared do not have the interests of the king and country completely at heart, and she has no shame in admitting it. Her eyes must be everywhere. These "eyes" have, on occasion, belonged to beautiful young women, totally loyal to her and invariably coming from Anjou. René regards her "recruiting" as a somewhat dubious activity, but Yolande see it as a justified defence of the kingdom. Isabelle agrees with her. Women are much more practical in these matters.

Yolande has written to Isabelle that Agnès is ready to return to her court in Lorraine; she has taught her all she can. Agnès has no idea of the old queen's hopes and plans for her, apart from her duty to her king and country. Yolande must leave it to Isabelle to ease into Agnès an understanding of the king's need for her, should he find in this pure maid the great love his own mother-in-law feels he has unconsciously been waiting for. Handled carefully, Agnès Sorel could be the saving of their disconsolate king.

Although Yolande is as confident as she can be that she has paved the way for the king's future happiness, she is far less confident that her son René is safe. As ever, she relies on letters, but they can be horribly delayed. None of them gives her any hope that there is an improvement in his fight for his kingdom.

At last, towards the end of 1441, a letter arrives from him.

> Here I am, still in Naples. Alfonso has laid siege to the city and for the past seven months we have held out, the citizens displaying extraordinary courage. To see my brave Neapolitans suffering is hard. Most have sent their families out of the walled city, and only the fighting men remain. The royal castle was built long ago to withstand just such a siege, and there are a number of small tunnels through which some food has been able to come in—and a little gunpowder. But as the weeks pass, it becomes harder for our men on the outside to supply us. Finally, today, five of my senior captains asked to see me.
>
> They came with great regret and hesitation, to inform me that food and gunpowder are in short supply, and our situation here has become untenable. And they made clear that, for all our sakes, I must not be taken prisoner. Pressure would be put on the King of France to pay a great ransom for my life, or for the lives of my citizens. How terrible it was for me to hear them say there is nothing more I can do here, and to know they are right. They requested that I leave while there is still a way out, and handed me a document signed by all the captains saying it would be

better for them if I was not in the city when they were obliged to open the gates. I feel almost numb with the realization—and to be honest, I have felt it coming for some time—that I must give up my kingdom and leave my good men to their fate. With deep regret, I have agreed to their request. I am to use an old escape route long prepared, it seems, by past rulers.

Yolande reads this passage again and again, feeling the raw pain of her son—knowing how his men will be treated by her cousin, their conqueror. And for René to be pushed out by his captains! Not only to save himself, but because they would be made to suffer more if he was captured. *My poor son!* How she wants to hold him; tell him that life is not full of heroes; that battle is not a noble art; that death can come quickly, without justification or preparation. Has he not learnt that lesson yet? After his treatment at the hands of Duke Philippe, how can he still believe in chivalry?

She reads on:

I asked for our soldiers to gather in the parade ground and our chaplain to say Mass before I left. Every man removed his helmet or head covering, knelt and received Communion. After the service, I walked through the ranks, shaking hands, patting familiar backs, trying to smile and to control my tears. I had no need to say anything; they know I am leaving, and they know why. Many of the men could not hold back their own tears. They can see I believe they have done their best—we all have—but now the end has come: the end of my kingdom, the end of their freedom, the end of our many hopes and dreams. None of us has any doubt as to the future of a city that has defied a man who considers himself the rightful ruler. Alfonso d'Aragon will take his revenge, of that we are certain.

She waits anxiously for the next courier. What has happened? Has he escaped? She paces the corridors and wrings her hands. Anxiety for René destroys the serenity Yolande has enjoyed for some time here at Saumur. For the past two weeks she has felt her heart pounding, dreading and yet longing for news to reach her.

At last—a courier. Trembling, she opens the packet. It is from René, in his own hand. He is alive!

Maman, I am safe—but a shell of a king, and so ashamed.

When I made to bid my good captains farewell, I had no speech left—my throat and tongue were dry; only my tears continued to flow. I stood on the ramparts and waved as they saluted me in unison. Once I had turned, I could not look back. Two of my captains led me gently through a series of chambers within the ramparts, doors opening and locking again behind us, until we came to a small room with a well in the centre. They removed the lid, and looking down, I saw a narrow metal ladder. They put a strong leather apron over my head covering my front and another covering my back, which they tied around my girth. Both captains knelt down before me and I placed my right hand on their heads for a moment. No one spoke. I climbed into the well and descended the metal staircase. After some minutes, the rungs came to an end and the tunnel made a turn to the right. I sat down as I was instructed, pushed off, then leant back with my head slightly raised. Soon I felt myself sliding down a smooth path inside the tunnel. I could smell sea air as I slid, gaining speed. After some minutes, the tunnel levelled out again, but not enough to stop my descent, although I did slow down. I descended for a while longer, and whenever I gained too much speed, the tunnel would level again. Suddenly I saw a speck of daylight ahead, and soon after, I arrived at the bottom, my feet resting in soft sand.

Hands pulled me gently out and helped me stand. As I blinked in the bright sunlight, I heard a man say: "All is well, sire, you are safely outside the city. We have been sent by your friend Jacques Coeur. His ship is waiting a little further out in the harbour. We are ready to row you to her. She is a good, steady vessel. All will be well." They were talking to me as if I were a child or an idiot—so I must have given the impression of being one or the other, or both. They removed my leather aprons, which had kept me from damage during my descent of the tunnel, and gave me some water to drink. Slowly I felt myself returning to my senses. The fresh sea breeze on my face helped, but looking back up at the fortress of Naples I saw a small group on the ramparts watching out for my safe departure and waving. I could only hang my head.

My poor darling son! thinks Yolande. *Oh, the anguish I feel for him!*

It seems that one of Jacques Coeur's innocent-looking merchant ships was waiting for René at anchor, a ship in fact well armed, as was her crew. As soon as René climbed on board in Naples, the order was given to set sail. Not long afterwards, Alfonso d'Aragon arrived with his forces and took possession of his kingdom.

The House of Anjou will never return.

René is safe. Yolande can breathe again. But mixed with the relief is the misery of it all. Yet another wasted effort; more lives lost in vain, and the Anjou fortune as well. There are no circumstances she can imagine that will enable another of the Anjous to turn the Aragons out of Naples after this. The spell is broken; the chimera has evaporated.

But he is on his way home, at least. It makes her smile a little, but sigh a little too, to learn that he has tarried in Italy to absorb art and to befriend the great and the good there. And she understands the shame he feels that keeps him from her.

Somehow the knowledge that René is safe has allowed Yolande to breathe normally again and loosen the tight reins that have held her in control for so long. Through her willpower alone she has forced herself to live on and resolve the greatest of her problems—the safe return of this most precious of her children. Now she feels her days are running out and there is not much of her life left. How well she remembers this same time before Louis' death, when he forced himself to dictate to her his testament and last love letter. Now she too wants to leave some words for her children and theirs, to act as a guide when they are in need, and to help them understand her actions, some of which might otherwise seem strange to their thinking.

She writes:

For my children and grandchildren, and then theirs:

First of all, I made it my mission to be of service to my husband, a man for whom I had the greatest respect as well as a deep, enduring, passionate love. When he died, I knew there would never, could never be another man to share my life. He taught me many things; the first, to give my complete loyalty to France, and by that, he made me understand, to the monarch. And he took me with him to his territories and showed me how to rule as his regent when he would need to be elsewhere.

When the young prince Charles came to us, he was most unlikely to inherit the throne, and I taught him the same values I passed to you, my own children, values worthy of a prince. When he became dauphin, the very nature of his position left him open to the envious and to others who wished him harm, often spreading damaging and mendacious tales about him.

Despite his coronation and unction, still he has had to continue to battle for his rightful position, fighting enemies close by him as well as from outside his kingdom. He found himself struggling for survival, which made him even more impenetrable to his people. Charles VII has become an inscrutable king, unfathomable to many, shaped by his own experiences. But shaped too by the love and wisdom I have poured into him since he came to us as a raw lad of ten, aching with insecurity and the lack of any affection or attention. You, my children, joined me in this and embraced him like a brother. I can do no more for my king—it is up to others now, and I trust I have trained well those I could. You, my children, know him in the way children find out one another's strengths and weaknesses. I know that nothing he does will surprise you, because you know both sides of his character, the good and the bad.

I have made some difficult decisions during my life, but always in the interests of France and her rightful king. If ever you doubt any of my past actions, I say only this: ask yourselves if what I have done was in the honest belief that it would help the kingdom and the king; for that has been the sole motive throughout my adult life as taught me by your father.

Now I look out at the leaves on the trees turning yellow and gently falling. I have had my bed moved to the window of this beautiful boudoir at Saumur that you all know so well, in order to see the carpet made by these honeyed shapes in my high courtyard garden, and they give me much pleasure, reminding me of that fabled "douceur Angevine." October is almost over and autumn has arrived late. I feel like the season, crisp and golden. I know I am nearing the end of my life, and to be surrounded by such beauty brings me great contentment.

Each day I see a blue sky, a few small clouds, and at night, when they close my shutters and draw my curtains, I have the warmth of the fire and the company of my faithful old wolfhounds Jason and Nestor, both descendants of the original two who ran alongside me on that journey from my home, and theirs, in Aragon to my wedding to your beloved father in Arles. My silky grey *levrettes*, Aurora and Electra, also descendants of the original three my mother sent me, lie beside my bed, their long noses outstretched on the ground and their adoring, impenetrable dark eyes gazing up at me. I have always felt closer to my dogs than to most people—they never complain and they make me feel they understand what I say. When I am sad, they know and put their heads on my lap, or just lie at my feet, and I am comforted. All my life it has been thus, and you, my children, I know feel the same about your dogs—more like friends than animals.

In the evenings, I have one of my musicians quietly play the mandolin in a corner of my boudoir, and if I want to be entertained with a little chess or cards, I ring for one of my ladies to come. They are all dear women, not close to me, but kind and accommodating. Mine is a peaceful existence here in my favourite of all my houses.

My work in this life is done. I have placed the chessmen on the board and taught the players. Now it is for you and others I have taught to make their moves. The end game especially would interest me, but I must watch silently from above.

Although none of you, my children or grandchildren, is with me at this time, I am content. You have your own lives to live just as I have lived mine, often alone after the death of the only man with whom I wished to share it. Happy memories sustain the long hours that remain until nightfall; somehow I know I shall not see the morning.

I believe I can go to my Lord above knowing I have done all I could with the intelligence and the courage He gave me to do my duty to my king, my adopted country and my own family. Here at Saumur, the serene château of my youthful marriage, the home I shared with my beloved Louis and our children, it pleases me to dwell on my memories, to thank God for the safe return to France of my treasured son René, and to prepare to meet my Maker.

Acknowledgments

I am grateful to my friend Philippa Gregory for convincing me to write an historical novel rather than another history book. Nevertheless, all the events in *The Queen of Four Kingdoms* did take place. Every character in the story—excepting some household staff—actually existed with birth and death dates as given. In other words, the history within the book is as accurate as I can ascertain.

During the past seven years spent in my quest to unravel and reveal the family saga of my trilogy, I have been aided and abetted by a number of skilled sleuths to whom I am deeply grateful: most of all to my brother Freddy, who has been my greatest supporter, adviser, gentle critic, always encouraging and invaluable with logistics; with regard to genealogy, Leo van de Pas is the best and has generously helped me throughout, as well as providing the family tree of Charles V, his siblings and their children and my descent from many of the book's characters enclosed in my website; and to Philippe Charlier, the French pathologist, whose original research will become more apparent in the second volume.

I am indebted to Marchesa Barbara Berlingieri for helping my researches in Calabria; to Anna Parkinson—always willing to find answers for my most obscure questions; my thanks go to Jean-Charles de Ravenel for his help with translations from medieval French; much gratitude goes to Susan Opie, my inspiring, generous personal editor for helping me understand the difference between writing history and a novel; to Jill Hamilton, whose writing and practical experience is always given generously and instantly; to Daphne Weir, whose kindness and advice I value enormously; to Lente Roode, for helping me know her cheetahs; to Professor Philip Bobbitt, for explaining money lending and financial transactions in fifteenth-century France; another I wish to thank warmly is Kate Maxwell, who helped with the initial research, and her husband Gregor, especially for translating some of the more difficult notes written in old French; Wayne Sime is due my thanks for his information on the medicinal use of mercury; also A. E. Curry, for giving me leads for research in Normandy.

Robert J. Knecht, Professor Emeritus of French Renaissance history has been a great help in the past and again here for the useful leads he has given me; thanks must go to Professor José Baselgar and his son for their expertise on medieval poison; Michael Browne and his wife Jane Baile deserve my gratitude for sharing their knowledge of medieval cuisine in France; my sincere gratitude goes to Gonzague St. Bris for urging me to write the story of Agnès Sorel, his insider knowledge on the subject and for his generous hospitality.

Perhaps most of all, my gratitude must go to Sibilla Clark, who has allowed me to hibernate in her cottage for a number of years during the winter months, so that I may write in peace.

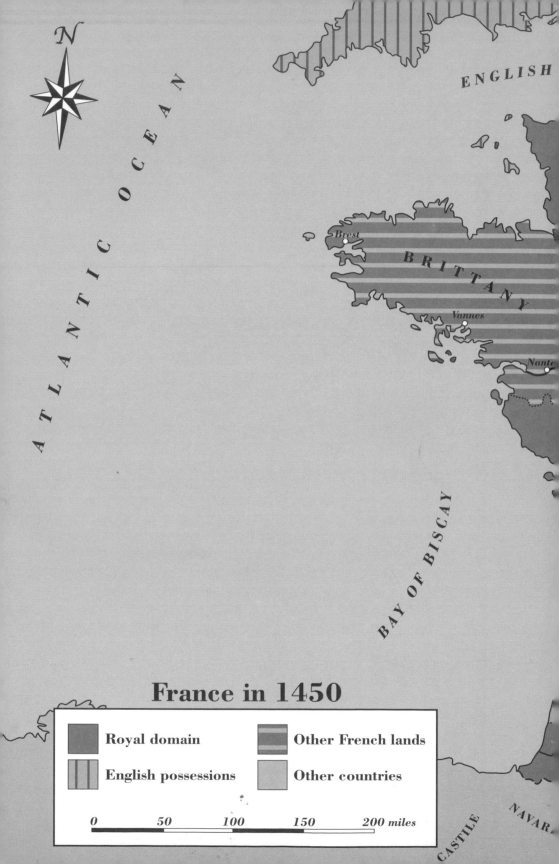

N

A T L A N T I C   O C E A N

ENGLISH

Brest

B R I T T A N Y

Vannes

Nante

BAY OF BISCAY

France in 1450

Royal domain		Other French lands	
English possessions		Other countries	

0   50   100   150   200 miles

CASTILE

NAVAR